CAFÉ AU LAIT

A ZION SAWYER COZY MYSTERY

Volume 2

ML Hamilton

www.authormlhamilton.net

CAFÉ AU LAIT

First print

January of 2017 marks seven years since I began this experiment as an author. It began with a New Year's resolution and 31 books later, I am still in love with it. None of this would be possible without my readers and my family, both of whom keep me focused, keep me living the dream. Thank you!

"I wake up some mornings and sit and have my coffee and look out at my beautiful garden, and I go, 'Remember how good this is. Because you can lose it.' "

~ Jim Carrey

CHAPTER 1

Zion stared into the mirror over the sink in her bathroom. Once upon a time, she'd had her hair straightened every four weeks, burnished with an auburn wash, slathered on hair oils and leave-in conditioners to keep it from going rogue (as her best friend Becks would say), but now she didn't care.

She didn't have a permanent monthly hair appointment, she didn't even have a stylist. She got her hair trimmed when it got in the way, braided it in a French braid when she worked, and otherwise didn't worry about it. Today, she tied the end with a floral scrunchy and walked into the bedroom to slide on a pair of pale pink capris and a hot pink t-shirt that said *Caffeinator* on it.

The *Caffeinator* was the name of the coffee house her biological mother, Vivian Bradley, had left her. Once Zion had taken over, she'd decided the employees needed a uniform. Since Vivian had trended toward pink for everything in the store, Zion felt it was a tribute to her to stay in that theme, but she'd limited it to a t-shirt. No sense going all crazy about it.

Staring at Vivian's picture on her dresser, Zion realized she was starting to look a lot more like her. Once she'd let her hair go to its natural red/orange color and allowed the curls to return, and once she'd stopped wearing so much foundation to hide her freckles, Zion actually felt more comfortable in her own skin. In San Francisco, she'd been so caught up in the latest fashion trends, wearing tight skirts and blouses that were not made for a woman with curves.

Sinking down on the bed and slipping her feet into her socks and sneakers, she couldn't deny she didn't miss six inch heels and punishing pointed toes. She felt free and relaxed and she wasn't worried how she was going to pay the rent on a studio in the Sunset that took up two thirds of her paycheck.

She looked at the other pictures on her dresser. Her adoptive mother and father – the two people she really thought of as her parents – Gabrielle and Joseph Sawyer had taken her in as an infant and raised her as their own. She adored them. Her father, Joe, still worked as a hospital administrator, but her mother, Gabi, was a retired nurse. They lived in San Bruno and while Joe worked, Gabi was reinventing herself. She'd tried a number of hobbies – canning and macramé and reupholstering – but piano was the one she'd stuck with for the longest. Until recently.

Joe had told Zion that Gabi had decided piano was too archaic and sedentary. She was into yoga now, which meant a whole new diet, a new wardrobe, and a new way of thinking. Zion had called her mother just to see how deep into this pastime she'd gotten, but at the first *Namaste*, she'd known Gabi was fully committed.

Zion smiled now. She missed them both and not being able to see them regularly was the one negative to this whole life change. Well, that and her best friend, Rebekah Miles. She missed morning coffee breaks with Becks or discussing what hotspot they were going to for lunch, or who they were dating, although in the last few months she'd been in the City, Zion's social life hadn't been any too exciting.

What she didn't miss was her job as an administrative assistant in an insurance company. Answering phones, taking member complaints had about drained her soul. She'd hated it and after three years with no chance for advancement, she'd decided it was time to make a change.

Vivian's death and the fact she left everything to Zion had given Zion a way out. She hated that Vivian had died so needlessly, but she felt grateful for the fact that Vivian had thought of her, had entrusted her to build the dream she'd started here in Sequoia.

In addition to the cottage, she'd left Zion the coffee shop, both free and clear of a mortgage. Zion had decided to stay on for a trial period. She'd told herself to give it three months. Well, it had been two now – it was the middle of July – and Zion didn't think her plans were going to change in another month. She liked Sequoia. She liked the people who lived here. And she liked owning a coffee shop. She didn't plan to go home, although Becks kept thinking she would when she got over her *Betty Homemaker* virus.

Rising to her feet, she walked over to the cat bed in the corner of the room where her kitten Cleo was stretched out on her back, her paws flexing in her sleep. Zion smiled at her. She loved the little black ball of fluff. She'd been only six weeks old when Zion had found her on the back porch of the cottage. She and Gabi had fed her with a bottle for a few weeks until she could eat on her own. Cleo still seemed small to Zion, but the vet assured her she was growing normally now. Zion didn't know. She'd only had dogs growing up and her experience with cats was limited.

Bending down, she scratched Cleo's belly. The kitten made a noise, stretched all four legs as far as they would go, and rolled over. "Breakfast," Zion told her and Cleo rose, immediately climbing out of the cat bed and following Zion into the hallway.

After giving Cleo a dollop of wet food next to her dry kibble and cleaning and refilling her water bowl, she made herself a piece of toast with butter, downed it with a cup of hot tea from her Keurig maker, and snatched up her keys and purse, headed for the door.

"I'll see you tonight," she called to the kitten, then she was out in the cool morning air, walking to her car in the driveway. The sun was just peeking over the redwoods, but the air had a stillness about it that Zion was beginning to recognize. Sequoia never got unbearably hot like she heard the valley could get, but it had definitely made it into the 90's some days this month.

She liked the drive into Main Street. As she drove past Tate Mercer's house in the middle of the road, she glanced at his windows out of habit. The curtains were still drawn and his pickup was in the driveway, so he hadn't left for his hardware store. She liked Tate a lot.

An ex-cop, he had a quiet, calmness about him that she respected, but she also knew something bad had happened to him in a previous life. He'd quit the force, moved away from LA and a marriage, choosing to lead a much more sedate lifestyle here. He was dependable and steady, but she sensed a darkness lurking inside of him that scared her a little. He played things close to the vest and didn't give more of himself away than was absolutely necessary.

Unlike David Bennett, her current…well, beau, maybe? They'd been on a number of dates. David was the lawyer who'd helped her figure out Vivian's estate. He was tall, dark haired, handsome, and very smart. He was also funny and sweet and honorable. He wouldn't agree to going on a date with her until Vivian's affairs were completely taken care of to his satisfaction. She respected that about him and she wasn't opposed to taking things slowly. She didn't have the best track record when it came to love, so going slower might just be the ticket, she decided.

Thinking about David set up a pleasant distraction until she arrived in town and drove down Main Street to the municipal parking lot, pulling into her regular space. She'd noted the lights were on in the *Caffeinator* and Dottie Madison, her morning barista was already in place, helping customers. Climbing out of the car, Zion snatched her apron off the backseat and tied it around her.

Another car pulled in next to her and a middle aged woman with platinum blond hair got out. She wore a lot of makeup and her nails were long and painted with flags on them. She smiled at Zion.

"Good morning," she called, waving.

Zion grabbed her purse, shut the car door, and pressed the lock, then walked over to her. "Good morning, Trixie."

Trixie Taylor owned *Trinkets by Trixie*, a souvenir shop three doors down from the *Caffeinator*. She'd been a dental receptionist until her two kids left for college, then Trixie and her husband Joe had decided to open up the store.

"How are you this morning, Zion?"

"Good. And yourself." They started walking down the street to their shops.

"I tell you with that rock show opening up tonight, I'm about as busy as they get. Everyone wants a t-shirt or a refrigerator magnet that says Sequoia on it."

Zion laughed, fussing with the strings on her apron. "Yeah, it's been busy in the *Caffeinator* too."

"I'm not complaining. I mean money's money, but have you ever seen so many piercings or tattoos in any one spot before?"

"They're giving Deimos a run for his money, that's for sure." Deimos was Zion's afternoon barista, a young man in his late twenties who tended toward alternate living.

"When they floated the idea of *Redwood Stock*, I wasn't too sure, but it's done what they said. It's brought us a lot more business. Still, we usually have families renting cabins during the summer. It's a lot more quiet. I heard Sheriff Wilson had to break up six fights last night alone, and there were a couple of drug overdoses out at the county fairgrounds where they're holding the festival."

Zion sighed. "That's too bad. I hate to hear that."

They paused in front of Trixie's door.

"Well, I guess you can't have everything," Trixie said, then she touched Zion's arm. "How'd your mama like the glass hummingbird?"

Zion smiled. "She loved it."

"I'll have some new stuff right around September. You come in then and get your Christmas shopping done early."

"I will."

Trixie unlocked her shop door and stepped inside. Zion continued down the street, waving to Carmen through the windows of the *Knitatorium,* and then she pushed open the door of the *Caffeinator.* The bell above the door tinkled. Immediately, she was swamped with delicious smells – cinnamon, coffee, brown sugar. She loved this moment in the morning when she stepped inside and Dottie was filling the glass cases with sugary goodness.

A few customers sat at the wrought iron tables and a couple with two pre-teen kids were gathered in the lounging area. Dottie came through the swinging doors of the kitchen, carrying a tray of donuts, her face bursting into a smile.

"Hey, sweet girl, am I glad to see you."

Zion moved around the counter, pulling her purse off her shoulder. "Has it been busy?"

"A little bit," said Dottie. Dottie Madison was nearly as round as she was tall with a head of puffy curls which this month were dyed a brilliant red in honor of the 4th of July. She wore glasses, but they mostly hung off a beaded chain affixed around her neck. She had to be in her late fifties or early sixties, or so Zion guessed, but she had more energy than Zion had ever had in her lifetime.

Dottie did most of the baking and liked to come in much earlier than anyone else. She liked working the counter when fewer people were around so she could get her recipes made without fuss. She'd been teaching Zion to bake for the last two months and Zion found she actually had an affinity for it.

"What needs doing?" Zion called over her shoulder as she went through the swinging bar doors into the back where the kitchen and her office were located. She stashed her purse in her desk and came back out.

"Take the orders while I get these drinks made," said Dottie, pointing at the small line that was building in the center of the store.

Zion gratefully did as she was asked. The idea of boss and employee had been a loose concept from the beginning. Not that Dottie, Deimos and Tallah, her part-time teenage help, didn't treat her with respect, but Zion clearly was new at owning a business and they were the experts. Besides that, Zion had never considered herself boss material anyway. She'd much rather they all worked as a team, had each other's backs, and truth be told, that damn espresso machine had never liked her to begin with, so she had no problem deferring to those with more skill.

As she took orders and helped Dottie distribute drinks, she couldn't believe how happy she was, so far from the hustle and bustle of everything she'd known in the City.

* * *

At noon, Deimos and Tallah arrived. Tallah, a high school junior now, was the daughter of Zion's new friend, Cheryl Ford who ran the *Bourbon Brothers Barbecue* two doors down. Tallah had applied for the part-time barista position in May, wanting to get away from the family business. Her father Dwayne wasn't happy about it, but Cheryl pretty much got her way in that family and she didn't see any harm in the straight-A student going to work for someone else.

Zion was grateful to hear her two employees enter the coffee shop now. Tallah could work the espresso machine almost as well as Deimos and Dottie already had her purse slung over her shoulder, ready to hightail it out of there. The traffic had been steady all day and Zion had barely had time to take a bathroom break. The *Redwood Stock* festival had certainly brought a lot of colorful, interesting people to Sequoia, and they all wanted coffee to keep themselves awake for the opening act tonight.

Deimos burst through the bar doors of the kitchen as Zion was just removing a tray of chocolate chip cookies from the oven. "Heya, boss lady," he said.

Deimos was tall and lanky, had shaggy blond hair, and wide blue eyes that looked at the world with wonder and delight. Deimos and Dottie had been the only reason Zion had even considered keeping the coffee shop. Between the two of them, they understood the business completely and they were dedicated and dependable.

"Hey, Dee, am I glad to see you."

He'd grabbed an apron from under the counter and began tying it around his waist. "Were you slammed all day?"

"Yep. Haven't even had a chance to visit the facilities," she said.

Deimos finished tying his apron and grabbed a pot holder. "Well, give me that and go."

"Thank you!" said Zion, relinquishing the cookie sheet to him.

Tallah entered the kitchen a moment later. "Where do you want me to start, Zion?"

"Can you put a new batch of cookie dough on that clean cookie sheet and pop it in the oven?"

"On it," said Tallah, going to the sink to wash her hands.

Dottie poked her head through the doors. "You want me to stay? It's still slammed out here."

"No, go home," said Zion, easing past her and laying a hand on her shoulder. "You haven't had a break either. Dee and Tallah are here now."

"Heya, Dottie girl," called Deimos, following Zion back into the coffee shop.

Dottie planted herself firmly in front of Deimos, wagging a finger in his face. "You be careful at that festival tonight. You hear me?"

"I'm always careful," he said, heading for the display case and bending to put the cookies onto the tray inside. "Don't worry about me, dude."

"I always worry about you, *dude*," said Dottie, swatting his rear end with her purse where it jutted out of the display case. "No Mary Jane!"

Zion watched them as she eased around the end of the counter and headed for the bathroom.

"Mary Jane? Seriously, Dottie, we broke up a long time ago," she heard him say as she pushed open the door.

"Mmhm, keep telling yourself that, Dee, but you still watch out!"

Zion took care of business and straightened her braid, then washed her hands and returned to the restaurant. By the time she got back, Deimos and Tallah had cleared all the customers and were both rushing around preparing drinks. Zion couldn't deny she was pleased with their proficiency.

Grabbing her phone from under the counter, she looked at the time. Past noon. Her stomach rumbled as if it knew the time as well. "I'm gonna just go get lunch, if you guys have this under control."

Deimos held up a hand, since the noise from the espresso machine made talking difficult and Tallah gave her an encouraging nod. Detouring into her office, Zion grabbed her purse out of the desk, noticing that David had called her.

She dialed him back as she crossed the coffee house again, headed for the front door. He answered right away.

"Hello?"

"Hey, David, I missed your call."

"Hi, Zion, yeah, I called about an hour ago. I thought you might be on your lunch break."

"What's up?" She got a little flush of pleasure thinking about him.

"I just wanted to confirm that we're on for dinner tonight."

"Definitely. Where are we going?"

"I think *Corkers*, if that's okay with you. It's the opposite direction from the festival."

"Sounds good. Pick me up about 6:30. That'll give me a chance to get a shower after work."

"See you soon," he said and disconnected the call.

Yeah, David Bennett was a definite plus to living in Sequoia. She really enjoyed his company. Walking two doors down to the *Bourbon Brothers*, she smiled as a couple held the door for her. The interior of the restaurant was crowded with people and Zion wondered if she should just back out and go somewhere else for lunch, but this was the closest location without taking her car out of the parking lot.

Cheryl, Tallah's mother, saw her and waved her to the counter.

"Excuse me," said Zion, easing through the line of people waiting to place their order. Cheryl lifted the counter and motioned her through, giving her a quick hug.

Daryl, the younger Ford Brother, beamed a smile at Zion. "Hey, girl," he said brightly. "How are you today?"

"I'm good. You guys are sure slammed."

"Yep, this festival has put us in the black a week earlier than usual," he said.

Cheryl put her hands on Zion's shoulders. "I set us up a table in the kitchen away from the madness out here."

Zion nodded and let Cheryl lead her to the swinging door. The smell of smoked meat and barbecue sauce made Zion's stomach rumble again. Dwayne, Cheryl's husband, waved his spatula at her.

"How's it going, Zion?"

"Good," she called back. "How are you, Dwayne?"

"Peachy keen. My girl doing right by you?"

"Tallah's the best," Zion said. "Always prompt. Works hard. She's a great kid, Dwayne."

Cheryl smiled at her and motioned to the card table set up in a back corner of the kitchen. Zion had to sidestep as Alfred, the other cook, came out of the walk-in refrigerator, carrying a huge tub of coleslaw.

"Sorry, Al," she said with a laugh.

"Watch out!" he scolded mildly. "Coleslaw waits for no man."

Finally Zion dropped into her chair at the table.

"What're you thinking of having today?" asked Cheryl.

"I want a barbecue pork sandwich with chips," said Zion firmly. She'd been thinking about it all morning as she and Dottie rushed back and forth. She felt sure she'd worked off the calories already.

Cheryl went to get their food while Zion watched the huge Dwayne and the small Alfred dance back and forth at the grill, whipping up meals as if it were an intricate ballet. A young Hispanic man came into the kitchen, loaded down with a bucket of dishes. He deposited it in the sink, then grabbed a new bucket and went back out.

The Ford brothers had hired the young man when Tallah had come to work for Zion. He had an equally young wife and a new baby. Cheryl liked to fuss over the baby, lamenting that Tallah didn't need her mother as much as she used to and she missed mothering something.

Cheryl Ford was about fifteen years older than Zion, but it didn't seem to matter. They'd hit it off right away. And although she was reaching middle age, Cheryl Ford had a figure that made many men take notice. What Zion liked most about her was her direct way of speaking. If you wanted to know what was on Cheryl's mind, she had no problem telling you. Zion respected that.

Cheryl returned with two baskets and placed one before Zion. Then she went back and grabbed two large glasses of iced tea and set them before the baskets. Finally she took a seat. She wore her black hair cropped close to her scalp. Zion would have never been able to pull it off, but she thought it was a very becoming look on her friend.

Her daughter, Tallah, was a different matter. Tallah's hair went to below her shoulderblades. For a long time she'd worn it in braids, but lately she'd just left it free. It was glorious, full and thick, and curling. Part of Zion accepting her own natural hair color and curl had to do with how Cheryl and Tallah accepted who they were. Although, a small nose ring let everyone know that Tallah was still a teenager.

"So, you gonna catch a show at the festival?" asked Cheryl, lifting her sandwich and taking a bite.

Zion's mouth was already full of the delicious meat, so she didn't speak right away, holding up a hand to indicate she needed a moment. Taking a sip of her iced tea to wash it down, she shook her head. "It's not really my thing, but Dee's all fired hot to go."

"I'll bet," said Cheryl with a laugh. She glanced toward the order window. "It's sure helped with business."

"Yeah, it has."

"Things got a little rough in here last night."

Zion lowered her sandwich. "What do you mean?"

"Group of kids, about Dee's age, came in just before closing. They ordered food, no problem, and a couple pitchers of beer." She thought, then took a sip from her straw. "There were four boys and three girls. Everything was fine, then all of a sudden two of the boys got into it, bumping chests, acting like they're gonna fight."

Zion forgot her sandwich. "What did you do?"

"I called Sheriff Wilson, but He-man over there gets out his bat and goes into the restaurant."

"I'm not putting up with that crap in my establishment!" said Dwayne over his shoulder.

"You didn't know if they had weapons or not."

"She-et, woman, they were just some punkass kids, fighting over a girl."

"Fighting over a girl?" asked Zion.

Cheryl nodded, pushing the coleslaw around in the basket with her fork. "You met Merilee Whitmire yet?"

"I don't think so."

"She grew up here. I think she's friends with Dee. Nice girl, but the last few years…I don't know. She's gone kinda hippy dippy, if you know what I mean."

Zion figured she did. Many of the young people around Dee's age, and Zion's for that matter, who had stayed in Sequoia sometimes seemed a little lost, like they didn't know what to do with their lives once formal schooling was done.

"They were fighting over her?"

Cheryl gave a wry shake of the head. "Not really fighting, just a lot of chest bumping. As soon as Papa Bear got out there with his bat, it was over. By the time Sheriff Wilson arrived, they'd already left to go back to the motel on the highway. I guess they're all here for the festival from out of town. Merilee was the only one I recognized."

"Trixie told me there were about six fights out at the county fairgrounds that the sheriff had to break up."

Cheryl shrugged and took another bite. "What you gonna do? It's a double edged sword. The festival brings a lot of business to us, but it also brings a few problems. It'll be over in three days and then things will get back to normal."

"I bet Tallah wanted to go."

Dwayne snorted loudly.

Cheryl shot a glance at him, then nodded. Leaning forward, she dropped her voice. "I'm letting her go to a show on Saturday, during the day. It's *Anaconda Glee Club*, her favorite band. I actually don't mind their singing. They like to harmonize, so it's tolerable. She's going with a couple of girlfriends, but I'm driving them and picking them up."

"*Anaconda Glee Club*?" asked Zion, smiling. "Wow, that's a name, isn't it?"

Cheryl held up a hand.

"It's the devil's music," grumbled Dwayne.

"You said it, boss," answered Al.

Cheryl shook her head. "He'd put that girl in a bubble if he could."

"Damn straight I would. She-et, I don't see no need for bopping along to screaming banshees with greasy hair and wild drugged-out eyes. In my day, we had real music and our guys could actually play the instruments."

Cheryl and Zion burst into laughter, drawing a glare from Dwayne.

CHAPTER 2

Tate opened the *Hammer Tyme*, his hardware store, exactly on the hour. His one employee, Logan Baxter was waiting for him, leaning against the side of the door, his skateboard fixed under his foot.

"Hey, Logan," Tate said, smiling.

"Hey, Tate," said the boy. Logan was supposed to be a senior in the fall, but his mother had stage 4 cancer, so Logan had quit traditional high school. He went two days a week during the year to an alternate school just to get his diploma. As soon as summer started, he'd come back on full-time.

Tate unlocked and pulled open the door, then wended his way through the dim interior to the counter and lifted it, Logan on his heels. Reaching into the storeroom, Tate threw the light switch and the fluorescent track lighting came on. Logan disappeared into the storeroom to stash his lunch and then came out, going to the window and pulling up the blinds. He reached over and turned on the *open* light as Tate began counting out the money for the cash register.

The routine soothed Tate. The extra traffic in town due to the festival had made sleeping difficult the last couple of nights. Tate found himself spending a lot of his downtime in his favorite recliner with an open book. He'd be glad when the festival was over, despite the increased business.

He'd been surprised a hardware store would attract the attention of concert goers, but many had wanted flashlights or coolers. Logan had even suggested he stock a few portable lawn chairs, which he had. They'd flown off the shelves.

Logan came around the counter and grabbed the duster, then began on the shelves closest to the register, passing the duster over the inventory. Tate finished counting the money and closed the register, watching the boy.

Logan didn't like to talk about his mother or her cancer, and Tate respected that, but he felt sorry for the boy. He had way too many responsibilities on his young shoulders. Tate hated that Logan wasn't going to regular school. He was going to be a senior in the fall and he should be at school for his senior year.

The buzzer over the door sounded and Tate turned his attention away from Logan. A wiry older man entered. He had thinning grey hair, weathered skin, a hooked nose, and rounded shoulders. He wore overalls with a plaid shirt and worn work boots. He looked around the store, taking it in from behind black rimmed glasses. Tate thought he'd been in the store a few times over the last two years.

"Can I help you?" Tate called, lifting the counter and stepping out from behind it.

The man looked over at Tate. "I just need some random shit to keep things held together out at the fairgrounds. I don't wanna drive down to Visalia." He backtracked and grabbed one of the baskets by the door to hold his stuff.

"You work at the fairgrounds?" Tate asked, leaning against a shelf as the man started putting boxes of nails and screws into his basket.

"I'm the head of maintenance." He held out his free hand. "Walter Kennedy, but most folks call me Walt."

Tate took his hand and shook it. "Nice to meet you, Walt. I'm Tate and that's Logan." He pointed over his shoulder to the boy dusting. Logan lifted the duster in salute. "Guess things are pretty crazy out at the fairgrounds, huh?"

"Man, I'll tell you, I hate these things. Give me a good garden show anytime, but a rock concert? The sort of people that damn thing attracts are nuts. They're selling marijuana pipes out there and t-shirts with vulgar sayings on them. And the acts aren't much better. Like *Ironbound* and *Oblivion*. What the hell is that? And the worst one, the headliner, is that *Anaconda Glee Club*."

Tate laughed. "Anaconda what?"

"*Anaconda Glee Club*." He leaned close. "They were out there yesterday morning, doing a sound check. They play tomorrow during the day and then again at night. Bunch of freaks, dressed in black with tattoos and piercings. And they're all assholes, every last one of them."

"How so?"

"They started bitching about the height of the stage, then the barricade, then the backstage accommodations. What the hell did they expect? A ritzy hotel? You want that, go play in Frisco or LA."

"Pretty annoying, huh?"

Walt shook his head. "I don't got time for that crap. I keep the toilets running and the lights on. I don't give a damn if they got refrigeration for their imported beer."

"Well, it'll be over on Sunday, so only three days to go and it's helped with business in the area. I've sold more in the last few days than I have in months."

Walt gave a disgusted shake of his head. "I moved up here to get away from freaks and druggies. Then we go and invite them in. I don't care if it's good for business. It encourages the wrong element. They all need to stay the hell away. If I could, I'd make sure they never came back again."

Tate raised an eyebrow at that, but he left it alone. Walter Kennedy was clearly a cantankerous old man who didn't want to be bothered with any deviation from his normal routine. Tate wasn't going to convince him otherwise.

"Sheriff was out at the fairgrounds six times last night, breaking up fights," said Walt, "and the damn festival was only just starting. What you think it's gonna be like tonight when all those druggies come out for the show?"

"Who's playing tonight?" asked Tate.

"Don't know and don't care."

"*Oblivion*," said Logan. "They're kinda heavy metal/punk. Sure wish I could go. Bunch of guys from the school are going. *Oblivion's* not sold out like *Anaconda*."

"So *Anaconda's* big?" asked Tate.

"Yeah, pretty big. They got a traditional record deal. They actually tour around the country. The other bands aren't that big. I mean they're big here, but they don't really play stadiums. *Anaconda* does. I was kinda surprised they agreed to play *Redwood Stock*."

"Hm," said Tate. Walter had wandered away, placing various items in his basket, so Tate focused on Logan. "Why don't you get tickets for tonight?"

Logan shook his head. "I can't afford it."

Walt made a scoffing sound. "Yeah, you know how much those damn tickets are? You gotta sell a kidney to get one."

Tate thought about that one for a while. Maybe he could go out to the fairgrounds and buy Logan a ticket himself. He hated that the boy never got to do anything fun and if his friends were going, he might really enjoy a night just to be a kid. How much could it be? Especially if they were just a local California band.

"Say, Walt, you know when the box office opens?"

Walt gave him a disparaging look. "You're not thinking of going out there, are you? I mean, I'm not kidding when I say they're a bunch of druggies and thugs."

Tate shrugged. "Just thought I might check it out."

"Whatever, man. I seriously don't think it's your sort of thing, but who am I to judge? The box office opened at 8:00 this morning."

Tate glanced at his phone. 10:15. He'd go over at lunch and see if they had any more tickets for *Oblivion*. No matter how much it cost, Logan deserved it. He deserved so much more than Tate could give him that this seemed like a small enough gift.

* * *

The parking lot was already filled when Tate pulled into it. When he told the guy at the parking booth he just wanted to buy a ticket for tonight's show, the kid waved him through. He drove around for a long time, trying to find a space.

People were moving toward the fairgrounds, carrying coolers and lawn chairs, all normal accessories, but their clothing and hairstyles were anything but normal. Some sported full body tattoos with piercings not just in their noses or ears, but all over their faces. Their hair was every color of the rainbow. In fact, one adventurous fellow had rainbow colored hair nearly to his ass.

Tate finally parked the truck and climbed out. He understood what Walt had said. He definitely wasn't the type for this adventure and he was way too old. He had second thoughts about sending Logan here after dark, but then remembered how he'd fought with his dad to see concerts when he was Logan's age. Besides, most of these ragged concert goers wore peace signs all over their clothes.

He found the box office and waited in line behind a couple that couldn't keep their hands off each other. He tried to look everywhere but in front of him. They were grinding against each other, and he'd seen way too much of their tongues for his comfort level. Interesting enough, they both had tongue piercings. He couldn't help but wonder if they'd ever gotten entangled with one another.

"Gonna catch a concert?" came a familiar voice behind him.

Tate glanced over his shoulder to see Sheriff Wilson strolling toward him from his patrol car. It was parked in the red zone before the fairgrounds entrance. Sheriff Wayne Wilson was a thin man with a chest that rolled inward rather than out. He had a pencil-thin moustache on his upper lip and a severe widow's peak, and he always hooked his thumbs through his belt.

Beside him was his deputy, Samantha Murphy. Sam's grey hair peeked out under her sheriff's hat and the lines around her eyes were more evident in the bright sunlight. She gave the couple a look and sighed.

"Knock it off, will you?" she scolded them. "You're in public for God's sakes."

The young man turned, giving her a glare, but it cooled the moment he saw her badge and uniform.

Sheriff Wilson chuckled, holding out his hand for Tate to shake.

"Sheriff," said Tate, shaking Wilson's hand, then he nodded at Murphy. She tipped her hat at him. "I hear you've been busy."

Wilson rocked on his orthopedic shoes. "Out here six times last night and they didn't have any music going, just vendors selling crap. Gonna get worse once the concerts start tonight." He jerked his chin at the box office. "You getting tickets for this noise fest?"

"No, I thought I'd treat Logan to a concert. He likes the band playing tonight. *Oblivion*?"

"That's nice of you, Tate," said Sam. "That boy doesn't get to be a kid very often."

"That's what I thought." He cast an eye on the couple in front of him. The young man had such large gauges in his ears, his lobes hung down to mid-neck. "I'm just hoping it'll be safe."

"I went to plenty of concerts in my day," said Wilson, smiling in remembrance. "Not a one of them was safe, but I loved it. He'll be fine. He's got a good head on his shoulders, but he needs to blow off some steam, throw his body around in that mosh pit or whatever they call it."

The young man in front of them gave Wilson a bored look, as if to say he was too old to live. Tate shared a smile with the sheriff. Tate himself was probably too old to live. "I went to some rough concerts myself," he said. "One time I got so drunk, I wound up in the medical tent for the whole night."

Wilson and Sam laughed with him. "Do you even remember anything about it?" asked Wilson.

"Not really. And when I got home, my dad tanned my hide." Tate's smile faded in memory. Thomas Mercer was a *spare the rod, spoil the child* sort of parent. Tate's mother had never opposed him and Tate couldn't deny he resented her for that. Even now, she accepted that her role was to back up Tom Mercer in everything he did. She'd never had her own life, fulfilled her own dreams.

"The one that's really got us worried is this *Anaconda Glee Club*," said Sam. "Last concert, two kids got stabbed."

"Yeah, Walt mentioned them. Logan said they were different than the others, that they headline stadiums. Why'd they agree to do our small town gig?"

"Their lead singer or guitarist, I don't know what he is, grew up around here," said Wilson. "Sabrina Clark, she's the event's planner for the fairgrounds, thought up the whole idea and presented it to the Chamber of Commerce. She went to high school with this guy, some cat name."

"Some cat name?" asked Tate.

"Jaguar," said the kid in front of them through clenched teeth. "His name's Jaguar and he's the lead singer and guitarist both."

"He plays rhythm guitar," said the girl. Her lashes were so long they stuck together as she blinked. "Maximus Starr is the lead guitarist."

"Right," said Wilson, then he gave Tate a disgusted look.

Tate lowered his head to hide his smile and the line finally moved forward.

"Hey, you know what, I'd sure like your opinion on the set-up in there. This *Anaconda Whatever* has been complaining about the way things are arranged," said Wilson.

Tate gave him his *I'm-not-in-the-business-anymore* look, but he knew it did less than no good with Wilson. "I'm not sure I'd be too good at that. I never worked many concerts during my time."

"But you know security. What do you say? Just a few minutes. I'll buy you a beer."

Tate stared at the line in front of him. If he went inside and looked things over, he'd feel better about sending Logan here tonight. Maybe it wasn't such a bad idea. "Okay, but I gotta get back to the store. I'll take a soda, rather than a beer."

"You got it. We'll meet you inside the gate when you're done here." Wilson tipped his hat and he and Sam Murphy wandered off, disappearing around the corner of the ticket booth.

The kid in front of Tate turned around and gave him a once-over. "You a cop too?"

"Was. In LA."

The kid nodded, tonguing the silver stud through the center of his lower lip. It made Tate want to squirm. "Nice you buying a ticket for that kid."

Tate shrugged. "You think it's safe? I mean he's only seventeen."

"*Oblivion*? Yeah, they're cool," said the girl. Her hair was bright pink on top and candy cane blue on the bottom. She also had a silver stud, but it went through the middle of her upper lip, and a thick, silver ring hung from her septum.

"Dude, *Redwood Stock* is all about the peace and love," said the boy. "People come out here to smoke the ganja and chill."

Tate nodded. So much was wrong with that sentence, but he wasn't going to correct the kid. The line moved forward and another window opened up. The boy draped his arm around the girl's shoulders and moved to the new window, holding up two fingers to Tate.

"Peace, out," he said without turning around.

"Peace, out," Tate muttered under his breath. He was only 33, but he suddenly felt 63.

A moment later, he was at the window. The older woman smiled at him. "What can I get you, sweetie?" she asked.

Tate reached for the wallet in his back pocket. "Do you have any more tickets for the *Oblivion* concert tonight?"

"Sure do." She made some clicking sounds on the computer, her eyes fixed on the monitor.

"So, what about tomorrow night?" Tate asked just out of interest. "*Anaconda Something*?"

"*Anaconda Glee Club*?" said the woman, then she laughed. "Isn't that the craziest name? I tell you what. The things these kids come up with now."

"Yeah. Do you have tickets for them?"

"No, they've been sold out for weeks. They even added a matinee show tomorrow afternoon. The kids just love them. I don't think they're half bad myself. They actually know how to sing."

"You've heard them?"

"My granddaughter loves them. I hear them all the time when she comes over."

Tate smiled at her. "Is she coming to the concert?"

"No, I couldn't afford those tickets." She clicked on the computer some more. "So, how many tickets do you want for *Oblivion*?"

"Just one." Tate pulled his credit card from his wallet and passed it through the slot in the window.

The woman took it and slid it across her keyboard, then she clicked some more. Tate leaned back and looked at the poster next to her window. A group of four men in their mid-twenties posed in front of a fountain. The water in the fountain was shooting over their heads. All four men had torn jeans, ragged t-shirts, and tattoos. One had full sleeve tattoos in brilliant colors running up and down his arms. Across the bottom were the words *Anaconda Glee Club*. They didn't look like any glee club Tate had ever seen. He blew out air, hoping he wasn't making a mistake sending Logan to this place.

The woman passed him his card and a rectangular ticket with *Redwood Stock* emblazoned across the front of it. "Enjoy the show," she said.

Tate put the credit card back in his wallet and picked up the ticket, studying the date and time stamp on the end of it, then he slipped it into the money slot on his wallet and put the wallet in his back pocket again.

Stepping away from the window, Tate made his way to the entrance. A young man in a black t-shirt and slacks with the words *Sequoia County Fairgrounds* on the upper right corner blocked the way. He was clean-cut and clean shaven, very different from the fairgoers moving through the gate on either side of him.

Sheriff Wilson stepped up to the young man and said something in his ear, then motioned Tate inside. The attendant pushed the turnstile down and Tate walked through. He stopped Tate on the other side and picked up a metal detector wand, waving it over his body.

"Just gotta be sure," he told Tate.

Tate nodded. That was fine with him. The more he saw, the better he felt about Logan coming here. After the attendant finished, Tate joined Wilson and Sam waiting next to an information booth.

The fairgrounds stretched on before him with planter beds sporting marigolds and small redwood trees. A bank of bathrooms were arranged to their left next to the fairground offices. A security kiosk sat smack dab in the middle of the asphalt area. Beyond that were wooden booths or covered awnings, marking off vendors. Some sold food, others clothing, and quite a few displayed jewelry.

As he wandered beside the two sheriff's officers, he saw a booth that sold crystals and crystal balls, proclaiming them *the pathways to the beyond.* The prices on the bits of glass were *beyond* anything Tate had seen in a long time. The number of tie dyed clothing vendors was staggering. He gaped in shock when he saw one whole booth dedicated to tie dyed underwear. Of course, there were a number of shops that sold pipes and bongs and other drug paraphernalia. It was billed as tobacco products, but Tate wasn't a fool, especially when he saw a cookbook for baking ganja brownies.

He marked the black uniformed security guards with their embroidered badges on their right breast pockets and their walkie talkies hanging from their belts. A few drove by in golf carts, the crackle of their radios fading into the distance. There seemed to be a large security presence.

They passed a first aid station and already there were a few people inside, lying on cots. Tate figured they'd either not eaten today or had gotten overheated. The day was in the low 90's and a sheen of perspiration was coating Tate's skin.

"What do you think?" asked Wilson.

Tate glanced around, looking for exit signs as Wilson stepped up to a vendor and took out his wallet.

"What'll you have?" Wilson asked him.

"Water, please," said Tate, immediately marking where the emergency exit was located closest to them. It was manned by a security guard. Good.

Wilson bought three water bottles and distributed them around the group.

"Please recycle," said the vendor, her hands covered in henna tattoos.

Tate smiled at her as he open his bottle, then he focused his attention on Wilson. "Where's the concert venue?"

"This way," said Wilson, pointing with his bottle.

Tate followed him and Sam to the left. Signs appeared pointing the way to an open air stadium blocked off with cattle guards. Folding chairs set up in front of a stage indicated where the audience would be. There was little open ground between the first row of chairs and the raised edge of the stage. In fact, there was no barricade between the audience and the performers, except the height of the stage and Tate himself felt he could probably scale it. This certainly hadn't been well prepared ahead of time. Clearly, the Sequoia Fairgrounds didn't hold many concerts. He could understand why the bands were complaining.

He turned a full circle, taking another sip of his water. "I don't know. I think you need to back up the audience another couple of feet and get some more cattle guards between them and the stage. Anyone can climb up on that stage if they're determined. Then I'd station some of your officers in the area between the stage and the audience."

Wilson nodded, one hand on his hip as he surveyed the situation.

"You do have officers scheduled to man these concerts, right?" Tate asked.

"Yeah, but you think I need more than two?"

"Not if you bring in some of the security personnel, but you've got to do something about blocking off that stage."

"Finally, someone with brains around here," came a voice behind them.

Tate turned to see a man about his own nearly six foot height standing on the other side of the cattle guard. He had two burly men behind him, both with shaved heads and muscles bulging. They wore identical khaki pants and black polo shirts, their hands clasped before them. The man himself was in his mid-twenties, sporting a dirty blond beard and spiky bleached blond hair, colorful tattoos covering his arms from his wrists disappearing under his tie dyed t-shirt. His jeans were torn at the knees and he wore Converse sneakers. He might have been handsome if he didn't have piercings covering both ears from lobes to upper cartilage.

"You one of the performers?" said Wilson, moving toward him.

Sam and Tate followed, Tate's attention drawn to the tattoos. He himself had a tattoo, a panther snaking along his inner arm, but that one tattoo and the pain of getting it had been enough for him. Dear God, how long had it taken for someone to tattoo both of this guy's arms?

"I'm Jaguar," said the younger man. "I'm the lead singer for *Anaconda.* I've been complaining about this set-up since we got here, but no one listens."

"Well, Mr. Jaguar…" began Wilson.

"Just Jaguar," corrected the younger man.

"Just Jaguar," said Wilson with an edge to his voice. "That's why I brought Tate out here. He's giving us some ideas on how to make things safer."

Jaguar nodded, looking Tate over. "You a security specialist?"

"No, I own a hardware store."

Jaguar's blue eyes narrowed. More than anything about this guy, his eyes were remarkable. Of course, he'd enhanced them with mascara or eyeliner, or honestly, Tate didn't know or care.

"A hardware store," Jaguar said, his voice dripping with sarcasm. "So glad you're taking my safety seriously, officer."

"Sheriff, Sheriff Wilson," said Wilson, removing a card from his breast pocket and holding it out to the rockstar.

Jaguar snapped his fingers at his bodyguards and one stepped forward, taking the card from the sheriff. Tate frowned at that. What an asshole thing to do. He had an immediate and visceral dislike of the arrogant idiot.

"All righty then," said Wilson, hooking his hand in his belt. "We'll just get back to our surveillance and let you get back to whatever it is you do."

Jaguar didn't look happy. "I have some ideas if you want to hear them."

"I'm sure you do." Wilson motioned Sam up beside him. "Deputy Murphy here will be happy to go over everything with you."

Before Jaguar could protest, Wilson jerked his head back toward the stage and motioned for Tate to follow him. "Asshole," Wilson muttered under his breath.

Tate chuckled.

"Give me any other thoughts you have about this concert," he told Tate. "And I still owe you that beer. Probably with a barbecue sandwich at the *Bourbon Brothers*."

"I'll take it," said Tate, smiling at him.

* * *

Tate got back to the hardware store around 1:30. He'd texted Logan to see if everything was all right and the boy had assured him he had things under control. When Tate walked through the door, he was surprised to see so many dreadlocks and piercings crowding his store, buying the rest of the lawn chairs and coolers and flashlights.

Logan had a line going to the register, but everyone seemed to be patiently waiting. Tate felt even better about getting Logan the ticket, since he'd become such an asset to Tate's business. As Tate went to the counter and slipped under it, Logan shot a glance at him, pulling a basket to the side and off loading its contents. "Are there any more chairs in back?"

"I'll go look, but I think I pulled out everything we had."

"What about styrofoam coolers? I thought I saw some of those."

"I'm on it."

Tate left Logan at the register and went into the storeroom, walking down the shelves and searching for the coolers. He found a stack behind some Christmas lights. He didn't remember putting them there, but Logan had obviously remembered. There were no more chairs, though. He carried the coolers back into the store and set them on the end of the counter where customers could grab them when they went to the register. Looking over at Logan, he wondered if he should get a second register. It might come in handy on the rare occasions that the place got busy. Then he and Logan could ring customers up together.

Glancing out at the store, he noticed Bill Stanley, one of his most loyal locals, edging his way through the crowd. He gave Tate an aggravated look.

"Hey, Bill," Tate said in greeting. "What's up?"

"I need a new chain for my chainsaw. I've got the size right here." He held up a piece of paper. "Can you help me?"

"Sure." Tate lifted the counter and stepped out into the store, sidestepping a green haired woman who looked like something from a fairytale. She actually had wings affixed to the back of her sundress.

Bill eyed her, then shook his head. "I can't wait for this *Redwood Stock* to be over."

"Yeah, but business sure is good," said Tate, leading him to the chainsaw accessories.

"I guess, but I just want to come in for my stuff without dealing with all of this."

Tate found what Bill needed. "Anything else?"

"No. I came in earlier, but you weren't here. Logan said you went to lunch."

"I actually went out to the fairgrounds."

"It's a mess, isn't it? I heard there were fights out there."

Tate shrugged. "It seems to be under control now. I was pretty pleased with the security."

Bill gave the line a jaundiced eye. "I should have just stayed home."

"Go ahead and take it. You can pay me when you come in next time. That way you don't have to wait in line."

Bill's face brightened. "You sure?"

"Yeah, go ahead."

"Thank you. I appreciate it." Without hesitation, Bill turned and left the store with his purchase.

Tate went back to the counter and ducked under, but Logan seemed to have everything under control, so he went into the storage room, looking for more flashlights and lanterns. People also wanted batteries and he knew he had more of those somewhere in the back.

By 2:00, Logan had the customers cleared out. Tate leaned against the counter, breathing in the silence, as Logan ran a hand over his face, wiping away the sweat. The interior of the shop had gotten hotter over the last few hours.

Removing his wallet, Tate took out Logan's ticket and laid it on the counter, pushing it over to the boy. Logan's eyes widened when he saw it, then he picked it up, staring at it in awe. "What's this?" he asked Tate.

"For you. For tonight. You said some of your friends were going. I thought you might like a ticket."

"You got this for me?"

"Yep."

Logan gave him a bewildered look. "For me?"

"Yes, Logan. I wanted you to have a night out with your friends."

Logan's face lit up. "Seriously? I don't know what to say."

"Say you'll go. I know it isn't *Anaconda*, but it's still a concert."

"It's awesome, Tate." He faced his boss and gave him a tense smile. "I don't know what to say," he repeated.

"Don't say anything. It's a bonus for how hard you work for me and I want you to have fun."

"I will," said Logan, beaming. "Dude, will I ever! I'm just so stoked."

"Good." Tate bit his bottom lip. He didn't want to cross the line with Logan. Logan didn't like it when he got fatherly with him, but he still worried about the kid. "Be careful, okay? I mean, I looked the place over and it seems all right, but some of those fairgoers look a little rough."

Logan gave him a patient, condescending smile. "I'll be fine. I know how to take care of myself."

Unfortunately, Tate knew that was true. Few seventeen year olds were more mature than Logan was and for some reason, that made Tate feel sad.

CHAPTER 3

Zion found David waiting at the counter, chatting with Dottie when she came in the next morning. David's face burst into a brilliant smile. He wore a casual polo shirt and chinos. He looked like he was off for a round of golf.

Their date the previous night had been nice and low-key. *Corkers* had been crowded, but David easily secured a table. As one of the few lawyers in town, he got special amenities on occasion. They'd returned to Zion's cottage, shared a few kisses on the couch, then he'd left. For some reason, Zion just wasn't ready to take the relationship any further yet.

She knew Rebekah thought she was crazy, but then Zion had always thought Rebekah threw everything into her relationships maybe just a bit too fast. She didn't wait for them to develop into something deeper before she was agreeing to move in with a guy. So far, Rebekah had lived with five different guys. Every time the relationship went south and Rebekah found herself homeless again. It was exhausting and Zion didn't have any desire to try it.

"Hey," she said, smiling at him.

"Hey, yourself," he answered, putting an arm around her waist and giving her a light kiss. "Thought I'd stop by for some coffee and one of Dottie's famous cinnamon breadsticks."

Zion glanced at the perfectly browned confection on David's plate. The smell was heavenly and Zion knew it drew people into the shop.

"Morning, Dottie."

"Morning, sweet girl," said Dottie, bending to place a tray in the display case.

Zion slipped out of David's embrace and crossed around the counter, taking her purse into the office and placing it in her desk, then she returned and grabbed a clean apron from under the counter and tied it around her waist.

The bell above the door jingled and Tallah walked through. Zion was surprised to see her. Usually Tallah worked the afternoon shift with Dee. "Hey, Tallah? What's up?"

"Morning," the girl said, waving at everyone. "Remember I swapped shifts for today, Zion."

"Oh, right, you've got the concert this afternoon."

"Yep." She beamed happily, crossing around the counter and going in back to deposit her stuff. When she returned, she also took an apron and tied it around her waist, then went to the sink to wash her hands.

"You're leaving at noon?"

"Yeah, the concert starts at 1:00."

"You be careful out there, young lady," said Dottie.

"I will," Tallah promised. "It's just a day show and I'm going with a bunch of friends. We'll be fine. Besides, Mom's driving and picking us up."

"That's good," said Dottie, going into the kitchen to prep some more baked goods.

"Are you excited?" asked Zion.

Tallah opened her eyes wide. "Are you kidding me? I'm so excited. I've never seen *Anaconda* live. It's gonna be epic."

David and Zion laughed.

"Has anyone heard how it went last night?" asked Zion. "Any more fights?"

David shook his head. "I haven't heard anything." He took a sip of his coffee. "I didn't get called down to the courthouse to bail anyone out or anything."

Zion playfully slapped his arm. "You're terrible."

He chuckled and took a bite of his cinnamon breadstick.

The bell jangled above the door and a large group entered. David wrapped his pastry in a napkin and grabbed his coffee. "I'd better get out of here," he said, bending over the counter to kiss Zion's cheek. "Talk to you later. Maybe we can catch a movie tonight?"

"Sounds good," Zion said, waving him off.

As he slipped out the door, another group entered. Zion shared a look with Tallah, glad the girl had come in early after all.

* * *

At 11:30, Deimos entered the coffee shop. The customers had been steady all day, but they were tapering off now. Cheryl followed Dee in and he held the door for her.

Zion looked up from taking an order and waved at her friends. "Hey, Dee, Cheryl."

"Hey, boss lady," said Dee, coming around the counter and grabbing an apron. "Looks busy in here."

"All morning."

"Hey, Zion. I'm glad to see that girl of mine working for her keep," said Cheryl, giving her daughter a pointed look.

Further conversation was cut off as Tallah ran the coffee grinder. Zion figured she did it to stop her mother from commenting about her behavior in front of strangers. As soon as she finished, Dee had washed his hands and was taking the next order.

Dottie came through the bar doors, her purse slung over her shoulder. "How was the concert last night, Deimos?"

"Awesome," said Dee, running a credit card. "Not as good as tonight's though." He jerked his chin at Tallah. "You're going to see *Anaconda* now, right?"

"Right," she said. She'd been smiling all day, she was so excited "I can't wait to see them perform *Edge of Nothing*." She started to sing, "The next day I thought my heart had broken, I thought my heart had burst into flames."

Dee picked up, "I was standing on the precipice, standing on the edge of nothing."

Tallah joined him and they began to harmonize. "She was my lover, my lover, my pilot, my dream."

A loud clapping sound came from the front door. Although the room was crowded, Zion could see a young man had entered, backed by two burly guys in black. Tallah gave a scream, covering her mouth with her hands and dancing excitedly in place.

"Holy shit!" breathed Dee, his eyes bulging.

"That was awesome," said the man. He had white blond hair, a dirty blond beard and moustache, and full-sleeve tattoos on both arms. Piercings ringed his ears from the lobe all the way around to the top. He wore torn jeans and a black t-shirt with a green snake winding around his abdomen. The band name, *Anaconda Glee Club*, was emblazoned around the bottom of the shirt in red stylized letters.

The two burly guys moved to either side of him and glared menacingly at the crowd as he made his way to the counter. Tallah still had her hands over her mouth when he stopped before the register.

"Maybe you two should be backup singers tonight," he told Tallah and Dee.

Cheryl and Zion exchanged a look and Cheryl mouthed the word *Jaguar* to her. Zion wasn't sure what that meant.

"Holy shit!" said Dee again, staring. "I can't believe it's you."

The man smiled. His teeth were surprisingly even and white. "In the flesh. So, are the two of you coming to our concert?"

Tallah nodded her head vigorously, still covering her mouth with her hands.

"Yeah, tonight," said Dee. "Dude Jaguar, you're on in like an hour. What are you doing here?" Then his face drained of color. "I mean, dude, you're here! Holy shit!"

Jaguar laughed.

Zion realized all movement had ceased in the coffee shop, everyone staring in rapt adoration at this man with the many tattoos. She hadn't heard of *Anaconda* before *Redwood Stock*, but Tallah and Dee sure thought this guy was a big deal.

Dottie cleared her throat. "Maybe he wants coffee," she suggested to Dee.

"Oh, yeah, dude, do you want coffee?"

Jaguar's remarkable blue eyes lifted to the menu above Dee and Tallah's head. "What do you recommend?"

Dee just gaped at him, his eyes wide. He didn't seem to be able to speak coherently. Zion started to move to intervene, but Tallah stepped forward. "What about tea? Anything with milk will ruin your voice."

He dropped his gaze to her. "Smart girl. I'm partial to café au lait, but you're right, the milk isn't good for the pipes. Surprise me with a tea choice."

Tallah went to prepare it, her hands shaking. A few of the customers eased forward, glancing at the burly men. "Can I have your autograph?" asked a girl with purple hair.

"Sure," said Jaguar.

Zion wished he'd move away from in front of the register, but more people were now getting up the courage to ask him for autographs or to take a selfie with him. Tallah set his tea on the counter, putting a protective sleeve on it. He gave her another smile.

"Anything else?" she asked, her voice quavering. "Do your bodyguards want something?"

He snapped his fingers at the men. "Order whatever you want," he said.

Both ordered black coffee. Tallah got that too because Deimos didn't seem able to do anything but stare. Zion went to the register and pushed him out of the way, ringing up the sale. She told Jaguar the amount. He snapped again and one of the bodyguards handed Zion a twenty. She frowned at that. She didn't like the snapping. What a jerk!

Tallah held the coffee out to the guards as Jaguar turned back to the counter. Zion offered him his change, but Jaguar waved it off. "Keep it," he said.

Zion stuffed the remainder into the tip jar, motioning the next customer to the register. She wasn't impressed with the rockstar one little bit.

Jaguar took a sip of his tea and nodded. "Good. I like mint."

Tallah beamed.

"So, you didn't say if you were going to my concert or not?" he asked her.

"I am. I'm going to the one in an hour."

"Ah, well, I'm glad to know I'll have at least one friend in the audience." He snapped his fingers again. "Give her two backstage passes," he told the guard on the left.

The man stepped forward and held out the passes.

"Just show those at the door and they'll let you back," said Jaguar. "I look forward to seeing you."

Tallah smiled, breathing a little too fast.

Dee finally recovered. "Can we get a picture, Jaguar dude?"

"Sure," said Jaguar, taking another sip.

Tallah and Dee raced around the counter, poising next to the rockstar. Zion marked he held the *Caffeinator's* cup out so the logo was visible. Maybe she could use this visit for marketing purposes and his obnoxious behavior toward his bodyguards would be worth something after all.

As soon as the picture was finished, he headed toward the door, holding up a hand. "Later gators," he said and exited with his bodyguards flanking him.

The room exploded in excited conversation. Tallah and Dee were staring at Dee's phone, then they both danced in place excitedly. Dottie shook her head. "I'm going home. That's enough excitement for this old woman," she said. She stopped by Dee and Tallah. "You be careful at that concert, both of you," she scolded.

"We will," said Tallah. "Send the picture to me," she told Dee.

"Bye Dottie," Zion called to the older woman.

"Later gator," mocked Dottie, waving over her shoulder.

As Zion rang up a customer, Tallah wandered back to the counter, staring at the backstage passes.

"No, you don't," said Cheryl, "just hand those over right now."

"Mom, he gave them to me."

"No sixteen year old daughter of mine is going backstage with tattooed and pierced rockstar. What do you think your father would say?"

Tallah gave her mother a disbelieving look, then she turned to Zion, appealing for her interference.

"Don't look at me. I don't think you should go either. He's too old and I don't like the way he treats people, Tallah," Zion said.

Cheryl gave her a grateful nod behind Tallah's back.

Dee came around the counter. Tallah focused on him, sensing an ally. "Tell them it's harmless, Dee."

Dee went to the sink to wash his hands again. "I can't do that, dude. I love me some Jaguar, but he shouldn't be hitting on no sixteen year old kid."

"He wasn't hitting on me. He was being nice."

Dee gave her a level look. "You're a smart kid, Tallah. You're too smart not to know when a guy's hitting on you. Listen to your mom. She knows best."

Cheryl held out her hand. Tallah huffed, then slapped the backstage passes on her palm. "Fine." She looked at the time on her phone and untied her apron. "We better get going or we're gonna miss the concert," she said.

Zion took the apron from her and gave her a smile. "Have a good time," she told the girl.

"Thanks. See you tomorrow."

"See you tomorrow," said Zion, watching her wend her way through the crowd to the door.

Cheryl paused in front of Dee, holding out the backstage passes. "Knock yourself out," she told him.

He stared at them, then he reached for them and threw his arms around Cheryl's shoulders. "Thank you!" he said excitedly.

Cheryl patted his back. "No problem. Thank you for supporting me." She waved at Zion and extricated herself, moving toward the door. "See you tomorrow," she called.

Zion rang up the next customer as Dee made the drinks. They fell into an easy routine until they had most of the customers served and the line had dwindled. A few people sat around at the bistro tables, but most had taken their coffee and sweets to-go.

Just as Zion rang up the last customer in line, the bell jangled and a young woman entered. She had long blond hair, hanging to mid-waist and held back with a floral crown. Tattooed stars circled from her cheekbone up around her left eye to her brow ridge. Earrings dangled from multiple holes in both ears and she had a small nose ring like Tallah's in her right nostril. She wore a long, flowing tie-dyed skirt with a teal peasant blouse and sandals. Her toenails were painted black with white stars.

"Hey, Dee!" she shouted above the sound of the grinder.

Dee glanced over his shoulder. "Hey, Merilee. Give me a minute."

"Sure," she said.

Zion thought the name sounded familiar, but the girl didn't acknowledge her at all, so she busied herself with wiping down the counter. Dee set a coffee drink on the pick-up counter and called out the name of the customer, then he leaned on the counter in front of Merilee.

"This is my friend, Merilee," he told Zion.

Zion held out her hand. Merilee gave her two fingers and shook half-heartedly. "Nice to meet you," said Zion. She knew she'd heard the girl's name before, but she couldn't place where.

"You want something to drink?" Dee asked her.

"Naw, I just wanted to see what time you wanna meet for the concert."

"Dude," Dee gushed. "You should have been here just half-an-hour ago. Jaguar was here."

"Shut up!" said the girl, pushing Dee's shoulder. She was pretty if you didn't look too hard at the tattoo on her face.

"Yep, and he gave me these." He took the backstage passes out and laid them on the counter. "Well, he gave them to Tallah, but her mom didn't want her to go."

Merilee stared at the passes in wonder. "Backstage? We're going backstage?"

"Yep. What you think?"

"That's awesome." Her eyes twinkled as she stared up at him. "Can you believe it? We're going backstage with *Anaconda*."

"I know."

"Wait." Merilee tilted her head. "Why'd he give them to Tallah? She's what? Thirteen?"

"Sixteen." Dee shrugged. "Dude sees a pretty girl and doesn't stop to think she might be under aged? How'm I supposed to know?"

"What time do you wanna leave?"

"This one's gonna be crowded. I wanna be up front. I say we get there an hour early."

"You're gonna pick me up, right?"

"Right. Everett ain't gonna be there, is he?"

She waved a hand. "I told him to get out. He picked a fight with Gunner the other night. We were just getting something to eat and he got all possessive. I don't need that shit."

"Word," said Dee. "I don't need it either, Merilee. I ain't looking to get mixed up in your love life."

Zion glanced over, concerned. Some part of her felt responsible for Dee. Merilee met her look and scowled at her. She leaned up on the counter, bringing herself closer to Dee. "We'll talk about it later." She jerked her head toward Zion.

"Whatever you say. I'll pick you up at 8:00."

She tapped her hand on the counter. "See you then." A moment later, the bell jangled as she left the coffee shop.

"I didn't mean to listen in, Dee," said Zion.

"No worries, boss lady. It's your shop. Merilee's good people, she just gets mixed up with the wrong guys."

"So the two of you aren't…"

Dee looked over at her. "Aren't what?"

"Romantically involved?"

"Shit no. Merilee is way too much work. We grew up together. She's like my little sister."

Zion nodded. "Good to hear." She didn't add anything else because she didn't want to push Dee too far, but Merilee seemed like she might be a whole lot of trouble, just the same.

* * *

Zion saw Tate getting out of his truck as she drove down the street to her house. She pulled to the side and rolled down her window.

"Hey, stranger, I haven't talked to you in a while. You haven't been in the coffee shop lately."

He turned and smiled at her, walking toward the Optima. "Hey, how are you? Yeah, sorry, it's been crazy busy at the store. I'll bet you've been busy too."

"I have. Come down to the house and have a beer." She jerked her chin toward the cottage at the end of the street.

"Sounds good. Just let me put on some clean clothes. I've been digging through the storeroom all day and I feel like I've got cobwebs in my hair."

"No problem. See you in a bit." Zion drove the rest of the way to the cottage and pulled into the carport. Climbing out of the car, she grabbed her purse and walked to the mailbox in front of the gate, opening it and pulling out the collection of bills and advertisements. She leafed through them as she pushed open the gate and walked up the granite walkway to the small porch. Shaking her keys, she found the one for her lock and opened the door, dropping the keys into her purse. She stashed the purse in the coat closet, smiling as she heard the jingle of Cleo's bell.

Bending down, she scooped the little cat into her arms and cuddled her as she walked to the kitchen to set the mail on her desk. She'd go through it later. Then she made her way to her bedroom where she exchanged her capris and *Caffeinator* t-shirt for shorts and a tank top. Cleo wound around her legs as she went back into the living room. As she crossed for the kitchen, a knock sounded at the door.

She detoured and opened it for Tate. "Come in," she said, backing up.

He entered the house and reached down to pick up Cleo, carrying her with him to the kitchen. Zion fetched them both a beer from the fridge. They had a beer together maybe once a week and Zion found she looked forward to catching up with the ex-cop.

"She's getting so big," Tate said, taking a seat at the table.

"I know." She handed Tate the beer and opened her own, then grabbed Cleo's bowl and a new can of cat food. "After I feed her, you wanna go sit outside for a bit?"

"Sounds good."

She put the food in the bowl for the cat and set it on the floor. Tate released Cleo. She hurried over and began eating. Grabbing her beer, she and Tate went out the door and down into the yard. They took seats in the loungers Zion had placed in the yard to look over the redwood trees. This late in the evening, the weather was pleasant.

"I'm so glad the heat tapers off at night here," Zion said, taking a sip of her beer. She was beginning to really enjoy the quieter times, the sounds of birds rather than cars. Sometimes she missed the City, but other times, like now, she felt content.

"Me too." Tate sighed, obviously releasing the tension of the day. "So, you would not believe how busy the shop has been."

Zion curled her legs to the side and turned toward him. "Really? What are people buying?"

"Lawn chairs and coolers and flashlights. I totally missed the boat on this festival. I didn't stock enough. Logan warned me it might be big, but I just didn't think it would be. Who comes out here for a festival?"

"People on vacation. It's a great retreat. You get away from the rat race, but you still get to do something entertaining."

"I guess. I bought Logan a ticket for last night's show."

"Who was playing?"

"*Oblivion.* I've never heard their music, but Logan said they were good. I'm glad he got to go."

"He doesn't get to do many kid things, does he?"

Tate shook his head. "I wish I could do more for him."

Zion laid her hand on his arm. "You do a lot."

He looked down at her hand and then gave her a wistful smile. She studied his panther tattoo, then pulled her hand away when she realized she was tracing it with her fingers. A blush heated her cheeks. She couldn't deny it – she got along so well with Tate that she sometimes wondered if there might be more between them, but he was a cop with a secretive background and she didn't need that. Better to stick with her lawyer.

"So, Jaguar came into the coffee house today."

Tate lowered his beer and gave her a skeptical look. "Jaguar? The singer from *Anaconda*?"

"Yeah, you know who he is?"

"I met him out at the fairgrounds when Sheriff Wilson ask me to look over the security there. He's a piece of work."

"You could say that," she said, giving a laugh. "He liked Tallah."

Tate shuddered. "Did he understand she's only sixteen?"

"Did he care?" asked Zion. "He gave her backstage passes."

Tate sat forward in alarm. "She's not going to the concert, is she?"

"She went to the one this afternoon, but Cheryl took the backstage passes away from her."

Tate relaxed again. "Good. Shit, Dwayne would lose it if anything happened to his little girl. I mean, there would be one dead rockstar in Sequoia."

They both laughed at that. Dwayne loved three things – his wife, his daughter, and his restaurant – mess with any at your own peril. "Cheryl gave the passes to Dee. He's going to the concert tonight."

"Huh. I kinda like thinking that Jaguar's sitting there expecting Tallah and he's gonna get Deimos instead."

They laughed again.

"What's so funny?" came a voice at the side gate.

Zion leaned forward, setting her beer on the little table between the loungers. "Hey, David." She rose and hurried around the side of the house, unlatching the gate and opening. "Come in."

"I heard your voices when I came to the door." He bent and kissed her on the cheek. "Nice night to sit outside."

"Yeah, I haven't seen Tate in a while, so I invited him to have a beer. You want one?"

He held up a bottle of wine. "I brought this for dinner, but I might be persuaded to have a glass before we order the pizza."

Zion took the bottle and shut the gate, stepping around David to head for the back door. "Go sit down. I'll bring you a glass." She tapped the top of Tate's lounger as she passed. "Another beer?"

"Sure," he said, rolling to his feet to shake hands with David.

Zion hurried up the back stairs and into the kitchen, setting the bottle of wine on the counter. She fetched another beer from the refrigerator and grabbed the opener. Cleo wound around her legs as she worked to get the cork out of the bottle. Looking out the window, she noticed that David had taken a chair from the patio and set it up in front of the loungers. He had his hands folded on his lap, his hair perfectly coifed. He still wore his khaki chinos and polo shirt, while Tate was in faded jeans and a navy t-shirt. Tate's brown hair was a bit mussed and he had a five o'clock shadow on his jaw.

Back in San Francisco, David was definitely the man she would have chosen to date. He was polished and educated, had money and prestige. Rebekah thought he was a catch and kept encouraging her to move forward in the relationship and yet, Zion kept hesitating. Besides a few make-out sessions, she'd never let him stay the night. Maybe she was taking it too slow. They'd been dating for two months now. Maybe it was time to take it to the next level before he got bored and moved on.

Still, as much as she liked him, she couldn't deny she felt more at ease with Tate. They laughed more, enjoyed a lot of the same things. David belonged to the Zion she once was – fashion conscious, status obsessed; while, Tate appealed to her new life – comfort and ease and simplicity.

She popped the cork, then poured the glass of wine, picking it up with Tate's beer. Cleo raced out the door when she opened it and down into the yard. Zion didn't like her going out this late, but as yet she'd never left the yard and always allowed Zion to pick her up and bring her in when it was time. She dreaded the moment when the fenced part of the world was no longer enough for her little black cat.

She handed David the glass of wine and offered Tate his beer. They both smiled at her.

"Thank you," said David, taking a sip. "Man, I'm beat."

"Busy day?"

"Two wills, a probate case, and one contention."

"Someone was contending a will?"

David nodded, setting the glass on his thigh. "Family didn't think the assets were properly distributed. The new wife was getting *too much*." David made air-quotes at *too much*. "I tell you, I wish these older men would stop wanting the new latest model all the time."

Tate gave him a commiserate smile. "Seems to be going around." He shot a look at Zion.

"What?" asked David.

"Jaguar came into the coffee shop today and took a liking to Tallah. He gave her backstage passes," said Zion.

"Jaguar? Is he one of those singers at the fairgrounds?"

"Lead singer for *Anaconda Glee Club*," said Zion.

"*Anaconda Glee Club*? Now they're just making this stuff up."

Tate gave a laugh. "Just shove three words together and you've got yourself a band."

David shook his head, then he considered. "Wait. You said, Tallah? Tallah Ford?"

"Yep."

"She's what? Fifteen?"

"Sixteen."

"And how old is this Jaguar character?"

"Probably Zion's age," said Tate. He himself was in his early thirties. David had to be around the same age.

"So, late twenties?"

"That's what I figure, but who knows? With rockstars it's the miles not the years, I figure."

"Yeah, you're right," said David. "All I know is I'll be glad when they're gone."

"You and everyone else in Sequoia," said Tate.

David's attention focused on Zion. "So what sort of pizza do you wanna order? And did you pick out a movie?" The dismissive way he said it let Zion know that he was done with socializing. Tate sensed it as well. He leaned forward on the lounge chair.

"I better get going," he said, climbing to his feet.

"Do you want to get a pizza with us?" asked Zion, surprisingly reluctant to have him go. If he stayed, it would put off any decisions Zion had to make about taking her relationship with David to the next level. "We could watch a comedy or something."

"No, I don't want to interrupt your date." He picked up both bottles of beer and moved toward the house.

Zion gave David a significant look. David seemed bewildered and didn't say anything. Zion grabbed her own beer and followed after Tate, scooping up Cleo where she was nosing through the bushes near the house.

"You're not interrupting anything. We were just going to have a quiet night at home."

Tate turned to face her, then his eyes rose beyond her to David. "Another time," he said, smiling at her, but he had a wistful look on his face.

She wasn't sure, but sometimes Zion thought she sensed he had feelings for her that went beyond friendship. Still, she was dating David. David was her sort of guy, not Tate. Tate had demons, she saw them whenever she looked in his eyes, and she didn't need to get mixed up in that.

"Okay, another time," she said.

David came forward and laid an arm around her shoulders, his wineglass in his other hand. "Thanks for stopping by," he told Tate.

Zion frowned, not liking the proprietary sound of his words. She'd been the one to invite Tate over and it was her house, not David's. Tate gave a nod and turned, going up the stairs and into the house. He poured out the rest of the beer in the sink and placed the bottles in her recycle bin.

"Talk to you soon," he said and headed for the door. David followed after him, setting his wine on the kitchen table as he went. Zion noticed it wasn't even a quarter drank. She sighed and put Cleo down.

A moment later, David was back in the kitchen, beaming at her. "How about a veggie pizza with low fat mozzarella?"

Zion's answering smile felt stiff. "Sounds awesome," she said.

CHAPTER 4

Tate found himself trapped behind the sedan, gunshots pinging off the metal on the car's opposite side. The passenger door's mirror shattered. Glass rained down on the asphalt, sparkling in the light from the street lamp. Tate's hands held the gun so tight, his knuckles ached with the tension, and still the bullets pinged off the car.

A moment later he heard the whoosh as the driver's side tire took a hit and began deflating. The street light exploded and darkness fell. Screams could be heard coming from behind him, coming from the houses along the street.

Try to count the bullets, he told himself. *Try to count how many he fires off.* But the percussion of the gun just kept on, never hesitating, never lessening. Tate knew if he didn't move he was going to be picked off as the gunman moved his way around the car.

He closed his eyes, took a deep breath, and…

Tate reared up out of the bed as the phone on the nightstand rang. For a moment, he went to reach for his gun, but he was smart enough to lock it in a gun safe every night. He didn't need to shoot someone by accident.

He tented his knees and raked his hands through his hair, then he fumbled for the phone and glanced at the display. Zion's name flashed at him and his heart picked up speed. It was 4:00 in the morning. Something was wrong. She'd never call him at this hour if something bad hadn't happened.

He thumbed it on and brought it to his ear. His t-shirt was damp with perspiration. "Zion?"

His voice came out husky with panic and sleep.

"Tate, I'm so sorry to wake you up."

"What's wrong?" He ran his hand through his hair again, then down over his jaw.

"Dee's been arrested."

It took a moment for Tate's brain to work out the words. "What?"

"Deimos? He's been arrested. He just called me. He's being booked at the sheriff's office right now."

"He called you?"

"Yes, he said he couldn't think of who else to call."

Tate shook his head to clear it. "Zion, hold on a moment. I'm really confused. What the hell has Dee been arrested for? Pot possession?"

The line went silent and Tate waited for her to come back on. "Murder. He's been arrested for murder."

Tate was sure he hadn't heard that right at all. "Deimos, your peace and love barista, has been arrested for murder? Who was murdered?"

"I don't know. He couldn't tell me much. He just told me they arrested him and why, then he asked me to come down and see if I can bail him out."

"It's likely to be a hefty bail, Zion. Do you have that?"

"No, I have to go see a bail bondsman. I don't want to do that alone, Tate. Can you go with me?"

"Yeah, let me get dressed and I'll come pick you up. What are you going to put up against the bond?" He shoved back the covers and rose to his feet, stretching.

He could hear the tension in Zion's voice and he hated it. Something about this woman brought out protective instincts in him. He thought he'd buried those feelings long ago. Cherise, his ex-wife, had pretty much destroyed them, or so he'd thought. Not that Zion needed him very often. She was amazingly self-sufficient.

"The cottage. I could use the coffee shop, but I can't chance losing it. At least I could find a new place to live if I lost the cottage."

Tate felt bad about that, but he didn't think Dee would ever betray Zion's trust. Then again, he'd never expected Deimos to be accused of murder. Something definitely had to be wrong there. "I'll be there in a minute, Zion. Hold tight, okay?"

"Okay," she said, her voice quavering.

Tate longed to pull her into his arms and chase the fear away, but that wasn't his right. Come to think of it, he was surprised she'd called him and not her lawyer boyfriend. In fact, why wasn't her lawyer boyfriend there with her right now?

He went into the bathroom and splashed water on his face, tugging the damp t-shirt off and tossing it in the laundry hamper, then he decided he'd just jump in the shower. He scrubbed quickly and toweled off, going into his room to pull on a clean pair of jeans and t-shirt. He tugged on his socks and slipped his feet into his sneakers, then grabbed his keys and wallet, hurrying to the door.

The neighborhood was silent as he climbed into the truck and started it, pulling out of the driveway and turning toward Zion's house. She came out as soon as his lights passed over her front window.

She was wearing jeans, a pink t-shirt, and a hoody. Her red hair was wound up on top of her head, but loose curls had escaped to wind around the nape of her neck. Tate had to admit he liked her natural hair color and curls better than the auburn tones she'd had before. In the past, she'd straightened her hair, but it was obvious curly suited her best.

She climbed in the passenger seat, clutching her purse on her lap. Her face was freshly scrubbed and free of makeup, but he liked her best this way. She had an intriguing pattern of freckles over her nose and cheekbones. For a moment, he had an image of her, rumpled from sleep, and it was almost irresistible. Why the hell wasn't David Bennett locking this one down?

He forced the thought away and gave her a tense smile. "You okay?"

She shook her head. "I don't know. I can't get my head around it."

"We'll go over to the sheriff's office first, then the bail bondsman. We need to see if Deimos qualifies for the standard bail or if he's going to have to wait for a hearing before a judge."

Zion nodded, staring out the windshield.

Tate wheeled the truck around and drove back down Conifer Circle, headed for the highway and town. Zion sat quietly for a bit, then she shifted and looked at him.

"Thank you for coming with me," she said.

He glanced at her. "No problem. I'm happy to do it."

"Happy? It's four in the morning."

He shrugged. "Sleeps overrated."

That finally got him a laugh. "I just can't believe Dee would harm anyone, let alone murder someone. There has to be something wrong." She laid her head against the back of the seat. "I wouldn't have the first clue how to go about getting him out without you."

Tate tapped his fingers on the steering wheel. *Don't ask it. Don't ask,* he told himself, but a moment later, he found his mouth opening and the words tumbling out. "It's really not a problem, but can I ask why you didn't call David?"

She stared down at her purse for a moment and he thought she wasn't going to answer. Finally she said, "I don't know."

He took that in, but he didn't comment.

She tilted her head. "I didn't even think of it. When Dee called, I just reacted and you were the first person I thought to call. Should I call him? Can he represent Dee? I didn't think he was a criminal lawyer."

"He's not, but he might know someone. Still, don't call him yet. Let's see what's going on first."

Zion nodded. "Good idea. No use ruining another person's night, right?"

Right, he thought, but he didn't say it.

The sheriff's office was in a strip mall on the edge of town. It shared the mall with a dry cleaner, a Chinese restaurant, and an auto parts store at the opposite end. In between the sheriff's office and dry cleaners was the bondsman aptly named *Bonds, Just Bonds.*

Tate parked the pickup and they got out. He held the glass door on the sheriff's office for Zion. The waiting room was sparsely populated with metal chairs sporting cracked vinyl seats, a long counter across the back wall with a frosted glass barrier, and a door to the left that led into the actual sheriff's station. A water cooler, a few metal end tables, and a dusty silk plant made up the rest of the furnishings. Tate noticed the magazines on the end tables had been updated to ones just two years old.

He pressed the button on the counter and glanced over at Zion. She had her arms wrapped around her middle, looking tense. The urge to hug her was so strong, Tate curled his hands into fists.

"It's going to be okay. This has to be a mistake," he told her.

She nodded, her green eyes darting to the window as it was pushed open. Emilio Vasquez, one of Wilson's deputies, looked out. "How can I help you?" he asked.

In his early forties, Emilio was tall and lean with slicked back black hair and deep-set dark eyes. He wore a neatly trimmed anchor beard. Tate thought he might like to try that, but whenever he grew out a beard it seemed patchy and it itched.

Zion tilted up her chin. "I got a call from Deimos Hendrix that he was arrested."

"And you are?"

"His employer," she said, stepping closer to the counter. She was nervous, but Tate had to admire her ability to tamp down on her nerves for Dee's sake.

Emilio's eyes shifted to Tate. "Hey, Tate."

"Hey, Emilio."

Emilio placed a book in front of Zion and pointed to a place for her to sign, slapping a pen in the binding. Zion signed her flourishing signature, then shoved the book back through the frosted window. Emilio reached under the counter and pushed a button.

The door next to them buzzed and Tate walked over, pulling it open. Emilio met them on the other side. "I need to look in your bag and frisk you both."

"What exactly do you think I have, Deputy? A file to break Deimos out?" she said, giving him a challenging look from her green eyes.

Emilio and Tate exchanged an amused look. "I can't take the chance on that, Ms. Sawyer," he said levelly.

Zion held out her purse, her expression still challenging. He peeked inside, then passed it back. Motioning for her to turn around, he gave her a brief, respectful patdown. Tate turned so he could do the same to him. He had no interest in making this man's life harder than necessary. He'd dealt with too many uncooperative people in his time on the force and he knew what it was like.

Once he was done, Emilio motioned for them to follow him. Tate marked that the precinct was down to a skeleton crew this early in the morning. Emilio entered the narrow, dank hallway leading to Sheriff Wilson's office.

He knocked on Wilson's door. A moment later, Wilson said, "Yeah?"

Emilio pushed the door open and poked his head inside. "Ms. Sawyer is here to see Dee, Sheriff."

"Let her in."

Emilio stepped back and motioned Tate and Zion through the door. Sheriff Wilson rose as they entered. His uniform was rumpled and there was a coffee stain on his right breast pocket. He had a five-o'clock shadow and his eyes looked bruised.

"Tate," he said, acknowledging him with a nod.

"Sheriff."

"Ms. Sawyer, please have a seat." He motioned to the two metal chairs before his desk.

Zion sank into one and Tate took the other. She clasped her purse on her lap, but she sat forward in the chair, her back stiff. "Sheriff Wilson, Dee called me and told me he'd been arrested."

"Well…"

"For murder?"

"He's a suspect in a suspicious death."

"Whose death?" demanded Zion.

"Merilee Whitmire," said Wilson, taking his seat again.

Zion slumped back in her chair. Tate glanced at her, then at the sheriff. "How'd she die?"

"Drug overdose."

"And you think Dee had something to do with it? How?"

"He was with her when she went into cardiac arrest. "

"And that makes him culpable or something? If it was a drug overdose, how is that his fault?" demanded Zion.

"They were both smoking dope, pot, in his apartment. Now she's dead."

"She overdosed. You said it yourself."

"I said he was a suspect in a homicide, Ms. Sawyer. We're waiting on an autopsy."

Tate knew that meant they had more evidence against Dee than just the pot.

"I want to see him," Zion demanded.

Tate put a hand on her arm. "He asked Zion to bail him out. Has he asked for a lawyer?"

"He did. Right away. We called the public defender's office. They'll send someone over tomorrow, but he hasn't been arrested. We just brought him in for questioning."

"I still don't understand," said Zion. "If they were both doing pot, why are you thinking this is anything more than an accidental death?"

"I can't reveal that at the moment."

Zion turned to Tate. He didn't know what to say. Something had triggered Wilson to bring Dee in for questioning, but he wasn't giving up that information right now. Tate drew a deep breath. He knew Sheriff Wilson wanted him to come on as a consultant, but he'd left police work behind. If he asked for information now, Wilson might get the wrong idea. Still, he couldn't deny the pleading look on Zion's face.

"Sheriff, this is obviously something more than a drug overdose. I've never heard of anyone overdosing on pot."

Wilson considered them for a moment, pressing his tongue into his molars. His chair groaned as he leaned back in it. "The doctors in the emergency room are suspicious. They've never seen a pot overdose either. The coroner will be doing an autopsy tomorrow and hopefully we'll know more."

"Can I see Dee?" Zion demanded.

Wilson leaned forward in his chair and picked up his desk phone receiver. He punched a button and waited. "Vasquez, will you escort Ms. Sawyer to see Deimos Hendrix?" He listened, then said, "Thanks," and hung up. "Look, Ms. Sawyer, I have a dead girl here. I had to tell a father that his daughter would never come home again. I'm just doing my job."

Zion didn't answer.

Emilio opened the door and motioned to them. "Come with me," he said.

Zion rose and stared down at Wilson. "I understand that, Sheriff, but you're looking in the wrong place." Then she turned on her heel and followed Emilio to the door.

Tate pushed himself to his feet. "Thanks, Sheriff," he said.

"Anytime you wanna come on and consult…"

"Yeah, I know. I'll think about it," he said, but they both knew he wouldn't.

* * *

Dee looked like hell. His hair was a mess, tangled and standing on end, his clothes were tattered and dirty, and he smelled of sweat and something sickly sweet. Tate figured it must be pot. He had his hands shoved into his hair, holding his head on either side, his elbows on the metal table.

Emilio let them into the interrogation room, then touched Tate's arm. "I'll be right outside this door."

Tate nodded, knowing both Sheriff Wilson and his deputy would be watching through the two-way glass.

Dee jumped to his feet as Zion stepped inside, throwing his arms around her. "I didn't think you'd come."

She patted his back, wrinkling her nose at the smell. "Of course I came."

"Tate, dude, I'm so glad to see you." He held out his hand and Tate took it, only to be pulled into a bear hug. Dear God, the kid needed a shower.

"Sit down, Dee, we need to talk," said Tate, releasing him.

Dee sank into the chair on the other side of the table, while he and Zion took a seat opposite him. Zion placed her purse in her lap and leaned forward, clasping her hands on the table. "What happened, Dee? Tell me everything."

Dee shook his head, screwing up his mouth in a grimace. "I wish I knew. It's all sort of blurry."

Tate looked around the room. Typical interrogation room – white walls, metal table, uncomfortable metal chairs, mirror on the back wall that functioned as a two-way glass. Two cameras in opposite corners let him know they were being recorded. Well, he didn't think Dee had anything to hide, so he wasn't that worried about it.

"Tell me what you remember. You picked Merilee up for the concert?" pressed Zion.

Dee nodded. "Yeah, that's right."

"What time?"

"Eight, like she said."

"What time did the concert start?" asked Zion.

"Nine."

"What time did you get there?"

"About 8:30."

"Did you stay for the whole concert?" asked Tate.

"Yeah, we were down in front, dancing and everything, having a blast."

"What time did the concert end?" asked Zion.

"Eleven."

"Then what did you do?"

"We went backstage after the concert was over. I had those backstage passes Cheryl gave me."

"Right. What happened backstage?"

"We noshed and drank a beer. Then we smoked a couple of blunts."

When Zion closed her eyes, Dee leaned forward. "I know, I know, but it was only a couple of blunts. It wasn't a big deal."

"Merilee died of a drug overdose, Dee. It was a big deal."

"But I mean it wasn't like she did anything else. No one overdoses on weed."

"What time did you leave the fairgrounds?"

Dee stared at the ceiling, trying to remember. "One, one-thirty."

"Merilee went back to your apartment with you?" asked Zion.

"Yeah." He shivered. "I can't believe this is happening. I mean, Merilee was my friend. She had so much left to do, you know?" He buried his face in his hands.

Zion exchanged an aggravated look with Tate. "Dee, did you sleep with Merilee?"

Dee peered at her through his fingers. "Sleep with her?"

"Have sex," said Tate, giving him a level look.

"Yeah," he said, dropping his hands. He wouldn't meet Zion's gaze.

"You said you weren't involved with her like that, Dee," Zion scolded. "You said she had a boyfriend and another guy messing around her. You said she was too much work. You told me she was like a little sister to you."

"I know." He held up his empty hands. "It was after a concert and we were high, sooo…" He dragged out the last word.

"Sooo?" Zion said.

Tate placed a hand on her arm. This wasn't really the point. The girl was dead. That was what they had to focus on. "Okay, so you had sex, then did you do more drugs?"

Dee nodded, his face twisted with misery.

"What?"

"What?"

Tate drew a breath for patience. "What drugs did you do?"

"Oh, only weed. I don't do anything else. We smoked another blunt, then went to sleep."

"What time did you notice something was wrong?"

"Geez, Tate dude, it wasn't even an hour later. I woke up. I think it was like 2:15 and I could hear Merilee in the bathroom. She was really sick, puking and everything."

"Did you go in to check on her?"

Dee chewed on his inner lip.

"Dee, you need to tell me everything," Tate demanded.

Dee considered that for a moment, then he shook his head no. Zion slumped back in her seat.

"You didn't go in to check on her when you heard her being sick?"

"No." Dee's face scrunched up more and Tate thought he might cry.

"But you called 911?"

"Yeah."

"Why?"

"I heard a crash and went in the bathroom."

"So you went into the bathroom after you heard the crash, not before?" Tate realized he was sounding like a cop, hammering down every bit of information, every detail, establishing a timeline.

"Right."

"And what did you see? What made you call 911?"

Dee shuddered and tears filled his eyes. "It was bad, Tate dude. It was bad."

"What did you see, Deimos?"

"She was laying on the floor, having trouble breathing. Her face was turning blue."

"Okay. So you called 911 and then what did you do?"

"They told me to unlock the front door, so I left Merilee to do that." He closed his eyes, tears running down his cheeks.

"And then what? What happened after you unlocked the door?"

"I went back to check on Merilee. I think she was having a seizure. I put a pillow under her head and tried to make her more comfortable."

"Then what?"

"The paramedics arrived. They started working on her and she stopped breathing."

"In the bathroom?"

"Yeah." Dee rubbed his temples with both hands. "You should have heard them. They were so calm, trying to get her breathing again. Dude, I couldn't do that shit. I couldn't stay calm like that. I was a mess."

Tate nodded, then continued, "They took her to the ambulance?"

"Right."

"And where were you?"

"I followed them. They asked me if I was her husband or boyfriend and I lied. I told them I was her boyfriend. They let me ride in the front of the ambulance."

"Once you arrived at the hospital, what happened?"

"They took her into emergency. I followed them, but they wouldn't let me go in back with her."

Tate wished he had a pad of paper to write down the timeline. "When did you get to the hospital?"

"About 2:45."

"How long were you there before they told you what happened to Merilee?"

"Half an hour or so."

"Can you be more certain?"

"I remember looking at the clock over the nurse's station. It said 3:15 or so."

"So, the doctor came out and said?"

"No, Sheriff Wilson came in."

"Sheriff Wilson came in?"

"Yeah, he told me Merilee died in the ambulance on the way there. She never even made it to the emergency room."

Tate drummed his fingers on the table. "That's when Wilson brought you in for questioning?"

"Right."

"What did you tell him?"

"Same thing I told you, then I asked for a lawyer and asked to call Zion."

Tate pulled out his phone and glanced at the display. It was 5:30. "Go back to the concert."

Dee slumped in his seat, his expression bleak. "I'm exhausted, Tate dude. I feel so damn sad. Merilee's dead, dude."

"I know, Dee, but you're in a lot of trouble."

"Can we talk about this later?"

"I want to hear it before you forget."

"But I'm just so tired and my brain's mush."

"Just answer him," growled Zion, rising abruptly to her feet and walking away from the table.

Dee flinched and Tate glanced over his shoulder at her. He'd never heard her angry before.

"Ask your questions," said Dee.

"Did anyone come up to her at the concert? Did anyone give her anything?"

"No."

"Did she go to the bathroom by herself?"

"I walked her to the door. She went inside by herself."

"Did she tell you anyone gave her anything in the bathroom?"

"No."

Tate nodded. "What about when you went to the after party. Are you sure she didn't take anything except smoke some pot?"

"That's right."

"You said you noshed, right?"

"Right."

"That means they had food?"

"Right. The fairgrounds catered it."

"Who was the caterer?"

Dee considered that. "I don't know."

Tate left that alone. He could find out himself. "Did Merilee eat the food?"

"Sure."

"Did anyone else?"

"Everyone ate the food."

"Did she ever leave with anyone at the party? Did she go into a room with anyone?"

"No, she stayed with me the whole time."

"Okay," said Tate. "When you got back to your apartment, did you eat anything?"

"Maybe. We scrounged in the fridge, but that starts getting blurry."

"The time in your apartment gets blurry? Why?"

"Dude, we smoked some more ganja."

"You need to remember what happened, Dee."

"I don't."

"You need to try harder. You're a suspect in a murder!"

"You think I don't know that!" he yelled. "You think I don't know why I'm here!"

Zion turned and looked at him. He glanced at her, then slumped in the chair again.

"You think I don't know." He pointed at the two-way glass. "You think I don't know they're listening right now. Well, I didn't hurt Merilee. I would never hurt Merilee. She was my friend. She was my friend." He gave a hitching sob and covered his face. "I just want to go home. Please. Just let me go home."

Tate stared at the metal table, then looked up at Zion. Her expression was tormented as she stared at the young man sobbing on the other side of the table, then she met Tate's gaze and he knew he was going to be sucked into another case whether he liked it or not.

CHAPTER 5

Dottie was working dough in the kitchen when Zion arrived an hour later. Dee's public defender had shown up and Dee had been let go with the admonition to not leave town. Tate had taken Zion back to her house, so she could shower and feed Cleo, then she'd driven to the coffee house.

She felt fuzzy headed and unsettled. Placing her purse on the counter, she grabbed the coffee and poured it into one of the pink mugs with *Caffeinator* emblazoned across the front of it. She rarely drank coffee, preferring tea, but today seemed like a coffee day. Pouring a little milk into it, she stirred and took a sip, grimacing at the bitter taste.

Picking up her purse, she went into her office and stashed it in her desk, then she carried her coffee to where Dottie pounded the dough with floured fists. Dottie smiled at her, then glanced into her cup.

"Coffee?"

Zion nodded. "Look, Dottie, I need to tell you something."

Dottie stopped, staring at her. "What's wrong?"

"Last night, Dee…"

"Oh, God, I warned him about that concert." She grabbed a towel and began scrubbing the dough from her hands. "He's in the hospital, isn't he? Concussion? Dehydration?"

"Dottie." Zion laid a hand on her arm. "He was arrested."

Dottie placed her free hand on her heart. "Arrested?" She leaned close and dropped her voice. "For drug possession?" she asked as if Zion didn't already know that Dee smoked pot.

Zion shook her head.

"For what?" The color faded from Dottie's face.

"He's a suspect in a murder."

To Zion's surprise, Dottie started laughing. "Geez, you scared the bejesus out of me, sugar." She pushed back the unnaturally red hair from her forehead. "I thought you were serious."

Zion didn't say anything, just stared at her grimly.

Dottie's smile faded. "You are serious?"

Zion nodded.

"Who?"

"Merilee Whitmire."

Dottie's expression grew angry. "I warned him that girl was trouble. I told him to stay away from her."

"Well, she's dead, Dottie."

Dottie stopped in mid-tirade. "How?"

"Sheriff says overdose."

"Wait. So how is that murder?"

"That's what I said. Tate says that means there's more to her death than the sheriff is telling us."

Dottie nodded, her eyes going distant as she thought, then she gave Zion a bewildered look. "Wait. How do you know all this?"

"He thought he'd been arrested, so he called me to come bail him out."

"He called you?"

Zion nodded.

"Before he called me?"

"I don't think he wanted you to see him like he was, Dottie. And he thought he needed bail."

"Why was Tate there?"

"I thought he needed bail too and I didn't know how to get it for him. I asked Tate to come."

Dottie nodded. "That was good. That was smart. Tate knows about these things. He was a cop."

"I know."

"Does Dee have a lawyer?"

"Public defender, but after things slow down this morning, I'm going to call David and see if he can recommend someone."

Dottie leaned on the counter. "I can't believe this. I warned that boy. So many times, I warned him he was going to get in trouble."

Zion gave her a grim smile. Dottie cared about Dee as if he were her own son. Dottie didn't talk much about her life, but Zion knew from Dee that she'd been married and her husband had died young.

Before she could answer, the bell over the door rang. She and Dottie looked out. A line of people had entered the coffee shop. Smoothing her hands down her apron, Dottie lifted her chin. "We better get to work," she said.

Zion followed her out, snagging a clean apron from beneath the counter, then she started taking orders while Dottie prepared the drinks. A girl with rainbow colored hair handed Zion a dirty ten, leaning close to the cash register.

"So, is it true?"

Zion looked up at her, pressing a button to open the cash drawer. "Is what true?"

"Did one of your baristas kill a girl at *Anaconda* last night?"

Zion gave her a glare. "No, it's not true." She looked over the crowd. True, morning was always their busiest time, and they'd been busier since *Redwood Stock* began, but it was even more crowded than usual. She handed the girl her change. "How did you hear something happened anyway?"

"It was all over the internet. They say Jaguar liked the girl who was killed. She went backstage, then her boyfriend killed her in a jealous rage."

Zion glanced over her shoulder at Dottie. Dottie gave her a worried look.

"That's just rumor," she told the girl.

"Mmhmm," said the girl, moving to the side to wait for her drink.

Clearly Dee shouldn't come in today, but that left Zion short handed and she was already so tired. Glancing into her own coffee cup, she held up a hand to the next customer and filled it again. It was going to be a long day.

* * *

Tallah walked in about ten. Zion was so happy to see her, she almost burst into tears. They'd had a steady stream of customers all morning. The baked goods were gone from the shelves and Dottie was frantically trying to bake up a batch of her cinnamon breadsticks. Zion had been forced to brave the temperamental espresso machine herself, but the gadget still hated her and complained whenever she tried to use it.

Tallah hurried behind the counter and grabbed an apron. "Mom said you were slammed, so I came in early."

"You are the best thing I've seen all day," said Zion.

Washing her hands, Tallah began making the next drink. "Mom is freaking out over what happened."

"Why?"

"She feels like she's responsible. She gave Dee the backstage passes."

"That's silly. How did you hear about it?"

"It's all over the social media sites. The *Anaconda* manager released a statement, saying the band was cooperating with police, but weren't involved in anyway with Merilee's death."

Political spin, thought Zion.

"Mom feels really bad. Merilee used to come into the restaurant all the time."

"I know, she told me."

Dottie came out of the kitchen. "I got two batches baking and another of cookies ready to go in." Her face burst into a smile when she saw Tallah. "Hey, sugar, it's sure good to see you."

"Mom said you guys were getting slammed," Tallah told Dottie, slapping a sleeve on a cup and placing it on the pick-up counter. "Dillon, your caramel macchiato is ready."

"Dottie," said Zion, ringing up a new order. "Do you think you can take over? I think I better call Dee and tell him not to come in."

"You got it," she said, stepping up to the register.

"While I'm at it, I'm gonna give David a call and see about getting Dee a lawyer."

"You take your time. That's more important right now. I've cleared my schedule for the day. I'll stay to closing if you need me," said Dottie.

Zion patted her shoulder, then hurried to her office, shutting the door. She picked up the office phone and dialed Dee's number. He didn't pick up. Zion decided not to leave a message, but this worried her. Dee had been almost inconsolable on the ride home this morning.

She dialed David next. He picked up on the first ring. "Hey, this is a nice surprise," he said brightly.

"It might not be after you hear what I need to ask you." She hesitated. She couldn't believe she was about to ask him for the name of a criminal attorney for her hippie barista. "Did you hear the news from the fairgrounds last night?"

"Nope. How did Dee like the concert?"

"He was brought in for questioning by the sheriff this morning, David."

That got his attention. "What?"

Zion told him everything. He listened attentively. That was another thing she liked about David. He was a good listener. After she finished, he blew out air. "Well, they obviously have more evidence than they told you or they wouldn't be thinking murder charges," he said.

"That's what Tate said."

David got quiet for a moment. Zion didn't know if he was thinking or if he didn't like her mentioning Tate. She knew how it might look to him that she'd asked Tate to accompany her last night rather than him.

"I've got some names. I'll call a few people and see who might be willing to represent Dee if it comes to that. Tell him to lay low until I get someone on board. We don't want him talking to reporters and inadvertently messing up his own case."

Zion knew that was good advice. If she could find Dee, that is.

"Thank you, David. I appreciate this."

"I'm happy to help, Zion. I can't believe Sheriff Wilson really suspects Dee of doing something wrong. Dee's many things, but he's not a murderer."

"I know that, and you know that, but Sheriff Wilson still has a dead girl on his hands."

"Such a shame," said David. "Merilee was such a pretty girl with so much potential."

Zion agreed, but even pretty girls with potential could get mixed up in the wrong thing. A knock sounded on her office door. "I gotta go. We've been slammed all day. I'll talk to you later."

"Zion?"

"Yeah?"

"Call me immediately if Wilson actually arrests him."

"I will."

"You wanna grab dinner or something?"

"I might beg off tonight. I've been up since 4:00 and I'm exhausted."

"I understand. I'll call you later, then."

"Talk to you soon." Zion disconnected the call and rose to her feet, going to the door and pulling it open.

Cheryl Ford stood on the other side, holding a wrapped sandwich and a bottle of water. Zion stepped back to let her inside. "I thought you might need someone to bring you lunch," she said, holding out the sandwich and the water. "I brought something for Dottie and Tallah too. They said for you to take your time. You can all eat in shifts."

Zion accepted the sandwich and water, hugging her friend. "Thank you. You're the best." She motioned to the chairs. "Come sit down."

Cheryl sank into a chair, while Zion assumed her original seat, unwrapping the sandwich. Pulled pork with extra sauce, her favorite. She took a bite, watching Cheryl fidget in the chair.

"It's not your fault," she told her friend around a mouthful.

Cheryl swiped a hand through her short cropped black hair, her diamond wedding ring twinkling in the overhead lights. "I gave Dee the backstage passes. He invited Merilee and she overdosed. Maybe she wouldn't have overdosed if I hadn't put her in that situation."

Zion set down the sandwich. "Both Tate and David said there's more to it than that. They think Sheriff Wilson's holding back information."

Cheryl shook her head. "Dee would never kill someone, Zion."

"I know that."

"He needs a lawyer."

"David's working on getting him one."

Cheryl looked down at her hands. "Dwayne is so mad at me for letting Tallah go to that concert."

"You didn't do anything wrong. Tallah's two years from being a legal adult. She's going to be making her own decisions. You have to trust you raised her right and I know you did. She's a great kid and she has a bright future ahead of her. Stop blaming yourself for this."

Cheryl gave her a wane smile. "I just think of Merilee. She came into the barbecue a lot. She was so full of life, so much future ahead of her, and she's dead, Zion. Just like that. One minute she was alive and now she's not. I can't help but think it could happen to anyone."

Zion rose and came around the desk, bending to hug her friend. "Tallah is going to be driving you and Dwayne crazy for the rest of your lives. Don't you worry about that."

Cheryl hugged her back. "Go finish your sandwich. I've got to get back before the lunch rush begins."

Zion released her and watched her walk out the room. It was tragic that someone so young as Merilee had died, but Deimos Hendrix was not the one responsible. Of that she was sure.

* * *

The outer door opened and a cacophony of voices filled the coffee shop. Zion looked up seeing a crowd pushing their way inside. She caught video cameras and microphones being shoved into the center of the circle, then spotted Dee's shaggy head.

She glanced over at Tallah and Dottie. "Tallah, go get your dad or your uncle, whichever one's available." Tallah headed for the back door that led behind the buildings on this side of the street.

Zion slipped around the counter and waded into the crowd, grabbing Dee's arm and dragging him forward.

"Do you have a statement to make?"

"What were you smoking?"

"Did you know it would kill her?"

"Did you wake up and find her dead?"

"Excuse me!" said Zion, pulling Dee behind the counter and around Dottie who wielded a rolling pin. Dottie stepped into the gap and brandished the rolling pin at the reporters, driving them back behind the counter again.

Zion dragged Dee into her office and slammed the door. "What were you thinking?"

"I have to work," he said. "I can't leave you in the lurch."

He'd showered and shaved. He'd even tried to slick back his hair, but the scuffle with the reporters had mussed it again.

"I tried to call you. Why didn't you answer?"

"I turned my phone off. It's been ringing all day."

Zion drew a deep breath for calm. "Where did all those reporters come from?"

"They were covering *Redwood Stock*, but I suddenly became more interesting. Dude, I still can't get my head around this."

She patted his arm. Suddenly she could hear Dwayne's booming voice in the coffee house and she breathed a sigh of relief. She didn't think there were many reporters brave enough to face down Dwayne Ford's more than six feet of toned muscle.

"That's right. Either order something or take yourselves off," came Daryl's voice.

Zion frowned. Both brothers had come? "Wait here!" she told Dee, then pulled open the door and went out.

Dwayne and Daryl stood shoulder to shoulder in the middle of the coffee shop, holding back the scrum of reporters and cameras and lookie-loos. Zion felt a rush of gratitude toward them. Reluctantly, the reporters were making their way to the door, glancing back over their shoulders for a peek at Dee.

Zion stepped around the counter, stopping beside Dwayne. He frowned down at her.

"She-et, girl, what the hell is going on?"

Zion shook her head. "Dee came to work. I tried to stop him earlier, but he'd turned off his phone. I guess they've been hounding him all day."

Dwayne kept one eye on the reporters as he responded. "He needs to get out of here for now. This is too hot and he doesn't need to draw attention to himself."

"I know. I need to find someone to drive him home."

Dwayne slapped his little brother on the shoulder. "Daryl'll drive him home."

Zion leaned around Dwayne to smile at Daryl. "Thank you both for coming. I know you need to get back, but I really appreciate it."

"Don't worry about it. Neighbors need to have each other's backs," said Daryl.

The rest of the reporters had left, so Daryl turned to face the counter. "Get me an iced coffee to go, little girl," he told his niece.

She rolled her eyes, but she moved to obey. Zion exchanged an amused look with Dwayne.

"I'll just get back to work," Dwayne said and headed for the door.

Zion waited to make sure the reporters had gone, then she walked around the counter, motioning Daryl to follow her. "You should probably leave out the backdoor."

Daryl grabbed his coffee and reached for his wallet.

"Nope. The coffee's on me," Zion told him. "For coming to our rescue."

"Thanks," he said and followed Zion into her office. Dee was pacing before the desk.

"Hey, Daryl dude," he said, offering the other man his hand.

They shook, then Daryl gave him a level look. "You need to lay low, Deimos. At least until this thing's over."

Dee's expression became crestfallen. "I need to work, dude. I can't just stay home. I need the money."

"I'll pay you for your regular hours, but Daryl's right. You can't come in here until you're cleared."

"I don't want charity, boss lady," said Dee.

"It's not charity. It's for all our sakes."

Dee looked so upset, Zion felt sorry for him, but he'd gotten himself into this mess. Everyone had warned him to stay away from Merilee. "I guess. I just don't know what I'll do with myself."

"Read a book," suggested Daryl. "Binge watch something on *Netflix*."

"Whatever you do," said Zion, pushing him toward the door. "Stay out of trouble."

He didn't answer, but he followed obediently behind Daryl as they made their way to the alley door and left.

* * *

By early evening, Zion was so tired, she wasn't sure how she was going to keep working twelve hour days. She might need to hire someone temporarily to cover Dee's shift, but she wasn't sure how she'd pay that person if she also gave Dee his regular wages. Still, she was exhausted, her feet hurt, and her shoulders felt stiff. She'd drank so much coffee, she had the jitters.

Around 4:00, she'd forced Dottie to go home. The older woman was lagging and Zion had caught her popping painkillers just to make it through. Thankfully, the traffic had finally died down, allowing her and Tallah to spell each other regularly.

She glanced at her phone. Almost 6:00. She'd decided to close at 6:00 tonight. During the summer, the coffee shop had been staying open until 8:00 to accommodate the tourists, but tonight she and Tallah were beat.

A handful of concert goers had come in after the matinee show and were sitting around on the couches, chatting and sipping coffees. The baked goods had gone shortly after Dottie left for the day and Zion hadn't had a chance to whip up anything.

She grabbed a glass of water and walked to an unoccupied bistro table, sitting down and putting her aching feet up on the chair opposite her. She didn't remember when she'd been so tired. When she worked in San Francisco, there were nights she and Rebekah stayed out late, dancing, but this was a different tired. Every muscle in her body hurt and she could hardly keep her head up.

The bell over the door jangled and a handsome young man walked in, looking around. He had blond hair, cropped short, but the top had been spiked up. He also had piercings in both ears and one in his lower lip. Colorful tattoos ran up his arms from the wrist to the shoulder. He wore a tank top and jeans torn out at the knees, and flip flops that had seen better days. He swaggered up to the counter.

"Where's Dee?" he demanded of Tallah.

"I don't know," she said, her eyes cutting to Zion.

Zion pushed herself to her feet, grimacing. "Can I help you with something?" she asked him.

He glanced back at her, his lip curling in distaste. "No, I want to see Dee." He focused on Tallah again. "Tell me where he is. I know he works this shift."

Tallah's panicked dark eyes flickered to Zion once more. Zion stepped closer to her, edging toward the counter opening.

"Tallah, will you go check the cookies in the oven?"

She gave Zion a bewildered look. They'd decided to wait until tomorrow to bake some more. But a moment later, her expression cleared and she nodded, hurrying through the swinging doors. Zion came around the counter and laid her hand on Dottie's rolling pin, which she'd left on the counter behind the display case.

"I'm Zion, the owner," she told the young man. "I gave Dee the day off."

His jaw clenched and a muscle bulged. "Give him a message, will you?"

"Sure," said Zion, tightening her hold. The rest of the people in the shop sensed the tension and were gathering their belongings, headed for the door.

"Tell him that when I find him, he's dead."

Zion's fingers curled around the handle. The bell jangled as the customers hurried out of the shop. "Why? What did he do to you?"

The young man took a step closer to the counter and Zion picked up the rolling pin. "He killed my girlfriend!" he growled, then he seemed to notice the rolling pin and leaned away. He nodded, easing back a pace. "Just tell him for me, okay?"

Zion didn't respond, refusing to look away. After a moment, he turned and headed for the door. Zion waited until he opened it, then she raced around the counter, rolling pin in hand, and hurried across the dining room. When she reached the door, she looked out, but the young man had disappeared. Throwing the lock, she turned to face Tallah.

The girl stood in the doorway, her phone in hand. "Do you want me to call the sheriff's office?"

Zion shook her head. "No, but you did really good, Tallah. Thank you."

Tallah lowered the phone. "Man, that was scary."

"Yeah," said Zion, breathing out. "Do you know who that guy was?"

"That's Everett Hughes, Merilee's boyfriend."

Zion nodded. "That's what I figured."

"Are you sure I shouldn't call 911?"

Zion moved back to the counter and settled Dottie's rolling pin on the display case. "Yeah, I'm sure. I'll give Sheriff Wilson a head's up on their direct line." She moved around the counter, untying her apron. "Let's clean up and get out of here early. I'm beat."

Tallah didn't need to be told a second time. She shoved the phone in her pocket and set to work taking apart the hated espresso machine. Zion rubbed the back of her neck and looked toward the coffee shop door. Damn, Dee really knew how to get himself into a heap of trouble.

CHAPTER 6

Monday morning dawned with a glorious blue sky and a promise of oncoming heat as the day progressed. Logan met Tate at the door of the *Hammer Tyme*, his young face alight with excitement.

"Did you hear the news?"

"What?" Tate frowned. What more had happened?

"The sheriff told *Anaconda* not to leave town yet. He wants to question them about Merilee's murder."

"Really?" Tate unlocked the door and they stepped inside.

Logan immediately veered off to open the blinds, while Tate walked to the back and flicked the switch, turning on the track lighting.

"They agreed. I guess they don't have anything scheduled for a while and most of them are from this area, so it gives them time to see their families," finished Logan.

Why was the sheriff targeting *Anaconda* if he suspected overdose or that Dee had something to do with it? Even Sheriff Wilson had to know that last idea was silly. Deimos Hendrix might be many things, but Tate just couldn't peg him for a murderer. Still…

He shook his head. This wasn't his case and he wasn't getting dragged into it. "Well, I'm sure they have enough money for lawyers," he said, going into the back to get money from the safe.

Logan followed him. "Why would the sheriff question the band though?"

"I don't know," Tate lied. He didn't want Logan getting too caught up in it either. "Hey, can you vacuum the floors real quick?"

"Sure," said Logan, grabbing the machine and carrying it out into the store.

Tate paused at the safe. After he figured out the books for the month, maybe there would be enough left over to give Logan a raise. The kid did everything he asked and he did it with enthusiasm. Tate didn't know what he'd do without him.

After the excitement of the weekend, Monday wasn't as busy. They got a few customers, and Bill Stanley made his daily appearance, picking up LED light bulbs because his wife wanted to be more energy efficient. He hung around, wanting to talk about the festival, then the murder.

Tate tried to stay out of it, but after he'd counted the money in the cash register three times without Bill making any effort to leave, he figured he was going to have to say something more than "Huh".

He actually felt grateful when the buzzer went off and Sheriff Wilson entered the store. Wilson removed his sheriff's hat and held it before him as he approached the counter.

"Morning, Bill," he said, ducking his head at the older man.

"Morning, Sheriff," said Bill.

"Logan," said the sheriff.

"Sheriff Wilson," said the boy, his eyes dancing with excitement.

Tate felt a sinking in the pit of his stomach as Wilson's attention shifted to him. "Can I have a word with you in private, Tate?" he asked.

"Sure," said Tate, lifting the counter for the sheriff to walk through.

They made their way into the storeroom, where Wilson sank into the plastic chair at the table, laying his hat on its surface. Tate motioned to the coffee maker.

"Can I get you a cup?"

Wilson looked tired and the lines in his face seemed more prominent. He ran a hand through his thinning hair and over his moustache. "That'd be great," he said.

Tate poured them both a mug, then carried it to the table, taking a seat across from the sheriff. He slid the coffee over to him. Wilson picked it up and took a sip, sighing loudly.

"What can I do for you, Sheriff?" asked Tate. "You look like you've been up all night."

"Because I have. Then first thing this morning, I had to go out and tell Roger Whitmire his daughter was murdered."

"Murdered? You got the autopsy back?"

"The toxicology report will take another week or so, but Angela, she's our coroner, believes Merilee was poisoned."

"Poisoned? How?"

"Either something she ate or something she smoked. She'd been vomiting, so there was nothing on her stomach, but a biopsy of the tissue in her stomach and lungs revealed arsenic."

"Arsenic?" Tate leaned back, frowning. "Arsenic?"

"That's what Angela says."

"Where would someone get arsenic?"

"Some rat poisons used to have it, but mostly it's found in older pressure treated lumber."

"If she ate it, wouldn't she know there was something wrong with the food?"

Wilson shook his head. "According to Angela, arsenic has a garlic smell, but she also could have smoked it. Deimos told me they were smoking pot both at the afterparty and at his apartment."

Tate blew out air. This didn't look good. Sequoia had old buildings. It wouldn't be hard to find pressure treated lumber where arsenic had been used as a preservative. Besides that, he'd just bet a lot of people had old bottles of pesticide or rat poison with arsenic in it lying around their garages.

"You can't believe Dee did this, Sheriff?"

Wilson toyed with the handle on his coffee mug. "I don't, but right now I don't have any other suspects. I did tell *Anaconda* to stay in the area for a few days, but I'm not going to be able to keep them here for much longer than that if I don't make an arrest."

Tate felt the sinking feeling in the pit of his stomach again. He was pretty sure Wilson hadn't just come by to talk shop with him. "How did her father take it?"

"He's a mess. She was his only child. The mother died of a heart attack a few years ago, so it's been just him and Merilee. God, I hated telling him."

"I know."

Wilson stared into the coffee. "Here's the thing, Tate."

Tate braced himself. He had to say no. He had to make sure he didn't get sucked into this again. He was sorry Merilee had been murdered, but he wasn't a cop anymore. He ran a hardware store now.

"I need your help."

Tate looked out into the store. He could see Bill Stanley and Logan trying to eavesdrop without being obvious. "Sheriff…"

Wilson held up a hand. "Please hear me out."

Tate blew out air. "Okay." He could at least offer Wilson a few suggestions for investigation, the way he had with Vivian Bradley's murder.

"I want to deputize you. I don't have the manpower or the experience to take on this case. I need some help."

"Sheriff, I…"

"I told a man his daughter was dead today, Tate. I owe him closure. I owe him a chance to make her murderer pay." He held up a hand. "I'm not asking for you to come on full time. Just do a little investigating in your spare time. I can even free up a little money in the budget to pay you, but I need your help."

"I gave up being a cop two years ago."

"I know, but besides Vivian Bradley's murder, do you know how many murders we've had in Sequoia, Tate?"

Tate shook his head.

"Three. Three murders in over a hundred years. Now, I know we're growing and with that growth comes an increase in crime, but my people aren't used to handling crime of this nature. You are. You know how to conduct an investigation and if I deputize you, it'll be completely legal."

"I don't want to investigate. I came here to work my hardware store and forget about being a cop."

"I know that and under normal circumstances, I would never ask this of you, but these aren't normal circumstances." He tapped the table with his fingers. "Think of it this way. If you help me, you can prove that Deimos didn't have anything to do with it."

Tate gave him a dissatisfied look. "That's low, Sheriff."

"I'm desperate, Tate. I don't have time to be polite. I wouldn't ask if I didn't really need your expertise." He leaned forward, his expression intense. "There's a twenty-four year old girl in the morgue, Tate. She has no business being there. You've got to care about that. You've got to realize that isn't right. Help me find her killer. Help me solve her case. And help me give a father the closure he needs."

Tate closed his eyes briefly. He should have known this would happen after he helped solve Vivian Bradley's case. Still, if he took on the job, he'd have enough to give Logan a raise. He looked out at the store again. Logan's head snapped forward as if he hadn't been listening to their discussion. Logan deserved a raise.

And damn it, Merilee deserved justice even more.

* * *

Tate walked down to the *Caffeinator* later in the afternoon. They hadn't had more than a few customers, so he felt safe leaving Logan in charge. The sun was blazing overhead and it had to be at least 90 degrees. No breeze wafted through the town and Tate felt a prickle of sweat bead on his forehead.

He had finally agreed to Wilson's request, but he felt almost sick about it. He didn't want to investigate. He didn't want to play cop. He just wanted to work the hardware store.

And now that he'd agreed, he knew this wasn't just a one-off. Now that Wilson had deputized him, he wasn't going to let Tate go back to his quiet life of retirement. Either Tate was going to have to pull up roots again and move, or he was going to have to accept that this was his life now.

The most worrisome part, however, wasn't the fear that the nightmares would return, or that he was doing the very thing he said he wouldn't do anymore. The most worrisome part was the flutter of excitement he felt in his stomach when he thought about working a case. It was addictive. Nothing quite matched the rush of solving a murder.

And it's not like it would take too much of his time. As Wilson had said, Sequoia only had three murders in a hundred years. But what if Wilson started wanting him to help with things like break-ins or accidents? He might have to hire another person to work the afternoons with Logan.

He squashed those thoughts as he pulled open the *Caffeinator's* door, a blast of cool air hitting him. The shop was filled with people and he was surprised to see Dottie making pastries still. She usually left by noon.

Tallah manned the espresso machine and Zion worked the cash register, taking orders and ringing up purchases. He almost walked back out again. This was clearly not a good time, but he needed to talk to Dottie. And, if he were honest with himself, he wanted to see Zion.

She brushed back a strand of curling red hair. She had it up in a ponytail, but wisps were tickling the sides of her face. She wore a *Caffeinator* apron and pink t-shirt, her face flushed from her exertion. He couldn't deny that out of all the women in the world, she was the one that made his heart beat a little faster. He hated that David Bennett got the privilege of spending quality time with her, while he was relegated to the *friend zone*.

He grimaced as he thought that. Logan had admonished him that the term *friend zone* was so over now. Tate didn't want a lecture on slang from his young employee, but Logan felt it was his duty to keep his boss abreast of all the latest terminology.

Tate walked to the opening of the counter where Dottie was rolling dough. She smiled up at him, her bright red hair highlighting the pink in her cheeks. "Hey, sugar, what are you doing down here this time of day?"

"I need to talk to you," he said, then he nodded at Zion. Zion gave him a quick wave. "But, I didn't think you'd be here. I was coming to get your number from Zion. Why are you still here? I thought you got off at noon."

Dottie wiped the back of her wrist against her temple. "Zion needs me right now. Without Dee, we're slammed."

"Have you talked to him?" he asked her.

Tallah turned, bringing a coffee order to the pickup window. "Hey, Tate," she said.

"Hey, Tallah, working hard?"

"You know it," she said and went back to the machine.

"I talked with him this morning. He's a mess. He doesn't know what to do with himself since he's not working and he feels horrible about Merilee," answered Dottie.

"Yeah, I'll bet he does. Did he say where he was going to be today?"

Dottie gave him a narrow eyed look. "You got a bee in your bonnet, sugar. I can see that. What's up?"

Tate shot a stunned look at her. She'd read him so easily. He knew she was protective over Dee, so he didn't want to worry her. The sound of voices in the coffee shop was loud, but he still dropped his voice so only she could hear. "Sheriff Wilson deputized me."

Dottie reared back, her hands stilling on the rolling pin. "Are you investigating Dee?"

Tate chewed on his inner lip. He could hear the accusation in her voice. She wasn't calling him *sugar* now.

"Look, Dottie, I don't believe Dee had anything to do with her death, but I need to talk to him. Do you think you could call him and ask if he'd meet with me?"

She studied him a moment, searching him with grim evaluation. "You sure you believe he's innocent?"

Tate met her gaze. "There's no part of me that thinks Deimos Hendrix could be capable of murder. Not one part."

She nodded, then reached for a dishtowel, wiping her hands. "Hey, sugar," she called over to Zion. "I gotta take a quick break."

"Sure," said Zion, ringing up the next customer. She gave Tate a speculative look. He just smiled at her.

Dottie disappeared through the doors leading to the back. Zion finished ringing up the last customer and walked over to him. "What's going on?" she demanded.

Tate shifted weight. He wasn't sure how she would react to his being on the case. "I need to talk to Dee."

"Why?"

Tallah brought another drink to the pickup counter and stopped to listen too.

"Wilson deputized me and asked me for help on this case."

Both women gave him a dirty look. "Dee didn't hurt anyone," said Zion. "He wouldn't do that, Tate."

"I have to talk to him, Zion. He was with Merilee when she died."

Dottie came out of the back room, her expression troubled. "He said he'd see you whenever you want." She passed him a slip of paper. "Here's his address. He's in a bad way, sugar. Please go easy on him."

"I will," said Tate, picking up the paper. He gave Zion an apologetic look. "I'm sorry. I have no choice."

She didn't seem convinced.

He turned and started walking toward the door.

"Wait," she called after him.

He stopped and turned. She was untying her apron. "Let me get my purse. I'm coming with you."

He glanced around the shop. "It's too busy in here, Zion. I promise you I'll go easy on him."

Zion hesitated, but Dottie motioned to her. "Go, we've got this. Dee will feel better if you're there."

Zion handed Dottie the apron and ran into the back. Tate breathed out a sigh. This is not what he needed right now. Especially not Zion. She was going to want to help him investigate. *He* didn't want to investigate, and he sure didn't like the idea of Zion getting involved.

She appeared from the back, her purse slung over her shoulder. She raced around the end of the counter and met him in the middle of the floor.

"I can handle this by myself," he told her.

"Then you won't mind my tagging along. I've been meaning to see how Dee is anyway." She started for the door.

"I'm the one doing the investigating, Zion," he called out, jogging to keep up with her.

"Of course you are, silly man. I wouldn't dream of getting in your way." She pushed open the door and stepped out into the heat.

"Right," Tate said skeptically, but he followed.

* * *

Dee lived in a single building apartment on the edge of town. Staring up at it, Tate figured it had probably been a motel in its previous life and had been converted into permanent rentals. The wood siding was cracked and some shingles were missing. A number of doors on the first floor were open, the screens blocking insects from coming inside, but the tinny sound of mariachi music drifted out. He could smell garlic and onions cooking and children rode bikes on the dried lawn in front of the building. An empty swimming pool off to the left sported caution tape and the gate was padlocked shut.

Tate gave Zion a shrug and they climbed out of his truck. She met him on the curb, holding her purse close against her side. Tate looked at the slip of paper Dottie had given him. "He's on the second floor," he said, motioning to the concrete stairs.

A sign between the floors proclaimed the place the *Royal Redwood Resort*, but there was nothing royal or resort-like about it, and the redwood seemed skeptical. The stairs were more or less intact, but someone had helpfully spray-painted a penis leading up to the landing.

Tate placed a hand on Zion's back to direct her in front of him. The open door nearest the stairs revealed a man lying on a couch in nothing but his tighty whities, sipping a beer and listening to the television at the highest volume setting. He lifted the beer to salute Zion as they walked past.

They came to Dee's apartment, smack dab in the middle, right over the *Royal Redwood Resort* sign. Dee's door was closed, his curtains pulled shut. A welcome mat made of tires had seen better days. The ends looked like they'd been chewed by a dog. A rusty plant holder and a dead plant made up the rest of his entrance.

Tate knocked on the door, giving Zion a weak smile. She hadn't said anything on the ride over here and now she looked like she just might bolt.

"Yeah?" came a voice behind the door.

Tate leaned close. "Dee, it's Tate. Open up. I want to talk to you."

"Give me a second," came the response. A moment later they could hear someone unhooking a chain and turning the deadbolt, then the door opened and a cloud of smoke wafted out.

Zion waved her hand in front of her face, grimacing. The smell was overwhelming – the sickly sweet tang of marijuana. Dee looked like hell. His hair was a tangled mess, his face had multiple days growth of beard, and he wore a ragged pair of cut-offs and a wife beater tank top. His bloodshot eyes widened when he saw Zion.

"Dude, you didn't tell me you were bringing the boss lady!" he scolded.

Tate didn't answer. He hadn't known he was bringing the boss lady himself. Dee stepped back and motioned them inside. Tate walked into the apartment, stopping in the middle of the small living room. Besides an orange, broken-down sofa, a lawn chair, and a basket chair, there was a flat screen television, two apple crates for a coffee table, and a lamp without a shade sitting on the floor. Tate could see through the haze of smoke into a galley kitchen with a two-burner stove, a small fridge, and a sink, and beyond that to a small bedroom, the mattress on the floor, the bedclothes wadded in a heap in the middle of the bed.

The smell of pot permeated everything and a cloud of smoke hung in the air. Tate could already feel a headache hammering in his temples. If the DEA were to walk in here, they'd get a contact high.

"Oh for heaven's sake," said Zion, moving around Tate and going to the window. She yanked back the curtains, causing Dee to make a mewl of protest and cover his eyes. Then she struggled to open the window.

"Hey!" Dee protested.

"You need oxygen in here. You're going to die from carbon monoxide poisoning!" she scolded, pointing a finger at him. Her eyes tracked over his appearance. "When was the last time you ate?"

Dee and Tate both looked down at the empty beer cans and pizza boxes scattered on the floor near the couch, then Dee shrugged. Zion reached into her purse and pulled out a paper bag, tossing it to him.

"Here. Eat this."

Dee opened it and lifted the bag to his nose, taking a long sniff. "Dottie's cinnamon breadsticks," he said wistfully, then dug one out. "You want something to drink."

Tate and Zion both looked at the sink, overflowing with dirty dishes. "We're good," Tate said, speaking for the both of them.

Dee backed up and fell onto the couch, eating the breadstick in three bites. "I miss Dottie so much." He sighed and reached for another one. "I miss the coffee shop. I miss the customers. I miss the espresso machine."

Zion walked over and took the lawn chair, sitting on the very edge of it. That left Tate with the couch next to Dee or the basket chair, and he wasn't going to try rolling out of that. God only knew what diseases had been caught in the fabric.

"I know you miss everyone, Dee, but Tate's here to help you." She nodded at Tate to begin.

Tate wasn't sure where to start, but he drew a deep breath and exhaled. Not a good idea. Smoke tickled the back of his throat and he coughed. Zion gave him an aggravated look.

"I guess I should start by telling you Sheriff Wilson deputized me."

That surprised Dee. His eyes went wide. Tate guessed Dottie hadn't told him why he wanted to talk to him.
He walked over and took a seat on the other end of the couch from Dee.

"Dude, you're Johnny Law now?"

Tate had been Johnny Law in the past. What he was now, he wasn't sure. He didn't want to be anything to do with the law, yet here he was. "I guess. So, um, he asked me to look into Merilee's murder."

Dee slumped back on the couch, the paper bag resting on his belly. "So it was a murder?"

Tate nodded. "Poison."

"Poison? What kinda poison?"

Tate shrugged. He wanted to see if Dee slipped and came up with it on his own.

"How was she poisoned?"

"It was either in something she ate or something she smoked."

Dee's expression was horrified. "Something she smoked? No, Tate dude, don't say that. I gave her the blunts. I smoked them myself. I couldn't stand it if something I gave her caused her death."

"You smoked everything she did?"

"Yeah."

"She never smoked anything different?"

"No, dude. We were together all night."

Tate clasped his hands between his knees. He really didn't want to touch anything in Dee's apartment. "Dee, I need you to go over the whole night with me again. Do you think you can do that?"

"I don't know. I was pretty wasted."

"I need you to try."

Dee glanced at Zion and she nodded. "Okay. What do you want to know?"

"You told me that Merilee never left your side at the concert, except to go to the bathroom, right?"

"Right."

"Was she in the bathroom an unusual amount of time?"

"No, dude, I mean, it was crowded, so she had to wait, but I could see her standing outside for the most part. No one talked to her and she didn't leave."

"Okay, so then you went to the after party. Did you know anyone else at the after party?"

"*Anaconda* was there, dude. It was their after party."

Tate fought for patience as Dee screwed up his face in concentration.

"You know, Jaguar and Maximus and Ricky…"

Tate shook his head. "Hold on. Do you have some paper and a pen?"

They all looked around the apartment again. There didn't seem to be any writing implements. Zion huffed, then opened her purse and pulled out a pad and a pen, flipping open the cover.

"Say those names again, Dee," she told him, poised to write them down.

"Jaguar and Maximus…"

"Hold on. You need to give me a little more than that. Jaguar does what with the band?" asked Tate.

"He's the lead singer, rhythm guitarist," said Dee.

"Is that his legal name?"

Dee shrugged. "Dude, how would I know?"

Tate exchanged a look with Zion.

"We can find that out later," she told him.

"Okay, go on," Tate said, rubbing his left temple. At least the air had cleared a little.

"So there was Maximus Starr. He's the lead guitarist. And Ricky Sinister. He plays bass. And Steele Torpedo, the drummer."

Tate rubbed his fingers under his eyes. God, he didn't want to get caught up in this. It was like some fantasy role playing game online, not real life. "I'm guessing these are all stage names."

Dee shrugged again. "Dude…"

Tate held up a hand before he could add anything. *Dude* seemed response enough. "Who else was there besides these…um, guys?"

"Some other fans and a couple of the guys had their girlfriends. Uh, some dude who said he was the manager. He introduced himself to us."

"What was his name?"

Dee screwed up his face in concentration again. "I can't remember. I was pretty wasted by then. I think it started with an R or something."

Zion scribbled on her pad, then she pulled out her phone and began typing into it. After a moment, she said, "Desmond Hifler?"

Dee snapped his fingers. "That's it. Desmond Hifler."

Starts with an R? thought Tate. Shit. This was like pulling teeth.

He focused on Dee again. "How many other fans would you say were backstage with you?"

"Maybe six or seven. I didn't talk with them much."

"You said it was catered."

"Yeah, the fairgrounds hired someone or I thought that's what they said. It was pretty righteous. They had salmon and finger sandwiches, and these shrimp cocktails with the biggest shrimp you've ever seen."

"What did Merilee eat?"

"She got a plate of stuff. I know she ate the shrimp, but so did I."

"Who gave you the blunts?"

"Dude, Jaguar had some good ganja. We smoked a few joints with him."

"Did Merilee go off with any of the men?"

"No, she stayed with me."

"And you shared the blunts with her? She didn't smoke anything that you didn't?"

"That's right."

"What about food? Did she eat anything you didn't?"

"I don't know. Dude, I wasn't really paying attention to what she ate."

"Did she drink anything?"

"They had beer, but it was in bottles and we had to open it ourselves."

"So, no hard alcohol, nothing in a cup?"

"No, she had a beer. So did I."

"How did you get home?"

"Uber."

"Did she act sick on the ride?"

"No. We came back here and…" His voice trailed off, his gaze shifting to Zion.

"And you had sex," pressed Tate.

"Yeah." He lowered his head.

"Zion said she had a boyfriend and another guy who was messing around her."

"I know."

"But you slept with her anyway?"

"Dude, don't judge."

"I'm not judging, Dee. I'm trying to establish what happened. I need you to be honest with me."

"She said she was breaking up with him."

"What's the boyfriend's name?"

"Everett Hughes," said Dee.

"And the name of the other guy?" asked Zion.

"Gunner," said Dee. "Gunner Bishop."

Zion looked over at Tate. "They got into a fight about her in the *Bourbon Brothers*," she told him. "After her death, Everett came into the *Caffeinator* and demanded to know where Dee was. He threatened to kill him."

Dee made a face. "Like I need more problems," he moaned.

Tate ignored that, more alarmed that Zion hadn't told him this before. "Why didn't you say anything?"

"It didn't come up until now."

"Did he threaten you?"

"No, and I don't think he meant what he said about Dee either. He was pretty upset about Merilee's death. He said he was still her boyfriend."

"That's not what she said," grumbled Dee, staring at his paper bag.

"You said you ate something when you got back here. What did you eat?"

"I had some pizza in the fridge, but I ate it too."

"And smoked some more weed?"

"Just a little. We were pretty burnt out by this time."

Tate leaned forward, clasping his hands before him. "This is really important, Dee. Is there anything else that you can remember? Someone Merilee talked to, someone she went off with, something she did that you didn't do?"

Dee's expression was miserable. "If I could remember anything, don't you think I'd tell you? Don't you think I want this whole thing to go away? I've told you everything I can remember. Tate dude, I just don't have anything else. I can't figure it out. I keep racking my brain, trying to come up with something, but it's all just so hazy." He leaned forward, the bag tumbling to the floor. "Still, I'd never hurt Merilee, Tate. I'd never hurt anyone. You've got to believe me. You've got to prove me innocent."

Tate blew out air, meeting Zion's gaze across the smoky room. "I'll do my best, Dee. I promise."

CHAPTER 7

Zion gave Cleo a final squeeze and set her on the couch, then she went to the door and slipped outside. The sun was up and the stillness of the day promised later heat. Zion breathed in the fresh air as she hurried to the Optima and climbed inside.

Her phone rang as she started the car. She pressed the button and backed out of the driveway, glancing at the screen. Her mother's name flashed at her.

"Hey, Mom."

"Namaste, sweet girl," came Gabi's voice.

Zion resisted rolling her eyes. "What's up?"

"I was just calling to see how things are going. I haven't heard from you in a long time."

"It's been two days, Mom. How's Dad?" Out of habit, Zion glanced at Tate's house and marked his truck was in the driveway. She needed to text him this morning about the case.

"He's fine."

"And Rascal?"

"He's the best."

Zion laughed. Both of her parents favored the little terrier.

"How are things there? How's David?" Gabi asked.

"David's great, but everything else has been stressful."

"How so?"

Zion turned toward the highway leading to town. "We had a festival here this past weekend. *Redwood Stock*?"

"I heard something about it."

"Well, a girl was killed. Murdered."

"What? How?" Worry thrummed in Gabi's voice.

"Poisoned."

"That's awful. Does the sheriff have any suspects?"

Zion paused, merging onto the highway ramp. "Actually, Dee's a suspect."

"Dee? Your barista?"

"Yep."

"What?"

Zion glanced over her shoulder, then merged into the light traffic headed for town. "He was with the girl when she died. They went to the concert together and she collapsed in his apartment."

"Dear God. The sheriff doesn't really believe Dee is capable of murder, does he?"

"Right now he's the only suspect. Sheriff Wilson deputized Tate."

"Did he? Wow, a lot has happened in the last few days."

"It has."

"How's Dee doing?"

"Not good. We saw him yesterday." Zion signaled and pulled off on the Sequoia Main Street exit. "Tate and I, I mean. He's smoking a lot of pot and sitting around the house doing nothing. I can't let him come to work because everyone's just swarming him, wanting information. The girl's boyfriend threatened to kill him."

"Good lord. Poor guy."

"He's not used to doing nothing, and he feels so bad about Merilee."

"The girl that was killed?"

"Yeah. I guess they were friends, or more. I'm not really sure."

There wasn't much traffic in town, but as Zion drove down Main Street, she noticed a line was already starting to form outside the *Caffeinator*. She sighed.

"Is there anything I can do?"

Zion gave the phone a frown. What did her mother think she could do about Dee's problems? "No, Tate's working on the case." She pulled into the municipal lot and parked in her usual spot.

"That's good. Tate's good with this sort of stuff."

"Yep. Hey, Mom, I gotta go. There's a line outside the coffee shop already.'

"Okay, sweetie. Take care. I'll talk to you soon."

"Talk to you soon," Zion said, then turned off the car, grabbed her purse, and climbed out. Already she knew it was going to be a long day. Still, she paused long enough to pull out her phone and send a text to Tate.

Come see me before you open the Hammer Tyme. I'll treat you to a mint chip frappe.

She pressed send, then hoisted her purse on her shoulder and set off at a brisk pace for the *Caffeinator*.

* * *

The morning rush had just ended when Tate walked through the *Caffeinator's* door. His hair was still damp from his shower and his face was freshly shaved. Zion watched him walk toward her and thought about how he could make her smile just by seeing him.

Of course, David was better looking and he had a better job, but something about Tate always eased the tension inside of Zion. He had a calm demeanor and a steadying presence – if there weren't those shadows always lurking behind his eyes. She knew he'd seen things as a cop in LA that had made this quiet man walk away from a promising career. She just wasn't sure she wanted to know what those things were.

"Hey," he said, smiling.

Dottie and Zion both smiled at him. "What can I get you, sugar?" Dottie asked him.

"I promised him a mint chip frappe, Dottie."

"On it." She leaned close. "And a half dozen of my cinnamon sticks for the boy?"

"Yeah, but make it a dozen," he said, winking at her. "I can't resist them myself."

Zion took a few more orders while he stood by the pickup window, talking with Dottie about Logan and his plans for the future. Zion watched him surreptitiously, thinking there wouldn't be many people as concerned about a lost teenage boy the way Tate was. He acted almost fatherly toward Logan, protecting the boy, buying him treats. It endeared Tate to her more and more.

As soon as she'd finished taking the last of the orders and filled the easy ones, like hot tea or straight black coffee, she eased behind Dottie, placing her hands on her shoulders. "I'll just be in my office for a bit, okay?"

"You got it, sugar." Dottie patted her hand, sliding Tate's drink over to him. "Can you take those peanut butter cookies out of the oven for me?"

"On it," she said, motioning for Tate to come around the counter. "Let's talk in my office."

Tate gave her a skeptical look, but he followed as she made her way to the back. She motioned for him to take a seat. "I'll be right back," she said and hurried into the kitchen to remove the peanut butter cookies like Dottie had asked. The smell of warm cookies made her stomach grumble and she realized she hadn't eaten breakfast yet.

She dished the cookies onto the display plate, keeping four aside for her and Tate. These she put on a paper plate, picking up both. She delivered one to Dottie for the display case and carried the other into her office, pushing the door partially shut.

Tate's face lit up as he smelled the warm cookies. She sat down at her desk, putting the plate between them and fished two napkins out of her desk drawer, passing one to him, then she snagged a cookie and laid it on her own napkin, just waiting for it to cool enough to eat. Tate didn't bother with waiting, but broke it in half and plopped it in his mouth, closing his eyes in bliss.

"Dottie sure knows how to bake," he breathed once his mouth was no longer full.

"Actually, I made those. She's teaching me her magic."

Tate gave Zion an appreciative look. "They're wonderful," he said, snagging the other half.

Zion clasped her hands on top of her desk. "So, I have some thoughts about where to start with this case."

Tate stopped chewing, looked at her, then he reached for his frappe and took a sip, swallowing. "Zion…"

"Just hear me out. Dee's my employee. I need him back at work."

"I know that, but…"

"I also was very helpful when we solved Vivian's murder."

"Zion…"

"Please, Tate. Please just listen to me for a moment. You have a business to run just like I do and you don't really have time to investigate. I won't do anything behind your back, but I might be able to help you figure this out. It'll help both of us. You'll get back to the *Hammer Tyme* faster and I'll get my barista back. It's a win win." When he didn't respond, but just stared at her, she gave him her best puppy dog eyes. "Please."

He slumped in the chair. "Fine," he grumbled. "Tell me your ideas."

"First of all I think we should talk to Merilee's father. Then we need to go out to the fairgrounds and find out who catered the after party. And finally, we need to talk to the band members. They agreed to stick around for a few days, but they won't stay long. We've got a narrow window for talking to them. In fact, maybe we should move that to the top of the list."

Tate's brows rose, but he didn't respond.

"Finally, we need to interview both of the boyfriends." She grabbed the notebook out of her purse and glanced over the notes she took yesterday. "Everett Hughes, and the other guy who was interested in her, Gunner Bishop."

When Tate still didn't respond, she set the notebook down. "Say something!" she urged.

"I'm still stuck on *we*."

"Huh?"

"When did *me* become *we*."

"When my barista became a suspect." She held out an empty hand. "You know I'm good at this sort of thing, Tate."

"I don't know anything of the kind."

"We solved Vivian's murder."

"We got lucky, Zion, and I almost got my head bashed in."

"But that won't happen here. We just need to pool our resources. Think of it this way. With both of us working it, we'll get it solved that much quicker and then we'll be able to get back to our businesses."

"Sheriff Wilson is never going to accept you working with me on this."

"Sheriff Wilson doesn't need to know. You can do all the interrogating. You're good at that."

He narrowed his eyes. He wasn't buying her flattery the way David did.

"I'll just be the idea person."

"The idea person? And you aren't going to want to go out with me when I interview these people?"

"No, I want to go with you. I'll take notes. I'll be the silent partner. Like I did yesterday." She held up the notepad. "Remember how handy that was."

He gave a frustrated laugh. "You're impossible, you know that?"

She beamed at him.

He snatched another cookie and popped the whole thing in his mouth, chewing. "If I agree to this," he said around a mouthful, "will you promise not to investigate on your own?"

She crossed her heart with her index finger.

Tate shook his head. "Nope. I need the words. Will you promise not to investigate on your own?"

"I promise."

"And if Sheriff Wilson finds out, you agree to back off?"

"I'll agree to back off."

He shook his head again. "I'm going to regret this."

"No, you won't. I promise you." She could hardly contain her excitement. She hated that Merilee was dead, but the idea of trying to solve her murder was energizing. Solving Vivian's murder had given her a sense of purpose. Plus, it was fun to work with Tate. It meant she'd get to spend a lot more time with him and that was always a bonus. "So, what's first on the agenda?"

Tate stared at her notepad for a moment. "I need to call Merilee's father and see if he'll see us. Then I need to make sure the band doesn't leave town before I have a chance to talk to them. Finally, I'll put a call into the fairgrounds and ask them who did their catering. Beyond that, I'm going to open my shop and get to work." He pushed himself to his feet and snagged another cookie. "You need to get to work too. Your coffee house is packed."

"You'll let me know as soon as you find out anything, right?"

"Right," he said reluctantly.

"And you won't go interview anyone without me, right?"

"Right," he said again.

She held out her hand.

Tate stared at it, then looked into her eyes.

"Let's shake on our partnership," she said, moving her hand in a shaking motion.

Tate took her hand in his own and chuckled. "You're already making me regret this," he said grimly.

"Don't be silly!" she said, shaking his hand. "We're going to be the best team this town has ever seen."

Tate squeezed her hand gently. "Sure we are," he said. "Sure we are."

* * *

The espresso machine hated her. Zion was convinced of that. She'd made Dottie leave at her normal time. The older woman couldn't keep putting in ten hour days, but Zion missed her expertise the moment she walked out the door. Zion had never been able to work the machine the same way that everyone else seemed to.

Tallah kept shooting her worried looks as Zion fought with it. The teenager was better at working the machine, but she was on break now, sitting at one of the tables with a book. Zion was determined to force the machine into compliance if it was the last thing she did.

However, the noises coming from it were alarming. She could feel the eyes of the customers on her. She knew she was disturbing their tranquil afternoon, but if she couldn't figure out how to work this machine, she had no business running a coffee shop.

Tallah had tried to show her as patiently as she could, but it didn't matter. The machine hated her.

"Dear God, woman, that thing is in pain," came a loud voice and a tattooed male arm snaked out, turning dials and throwing switches.

Zion backed up, her started gaze coming to rest on Jaguar. His blond hair was in artful disarray, his jeans had holes at the knees, and he wore a pair of broken down hiking boots in brown leather. He'd come around the counter and was now pulling the espresso shot as if he did that every day.

She looked out into the dining room and found his two hulking bodyguards standing on either side of the door, glowering at everyone. The rest of the room, Tallah included, seemed to be frozen, watching the rockstar battle the espresso machine back into obedience.

"What were you trying to make?" he asked Zion over his shoulder.

"Café au lait," she said, still not sure what was going on.

He set the espresso aside and began steaming the milk. His hands flew over the machine with such familiarity Zion was impressed.

"You know how to make designer coffees?" she asked him.

"You think I was always a musician?"

Zion shrugged. She didn't know one thing about him.

He poured the steamed milk into a *Caffeinator* mug, then began pouring the espresso into the steamed milk. Finally he went back to the machine, poured milk into the steamer pitcher, slapped a thermometer into it, and began steaming up some foam for the top.

"I grew up in Sequoia. Went to school here. After school and during the summer, I worked in this coffee shop." He carried the steamed foam to the coffee mug and picked up a clean spoon, bending over the mug as he dropped the foam onto the top, creating a design.

Zion found herself mesmerized. So was the woman waiting for the drink. He ended with a flourish and pushed the coffee over to the woman, beaming a smile at her. She blushed and lifted it, staring at the heart on top.

"Thank you," she said and hurried over to her friends gathered on the couch. They all remarked on the coffee art and twittered in excitement.

Zion shook her head. "That was amazing."

"You have to treat your machine with respect." He reached back and patted the espresso machine. "It's a delicate piece of equipment and needs a little babying."

"It hates me."

He laughed, his eyes crinkling at the corners. Those eyes. Zion could see why any woman might fall for him just because of his baby blues.

"So you worked here? Who owned it?"

"His name was Peter Parkwold. You should have seen this place." He stared out at the coffee shop, shaking his head. "He was a huge fan of 80's action movies. You know, *Terminator*, *Rambo*, those kinds of flicks." Jaguar extended his hands as if he could see it. "Posters all over the walls, these horrible metal chairs and tables. The couch was this monstrosity – leather and hard and miserable to sit on, but it looked like a movie set in here." He winked. "A lot less pink."

Zion laughed, charmed despite herself. "So why did you come in today?"

Jaguar shrugged. "Wanted a café au lait myself. No better place to get it." He turned back to the machine and began working it again.

Zion wasn't sure she liked him invading her space, but he wasn't doing any harm and a few more customers had suddenly shown up, drawn by the limo waiting outside on the street.

"How long do you plan to stay in Sequoia?"

"My folks are here, so I thought I might take a little break." He looked over his shoulder. "Bruno, Maddog, you want something?"

"Just black coffee," the bodyguard on the right said.

Zion wasn't sure if she could tell them apart, they looked so similar, standing with their feet braced shoulder distance apart, sunglasses over their eyes, their hands clasped before them.

"Bruno?" Jaguar called.

"I'll take a mocha," said the other one. "With whipped cream."

"Coming right up," said Jaguar without turning around.

"I can do that," Zion said, feeling a little aggravated by this pushy man.

Jaguar jerked his chin at her customers. "Just take their orders. I've got this."

Zion gave Tallah a disbelieving look, but the girl didn't even notice she was there. She just sat staring at the man behind the counter as if she couldn't believe what she was seeing. Zion forced a smile for the young man waiting in front of the register.

"What can I get for you?" she asked him.

"I'll have a macchiato. Can you make a heart on mine too?" he called to Jaguar.

Jaguar waved a hand in the air to indicate he could.

The kid leaned close to Zion. "That's Jaguar."

"I know."

"He's huge."

"Yeah, well, he's making coffee right now. Will that be cash or credit?" she snapped.

* * *

Zion ran into Tate in the parking lot. She lifted a hand to smooth her tangled hair, then stopped herself. This was ridiculous. Tate didn't care that she looked like a hot mess. Having a rockstar barista sure drew customers. Their profit margin was up, but she was exhausted.

After he dropped a twenty in Zion's hand for the coffee he made for himself and his bodyguards, Jaguar meandered around the coffee shop, signing autographs and taking selfies with her customers. She and Tallah had raced around trying to fill everyone's orders. Not that he noticed how much strain he was putting on their operation.

Jaguar was a man who thought the world revolved around him and everyone should jump when he snapped his fingers. By the time he left, Zion was hoping that was the last she was going to see of him.

"I heard you had an interesting day," said Tate, smiling at her.

Zion relaxed, smiling back. The day was cooling off as the sun lowered and the air had a stillness about it that felt soothing. "It was a day, all right. I guess you heard Jaguar showed up and pulled some espressos."

"Yeah, Logan was all excited. It was all over Twitter or Instagram or WhatsitMessenger."

Zion laughed. "I should be glad of the extra money, but I'm tired." She looked around at the pleasant night, breathing in the fresh air. "You wanna come over and have a beer in the backyard? Maybe order takeout from somewhere?"

His smile dried and he shifted weight. "Beer? Um, tonight?"

"Yeah." She gave him a bewildered look. "I mean if you have plans, I totally get it."

"No!" he said quickly. "No, I cleared my calendar earlier in the day."

Zion frowned at that.

He shifted weight again. "Because it was full of nothing," he explained.

"Yeah, I got it." She nudged him with her shoulder as she unlocked her car and pulled the door open. "I'm just not sure it was worth getting."

He clutched his heart and swung around toward his truck. "Dagger through the aorta."

She laughed and dropped into the seat. "So, are you coming or not?"

"I'm coming," he said, hurrying to his truck.

He followed her out of town and to the highway. Zion didn't want to think too much about how happy it made her to think of spending the evening with him. After all, they were neighbors and partners on this case now. They should probably compare notes, make a plan of action. She gripped the steering wheel tighter. That was it. They would just work on the case a little and make it all official.

A few minutes later, she frowned as she pulled into her driveway. Her mother's car was parked under the carport. She pulled up behind her and set the brake. Tate had pulled into his own driveway and had parked his truck, but as she got out of the car, he was already walking toward her. Turning the corner of her house to meet him, she stopped dead.

Her mother and Dee were sitting cross-legged in her front yard on yoga mats, their hands palms up on their knees, their eyes closed. Her mother wore yoga pants, a neon blue tank top, and a blue headband, holding back her salt and pepper hair. Dee wore cutoffs and a wife-beater tank top, his hair spiked around his head. Both were barefoot and oblivious to the two people staring at them outside the fence.

Tate gave Zion an amused look. Zion hoisted her purse onto her shoulder and pushed open the gate. "Mom?"

Gabi opened one eye, whispering, "Shh, we're meditating."

"Why are you here?"

"You said Dee was in trouble, so I knew I was needed. I called him and told him I thought we should do some meditating. He agreed, so I went to his apartment and picked him up. Now, please don't interrupt." She closed her eyes again. "Hello, Tate," she said.

"Ms. Sawyer," answered Tate.

Zion stopped in front of her mother, squatting down to look her in the eye. "Does Dad know you're here?"

She opened both eyes this time. "Of course he does. He suggested I might be able to help. Dee said he's having trouble remembering everything that happened. Meditation can often unlock bottled memories." She made a shooing motion with her hand. "But you're disturbing our chi."

Zion looked up at Tate and shook her head. Then she pushed herself to her feet. "First it was the piano, now it's yoga."

Tate held out his hands. "It could be worse. It could be a cult."

"You sure it isn't," she said grimly.

Her attention was diverted to the street as David's silver Range Rover pulled up in front of the house. Zion sighed. She just wanted to have a quiet evening with Tate, now it was turning into a damn circus. What the heck? She didn't remember having plans with David.

She headed down the walkway and pulled open the gate for him. He glanced at the activities in her front yard and then bent, offering her a distracted kiss. "What's up?" he said, quirking a brow.

"I'm not sure. I just got on the scene myself."

"Hey, Mrs. Sawyer," he said, waving at Gabi.

"Hello, David," Gabi said, then she nudged Dee, whose eyes sprang open. He looked around in bewilderment.

"Whoa!" he said, then he focused on Tate. "Hey, Tate dude, how are you?"

"Fine. You look better."

"Man, this meditation stuff is the real deal."

"Come on," said Gabi, rising to her feet and grabbing her mat. "Let's go finish our meditation in the backyard. It's getting too crowded out here."

Dee scrambled to his feet. "You said the energy was better out here."

"It was until all these people started showing up." Without a backward glance, Gabi moved toward the house with Dee following obediently after her.

Zion offered David a smile. "I didn't know you were coming by tonight."

David gave a half-laugh. "I thought we'd have dinner together and maybe watch some Netflix again."

Tate wandered back toward them. "Hey, David," he said, holding out his hand.

David shook it. "Tate. You come by to say hi to Zion's mom."

"Um…" Tate looked at Zion uncertainly.

"No, we were just going to have a beer. It's been a long day. Jaguar came to the shop and caused quite a fuss," she told David.

"Oh, I see." He stood up straighter, then he slid an arm around her waist. "Mind if I join you. It's been a long day for me too." His eyes shifted to Tate. "You don't mind, do you?"

"No, um, actually, I should probably go. You got a lot going on here already."

Zion was disappointed. He was the only one she'd wanted to spend time with tonight and now he felt like he should leave. "That's silly. I promised you a beer."

"Let the man go, darling," said David. "If he feels uncomfortable, he feels uncomfortable."

Tate lowered his eyes, tucking his hands in his pockets.

Zion eased away from David. What was he thinking? He was the one making Tate feel uncomfortable.

"I really should go," Tate said, moving around them.

"But I thought we could talk about the case."

Tate hesitated at the gate. "We'll talk later. I'm really beat tonight, Zion, okay?"

She nodded miserably. This wasn't at all what she wanted to happen tonight.

"What case?" asked David.

She didn't answer him. She didn't really want to talk about it with him and she figured he'd tell her to stay out of it. "See you tomorrow," she called to Tate.

"Night, Zion," he said, waving as he walked through the gate. "Tell your mom I said good bye."

"I will."

"Later, David."

"Bye," said David, putting his arm around Zion again, then he turned her toward the house, urging her along. Zion went because she couldn't think of a good reason to rebel, but some part of her didn't like it just the same.

CHAPTER 8

Tate pulled into the parking lot of the strip mall, staring at the sheriff's star on the glass door. He couldn't believe he'd agreed to do this. It went against everything he'd been telling himself for the last two years.

He pushed open the truck door and stepped out. It didn't matter. He didn't have a choice. When he went to Dee's apartment, the decision had been final, but seeing him sitting on a yoga mat meditating had solidified that decision. He seemed like a lost little boy and if someone didn't step in, he'd wind up a lost little boy in prison. Deimos Hendrix would not survive prison.

He pulled open the office door and crossed to the counter, pressing the buzzer. A moment later, Sam Murphy pulled back the window and gave him an appraising look. "The sheriff's been expecting you."

Tate gave a chin nod.

Sam buzzed him into the back and Tate met her on the other side. Wilson appeared in the hallway leading to his office, a smile bursting across his face. He had his thumbs tucked into his belt, his sheriff's hat pushed to the back of his head.

"I'm glad to see you, Tate," he said, coming forward and holding out his hand.

Tate accepted it. "I need a copy of the case file."

Sam grabbed something off the nearest desk and held it out to him. "Just sitting here waiting for you."

"There isn't much yet, I'm afraid," said Wilson.

Tate flipped it open and winced. The autopsy pictures were on the top. He closed it again.

"Come on. Let me show you to your desk," said Wilson, clapping a hand on his shoulder.

"My desk?"

Wilson moved him to an open desk behind Sam's. It was a standard metal desk with a monitor on top and a leather desk chair in black. He'd had a similar one in LA. "We cleared this space out for you."

"Sheriff…"

"Don't say anything. I know you won't be here often, but we wanted to make sure you had a spot." He went around the side of it and pulled out a drawer. Reaching in, he drew something out and laid it on the desk surface.

Tate stared down at a shiny deputy's badge. Emotions crowded his throat. Turning in his badge had been one of the hardest things he'd ever done. He reached out and ran a finger over the surface, but he didn't pick it up.

"You might need that," said Wilson, smiling at him.

Tate glanced at him. "I really just came in to ask you a question, but I appreciate the desk and the badge."

"No problem. We got some paperwork for you to fill out too."

Sam picked up a second folder and held it out to him.

"To make it all legal and to make sure you get paid."

Tate accepted the second folder. "Thanks. I'll fill this out and get it back to you."

"Sounds good. Now, what was your question?"

"Do you have a list of suspects?"

Sam pointed to the folder in Tate's hand. "It's in here."

"What about the caterer? Dee said they ate food at the after party."

"We checked the food at the lab. No arsenic," said Wilson.

"Okay. So that's out."

"Sorry. The coroner's pretty sure she ingested it through smoking. Her THC levels were through the roof."

THC, the drug in marijuana. "And all that's in here, right?"

"Right," said Wilson.

Tate's gaze went to the desk. It might be nice to have a place in the sheriff's office to work. He could come in before the store opened and get things done and he'd have access to the sheriff's database.

He gave Wilson a sheepish look. "Mind if I take the desk for a spin while I read the file."

Wilson chuckled and stepped back, motioning for Tate to go in front of him. "Be my guest," he said. "I'll even get you your first cup of coffee."

"Will it be thick as lead and burnt?" asked Tate, setting the file on the desk and pulling out the chair.

"You know it will."

Tate sighed and sat down, sliding the chair in under the desk. "Bring it on," he said.

* * *

Tate fidgeted all morning. He'd called Merilee's father, Roger Whitmire, from his desk phone at the sheriff's office and asked for a meeting around noon, when he usually took his lunch break. That way he could get out there and back in time to relieve Logan for his lunch break. Roger had agreed. He wasn't working this week because of his daughter's death. He sounded like a broken man and Tate hated the thought of making things worse for him.

In a moment of weakness, he'd promised Zion she could work the case with him, but he didn't really want to get her involved. Not only that but it was getting harder for him to hide his feelings for her. He'd left her house last night because he didn't want to cause trouble for her with David, but he was beginning to think the lawyer wasn't right for her. He was too possessive. Although, Tate had to admit that if Zion were his, he probably wouldn't like another single guy hanging around her himself.

Still, if he asked her to go with him to see Roger Whitmire, that would give David another reason to suspect his motives. On the other hand, if he went without her, Zion would be mad at him. She might even refuse to talk to him and he didn't want that. Besides that, often a woman's presence helped smooth over a difficult discussion and Roger Whitmire was a man in need of a soft touch.

Bill Stanley entered the store, causing the buzzer to sound. Tate's head lifted and he blinked, realizing his thoughts were a million miles away. "Hey, Bill," he called.

"Hey, Tate, Logan," said Bill.

"Mr. Stanley," answered Logan. "Can I get something for you?"

"The wife wants me to paint the front porch. I need some wood paint that'll last even under a load of snow."

Tate smiled and lifted the counter, headed toward Bill. "She's got you working harder in retirement than you did at the job."

Bill scratched the side of his ever present ball cap. "To be honest, I've been thinking I need to get a job, so I can get some rest."

Tate laughed, then showed Bill where the wood paint was. He pointed to his favorite brand. "I think you'll get good coverage with this and it'll withstand our winters. Just pick out the color you want. It's already pre-mixed."

"Sounds good." As Bill drew out a pair of reading glasses from his pocket, Tate went back to the counter. He gave Logan a speculative look. "You think you can handle the shop if I head out to talk to Merilee Whitmire's father."

"Yeah," said Logan, excitement lighting his young face. "You know I can."

"I'm gonna try to keep it to my lunch hour, but I might be longer."

"No problem."

Tate looked over his shoulder at Bill. "You got this sale or you need my help."

"I got this," said Logan. "You go."

Tate nodded and headed for the door. He couldn't concentrate on anything. Might as well go do some sheriff department business. "See ya later, Bill," he called to the older man.

Bill lifted his hand, but continued to study the paint canisters.

Tate walked down to the municipal lot and climbed behind the steering wheel. He'd made a decision. It was better to keep Zion out of this. He would just be causing problems for her with David and she didn't need to get mixed up in a murder investigation. Besides, Sheriff Wilson wouldn't like it. This was his case to work.

He pulled out of the municipal lot and onto Main Street, but he slowed as he neared the *Caffeinator*. As he peered through the window, there didn't seem to be as many people today as there were on other days. She might be able to slip away for a while. He chewed on his lower lip fighting with himself.

It would go so much smoother with Roger Whitmire if Zion was there. She had a calming presence. And she could take notes so he'd just have to concentrate on his questions. That was good. It had certainly helped with Dee the other day.

But Tate knew all of that was just an excuse. He wanted to spend time with her and this was a non-threatening way to do it. Finally, he swerved to a stop before the coffee house and threw open the truck's door, climbing out.

The bell tinkled as he yanked it open and Zion looked up. She had her hair down today, the sides pinned back with sparkly barrettes. She beamed a smile at him. "Tate, how are you?"

"Fine." He gave Dottie a tense smile. This was wrong. He shouldn't be taking her away from the coffee shop, not while they were short handed. "Hey, Dottie."

"Hey, sugar, you want a mocha?"

"No thank you." He returned his attention to Zion. "I'm going out to interview Roger Whitmire," he said. "You wanna come?"

Her eyes grew wider and she gave Dottie a pleading look.

Dottie laughed. "Go play detective. That's the only way we're gonna get our boy back. I've got this until Tallah comes in."

"I won't be long," said Zion, untying her apron as she moved toward the end of the counter. "And as soon as I get back, you can go."

"Don't worry about it," said Dottie, shooing her off. "Go. I've got this."

Zion stuffed the apron under the counter. "Just let me get my purse," she said, racing into the back.

Tate gave Dottie another tight smile. God, he was an idiot.

"I hope you know what you're doing, sugar," Dottie told him with a lift of her brows.

Tate hoped he knew as well.

* * *

Roger Whitmire answered the door in a pair of paint splattered sweats. He was bald on top with a ring of hair from just above his ears down to his lobes. His remaining hair was grey and cropped short. He wore glasses and his jowls hung nearly to his neck. In fact, his whole face looked like it was melting down, increasing the dejected air he gave off. Tate felt his stomach tense as he looked him over.

"Mr. Whitmire, I'm Tate Mercer and this is my friend, Zion Sawyer." Tate held out his hand.

Roger Whitmire gave Tate a confused look, but he accepted his hand. "I thought you were coming by yourself, Mr. Mercer." He pulled at his sweatshirt. "I would have dressed better."

"You're fine, sir. I'm sorry I didn't tell you earlier, but Zion's helping me take notes on the…um, case." He didn't want to use the word *murder* where Merilee was concerned. Not with her father.

"Nice to meet you, Mr. Whitmire," said Zion, offering her own hand.

Whitmire shook hands with her, then moved back and motioned them inside his small cottage. The door opened on a living room with a wide front window. The curtains were drawn and the room was dark. A flat screened television hung from the wall perpendicular to the window and a massive brown sectional took up the rest of the room. A claw-footed coffee table and two claw-footed end tables were the only other furnishings, except for two brown jug lamps sitting on the end tables.

"Please take a seat," said Whitmire, returning to his spot in the middle of the couch.

Tate let Zion go in front of him and they sat close to each other on the side couch. "Mr. Whitmire," said Tate, "I want to tell you how sorry both Zion and I are for your loss."

Zion nodded vigorously. "If there's anything we can do for you, please let us know."

Whitmire crossed one ankle over his other thigh, stretching his arms out on the top of the couch. "There's nothing anyone can do, Ms. Sawyer. I just can't get my head around it. I'm not sure I ever will."

"I understand, sir," said Zion. She took the notepad out of her purse and gave Tate a pointed look.

Tate leaned forward, clasping his hands. "Mr. Whitmire, can you tell us anything about Merilee? What did she do for a living?"

Whitmire stared at his sock-clad foot. "She was taking a few classes at the JC, but she'd recently quit her job. She used to do nails at the salon in town."

"Why did she quit?"

"She said she hated being exposed to the chemicals. Lately she'd gotten really into environmental stuff. She was worried about global warming and such. That's what she was taking classes for, environmental science."

Tate nodded. "So, she didn't have a disagreement with her boss or anything?"

"No, she gave two weeks notice and they even gave her a party when she left."

"What about at school? Did she have any trouble at school?"

"No. She was getting good grades too." He looked over at Tate, his droopy eyes miserable. "She wanted to transfer to a four year university. She was thinking Humboldt State."

"Did she live here with you?"

"She stayed here some nights. She kept her clothes here, but a lot of the time she didn't come home. I figured she was with that boyfriend." He gave a shrug. "What could I do? I mean, she was twenty-five. I didn't really have a say, especially after her mother died."

"The boyfriend? You mean Everett Hughes?" asked Zion.

"Yeah, that's the one." Whitmire made a face. "I told her that guy wasn't good enough for her."

"Why did you think that?" asked Tate.

"He wasn't going anywhere, just smoked dope all day, but Merilee couldn't find a good guy to save her life." His face fell again. "Man, that's the truth of it. She was always dating losers. Like the one she was with when she died. That Deimos character. I remember when they were in school together. God, he was such a burner. Then he just got worse. Never made anything of himself. His name was Dean when they were in school, then he goes and changes it to Deimos. Who the hell ever heard of something like that?"

Tate and Zion exchanged a look.

"Was there anyone else she hung out with?" asked Tate.

"Not that I know of. She never had many girlfriends. It was always guys with her. They just flocked around her all the time."

"Do you know someone named Gunner Bishop?"

Whitmire thought about that for a moment, his foot jogging up and down. "Gunner Bishop? The name's familiar. Is he connected to this somehow?"

"I'm not sure. Apparently, Everett Hughes and Gunner Bishop got into a fight over Merilee at the *Bourbon Brother's Barbecue*. You don't remember Merilee talking about him?"

Whitmire shook his head. "She might have, but I didn't pay much attention." He sighed. "My girl and me didn't always see eye to eye. I didn't like the drugs or the guys. Didn't like it?" He made a disparaging sound. "I hated it."

"We know she smoked pot the night she died. Did she do any other drugs?"

Whitmire studied Tate's face, then glanced at Zion, watching her scribble on her pad. "To tell the truth, I don't know. I know about the pot, but I wouldn't bet my life she didn't do more. Merilee was a free spirit. She did what she pleased."

Tate could feel Whitmire's regret. Somewhere along the way he and his daughter had grown apart. Now it was too late. Tate didn't think you ever recovered from something like that.

"Is there anything else you can think of, Mr. Whitmire?" he asked.

Whitmire tilted his head. "Do you believe she was murdered?"

"The autopsy showed she had arsenic in her system. It came from either something she ate or something she smoked."

Whitmire shook his head. "No, it couldn't be something she ate."

"Why's that?"

Whitmire screwed up his face in concentration. "It just doesn't make sense. The sheriff told me it could have been something she ate at the after party or at that Deimos' place, but Merilee was real careful about what she ate. He said

Deimos told him they ate pizza, but Merilee wouldn't do that."

"Why not?"

"She had a gluten allergy. She never ate anything with gluten in it and whenever she went out, she was real careful about eating anything unless she was sure it didn't have gluten in it. I just don't see her eating anything. It had to be the weed. That's all I can figure."

The autopsy had been uncertain about the contents of Merilee's stomach since she'd been physically sick before her death. Tate wondered if they'd done a trace for gluten.

He shifted on the couch. "I appreciate you talking with us, Mr. Whitmire. I know how hard this is for you."

Whitmire nodded, but he still seemed lost in thought.

"If you think of anything else, you have Sheriff Wilson's contact information, right?"

"Right," he said, distractedly.

Tate rose to his feet and Zion rose with him. "We'll let ourselves out. Thank you again, sir."

Whitmire nodded once more.

"If you need anything at all," said Zion, backing around the coffee table, "don't hesitate to ask."

"Thanks," muttered Whitmire.

Tate touched Zion's arm and they turned, moving toward the front door. He pulled the door closed behind them and they started for his truck.

"Well, that eliminates one clue," said Zion.

Tate gave her a questioning look.

"We know Merilee was poisoned by a joint."

Tate nodded, but he wasn't convinced. He wasn't ready to eliminate anything at the moment. It was too early in the investigation. They still didn't know if marijuana was the only drug Merilee took. For all he knew, she might have injected the arsenic directly in her blood system. "Maybe," he said, and he didn't like the worry that was gnawing at him.

He just wasn't sure Dee was being straight with them. What else had he and Merilee done with *Anaconda*?

* * *

Tate dropped Zion off at the *Caffeinator*, then headed for the municipal parking lot to drop off the truck. Logan had everything under control when he arrived back at the *Hammer Tyme*. A few customers were milling around and Logan was helping a man pick out a leaf blower. Tate recognized the maintenance man from the fairgrounds, who'd come in for miscellaneous stuff before *Redwood Stock* began. He couldn't remember the guy's name, but he recognized the thinning grey hair, the weathered face, and the rounded shoulders.

"Can I help you find anything?" he said, walking up to him.

The guy turned, his basket filled with nails and screws and a new drill, one of the best that Tate carried. "Naw, I just thought I'd pick up a few things. You got pretty good stock here and it's nice not to have to drive into Visalia."

"Sorry, I forgot your name."

"Walt, Walt Kennedy."

"Right, Walt. How have you been? Bet you're glad the rock festival's over."

Walt made a disgusted face. "Bunch of hooligans. They couldn't get out of there fast enough for me. Hated every minute of it."

"Yeah, I guess there were a few problems."

"A few?" He glanced around to see if anyone was listening. "You know a girl died because of that mess out there, right?"

"I heard." Tate wasn't about to tell him he was working the case. "That's awful."

"Well, that's what you get when you do drugs with those thugs."

"What thugs?"

"The rockstars and such. That lifestyle, it's all about fast living and dying young. Poor girl. Then she goes and gets mixed up with the worst of the lot."

"Who would that be?"

"That *Anaconda Glee Club*. Wild parties every night. Drugs and booze and girls. Damn near had to burn the place down after their shows, it was such a mess. Puke everywhere. The night the girl died, they stopped up the toilet. Called me out at like midnight. I'd already gone home. That shit-assed punk, that Jaguar, he tells me to fix it." Walt made a fist. "I'll fix it all right. I'll shove my boot up his…"

Tate cleared his throat, making Walt stop his tirade. The older man glanced around again.

"Worst part is they're hanging around town for a few days because of the girl's death. Sheriff Wilson told them to stay in town."

"Well, I thought a number of them have family here."

Walt shook his head in disgust. "Family, bah! They may have started here, but they're a bunch of druggies now."

Tate shifted weight. "What do you mean? Did you see them doing drugs?"

"Yeah." Walt gave Tate a disbelieving look. "The pot smoke was so thick, I got high just being backstage."

"But did you see anything else? Did you notice them doing any other drugs?"

Walt thought about that for a moment. "Can't say I did." He scratched his thinning hair. "Doesn't mean they weren't doing it though."

"Right."

"I tell you, it's a damn shame that girl died. She's not the one that deserved it. That Jaguar, that's the one that should be sitting in the morgue. That's the one that needs to go."

Tate frowned. He wondered if Walt understood how bad that sounded. He understood Walt felt put out by Jaguar and his band, but wishing the guy harm for asking him to do his job seemed a little extreme. Maybe he needed to look at Walt Kennedy a little closer.

Sheriff Wilson had said arsenic could be gotten from old pressure-treated lumber. Tate wasn't sure, but he figured the Sequoia fairgrounds had probably been built quite a while ago. Most likely this was a red herring, but the cop in him knew that what he might think of as an illogical motive didn't necessarily mean it was illogical to a murderer, and Walt's malice toward the rockstar seemed out of proportion with the offense.

"Anyway, they'll be gone in a few days," said Walt, moving down the aisle, "and I for one will be happy to see them go. Good riddance, losers."

Tate blew out air. Well, that conversation just made his job harder. Logic suggested Merilee was the target because she was dead, but now he had to consider that she might not have been the one, which meant other people might still be in danger. Aw hell, and he had a business to run.

CHAPTER 9

Zion slowed as she headed down the street toward the *Caffeinator*. A black limo sat outside the front door, its windows tinted so dark, she couldn't see inside, but as she passed the *Knitatorium*, the passenger side door opened and one of Jaguar's bodyguards got out. The two men were so similar, she wasn't sure if this was Maddog or Bruno.

The man stepped back to the rear door and pulled it open. Jaguar sprang out, dressed in jeans with holes in the thighs and knees, and a t-shirt that had a snake curling around it. Did the guy own any clothes that didn't belong to the band?

"Morning," he called to Zion, then stepped up to the coffee shop and opened the door.

"Morning," Zion said, bewildered by his continued presence at her store. It only made more work for her and her baristas. "What brings you by? Did you want a café au lait?"

"Naw, I need to talk to you."

Zion looked over at the limousine. "That's not going to stay there, is it?"

Jaguar laughed. "No. Bruno, tell Maddog to move it to the lot down the street."

"On it, boss," said Bruno, ducking his head inside the passenger side door and talking with the invisible person inside.

Zion went through the open door, finding Dottie at her post rolling out dough for some magical confection. Dottie's face fell as she noticed Jaguar following Zion with Bruno bringing up the rear.

So far they had no customers, but if Jaguar was here for long, people would start flocking through the door.

"Morning," said Dottie with forced brightness. "Did you want a café au lait?" she asked Jaguar.

"Not right now," he said with a good natured chuckle. "Boy, I'm already a cliché." He tucked his hands into the pockets on his jeans. Zion marked he had a number of thin leather strips tied around his wrist like a bracelet. They matched the sleeves of tattoos on his arms. As she glanced over the tattoos, she noted some were of scantily clad women, but most were of musical notes or musical instruments. "I need to talk to Zion," he added.

Dottie nodded, but her expression remained troubled.

Zion went around the counter, motioning Jaguar to follow her. "Why don't we talk in my office? That way we won't be interrupted." She was more interested in not having people know he was here.

"Sounds good," said Jaguar. "Grab yourself a coffee, Bruno, and get something for Maddog. My treat."

Bruno shifted weight uneasily. "Maybe I should go with you."

"Naw, nothing to worry about here. Take a load off." He pointed at the couch as if he were telling a pet dog to go lay down. "This shouldn't take long."

Zion couldn't imagine what he had to say to her. It was only 7:00 in the morning, but already the day was starting off strange. Her mother had gotten up with the dawn, banging around the house until Zion woke, then a few minutes later, Dee had shown up at the door, wearing yoga pants. It was a sight Zion hadn't needed. Before she'd finished her shower, they were already in the front yard, doing yoga poses. Watching Dee sprawl his yoga-pants-clad body into *downward facing dog* was a sight Zion felt sure she wouldn't forget anytime soon. And now, she had an arrogant rockstar waiting on her doorstep.

Going behind her desk, Zion stashed her purse in a drawer and took a seat. Jaguar closed the office door and sat in the chair opposite her, bracing his elbows on his thighs. They sat like that for a moment, staring at each other, then Zion sighed. This was obviously going to be a long day.

"How can I help you?"

"I want a job."

Zion blinked. She was sure she hadn't heard him correctly. "Say that again?"

Jaguar lowered his eyes to his hands, staring at the palms. "Here's the thing, Zion." He glanced up, giving her the full force of his remarkable eyes. "I can call you Zion, right?"

"Sure."

"I want to work here like I did when I was in high school. This place grounds me." He splayed his hand across his chest.

Zion felt sure she must be having a stroke or something. He couldn't really mean that, could he? He rode around in a limousine, he had millions of dollars, he had two bodyguards who were his constant companions. "I'm sorry, I'm really confused."

He sighed, rubbing one palm with the thumb of his other hand. "*Anaconda* is stuck."

"Stuck? What do you mean stuck?"

"In a musical rut. We're not original anymore. We're not drawing them in like we used to."

"That's not true. You drew a massive crowd at *Redwood Stock*. You were the headliners."

"Think about that for a minute."

Zion did and she didn't see the problem.

"We headlined a concert in our hometown, a place that in the best of times is a tourist trap."

"I think you're being a little harsh," she began, but he shook his head.

"The last few albums we produced were flops. We took this gig not because we wanted to give back to Sequoia. We took it because we can't book anything bigger right now. We need a hit. We need something to go viral."

"How does that fit with working here at the *Caffeinator*?"

"The guys are hanging around town for a few days because Sheriff Wilson asked them to, but then they're leaving. They're heading back to LA. When they go, I'm staying here."

"Okay?" Why was this not making sense?

"My mom's sick. She has early onset Alzheimer's."

"I'm sorry, Jaguar." And she was too. She would hate for something like that to happen to Gabi. She still depended on her mother.

"Mornings are better. She remembers more things then." His face clouded over. "She remembers me then."

Zion nodded. She didn't know what to say.

"But the afternoons are bad. She doesn't remember anything and all she wants to do is sleep. I figured this was a good reason to take some time away from the band, get my head back on straight. It's not gonna be long before Dad and I have to put Mom in a home."

"Wow, that's gotta be a tough decision."

"Yeah." He stared at his hands again, rubbing his palm. "Thing is, Dad and I don't get along. Never have. We try in the mornings for Mom, but in the afternoons, we're just in each other's way."

"So you want to work here to get away from the house?"

"That, and because I think it might help."

"Help what?"

"Help me come up with a song or an album that will make the charts again. I think things have become too easy for us. We've lost our edge. We're a bunch of sellouts and the public knows it. That's why they aren't buying our latest stuff. They don't feel the passion anymore." He touched his chest again. "I need to get it back. I need to find that heat."

"And working here will do that?" She didn't know why this all seemed so crazy, except a limo had been sitting outside her shop this morning. Even if he didn't get his edge back, surely he had enough money to live comfortably for the rest of his life.

"Yeah. It's hard labor. I did it before. And I'd be going back to my roots. I need to check my privilege for a while."

Check his privilege for a while? *That* sounded so privileged. She was pretty sure this wasn't going to give him what he wanted.

"I don't know…"

"Hear me out. You're down a barista until this whole mess with the dead girl clears up, so we'll be doing each other a favor. You know I know how to work the machine and whatever you'd pay me, you can donate to a charity of your choosing. I'll fill your barista's shifts until he comes back and hopefully, it'll get me back to writing. In the meantime, you know I'll be a big draw for the customers." He gave her a sultry smile. "And I can sign a few autographs as well. It's a total win for you."

"It's a lot of work."

"I'm a good worker, Zion. I know it may not look like it, but I worked my ass off before I became famous."

"I have a young girl working for me, Jaguar. Tallah, the girl you originally gave the backstage passes to? I don't think you should be around her. She's only sixteen."

"I would never mess with a sixteen year old."

He acted affronted.

"Forgive me, but you've already flirted with her."

He laughed and shook his head. "I flirt with every female – old, young, but it means nothing. I'd never mess around a sixteen year old girl. Trust me."

She didn't. Not completely, but his expression was so earnest.

"Tell you what," she said, wishing she had more time to think this over, but Dottie couldn't keep working twelve hour days. Neither could she. She was exhausted and there was no telling when Tate might be able to clear Dee's name so he could return to work. "We'll give it a trial run, but I need you to understand that I'm the boss."

"Of course."

"And there won't be any snapping."

"Snapping?"

Zion snapped her fingers. "The way you do with your men. And they can't loom around the door. They have to stay inconspicuous."

"Got it," he said, amusement coloring his voice.

"And you stay away from Tallah."

"Yep."

"And if it doesn't work out, you agree to leave."

"Of course."

Zion chewed on her inner lip. God, she hoped she wasn't making a mistake, but she couldn't think of a good reason to turn him down. They did need an afternoon barista and he'd proven yesterday he could handle the espresso machine. If he refused to follow her lead, she'd just fire him or have him forcibly removed by the authorities. But he might be right. He might actually increase her customer flow.

"Okay, we'll give it a try," she said.

Jaguar sprang to his feet and held out a hand. "To becoming partners," he said.

Zion shook her head. "To becoming employee and employer," she corrected.

He gave her a sheepish look. "Of course, I'd never try to undermine your authority."

Zion just bet that wasn't true, but she wasn't going to argue with him. He looked like a little boy who'd just been promised a pony ride.

* * *

"He's going to do what?" demanded Dottie with a hiss. She and Zion stood in the kitchen while Dottie cut coffee cake into squares and placed them on a serving platter.

"He's going to take Dee's shifts until Dee can return."

Dottie looked over her shoulder toward the shop, but Jaguar and his men had left. He would be back at noon. "He's going to take Dee's *shifts*?"

"Right."

"He's going to take *Dee's* shifts?"

"Saying it with a different emphasis isn't going to change it."

Dottie huffed. "I was hoping that saying it with a different emphasis might make you realize how crazy it is. And how do you think Cheryl is going to like having her daughter work with a thirty year old womanizer? The girl has a crush on him."

"I'll talk to Cheryl, but I already warned Jaguar to stay away from her."

"The man's name is Jaguar. He's a predator."

"It's a stage name, Dottie."

"He flashed those baby blues at you, didn't he?"

"That's not why I agreed to it."

"Right."

Zion drew a deep breath and released it. "He brings in customers and we need them right now." She hadn't wanted to tell Dottie this, but she didn't know how else she was going to get her to see things her way. "I'm covering Dee's paycheck while he can't work. Now Jaguar wants me to donate his wages to charity. If I do both, I'll have to dip into Vivian's rainy day fund. I was saving that money for an emergency like if the HVAC or the espresso machine goes out."

Dottie stopped in mid-cut and looked up at her. "You're still paying Dee when he's not working?"

"He can't afford to go without a paycheck. And he might still need a lawyer."

Dottie set down the knife. "You can't do everything, honey. Much as I love Dee, he got himself into this mess."

"But I've got to help him get out of it. Jaguar's a big draw. This place will be full of customers." Plus she didn't add that Dottie couldn't keep working such long hours. Zion had caught her popping more painkillers just this morning.

The bell over the door tinkled and they both looked in that direction.

"I hope you know what you're doing, sugar," said Dottie.

Zion hoped she did too. Now she just had to convince Cheryl her daughter wouldn't be in any danger. Her face clouded over at that thought. It wasn't Cheryl she feared as much as Dwayne. Dwayne wasn't going to like this one little bit.

"Zion!" she heard Tate call.

Zion's eyes widened. She'd never heard Tate sound like that before.

"Seems like you got another problem on your hands," said Dottie, picking up the platter. "Guess you better have that little speech you gave me memorized." Then she pushed open the bar doors and walked out into the coffee shop. "Hey, sugar," she said to Tate. "Zion will be out in just a minute. Can I start something for you?"

She didn't hear what Tate answered, but she straightened her spine and closed her eyes, trying out one of her mother's mantras before she went to face the rest of the world. Geez, would everyone just take a number already.

* * *

Tate stood at the counter, giving her his cop's look as she stepped out. Dottie was preparing him his favorite mint chip frappe. A few customers sat at the bistro tables or lounged on the couch, but the morning crowd hadn't come in yet. Why was Tate here so early? He didn't open the *Hammer Tyme* until 10:00.

She smoothed her hands over her *Caffeinator* apron and pulled her braid over her shoulder, fingering the end of it. "Hey, Tate," she said with false brightness.

"Logan called me all excited, said he saw a limo out in front of the *Caffeinator* and Jaguar getting out of it."

"Wow, Logan was out and about early this morning."

"He went with his mother to her doctor's appointment," said Tate, then he narrowed his eyes on her. "Why was he here again?"

"Logan?"

Tate's expression never wavered. "No, not Logan, Jaguar. I need to talk with him and the rest of the band. They're suspects in Merilee's murder, Zion. You shouldn't be meeting with him by yourself."

"I wasn't meeting with him."

Dottie made a scoffing sound, then fired up the coffee grinder. Zion didn't mind the distraction. She knew Tate wasn't going to like that she'd hired the rockstar, especially since he was a suspect.

Once the coffee grinder stopped, Tate drummed his fingers on the counter. "You weren't interrogating him without me, were you?"

"Oh." She hadn't realized he might think that. "No, no, I wouldn't do that."

"Okay." His shoulders visibly relaxed. "I just wanted to make sure."

"She hired him to work Dee's shifts," said Dottie, pouring milk into the blender with a cup of ice.

"Dottie!" Zion hissed at her, but Dottie just turned on the blender.

The tension was back in Tate's shoulders, but he waited until Dottie finished before speaking. "You hired Jaguar to work Dee's shifts?"

She shrugged. "He said he needed the work."

"He *needed* the work?"

"Right."

"*He* needed the work?"

"Saying it with a different emphasis doesn't change it," said Dottie, sliding his drink over to him. She gave Zion a smug smile.

Zion gave it right back at her. "He told me that *Anaconda's* sales are down. He thinks his life is too privileged and he needs to get back to his roots, so he can write songs that will sell again. He said they had to play *Redwood Stock* because they couldn't book bigger gigs."

"So he wants to work in a coffee shop?"

"He worked here in high school. You know he's from Sequoia."

"Yeah, I know, but…"

She didn't want to tell him about Jaguar's sick mother. That seemed like something Jaguar should reveal himself, but Tate wasn't looking convinced. "He brings in a lot of customers and I need that."

"She's paying Dee's wages even when he isn't working," offered Dottie.

Tate's brows raised at that. "Why?"

"You saw how he lives, Tate. I can't let him go without his regular income."

"Jaguar wants to be paid too. He wants her to donate his wages to charity."

Zion put her hands on her hips and glared at Dottie. "Do you mind?"

"You're not telling him everything."

Tate leaned into her line of sight. "Jaguar's a suspect. Merilee died after being at his after party."

"You don't really think he killed her. What was the motive?"

"I don't know, but I don't like it. He shouldn't be working here, Zion."

The buzzer on the oven went off. Dottie ambled to the back to take the cookies out, so Zion leaned closer to Tate, dropping her voice. "Dottie can't keep working the hours she's been working, Tate. I caught her popping painkillers this morning before we even started. Her arthritis is acting up. Jaguar knows how to work the darn espresso machine. You know that thing hates me. And he's a big draw. It's a win win."

Tate picked up his frappe and took a sip. "Dwayne's not going to like that player working around his daughter. Have you thought of that?"

"I have and I told Jaguar he's to leave her alone."

"Right," he said skeptically. "The guy's a player, Zion."

"You need to stop saying that. Really," she warned him. "It sounds silly coming out of your mouth."

He sighed.

"So, what's the next step for the investigation?" she said, trying to change the subject.

"I want to interview the band. I called that Hifler guy."

"The manager?"

"Right. He's going to arrange for the band to be assembled at the hotel tomorrow around noon."

"Jaguar will be here at that time."

"Then I'll catch him here after I talk to the rest of band at the hotel."

"I want to go with you."

"Zion."

"You promised."

"That means you'll leave Jaguar alone with Tallah."

Zion considered that. "Nope. I'll have my mother come in and keep an eye on things while I'm gone. You're not getting rid of me that easily. Besides, the sooner we solve this case, the sooner Jaguar will be gone."

Dottie returned with another platter and bent to place it in the case, her free hand on the small of her back. Tate watched her, then he looked over at Zion. "Fine. I'll pick you up at noon. Just make sure Tallah isn't alone here with that guy."

"Scouts' honor," she said, crossing her heart.

He shook his head and turned away, grumbling something under his breath, but Zion didn't catch it and she sure wasn't going to ask him to repeat it.

"See you tomorrow," she called after him.

He lifted his hand as he walked out the door. Zion smiled to herself until she caught Dottie frowning at her, then she grabbed a rag and began scrubbing the counter.

* * *

Zion slipped out of the *Caffeinator* at 11:00 to go see Cheryl. The *Bourbon Brothers' Barbecue* was already full when she stepped inside the air conditioned interior. Daryl manned his usual spot behind the cash register and he waved at her as he took the next order. The smell of cooking pork and barbecue sauce wafted throughout the room, making Zion's stomach grumble.

She could see Dwayne and Al Wong, the short-order cook, through the window in the back. Dwayne looked up, spotting her, his heavy brows lowering in a scowl. Zion's mouth went dry.

"Is Cheryl in back?" she asked Daryl, stopping beside the register.

"Nope. She took Tallah shopping, but girl, you're in trouble."

"Did Tate come in here?"

"You know he did," Daryl said, taking a twenty from the customer and making change. "Go on back." He jerked his chin at the swinging kitchen door.

Zion was going to kill Tate. What did he do – go tattle on her the minute her back was turned? "He shouldn't have said anything. I planned to talk to Cheryl about it."

"He's worried about Tallah, Zion. Actually, he's worried about both of you with that playa."

"I wish you guys would stop saying that word."

"Nothing wrong with that word. Besides, Tate wanted to make sure we'd keep an eye on things."

Zion guessed she could understand that, although she hated Tate's heavy handedness. David would never treat her like this. She exhaled. Actually, she didn't know what David would say because he didn't know about it yet. Still, she was getting a little sick of men thinking they had a right to tell her how to run her business.

"You can't fault a father for worrying about the women in his life," said Daryl, reasonably. "Cut him some slack, girl."

Zion nodded. "I guess I should talk to Dwayne."

If she hoped Daryl would say no, she was wrong. "If you want Tallah to work her shift, you better."

"Fine," she said, walking around the counter and pushing open the kitchen door.

"You wanna tell me what's going on in that curly red head of yours," said Dwayne before the door had shut again.

"Look, Dwayne, I already told Jaguar he better steer clear of Tallah."

"What about you?"

"He's not interested in me."

Dwayne and Al exchanged disbelieving looks.

"Trust me. I will never leave Tallah there alone with him. If I can't be there, either Dottie or my mother will be. And if not them, then I'll make sure Cheryl is."

"The guy's a suspect in a murder, Zion."

"Tate doesn't really think he did it. I mean, it doesn't make sense. He didn't even know Merilee."

"Why do you want him working there?"

She told him what she'd told Tate. Dwayne listened as he continued to make sandwiches.

"Daryl told me you offered to pay Dee's wages even when he wasn't working. That's real nice of you. Not smart, but nice," said Dwayne.

"What else can I do? He needs the money."

Dwayne leveled a steady gaze on her. "I know you'll look out for my girl. I trust you," he said.

Zion felt a tightening in her chest. Hearing those words made her realize she finally belonged in Sequoia. She had people who cared about her, who respected her. It was more than she'd ever had working for the insurance company in San Francisco.

"That means a lot, Dwayne," she said.

He gave a terse nod. "You want lunch?"

"I wouldn't say no," she said. "I'll go pay Daryl."

"Naw, it's on me. If you're gonna be paying everyone's wages whether they work or not, you're gonna need someone to feed you."

Zion laughed and took a seat at the table she and Cheryl usually used when they ate in the kitchen. A moment later, Dwayne served her her favorite – a barbecue pulled-pork sandwich with coleslaw.

Jaguar had arrived by the time she got back to the *Caffeinator*. He had an apron on and his two bodyguards were sitting at a table before the windows. At least he was prompt, she had to give him that. Dottie was going over the orders and showing him how to work the credit card machine, but he looked up and smiled at Zion as she entered the store.

"Hey, I'm ready to work," he said.

Zion went around the counter and grabbed her apron, tying it around her waist. "Good. You work the espresso machine and I'll take orders. Dottie's going home." She gave the older woman a stern look.

Dottie hesitated, but after a moment, she removed her apron and went into the back to get her purse out of the file cabinet where she and Tallah stashed their personal belongings. When she came out, she grabbed the rolling pin off the counter and passed it to Zion.

"Use this if he gets frisky," she said, shooting a withering look at the rockstar.

He held out his hands and gave her an innocent smile. Dottie shook a finger at him and turned, leaving the coffee shop. Zion hid her own smile. Dottie was certainly fierce when it came to protecting those she took under her wing. She was grateful the older woman considered her worthy of that protection.

Tallah came in a few minutes later, but stopped dead, clasping her hands in front of her face. "Oh my God, it's true!" she squealed, jumping up and down, then she pulled out her cell phone and snapped off a few pictures.

Jaguar's body guards rose as if to intercept her, but Jaguar shook his head, waving them off. They subsided, glowering at the girl as she ran around the counter, grabbing Zion's hands.

"He's really working here," she stage-whispered.

Zion patted her hands. "Yes, but that's all. He's working."

"Oh my God, no one's going to believe this. I've got to post it on Instagram."

"Tallah, go put your bag away and come back out. I want to talk about your hours."

"My hours? Are you cutting my hours?"

"Go put your bag away."

As the girl went to do what Zion said, Cheryl pushed open the door and gave Zion a furious look. The look only grew darker as she fixated on Jaguar. Zion hurried around the counter and put an arm around her friend.

"Come into my office," she urged her.

Cheryl let herself be guided to the back. They found Tallah standing in the middle of Zion's office, texting someone. Zion shut the door and faced the mother and daughter. "Okay, listen. I've given this a lot of thought and I think I might have a solution."

Cheryl's brows lifted and Tallah looked up from her phone.

"Jaguar's going to take Dee's shifts until Dee comes back."

"Why?"

"Why? Seriously, Mom!" Tallah wailed.

"Why?" Cheryl said again, giving her daughter a *don't you dare* look.

Zion explained herself once more. She felt like she'd been doing it all day and she was tired. "Today I'll stay until closing. I promised Dwayne I wouldn't leave Tallah alone with him, but I'm hoping Tallah and I can change our shifts. If Tallah can come in during the morning and work with Dottie, I'll come in at noon."

"The morning?" cried Tallah. "Dottie gets here at 6:00."

"Right. You'll come in at 7:00. Just until Dee comes back."

"Seven? Seven!"

"She'll do it," said Cheryl with an expression that brooked no argument.

"Mom!"

"She'll do it!" Cheryl said more firmly.

"Good." Zion pushed her braid off her shoulder. "Good. That's settled."

Tallah didn't look like it was settled, but she had the grace not to pitch a fit right now. Changing Tallah to the morning would keep her away from Jaguar, but it would also keep Gabi away from the coffee shop, and it would let Zion work the case with Tate in the morning. It was a win/win/win as far as she was concerned. Now if she could just figure out how to get Gabi and Dee, and their yoga pants, out of her front yard, she'd be golden.

CHAPTER 10

Tate drove his truck down to Zion's house the following morning. He'd gotten a call late the previous night from Desmond Hifler, *Anaconda's* manager, that the band wanted to meet with him at 9:00. They planned to fly out of Fresno that afternoon to head back to LA.

Tate didn't like that they were leaving the area, but he didn't have any evidence to hold them either. At least Hifler had promised to give him their contact information and he still knew people in the LAPD who could serve an arrest warrant if necessary.

He parked the truck before Zion's house and climbed out of the cab, stepping up on the sidewalk. He opened the gate and went up the walk, a little surprised that Gabi and Dee weren't doing their yoga poses in Zion's front yard.

He knocked on the door and rocked on his heels, looking over the front yard. Gabi had a point. He liked the energy of Zion's cottage. He always felt at ease when he came here.

A moment later, Zion pulled open the door. She was wearing a black *Caffeinator* t-shirt and white capris, white lace sneakers on her feet. She'd braided her hair again and the end lay over her shoulder. Tate resisted the urge to pass the thick rope through his fingers. He liked her natural color and curl better than the fake wash she'd used before moving to Sequoia.

"Hey."

"Hey, come in." She backed up to let him enter the cottage. He could hear voices in the kitchen and recognized Dee's. "What's up?" she said.

"Cheryl said you switched shifts with Tallah. You're working the afternoons now?"

"Right." She tucked her hands in her back pockets. "I start at noon, but Dottie agreed to wait until I get back from going to interview the band with you."

Gabi poked her head outside the kitchen. "Tate, come in. I'm just making breakfast."

Tate smiled at her. "Sounds good."

Gabi disappeared again.

Zion shook her head. "Run. You don't want her breakfast."

Tate frowned. "What's wrong with her breakfast?"

"Trust me."

"Come on, you two," shouted Gabi.

Zion reluctantly turned and made her way into the kitchen. Dee was sitting at the little breakfast table, holding Cleo on his lap. Tate stopped to pet the kitten and then shook Dee's hand.

"How are you?" he asked the barista, trying to avoid looking at his skin-tight yoga pants.

"I'm getting healthy." He held up a tall glass filled with a green substance. "Haven't smoked the ganja in two whole days. Gabi says my memory might come back if I keep it up."

Tate wasn't sure how to respond.

"We're working on centering my chi."

"Okay."

Gabi came over to him and placed an identical glass in his hands. Tate held it up to the light and gave the green liquid a skeptical look. "Looks good. What is it?"

"It's a collard green smoothie with mango and lime."

"Collard greens? How inventive."

"It'll take the toxins from your blood," said Gabi.

Tate glanced over at Zion to find her making a face. "Wow, it sure is green."

"Fights cancer too and it'll help get you regular." Gabi patted her own stomach.

"Mom!" Zion scolded.

Tate fought a laugh as he lifted the smoothie to his lips. The smell was overpowering. He figured eating his front lawn might be about as appetizing. He took a tentative sip and shivered despite himself. He wasn't sure what he'd just drank, but a strange metallic taste lingered in the back of his throat.

"Good," he said dubiously.

Gabi beamed at him. "You can feel the toxins fleeing, can't you?"

"Yeah." He felt something fleeing.

Zion made a disgusted sound, but Gabi was undeterred and went to the blender, grabbing more greenery. Tate set the smoothie on the table near Dee's, hoping that maybe the barista would forget which one was his and drink them both.

"I got a call from Desmond Hifler. He wants us to interview the band at 9:00 instead of noon."

"Why?"

"They're heading down to Fresno to catch a flight to LA."

Zion looked at the clock on the wall. "Then we better get going."

"What about breakfast?" Gabi complained.

"It was real good, Gabi. Thanks," said Tate.

Gabi's gaze shifted to the full glass. "You haven't finished it." Her eyes widened. "I know, I'll put it in a travel mug."

"Uh," Tate began, but the look on Gabi's face stopped him. "Sure, that'd be real nice."

Gabi grabbed Tate's glass and hurried to the sink. Zion gave Tate an amused shake of her head and walked out of the kitchen. Tate looked down at Dee, who was smacking his lips.

"You can really taste the collard greens in this one, Gabs," said the barista. "Man, the toxins are heading for the hills."

Gabi smiled and handed Tate the travel mug. "Enjoy," she said.

Enjoy? Tate felt pretty sure health foods and enjoyment were about as far apart as two things could be. Enjoy, sure.

* * *

"*The Tumble Inn Beer & Breakfast*?" said Zion as they pulled into the parking lot.

Tate looked up at the sign sporting a frothy mug of beer, hanging above a massive Victorian mansion with a wide front porch. He'd driven by here a few times, but he'd never stopped to go in. "It's a microbrewery and hotel."

"Sure it is," said Zion, giving him a wry look.

They got out of the truck and walked up the path to the stairs. The *Tumble Inn* had gingerbread shingles painted deep blue with white trim. The porch sported lounge chairs and end tables, and a porch swing affixed to the rafters on the opposite end from the door.

As Tate pulled open the screen door and then the outer door, a bell tinkled. A long counter ran across the back wall and a few couches and armchairs were arranged around a stone fireplace in what had once been a formal living room.

A middle aged woman with grey streaked hair stood behind the counter. She was plump and had round cheekbones. Her eyes crinkled at the corners as she smiled at them. "How can I help you?"

Tate and Zion approached the counter. "I'm Tate Mercer and this is Zion Sawyer. We have an appointment to talk to *Anaconda*."

"Of course. They're in the breakfast room, right through those doors."

"Thank you," said Zion, following Tate as he headed toward the room she indicated.

Passing through a set of French doors, they found themselves in a sunny room, painted yellow, with round tables interspersed at regular intervals. Floral tablecloths covered the tables and a sideboard was piled high with silver serving trays filled with eggs, potatoes, and bacon. At the opposite end of the room was a bar and behind the bar a number of beer taps, but the bar sported a sign that said *Closed until 1:00PM.*

Gathered around a table were four men. Three of them sported spiked hair, ear/nose/lip piercings, and tattoos. The fourth rose to his feet. He couldn't have been more than five five, a paunch hanging over his suit pants, his tie stopping mid-stomach. He wore a suit jacket that wouldn't button all the way, and broken blood vessels marred his cheeks. His unnaturally black hair was combed over a bald spot on the top of his head and his eyes were red-rimmed. Tate figured this must be Desmond Hifler.

"Mr. Mercer," said the man, holding out his hand. "Or is it deputy?"

"Tate is fine," said Tate, taking the hand. Hifler's grip was clammy and Tate resisted the impulse to wipe his hand on his jeans. "This is Zion Sawyer."

Hifler extended his hand to her and Zion accepted it. "Nice to meet you." He pointed to the table. "This is *Anaconda.* Well, three fourths of it at any rate. I guess you'll be seeing Jaguar later," he said to Zion.

"That's right," she answered.

Hifler pointed at a tall, skeletally thin guy with blond hair, the ends of which were tinted blue. He had a bolt through his septum and another through his bottom lip. "This is Maximus Starr, the lead guitarist."

Tate and Zion shook hands with him.

Hifler then pointed to the guy on Starr's left. He was small and wiry. He wouldn't make eye contact, his eyes lifting to Tate's face and darting away. He had long bangs that completely covered one eye and he had tattoos on his neck.

"Ricky Sinister," said Hifler. "Bassist."

They shook hands, the man's hand light as a bird in his grasp. He wondered how someone so slight could hold a large instrument like a bass.

Hifler indicated the last guy with muscular shoulders on full display in a hot pink tank top. He wore shorts and his body was entirely covered in tattoos. Only his bald head showed skin. He drummed his fingers on the table. "And of course, Steele Torpedo, our drummer."

The drummer didn't offer his hand, just gave them a chin jerk and a "What's up?", while continuing to bang out a drumbeat with his index fingers.

Tate lifted his chin at him as well.

Hifler pulled out a chair for Zion. "Please take a seat."

She did so, removing her notepad from her purse. She began scribbling something on it as Tate took the seat next to her and Hifler returned to his breakfast.

"Thanks for agreeing to talk to us," said Tate, clasping his hands in his lap.

"Can we have your real names?" asked Zion, poised with pen in hand.

The band members all exchanged looks, then Starr shrugged. "Sure. I'm Maxwell Stark," he said.

Zion scribbled it next to his stage name, then looked over at the bassist, who still wouldn't meet her gaze. "And you?"

"My bourgeois parents gave me the name Richard Sinclair, but I prefer Ricky Sinister."

"Right," said Zion, scribbling. She smiled at the drummer. "And you?"

"Steven Torres, but Steven Torres is dead. I don't have a driver's license or credit cards. The only allowance I make to *the man* is my social security card and I'd get rid of that if I could."

Zion nodded. "Wouldn't we all," she remarked and went back to writing.

"What's Jaguar's legal name?" Tate asked Hifler.

"Jerome Jarvis," said Hifler.

"Thanks. Look, I know you need to get on the road, but I appreciate you giving me this time," he said to begin.

They nodded. The drummer continued his drumming and Tate tried not to get annoyed by it.

"I'm investigating the death of Merilee Whitmire."

"That's righteous bad," said Starr. "She was a pretty girl."

"You remember her?"

"Sure. We took pictures with her."

Tate glanced over at Hifler.

"Promo pictures. I can forward them to you."

"Please," he said.

"Do you have a card?"

He didn't have one yet, but Sheriff Wilson had promised to get him one. He motioned for Zion to give him a piece of paper and a pen. She handed everything over and he wrote down his personal email address. He needed to get an official one as well. Once he was done, he passed the slip of paper to Hifler and gave Zion back her pad and pen.

"The four of you grew up here in Sequoia, right?"

They glanced at each other and laughed a little. "We met in high school. Formed a garage band," said Starr. "Then things took off. Jaguar used to really have a vision, you know? He really knew how to lay down some tunes."

"Used to?" asked Tate.

Ricky Sinister shifted uneasily, shooting a quick look at Zion's pad. "We were always on the charts. For years. Now, I don't remember the last time we made it."

Hifler cleared his throat. "It's been a rough couple of years. We're not selling like we used to and the critics say the band's lost their edge."

Which didn't explain why Jaguar thought working in a coffee shop would help. Tate focused back on the case. "Did you know Merilee Whitmire? Did you go to school with her? I think she's about four years younger than you guys."

"Naw, I don't remember her. She woulda been a freshman when we were seniors," said Starr. "We weren't too involved at the school by that time. We'd already signed a record deal. It was a small time producer, but that was the start."

"Did you talk to Merilee when she came to the afterparty?"

"Sure. We talked with all the fans, signed autographs."

Ricky shot a look at Zion. "She wanted us to sign her…"

"Her?" Tate's brows rose.

Ricky motioned to his chest, his cheeks turning pink.

Zion sighed and continued to write.

"Did you sign her…" Tate motioned to his own chest.

They gave male barks of laughter, then sobered.

"Yeah," said Starr. "But that was it. I mean, she was with that guy. He had a girl's name."

"Deimos?"

"Naw, that wasn't it."

"Dee?"

"Right," said Torpedo, pointing at Tate, then going back to drumming.

Tate drew a breath for patience. "Did you see her drink anything?"

"They drank a beer," said Hifler. "I didn't see them drink anything else. Did you guys?"

They all shook their heads.

"What about eat anything? Did you see Merilee eat?"

"She and that Dee guy were making a big deal over the shrimp, but I didn't see her eat anything else," said Starr.

"What about drugs? Did they do any drugs?"

The guys shared a look, then all three shook their heads no.

Zion gave Tate a pointed look, making a joint motion with her fingers. He nodded. "I mean pot. Did you see Merilee smoke pot?"

"Oh," said Starr and there was more male laughter. "Yeah, she smoked a couple of blunts with us."

"Wait. You all smoked…um, blunts?"

"Yeah, you know, passed it around."

"So you literally smoked the same joints?"

"Yeah." Starr frowned in confusion.

"Did Dee smoke them as well?"

Starr leaned forward, his skeletal face twisting into a grimace. "We all smoked them. Everyone backstage."

"And no one got sick, except Merilee?"

"Right."

Tate slumped back in his chair. This didn't make sense. The beer had been in bottles and they'd opened them themselves, or so Dee had said. The food had been tested and it didn't have arsenic in it. Besides, both Dee and Merilee ate the shrimp. Everyone smoked the pot and when they got back to Dee's house, he smoked the same thing Merilee did. The only other thing Dee said she'd eaten was leftover pizza, but he'd had that as well. Still, the pizza hadn't been tested. Maybe there was something wrong with the pizza. He needed to find out where Dee got it.

"Is there anything else you remember about that night?" Tate asked the men.

They all shook their heads. He glanced over to Zion, but she simply closed the notebook and clicked off the pen.

Tate chewed on his inner lip, then turned to Hifler. This just wasn't adding up. He couldn't determine where Merilee had been poisoned – either at the after party or at Dee's apartment – and he couldn't rule out either place. Merilee had been the only one to get sick, so logic suggested she was the target, but how someone had poisoned only her and no one else didn't add up either.

"Has the band ever received threats of any kind?"

"From critics," said Hifler and they all laughed. Then he shook his head. "None."

"What about individual band members?"

"Nothing."

Zion frowned at him. He knew she didn't get where he was going with this.

"If you get any threats or you think anything seems suspicious, I need to know right away."

"Like what?" asked Hifler.

"Just anything that seems out of the ordinary. Even if you think it's trivial, contact me."

"Okay," said Hifler, clearly skeptical.

Tate rose to his feet and Zion followed him. "Thank you for talking with me."

A smattering of *no problem* and hand lifts answered him, then he and Zion made for the door. Unless he could somehow recreate the night Merilee died, this case was going nowhere fast and the hope of solving it was beginning to dim.

* * *

As soon as they got back into the truck, Zion turned to face him. "What are you thinking?"

"That I need to know where Merilee got poisoned and what was the method of delivery."

"It had to be the after party."

He started the truck. "Why do you say that?"

"Because otherwise, Dee did the poisoning and we know that didn't happen."

"They all smoked the pot at the after party. You heard them say they passed the joints around, and the food was tested. The only thing that wasn't tested was the pizza Dee said they ate at his apartment or the dope they smoked there."

"Dee didn't get sick."

"Dee doesn't remember what happened at his apartment. He said so himself. I need to search his apartment, Zion, and I need him not to be there."

Zion looked miserable. "You think he did it?"

"No, I don't think he did it, but I've got to narrow the poisoning window down somehow and his apartment is the only thing I can think of eliminating."

Zion faced the windshield, then she took out her phone and looked at the time. "It's 9:45. I don't have to be back at the *Caffeinator* until noon. Besides that, Jaguar won't be in until then and you wanted to question him."

"Right." He wasn't sure where she was going with this.

"Dee's at my house. I can call my mother and make sure he stays there."

"Okay."

She sighed and closed her eyes, then she looked over at him. "I know where he keeps his spare keys. He told me one time in case of emergency."

Tate stared out the windshield himself. If they found arsenic in Dee's apartment, he knew Zion would be devastated. So would he. He liked Dee, but he had to know. He had to search that apartment. Dee hadn't been arrested, so Sheriff Wilson hadn't bothered to get a warrant because he himself didn't think Dee was capable of murder. Tate knew that was a mistake. You never let personal feelings get in the way of an investigation. Dee's apartment should have been searched the moment he was brought in for questioning.

He pulled out his phone and dialed Sheriff Wilson's direct line. The sheriff picked up on the second ring. "What's happening? You got something?" he said.

"I'm going to search Dee's apartment. He's at Zion's house with her mother. I need you to get me a warrant, so we can do this legally."

"Shit," groused Wilson. "I was really hoping it wouldn't come to this."

"I don't think this means anything, except I've got to narrow down the window for her death. I need to be sure she didn't get poisoned at Dee's place."

"What if he destroyed evidence, Tate? This isn't going to narrow anything."

"I just need to get into that apartment, Sheriff. I need to check off one thing on my list."

"I'll get on the horn to the judge. You'll have your warrant by the time you get over there."

"Thanks. I'll let you know what I find out."

"I sure hope it isn't anything."

"You and me both." Tate hung up and turned to Zion. "See if Dee's still with your mom, but go ahead and tell him what I'm doing. I don't want him to be mad at you."

Zion dialed her mother and Tate pulled out of the parking lot, headed for Dee' apartment complex. He felt bad about this, knowing he was violating a friend's privacy. He'd never worried about it when he was a cop in LA, but then he'd never investigated a friend. He was personally involved in this, and that was how Sheriff Wilson had hooked him, he realized.

He listened to Zion's conversation with her mother, then he heard Dee's voice come through the line. "I'm sorry, Dee," said Zion, her voice heavy. "Tate doesn't think there's any other way to prove you're innocent."

Tate couldn't make out the actual words, but he could see the tension in Zion's posture. She hated this more than he did. "Put him on speaker," he said.

"Hold on, Dee," said Zion. "Tate wants to talk to you." She pressed the speaker button.

"Tate, dude, do you really have to go through my things?"

"I'm sorry about it, but I can't think of any other way. Something's bothering me about your side of the story."

"Ah, dude, I'm telling you I would never hurt Merilee. What do I gotta do to prove to you…"

"Listen to me," Tate said, his words coming out harsher than he'd intended.

Dee fell silent and Zion glanced over at him.

"When you brought Merilee back to your place, you said the two of you ate pizza you had in the fridge."

"Yeah, I always get hungry when I'm smoking blunts."

"Okay, but Merilee's father told us she had a gluten allergy. Did you get a gluten free pizza?"

Dee thought for a moment. "Oh, man, do you think that's what killed her? The gluten allergy?"

Tate fought for patience. "No, Dee, the coroner knows she was poisoned with arsenic. There's no debate, but she also didn't find any food in Merilee's stomach."

"But she was puking quite a bit, dude."

"Right, but do you remember seeing her eat the pizza? Do you actually remember her taking a bite of the crust?"

"She pulled some pepperonis off the top, then I told her to get her own slice."

"But did she take a bite of the crust?"

Dee went silent. Tate and Zion exchanged a look. Finally he exhaled. "I don't remember, Tate dude. That night is still all blurry to me."

"Where did you get the pizza?"

"*The Slice & Dice Pizza Pie*," said Dee.

"Did you order it that night?"

"No, it was leftover from before."

"How much was left?"

"Couple of slices. I ate most of it already."

"So you know you didn't order a gluten free pizza?"

"No, why would I?"

"Did you know Merilee had a gluten allergy?"

"We didn't talk about it. I don't know. I wasn't paying attention to that."

"Okay. Look, Dee. I promise we won't mess up anything in your apartment."

"Don't worry about it, Tate dude. I know you don't have any choice, and it's not like I got anything worth messing up anyway."

"You know I believe you didn't have anything to do with this, right?"

"Right."

"I'm gonna need the name of your dealer, Dee." While that angle seemed the most logical, it still troubled him. *Anaconda* had passed the joints around at the after party and no one else had gotten sick. Even Dee's private stash had been shared between him and Merilee. The coroner thought that was how she'd been poisoned, but no one could place a time when she smoked something they hadn't. He was missing something big and he knew it.

"Oh, Tate dude, no."

"I'm sorry. We can talk about it later, but I need to check this guy out."

"He wouldn't hurt Merilee."

Tate pulled up in front of Dee's apartment complex and put the truck in park. "Did he know Merilee, Dee?"

"Probably not."

"But you don't know for sure?"

"Not for sure. Pretty much everyone gets their pot from Jeremy. He runs a legitimate business, Tate. All legal and stuff."

Jeremy had to be the most non-threatening name Tate had ever heard for a drug dealer. "You wanna give me the last name now?"

"Give me a little time, okay? I need to let Dr. Jerm know you're gonna wanna talk to him. I can arrange it."

"That's great, Dee, but I still need his full name to run a background check. This is for Merilee's sake, Dee."

"Okay, okay, just give me a little time. Man, I wanna smoke a blunt now."

"Tell Mom you need to do more yoga," said Zion. "No blunts."

"I know, but whenever I get stressed…"

"No blunts!" said Zion firmly.

"Okay. You're right. Blunts is what got me into this mess. Yoga's gonna get me out. Gotta bounce. Dee out."

Zion gave Tate a shake of her head. "You know he didn't do this."

"I know. He doesn't have the ambition," he said wryly.

Zion held up a hand in agreement. "And that's the gospel truth," she said.

* * *

Zion found the key under the dead plant by the door and they stepped into the apartment. Tate immediately went to the kitchen and pulled everything out from beneath the sink, but he didn't find any rat poison. He did the same in Dee's bathroom.

Zion searched the living room, lifting the couch cushions, while Tate tackled the bedroom. He found a pipe and rolling papers in a drawer and he even found a business card for *Dr. Jerm's Herbal Remedies* with a phone number and for heaven's sake, a business license number. He pulled out his phone and entered the address into the internet search engine. It came up as a storage unit. No wonder Dee had to make contact with him. This guy wasn't exactly keeping a low profile, but he didn't have a storefront on Main Street.

Zion met him in Dee's room, staring at the mattress on the floor and the disarrayed bedclothes. "I hate that he lives like this."

Tate shrugged. "I don't exactly make my bed every morning myself."

"But do you sleep on the floor?"

Tate stared at the bed. "No." He held out the card. "Can you add this to your notes?"

She pulled the pad and pen out of her purse and took the card. "You know, we make a good team."

Tate rose to his feet and went to the closet opening the door. He wasn't touching that, no way. The more time he spent with her the harder it was to think of her with David. She was so different than his ex-wife, so easy-going and genuine. She couldn't hide her emotions no matter how hard she tried.

She put the card back in the nightstand as Tate rifled through Dee's clothes. A few pairs of jeans hung from hangers, but the majority of his clothes were wadded in a pile in the middle of the floor.

Zion wandered out of the room again, while Tate searched through the clothes. A moment later she called to him. Tate rose to his feet and closed the closet door, finding Zion standing in a corner of the kitchen. She pointed to a wall phone and attached to it was an answering machine.

Tate walked over to her. "He has an answering machine?" he asked, bewildered. No one he knew even had a landline anymore.

"Yeah, and listen to this." She pushed the button and a male voice came over the line. "I swear to God, you brain-dead idiot. Stay away from my girl. You come sniffing around her again and I'll kill you! You hear me, I'll kill you dead!"

Tate rubbed the back of his neck. Dee certainly wasn't telling him everything about his relationship with Merilee, that much was obvious. He looked at his cell phone, marking the time. He really needed to get to the *Hammer Tyme* and open up. Playing cop was interfering with his business, but the more he poked this case, the more it seemed there was to discover.

CHAPTER 11

Tate dropped Zion off at the *Caffeinator* at 11:00, an hour before she was scheduled to work, but she didn't mind. She felt nervous not being there to open the store. She was always the one to help Dottie get things ready for the day.

The coffee shop was busy, people occupied every table, and a small line waited at the cash register, but Tallah was handling the espresso machine like a pro and Dottie was ringing up sales as if she owned the place herself.

Zion waved to them both and hurried into her office, stashing her purse in the desk drawer, then coming back out and retrieving a clean apron from under the counter. She tied it on and moved up beside Dottie.

"You're early," said Dottie, glancing at her. "You're not supposed to start until noon."

"When's Jaguar getting here?" asked a teenage boy with eyes outlined in black eyeliner. "Heard he's gonna be making coffee, getting back to his roots. Man, that's bold."

Zion frowned at him, then looked at Dottie again. "Tate and I just went through Dee's apartment. Did you know he's been getting threats from some guy about a girl?"

Dottie gave her a worried look. "What's that boy gotten up to now?"

"I don't know."

"Who's the girl?"

"I don't know that either. Tate needed to get the *Hammer Tyme* opened and he dropped me off. I think he's gonna talk to Dee later tonight."

Dottie handed the eyeliner kid his receipt. "Coffee will be over there when it's ready. What's your name?" She picked up a grease pen and a cup.

"Rottweiler."

Dottie gave him an arch look, but she wrote on the cup. He gave her a cheeky grin and moved over to the pick-up counter. "I tell you, I hope you know what you're doing, hiring that rockstar to work here."

"So do I." Zion sighed.

"What'll it be?" Dottie asked a girl and boy behind Rottweiler. They both had tattoos on every part of their body that was visible. The girl even had music notes tattooed on her left cheek beneath her eye.

"I want a macchiato and he'll have a soy latte. Did you tell that guy when Jaguar's coming in?"

"Noon," said Dottie, punching in the orders. "Will that be all?"

The girl leaned back and looked in the display case. "Are those peanut butter cookies?"

"Yep," said Dottie.

"Oh, my gosh, I haven't had those since I was a little girl. This place is so fresh."

Zion and Dottie exchanged a look.

"You want a cookie?" asked Dottie.

"I want two. Are they vegan?"

"They're made with butter. Do you still want them?"

The boy leaned close and whispered in her ear. She nodded.

"It'd be better if they were vegan."

"Okay?" said Dottie, drawing out the word. Zion hid her smile. "So no cookie?"

"Yeah, no, we still want them, but it'd just be better if they were vegan."

"So would a lot of things, sugar," said Dottie, grabbing two cups. "Your names?"

Zion moved over and served up the two cookies, slipping them into a *Caffeinator* wax envelope. She handed them to the girl as the girl passed Dottie a crinkled twenty. Dottie made change, then shut the drawer and faced Zion.

"Do you know who called Dee?"

Zion shook her head. "I'm not sure, I didn't recognize the voice, but Merilee's boyfriend, Everett, came in here the other day, threatening Dee."

"Did you tell Tate about that?"

"Yeah."

"Was the person talking about Merilee on the message?"

"He didn't say that either. I just don't know. Do you know if Dee was seeing any other girls?"

"I didn't think he was seeing Merilee."

Zion sighed. "I don't know what to think."

"Let Tate handle it," said Dottie, putting her hands on Zion's shoulders. "He's the cop."

"He retired."

"And now he's back. You stay out of it. I don't want you getting hurt."

Dottie's concern warmed Zion and she smiled, patting her hand. "What needs doing?"

"We need another batch of shortbread if you're up for making it. And we could use a new jar of biscotti. The delivery came this morning."

"On it," said Zion, hurrying to the back to whip up her favorite baking recipe.

* * *

Jaguar and his two bodyguards arrived at noon to much fanfare. He came in carrying a guitar case and the entire coffee house stopped doing what it was they were doing to watch him, including Tallah. Behind Jaguar was a crowd.

Zion wasn't sure where these people had been lurking, but they appeared the minute the limo pulled past the coffee shop on its way to the municipal parking lot. People shouted at Jaguar to sign autographs or sing them a song. He stopped in the middle of the shop and held up his free hand.

"Now, listen up, everybody!" he said, the leather strips on his wrist sliding toward his forearm. "I'm here to work. If you want to buy coffee, I'll be happy to sell it to you, but beyond that, I'm just a regular guy doing his regular shift."

Dottie mouthed, *Yeah right!* Then she began untying her apron. She leaned in to speak in Zion's ear as she went past. "Remember the rolling pin," she stage whispered, then she snapped Tallah's rear with the bit of cloth. "Let's go, sunshine. I promised your mother I'd walk you over to the restaurant."

"But Dottie," Tallah whined, watching the rockstar as he wended his way through the people. "I'm just gonna stay and meet some friends here."

"No, you're not. I promised your mother. Now if she wants to let you come back, that's between you and her. Get a move on."

As Jaguar came around the counter, he stopped to let them pass. Tallah gave him a sultry smile and wave. He smiled back, but it wasn't anything more than he'd been giving his fans. Then he held up the guitar case.

"Can I store this in your office?" he asked Zion.

"Sure," she said and he disappeared in the back. A moment later, Tate pushed through the crowd, fighting his way to the counter. Zion smiled at him, surprised by how happy it made her when he showed up.

"Obviously, he's here," he said.

"Yep," she answered.

"I want to question him now if possible. I need to get back to the *Hammer Tyme*."

"Let me see if Tallah and Dottie will stay for a few more minutes."

The two women came out of the office, Tallah's face showing her disappointment. Zion intercepted them.

"Dottie, Tate wants to question Jaguar about Merilee. Will you and Tallah stay just until he's done?"

Dottie gave her a serious appraisal. "Sure," she said, reaching for her apron again and stashing her purse under the counter. "This murder investigation's getting old, though."

"I know. I'm sorry. I'll owe you big when this is over."

"You don't owe me, but it would be nice to get rid of that tattooed rockstar."

Zion smiled, patting her shoulder as she motioned Tate behind the counter. "I'll take notes for you," she told him.

He gave her a skeptical look, but he didn't argue. They found Jaguar, standing in the middle of the office, looking around.

"Brings back so many memories," he said wistfully. "I sure hope this gets my mojo back."

Zion motioned to Tate. "This is Tate Mercer. He wants to ask you a few questions. He's working Merilee Whitmire's murder case."

Jaguar's blond brows rose. "Really?" His eyes tacked over Tate's t-shirt and jeans. "You're from the sheriff's department?"

Tate pulled the badge out of his back pocket and showed it to Jaguar. "Sheriff Wilson deputized me."

"I see."

Zion retrieved her notepad from her purse in the desk, then patted her desk chair for Tate to sit down. "You sit here." She pointed to the chair on the other side of the desk. "You sit there, Jaguar." Glancing around, she spotted a step stool and yanked it over, sitting on the top step. "And I'll just take notes."

Tate gave her a wry look, but he took her spot at the desk. "I wanted to ask you about the after party when Merilee Whitmire attended."

Jaguar nodded. "Did you talk to the other guys today?"

"I did."

"Did they remember her?"

"They said they did. Do you remember her?"

"There were a lot of people at the after party, but I think I remember this Merilee chick. She was there with this guy with shaggy hair. They had backstage passes."

"Do you remember what Merilee and the guy did?"

Jaguar shrugged. "Nothing much. They ate a little food and drank a beer or two. I wasn't paying too much attention."

"Were you at the after party the whole time?"

"Pretty much. I think I left about midnight, but it was starting to break up then."

"Did you notice if Merilee went anywhere by herself?"

"I wasn't really paying attention to her, mate," he said again. "Not to be crude, but I was pretty wasted by the after party."

"What sort of drugs did you do?"

Jaguar considered that. "I drink mostly. Smoke a little pot, but I don't even do that much." He touched his throat. "Gotta protect the pipes, you know? I'm real careful about what I put in my body." He made a disparaging sound. "Well, except booze. I'm like my old man that way. I had my first beer with Pops when I was seven."

Tate gave Zion a look. She shrugged. She wasn't sure how that applied to anything, but who knew? She made a note of it.

"Do you remember seeing Merilee smoking pot?"

"Yeah, I think I remember them passing around a joint or two. I took a few puffs, then I left it alone. I always start coughing whenever I smoke."

"Did Merilee smoke anything or take anything by herself?"

"I wouldn't know that. I wasn't watching her. She was pretty into the guy she was with, so I left her alone. I don't go after girls that seem involved." He gave Zion a pointed look.

She wasn't biting. If he was trying to prove he wasn't a danger to Tallah, he was talking to the wrong person. She wasn't leaving the girl alone with him. Tallah didn't understand what a predator was.

"Is there anything else you can remember about that night? Anything strange that happened?" asked Tate.

"I wish I had more to give you, but it was a pretty standard after party. Actually, it was pretty tame. Some of them get wild, but that one was tame."

Tate exhaled, staring at the desk. "Okay." He looked up, pinning Jaguar with his gaze. "How long are you planning to stay here?"

Jaguar shrugged. "Not sure. My mom's not doing too good, so I wanna spend some time with her. Besides, I gotta get my mojo back. *Anaconda* is not gonna last if I don't come up with something fresh, something new. I need to check my privilege real bad and working here…" He looked around Zion's minimalist office. "…will probably do the trick."

Zion frowned at that, not sure she liked his disparaging comments.

Tate fought a smile, giving Zion a wink. "You can go back to work," he told the rockstar.

Jaguar rose to his feet and wandered out the door. Zion put the finishing touches on her notes and closed the pad.

"Arrogant ass," she muttered.

Tate laughed. "What did you expect? The guy rides around in limos." He gave her office a critical look as well. "Besides, you could liven this place up a little. Give it a fresh coat of paint." He pushed himself to his feet. "I know of a great hardware store in town that sells paint on the cheap."

She rose also and met his gaze. "I don't know. The owner's sort of a jerk. I've seen his office and it's a warehouse."

"Hey!" he said, laughing, then his laugh died off and his expression sobered.

Zion was suddenly aware of how close they were standing. The noise from the coffee shop filtered into the room, but for a moment, it seemed like they were the only people in the world. She stared into his brown eyes and found her gaze lowering to his lips.

He was breathing a bit fast and he shifted as if he could feel the sudden tension between them. She exhaled and took a step back. Maybe spending so much time together wasn't a good thing. Maybe she was getting confused by the ease of their friendship.

David was her guy. Wasn't he?

"I'd better get back to work," she said, pointing toward the door.

"Yeah, me too," he said and smiled.

Zion realized she liked his smile. It was genuine and low-key, just like Tate himself. David wasn't low-key, but David was a good guy. He was smart and handsome and accomplished and he didn't have that sadness lurking behind his eyes the way Tate did.

David was her guy, she told herself again, then she turned and headed for the door.

"Zion?" Tate called after her.

She stopped, but she didn't immediately turn around. Finally, she shifted.

"I need to talk to Dee again. Can you arrange for him to meet me at your house?"

She couldn't help but feel a stab of disappointment. She wasn't sure what she'd wanted him to say, but she wanted something more than to talk about the case. "Sure," she said. "I'll call him."

"Thanks," he answered.

Zion nodded, then went through the door, hurrying back into the coffee house. When she got back behind the counter, she was immediately swamped with people wanting orders, so she missed Tate as he fought his way through the crowd and out the door again.

* * *

By late afternoon, the coffee shop was still filled with people, but she had to admit that Jaguar was a whiz with the espresso machine. She'd finally had to press his bodyguards into service, having them call out names as the coffees came up and pulling baked goods out of the oven. She'd dipped into the frozen dough she and Dottie stored for just such an occasion, but she found that Maddog could drop cookies on a cookie sheet almost as well as she did herself.

She blinked in surprise when Beatrice and Carmen Sanchez appeared in front of her. Beatrice and her sister-in-law ran the *Knitatorium* next door. Beatrice had short grey hair that curled tightly against her scalp and glasses. She always wore elastic waistband pants in bright colors and knit sweaters. Zion wasn't sure how she stood the heat, but the sweater she wore today was short-sleeved. Her sister-in-law, Carmen had salt-and-pepper hair, cut in a short bob, and she wore blouses and pressed slacks with pumps. Carmen was the more stylish of the two.

"Hey, ladies," Zion said, smiling at them. She liked Beatrice and Carmen. Beatrice had a knack for saying inappropriate things, but Zion found her amusing.

Beatrice's eyes twinkled behind her glasses. "Hey, dear, how are you?"

"Good."

Both women cut their eyes to the rockstar adding whipped cream to the frappe he'd just finished pouring. "That's him?" whispered Beatrice.

Zion's brows lifted. "That's who?" she teased, surprised either woman knew the lead singer from *Anaconda*.

"The Jaguar," said Carmen, also leaning forward to whisper. "He makes the coffee now?" She looked him over. "So many earrings, so many tattoos. My granddaughter, she listens to his music all the time."

"We downloaded his album to our phones," added Beatrice and the two women giggled like school girls. "He's got a nice fanny."

Zion feigned a gasp, then smiled, enchanted by their infatuation. She leaned close to them as well. "You wanna meet him?"

Carmen straightened, putting her hand over her heart, her eyes going wide. Beatrice gave another giggle. "Really?" she said breathlessly. "Can you introduce us?"

Zion nodded. "Jaguar?"

The rockstar looked over. He'd been handing a pretty girl the frappe and the flirtatious smile was still on his face. "What's up?" he said, wiping his hands on his apron and walking over to her.

Zion motioned to the two women. "This is Beatrice and Carmen Sanchez. They own the *Knitatorium* next door."

Jaguar held out his hand. Beatrice clasped it between both of her own. "Nice to meet you, ladies. I guess we're neighbors for a little while."

They both tittered a laugh.

"They downloaded *Anaconda's* latest album to their phones," Zion told him.

Jaguar gently extricated himself from Beatrice and held out his hand for Carmen. She laid just her fingers in his grasp, her other hand still pressed over her heart. "I'm always happy to meet a fan."

More giggles. Zion fought her own laugh; they were too cute.

"My granddaughter, she listens to everything you do," said Carmen. "She's your biggest fan."

"Really?" Jaguar snapped his fingers at Bruno. The bodyguard rushed over from wiping up the counter. "Paper?"

Bruno pulled a pad from his back pocket and handed it to Jaguar. Jaguar reached for the pen on the cash register, placing the pad on the counter. "Tell me her name and I'll give her an autograph."

The two older women exchanged looks, then Carmen blushed. "It's Carmen."

Zion and Jaguar both frowned at that.

"Carmen?" asked Zion.

"She's named for me," said Carmen with a defiant glint in her eye. "It's Carmen, C-a-r-m-e-n."

Jaguar scribbled something on the paper, then finished with a flourish and tore it off the pad, handing it to her. "For Carmen," he said with a wry smile.

Both women looked at it, then they giggled again. Carmen clutched the autograph to her chest.

"Well, we should get going," said Beatrice, still staring at the rockstar. "We've got a business to run."

Zion didn't comment about the fact that they hadn't bought anything from her. It was pretty obvious they had one reason and one reason only for coming into the *Caffeinator*. Backing up, they both ran into a young man, waiting in line behind them.

"Sorry," muttered Beatrice. "Bye, Jaguar," she said, waving at him. Then her gaze cut to Zion. "Bye, Zion," she added.

"Muchas gracias," said Carmen, fluttering her autograph in the air. "Adios, Zion," she called after Beatrice, then they turned and scurried out the door.

The young man moved up to the counter. "I'll take what they had," he said. Jaguar signed his name again, tore it off and gave it to the young man, then he held out the pad to Bruno and moved back to making coffees.

Zion wanted to remind Jaguar that they'd agreed he'd stop snapping his fingers at his people, but a new wave of customers had just walked through the door. She was going to be out of supplies if this kept up for long.

* * *

Zion dragged herself out of Tate's car. "See you in a bit," she told him, weariness pressing on her. The whole ride home, she'd sat and stared out the window, not able to carry on a conversation. The nice thing about Tate was he didn't feel a need to fill the silence. She liked that about him. In fact, she was realizing there was a whole lot she liked about the guy.

"I'll just park, change, and head over. Tell Dee to wait for me," he said, leaning down to look at her through the open door.

She nodded and headed for her front door. She was glad her mother was still here. She didn't feel up to cooking for herself tonight. The steady stream of customers had lasted until closing. In fact, Zion had to tell them to leave. At least she had Bruno and Maddog backing her up. No one argued with those two hulking behind her.

Jaguar had mentioned he hadn't worked that hard in years and he felt like he was getting the privilege-poison out of his system. Zion didn't care. She wasn't sure she could take Jaguar working at the coffee shop if things didn't settle down really soon. Where were all these people coming from and why hadn't they left Sequoia yet?

She opened the door to laughter coming from her kitchen. Dee and her mother were making a salad and something green was bubbling on the stove. Zion scrunched up her nose at the smell. Turning, Gabi saw her daughter and came toward her, kissing her cheek. She had broccoli in one hand and a head of lettuce in the other.

"How was your day?" Gabi asked.

Zion dropped her purse on the table and picked up Cleo where she lay stretched out on a chair. She cuddled the cat against her face, enjoying the immediate rumble of her purr. "It was insane. I'm worried we're gonna run out of coffee."

Dee gave her a worried look. "You had that many customers?"

"It was crazy from the moment we opened this morning. Jaguar really draws them in."

Dee's face fell. "I guess you don't need me to come back."

Zion patted his shoulder. "I need you to come back and fast. I can't keep up this pace. I want my nice, quiet

Caffeinator back." She looked into the bubbling green pot. "What's this?"

"Brussel sprout soup," said Gabi, picking up a clean spoon and dishing up a mouthful. She held it out to Zion. "It is filled with antioxidants and vitamin C. It'll pep you right up."

Zion made a face. The smell was overpowering, weedy and a bit sour. "Mom, what's wrong with potato or chicken noodle soup?"

"You need to add a lot more green to your diet." She popped the spoonful in her mouth and smacked her lips. "I can feel the health just flowing through me. These are organic brussel sprouts, and then we have a kale and radicchio salad with a spritz of raspberry vinaigrette."

"So no Ranch?" Zion asked wryly.

Gabi's eyes widened and she took a step back as if Zion had said something foul. Zion laughed, despite herself. She noticed that both Gabi and Dee had a glass of wine.

"Is the wine healthy?"

"A glass of red wine a day keeps the blood flowing," said Gabi.

"Right."

A knock sounded at the door. Zion went to it, carrying Cleo. Tate stood on the other side in a pair of cargo shorts and a plain navy blue t-shirt. She tried not to notice that his legs were toned and his forearms were muscular. She especially didn't want to stare at the interesting tattoo of a panther that wound around the inner part of his right forearm.

"Come in. Are you hungry?" she asked him.

He reached out to pet Cleo, who pressed her face against his hand. "Sure, but I don't want to impose."

Zion laughed as she closed the door behind him. "Oh, you're not imposing. Just wait until you hear what we're having for dinner. You may change your mind."

Gabi appeared in the kitchen entrance, wiping her hands on a dishtowel. "Tate, it's so nice to see you. Come have a glass of wine with us."

Tate followed Zion into the kitchen. Zion settled Cleo back on her chair and went to pour the wine for herself and Tate. Dee gave him a worried look.

"I called Dr. Jerm."

Tate took a seat at the table. "Come sit down," he said, motioning to the open chair across from him.

Zion brought him a glass and picked up Cleo, sitting down with cat on her lap, while Gabi pretended not to listen by working on the salad. Dee sat down, his eyes downcast. Zion patted his hand.

"Tate's trying to help you, Dee."

"I know, but I just feel like everyone keeps looking at me as if they're trying to see guilt or something."

"That's not it at all," said Tate, resting his forearms on the table, the wine glass between his hands. "You called Dr. Jerm?"

"Right."

"What did he say?"

"He agreed to meet with you tomorrow morning at 9:00. That's what time he opens his shop."

"His shop?"

"The storage unit."

"Right. I need his full name, Dee."

"Tate dude…"

"I need his full name," Tate said firmly. "I have to run a background check."

"Dr. Jerm only has top notch stuff, Tate. He'd never risk his business by letting anything less than stellar get past him."

"I'm not talking about bad weed, Dee."

"I know. I know you mean arsenic, but he does quality control on everything he sells."

Tate frowned at that.

"He means he smokes it himself," Zion told him.

"Oh," said Tate. "Doesn't matter. I still need his name."

"Tate dude…"

"Just tell him," said Zion, feeling her temper snap.

Dee reared back and Gabi turned from the stove.

"Look, my coffee shop was a circus all day. I can't take much more of that. I want you to come back to work and if that means doing a background check on Dr. Jerm, the Pot Dealer, then we're going to do it." She caught herself and lifted her wine, taking a gulp.

Tate gave her a warm smile, but Dee and her mother just stared at her. She didn't often lose her temper, but there it was. She was exhausted and her feet hurt. She just wanted to eat some comfort food, not brussel sprouts, take a hot shower, and climb into bed.

"Jeremy Deluca," Dee said sullenly.

Tate took out his phone and punched something into it, then he put the phone away. "I'll pick you up at your apartment at 8:30 to go see Dr. Jerm. Be ready," he told Dee.

Dee nodded.

Tate met Zion's gaze and she nodded. There was something more important to discuss with Dee. With a sigh, Tate clasped his hands on the table. "Dee, we heard a phone message on your answering machine."

Dee looked up. Gabi stopped pretending like she wasn't listening and leaned against the counter.

"It was a man and he threatened to kill you if you didn't leave his girl alone."

Dee chewed on his inner lip, but didn't answer.

"Do you know who left the message?"

Dee nodded.

"I need to know, Dee."

"He didn't mean it. He was just blowing off steam."

"Tell me."

Dee drained his wine glass. "Everett."

"Everett Hughes, Merilee's boyfriend?"

Dee nodded again.

"Were you sleeping with her before the concert, Dee?" asked Zion.

He wouldn't meet her eye.

"Dee, it's important."

"She said she was leaving him. I thought we had something."

Tate slumped back in the chair. "You know this might be why Merilee was poisoned. Why didn't you tell me this before?"

"Everett wouldn't hurt anyone, especially not Merilee," protested Dee.

"What if he wanted to hurt you and Merilee got the bad pot by accident?" said Zion. She couldn't believe Dee was being this obtuse.

Dee's gaze lifted and met hers. Awareness dawned in his eyes, then he shook his head. "Everett wouldn't do something like this."

"You don't know what people might do, Dee," said Tate wearily. "People do some really surprising things."

"Besides, he's threatened your life twice now," said Zion.

Dee started to answer, then stopped.

Tate reached for his phone. "I need to tell the sheriff about this." He rose to his feet and went to the backdoor, pulling it open and stepping out onto the deck.

Zion gave Dee a stern look, but before she could say anything, there was a knock at her door.

She rose and went to answer it.

David stood on the other side.

"Hey, did we have plans?" she asked him.

He bent and kissed her lightly on the mouth. "I wanted to see you." His eyes went beyond her to the kitchen. "Dee's here?"

"Yeah, he's having dinner. You hungry?"

David nodded. "Sure."

Stepping back, she motioned him inside. He followed her to the kitchen.

"Hello, David," Gabi called. "Would you like a glass of wine?"

David lifted a hand to wave, but stopped mid-motion, his gaze fixing on Tate where he stood on the back deck, talking on the phone. "Why is he here again?" he asked.

Zion looked at David in surprise. Immediately she felt her temper rise. Twice now he'd made a comment about Tate being at her house. "He came over to talk to Dee about the murder investigation."

Dee gave David a sheepish look.

David frowned, his gaze sweeping over the table and the wine glasses. "But you're having wine?" He tried to put a touch of humor in his voice, but he didn't quite make it.

Gabi's brows rose and she turned her back, going to the stove. Zion shifted to face him. "It's been a long day, David, and we all thought we deserved a little break."

David held out his hands. "Look, it's fine, but I don't know why he has to keep coming here to question Dee. It might seem more practical to do it at the sheriff station or his house."

"What are you saying?"

"I just don't know why you have to be involved."

"Because I'm working the case with him."

David's brows drew down lower. "What?"

"I told you that."

"No, you didn't. You're not a cop, Zion."

"I know that."

"Do you?"

Dee made a choking sound.

Zion put her hands on her hips. She was so not in the mood for this tonight. "Look, David, I'm really tired. I've had a long day and I don't want to fight."

He looked away, his jaw tightening. "You're right. Let's not fight. We can talk about it another time."

Tate stepped back into the cottage, taking in the situation. Zion knew he sensed the tension by the expression on his face. "Hi, David," he said.

David just nodded without speaking.

"Well, I should go," said Tate, heading toward the kitchen door.

Zion glared at David, but she didn't tell Tate to stay. She knew David felt threatened by the other man, and to be honest, she wasn't sure he didn't have a reason. If she was being fair, she had to admit her relationship with the lawyer seemed to be stalled. She wasn't ready to take it to the next level and he clearly was. That had to say something, and that something probably wasn't good.

"Night, everyone."

"Good night, Tate," said Gabi.

"Night," muttered Dee, ducking his head.

Tate edged around David and headed for the front door. Zion broke her stare with David and went after him.

"I'm sorry," she said softly.

"No problem."

"Did you get a hold of Sheriff Wilson?"

"Yeah, but don't worry about it, okay."

"I want to go with you tomorrow morning."

Tate glanced beyond her to where David stood, his back to the living room. "That might not be a good idea."

"You promised," she reminded him.

Tate started to say something, then stopped himself. Finally he nodded.

Zion felt her shoulders released their tension. Why was this so important to her? True, she wanted Dee back at work and she wanted Jaguar gone, but it was more than that. She hated the thought of Tate going to question a suspect without her. She wanted to be in on the case. She wanted to figure out who'd killed Merilee and she wanted…she wrapped her arms around her middle, watching him walk out the door…she wanted to spend time with him like they had the last few days.

Oh, boy, she really didn't know what she wanted and this wasn't fair to any of them.

CHAPTER 12

Tate stepped out of the shower, toweled off, and got dressed. Running a comb through his hair, he stared at his reflection. The nightmare had returned the previous night and he'd spent a few hours reading in his recliner, the lights blazing in his house. This time when he'd crossed around the back of the car, stepping in blood, it hadn't been his partner, Jason, but Dee who lay crumpled on the ground. He needed to get a handle on this case. It was too slippery and too many people were potential suspects.

He knew he should go to see Dr. Jerm, the drug dealer, without Zion, but he was finding that hard to do. The more time they spent together, the more his attraction to her grew, but he knew he was causing her trouble with David. Not that he thought David was right for her, but he wasn't being fair. Zion had chosen the lawyer, so he should back off. Still, he sensed Zion wasn't as into the relationship as David was.

He brushed his teeth and went into the bedroom, grabbing his phone. Sitting down on the bed, he pressed the icon for his friend, Darcy Reyes, a technician for the LAPD. He hadn't talked to her in weeks. Usually he called to catch up, but he'd been more busy since the summer tourist season had started.

"Officer Reyes," came her cheerful voice.

Tate smiled. "Hey, Darce, what's shakin'?"

"Tater Tot!" she said. "You haven't called me in weeks. Did you forget I exist?"

"Not even a little. How are things going down there?"

She went silent for a moment, then her voice came on the line, much lower than before. "Tense."

"Why?"

"You hear about the shooting of that kid, Davonte Walsh?"

"I heard something on the news about it. He wasn't armed, right?"

"Right."

"Was it one of our guys?"

"Keith Poole," said Darcy. "He's on leave."

"Keith Poole?" Keith had been on the gang task force with him and Jason. "Was the kid a gang banger?"

"He was fourteen, Tate. He hung out with some of the bangers, but no one says he was one of them."

"Wow. How's Poole doing?"

"I haven't talked to him, but it's all over the news. The community's demanding answers and the mayor's talking about convening an independent council to review the department's handling of racial situations."

Tate couldn't deny he was glad he wasn't part of this anymore.

"Anyway, you might give Poole a call. Weren't you and Jason close with him?"

"He was on our gang task force. We went out for beers a few times, but I wouldn't say we were close."

"So, you didn't call just to see how I'm doing, did you?"

"Why would you say that, Darce? Of course I want to know how you're doing."

She made a disparaging sound.

"How's Mikey?"

Darcy had a five year old son that she was raising by herself. Tate admired her for it. He couldn't even keep a potted plant alive.

"He's great. He's starting to read."

"Kid's a genius."

She laughed. "You're trying to butter me up."

"You got me," he said, laughing with her. "Can you run a background check on a pot dealer out here?"

"Pot dealer?"

"It's supposedly a legitimate business. The business is called *Dr. Jerm's Herbal Remedies.* He runs it out of a storage unit. His name's Jeremy Deluca. I wanna know if he has any priors."

"You know I gotta run this during my off-time, Tater Tot."

"Yeah."

"Why are you running a background check? Thinking of going into business with him?"

"Nope. We got another murder here. Girl was poisoned at an *Anaconda* concert."

"*Anaconda Glee Club*?"

"You know them?"

"Yeah, I thought they were broken up actually. Their last few albums have flopped. Rumor has it the lead singer, Jaguar, was going solo."

"Not exactly. I mean, I guess they aren't doing as well as before. They had to play a festival we had here, but they were the headliners. Jaguar's working in my friend's coffee shop."

"Why?"

"I don't know. Something about getting his mojo back by working manual labor. I don't get those artist types."

Darcy laughed. "Come on. You remember what it was like down here with all those stars? Get a call and the lawyer was on premises before the ambulance. You'd have drugs and quinoa in the same cocktail."

Tate chuckled. "Yeah, I remember."

"Why are you working another murder? I thought you retired to go bear hunting or some such."

"The sheriff deputized me."

"Sucked you back in."

"Yep. So will you get back to me?"

"Sure. Give me until Monday. I'm only working a few hours today, then I'm picking Mikey up for baseball practice, and I have tomorrow off."

"Got it. Tell Mikey I said hi."

"I will. You watch out. Some of those bears might be armed."

"Right. Talk to you Monday."

"Talk to you Monday."

He started to disconnect the call, then on a hunch, he lifted it to his ear again. "Darce?"

"What's up, Tater Tot?"

"Can you run another background check for me?"

"Seriously? You're gonna get me in trouble, then I'll have to move in with you and hunt bears too."

"There's plenty of room. The bear carcasses only take up so much space."

"Who's this second check on?"

"Everett Hughes." He spelled the name. "I need any priors, also look for a sealed juvie record."

"Okay, got it. Just sit tight, okay?"

"Yep. Thanks again, Darce. You're the best."

"Right. You still owe me two bottles of primo wine from the last time you played cop."

"Oh crap!" Tate had completely forgotten he'd promised her wine for her help with Vivian Bradley's murder. "I'll make it a full case this time. Be on the look-out for it."

"I won't hold my breath," she said and disconnected.

Tate glanced at the time, then jumped to his feet. He had just enough time to grab a mug of coffee before he had to pick up Dee. The bigger question was if he planned to pick up Zion as well. If he was a good guy, he'd leave her behind and let her work things out with her boyfriend, but he'd decided a long time ago that he just wasn't that good.

* * *

Jeremy Deluca sat in front of his storage unit on a folding lawn chair, the legs of which were rusted. One of the plastic straps was broken, hanging down like a tail below him. He rose to his feet as Tate, Zion and Dee approached.

He was skinny, tall, stoop shouldered, with long brown hair and a wispy beard and mustache. In fact, it was the sort of sorry beard that made Tate wonder why some guys even bothered. He had on flip flops and his long toes curled over the front, a stained white wife-beater tank top, and jeans that hung low on his waist. Tate could see the tops of his boxers above the waistband of his jeans, and here he'd thought that style had gone out of fashion.

Zion instinctively moved closer to Tate, but Dee sprinted forward, clasping hands with the guy and pulling him in for a quick man-hug.

"Dr. Jerm!" said Dee, patting his back with his free hand. "How's it hanging, dude?"

"No complaints," said Dr. Jerm. Tate had to admit the nickname was apt as nicknames went. Deluca's eyes went beyond him and raked over Zion. Tate resisted the urge to put his arm around her in a protective gesture. "I thought you were just bringing Johnny Law, although I don't mind the company." He leered at Zion.

Dee frowned and released him. "Behave. This is my boss lady, dude."

Deluca held up his hands in surrender. "No problemo." He jerked his chin at Tate. "I need to see a badge."

"And I need to see your business license," Tate said, pulling his badge out of his back pocket and flashing it at the guy.

Deluca reached into the storage unit and pulled out a framed business license, handing it to Tate. Zion had taken her notebook out of her purse, so he handed her the license. "Can you write the number down so I can verify it?" he asked her.

She nodded without taking her eyes off the drug dealer. Today she had her red hair loose in curls to her shoulders, her usual capris in white, and a pink *Caffeinator* t-shirt. Her sneakers were pink lace with rhinestones on the toes. He tried to not get distracted by the smatter of freckles over her nose and cheeks or the way her green eyes shown in the sunlight. Damn, he had it bad. He liked everything about her, especially now that she wasn't hiding under so much makeup and hair products.

"Dee says you regularly supply him with marijuana," he said, forcing himself to focus.

"I provide the best medicinal herbs in the entire county. Nothing I sell leaves here without my rigorous quality assurance."

Tate smiled slowly. "What exactly does that mean?"

"I sample all of my products myself."

"Right." Just as Zion suspected. "Do you grow the marijuana yourself too?"

"No, I have a reliable source just north of here. It's an organic farm and they have a very good rating."

"Can you give me the name of your source?"

"You can understand why I'm reluctant to divulge this information. While marijuana is legal in California now, it's still illegal federally and I wouldn't want to cause a federal raid."

"You can understand that I have a dead girl in the morgue who was poisoned with arsenic. Unless you want me to turn over every inch of this place and your source, I suggest you play ball with me."

Deluca exchanged a look with Dee. Dee shifted weight.

"Tate's a good guy, Jerm. He'll be discreet."

"*Yerba Granja*." He pulled a wallet out of his back pocket and opened it, taking out a business card. A marijuana leaf was embossed on the front of it.

"Herb Farm?" asked Zion, crinkling her brow. "That's the name of the place? Seriously?"

Deluca shrugged. "I just source their stuff, top of the line. I'm telling you, no one has better herb."

"Did you sell your medicinal plants to *Anaconda* for their after party?" asked Tate.

"I mighta or I might not. I don't divulge client information."

"So, I'll need to get a warrant?" Tate looked into the storage unit. "Lot of boxes to search. Wonder what's inside all of them?"

"I run a legitimate business." Deluca looked at Dee. "You told me he was cool. I agreed to this for you."

Dee held out his hand. "Merilee's dead, Jerm. What do you want him to do? He's gotta find out who slipped her the arsenic. You didn't see it, Jerm. She suffered bad."

Tate sighed. Dee would probably need to see a counselor after this was over. He kept forgetting the poor guy had been there when Merilee died.

"I mighta sold some blunts to their manager, but it was top of the line stuff."

Tate glanced at Zion as she made some notes. Damn it, Desmond Hifler was in LA. It would be hard to compel him back to Sequoia without substantial evidence. "You rolled the joints yourself?"

"I did. Best of everything I've got."

"Could someone unroll them and add something to it?"

"I don't see how. It'd probably come apart."

Tate considered that. He didn't know much about pot, but he'd seen joints before and they were pretty tightly rolled. Besides, if Hifler had added the arsenic, he'd have been trying to poison his whole band, not just one girl. That seemed a little far-fetched.

Merilee had to be the target.

"Did you ever sell to Merilee directly?"

Deluca made a face, staring at the ground. "I don't like to divulge my client…"

"She dead. She's not your client anymore."

"I never sold to Merilee."

"She only smoked when she was at a party or we were celebrating something. Her pops was really against it and wouldn't let it in his house," said Dee. "Besides, she didn't really need to buy her own stuff."

Tate caught the underlying meaning behind Dee's words. With the string of men Merilee was dangling, she didn't need to get her own supply. He really needed to talk with Sheriff Wilson and see how his interrogation of Everett Hughes had gone, then he needed to locate Gunner Bishop, the other boy that had been interested in Merilee.

"If you hear anything or you remember something, you call me. Understand?" Tate said to Deluca. "You can leave a message at the sheriff's office and they'll get it to me."

Deluca gave a chin lift, but he wouldn't make eye contact.

Tate glanced at Zion. "Ready?"

She nodded and closed her notebook, shoving it into her purse. Dee gave Deluca another man-hug and the three of them walked back to Tate's truck. Tate found himself lost in thought. Something was niggling at the back of his mind, something that had been bothering him for days now.

Everyone they'd talked to said Merilee hadn't done anything different than the rest of the people she was with, and yet, Merilee was the only one who'd wound up poisoned. Clearly, she'd done something that the rest hadn't. She'd smoked something, taken something, or eaten something, but what was it?

There was no trace of anything in her stomach, the tox report pointed only to arsenic, and the autopsy had been inconclusive. He didn't remember reading in the report that she had injection marks anywhere on her body nor any other signs of drugs in her system. What had she taken that no one else had? And when had she taken it?

* * *

After dropping Zion and Dee off at Zion's house, Tate drove to the sheriff's office and pressed the button to get into the back. Sam looked up as he came through the door, giving him a jerk of her chin.

"What's up?" she asked.

"Is the sheriff in?"

Sam rolled back her chair and rose to her feet. No one else was in the office, but Tate figured they were likely out on patrol. "He's in his office. I'll show you back."

Tate knew the way, but he let her lead him. Better for her to interrupt the sheriff than him. She knocked at Wilson's door and leaned close, listening, then she opened the door and held it for Tate.

"Mercer wants to talk to you," she said.

"Tate, come in," came Wilson's voice. Tate entered the office, finding the sheriff sitting in his desk chair, leaning back with a foot on the edge of the desk. He was reading a file and his hat sat on the desk blotter before him. "Take a seat." He motioned to the chairs before his desk.

Sam tapped him lightly on the arm. "You want coffee?"

"No, I'm good," he told her, sliding into the indicated chair.

She nodded and backed from the room, shutting the door behind her. Tate clasped his hands, waiting while the sheriff finished reading the file.

"What can I do for you?" he finally asked, looking up.

"I wondered if you interrogated Everett Hughes."

"We hauled him in last night. Emilio took a shot at him. We asked him about the death threats and told him we wanted an alibi for the night the girl died."

"And?"

"He says he was out with some friends, drinking down by the river. I sent some of my guys to verify it. We also served a warrant on his parents' house. He still lives with them."

"Let me guess. No arsenic."

"Nope."

"What did he say about the death threats?"

Wilson shrugged, fingering the flap on the folder. "Just that. Threats, nothing more. He was pissed that Merilee was seeing Deimos too. He thought they were exclusive, but she said they weren't."

"How pissed was he?"

"He wasn't happy."

"Was he unhappy enough to poison her?"

Wilson looked up at a stain on his ceiling. "Can't exactly say for certain, but he swears he'd never hurt Merilee."

"But he threatened to kill Dee twice, Sheriff."

"Dee was sleeping with his girl. I've been known to threaten death on occasion, but I didn't mean it."

"So he's not a suspect."

"I didn't say that. Everyone's a suspect still. Unless you've eliminated someone."

Tate shook his head. "I'm having a difficult time narrowing down when she was poisoned and the autopsy is vague on that too. The window they gave me is between the concert and her death. She was around a lot of people during that time and everyone I've interviewed says she was never out of their sight. That she consumed the same things as other people did with no ill effects." He scratched his forehead. "Without being able to establish when she got the poison, I'm stumped."

Wilson shook his head. "That's not good."

"I know."

"Who's left on your suspect list?"

"Gunner Bishop, the other guy she was seeing, or, I don't know what she was doing with him. Then there's Desmond Hifler, the manager for *Anaconda.* Dr. Jerm said Hifler bought the drugs for the after party. I've got my friend in LA running background checks on Dr. Jerm and Everett Hughes. I'm gonna see if she'll look for any priors on Hifler too."

"He went back to LA."

"I know. Getting him back here's gonna be a pain."

"I've dealt with Dr. Jerm before. I hate to admit it, but he's pretty careful with his stuff. He knows one problem and I'll shut him down. Hifler's starting to look more and more promising by the minute."

Tate nodded. He was thinking the same thing, but he kept stumbling over the same problem. Motive. What could possibly be the manager's motive for poisoning a local girl? He just couldn't come up with one.

* * *

Tate made it on time to open the hardware store. Logan was waiting for him with his skateboard at the front door. Tate felt a stab of guilt when he saw the kid. He'd been putting a lot of responsibility on Logan lately and Logan had enough on his plate.

"Hey," he said, giving him a smile as he unlocked the door.

"Hey," said Logan.

"How's it going?"

Logan gave him a puzzled look and followed him into the store. "Huh?"

"I've been gone a lot, working this case for the sheriff's office, and you've had to pick up the slack. I just want to make sure I'm not putting too much on you."

"Tate, man, you gotta stop treating me like I'm some fragile flower." He turned to the right and began opening the blinds as Tate walked to the back and flipped on the lights. While they warmed up, Logan followed Tate into the storage room to stash his skateboard. "I got this. I mean, I run this place better than you." He gave Tate a wicked grin.

Tate grinned back. "True," he said, taking money out of the wall safe for the register. "But you can tell me if it's too much too. I won't think any less of you."

Logan grabbed the duster and waved it in the air, shaking off the dust. "Look, I'm serious. I'm good. Everyone's real patient when you're not here and it won't be forever. I mean as soon as you solve this case, we'll be back to normal."

Tate shut the safe and spun the dial, hesitating before answering the kid.

Logan picked up on it. "It is temporary, right? I mean you're not going back to being a cop, are you?"

"No," said Tate quickly, holding up a hand. "Nothing like that. It's just I've been sucked in on two cases already. I think it's safe to say Sheriff Wilson's going to come to me whenever they're short handed from now on."

Logan considered that. "You kinda like it, don't you?"

Tate paused, thinking about what the boy said. Did he like it? He liked the chase, he liked figuring out the puzzle, piecing it together even when it frustrated him. He'd felt more alive the last few days than he had in a long time, but he wondered if that had more to do with his red-headed assistant than the work. "I honestly don't know. I guess I miss parts of it. I miss figuring things out."

"You never told me why you left being a cop."

Tate's gaze snapped to Logan's face. No, he hadn't. He didn't like to talk about it, no more than Logan liked to talk about his mother's cancer. Maybe if he opened up, the boy would feel safer in confiding in him.

"My partner was killed. We were on a gang task force and we'd gone out on a call and…" His voice choked off. This was why he didn't talk about it. It was too hard. Still too fresh. Even after two years. He cleared his throat, forcing himself to continue. "He got shot." He tapped his own forehead.

Logan gave an involuntary shiver.

"I couldn't…I didn't want to keep being a cop without him."

"Man," breathed Logan. "Tate, I'm sorry."

Tate held up a hand. "I know. Thing is, I'm glad I left it, but helping out the sheriff here…" He shrugged. "I guess I kinda like feeling like I'm making a difference."

"I get that," said Logan. "I get that."

"But it's not fair to you."

Logan waved him off with the duster. "I'm good. I like running the store." He shifted weight. "But here's the thing. I'm going back to school in about a month. My senior year. I'll be here on weekends and after school every day, but I'm thinking I'm might want to go to the regular high school again. Mom thinks it's a good idea and she's doing okay right now."

"I think this is a great idea," said Tate and he did. He couldn't help the smile that blazed across his face.

"So I won't be working as much and well…you're gonna need some help."

Tate considered that. Could he afford to hire someone else to cover Logan's hours? Things were going well in the store and this past month had really gone a long way toward putting him in the black, even before the holiday season.

"I was thinking," continued Logan, running the feathers on the duster through his hand. "Bill Stanley's in here nearly every day. He's retired, but I think he's kinda bored. He might be willing to come in while I'm at school."

Tate hadn't thought of that, but it was a good idea. Bill had mentioned many times that he needed to get a part-time job just to get away from his Honey-Do List. He might be willing to work part-time to replace Logan.

"That's a really good idea, Logan," said Tate. "I'll talk to Bill the next time he comes in."

Logan smiled, his back straightening. Tate liked seeing this confidence in his employee and he realized Logan was growing up, right in front of him.

The buzzer on the front door sounded and they both looked toward it. Tate carried the money to the cash register, punching the button to open the drawer and glancing up at the young man who sidled into the store, looking around.

Logan lifted the counter and went out, carrying the duster with him. "Can I help you?" he asked.

The young man was around twenty-five or so with spiky blond hair, piercings in both ears, and full-sleeve tattoos from his wrists to his shoulders. He wore a *Redwood Stock* tank top and cargo shorts with Converse sneakers.

"Guy named Tate Mercer works here?" he said, jutting his chin at Logan.

Logan motioned to Tate behind the counter. "That's him."

Tate finished putting the money in the cash register, shutting the drawer, then slid his hand along under the counter to the gun safe, feeling along its edge. He didn't know who this guy was, but the way his gaze darted about the store had him a little alarmed. They hadn't been robbed before, but he wasn't going to take any chances.

The young man stalked toward the counter, then he stopped and ran his hand through his hair. "You're Tate Mercer?"

"Yeah, who are you?"

"Everett Hughes."

Tate casually reached into his pocket where he kept the fob for the gun lock and curled his fingers around it. He could see Logan watching the exchange as he dusted.

"How can I help you, Everett?"

The kid ran his hand through his hair, pressing down the spikes, but they popped back up again. "They hauled me into the sheriff's office last night for questioning."

Tate nodded.

Everett took a step closer to the counter and Tate pulled the keys out of his pocket, palming them. "They think I had something to do with Merilee's death, that I put poison in her pot or something."

"I'm not sure why you're here."

"They said you're working the case. They said I should call you if I know anything, remember anything."

"Okay?" Tate wasn't sure why he'd come here in person then. "Do you know something?"

Everett slapped his hands against his thighs, making both Tate and Logan jump. "I don't know shit. I don't know what the hell Merilee was doing. She was sleeping with me, then she goes off with that Deimos dude and then Gunner Bishop tells me she was with him. How am I supposed to know anything?"

"You sound like you were angry with her."

"I was. She was my girlfriend and she had all these other guys on the hook. Man, how do you think that feels?"

"Pretty bad."

"Yeah."

"Bad enough to kill?"

Everett went still, then he shook his head, tears glistening in his eyes. "No, man, I'd never hurt Merilee. I loved that girl. I loved her."

"You threatened to kill Deimos. Twice."

He waved that off. "That was all talk, man. Just talk. I didn't mean it. I never did nothing to Dee and he knows it."

Tate nodded. "That's what he said."

Everett swiped at his eyes with the back of his hand. "Thing is, I was drinking down by the river with some friends when Merilee died, but the cops, they think I had something to do with it." He stepped up to the counter and put his hand on it. "But I didn't. I didn't. I couldn't hurt Merilee."

"Then why are you here?"

"I need you to figure out who killed her. I need you to solve this."

"I'm doing the best I can. I'm interviewing suspects."

Everett made a disparaging sound. "Yeah, me and Dee. That's your suspects. Seriously? Dee couldn't hurt anyone. The dude's scared of everything. Besides, Merilee was throwing me over for him. Why would he hurt her?"

Tate shrugged, still not releasing the fob. "You have any other ideas? What about Gunner Bishop? I know the two of you got into a squabble at the *Bourbon Brothers* over her."

"It was just a bunch of yelling and chest bumping. I don't think she was into Gunner. I mean, he thought she was, but he thinks every girl's into him. Merilee was just using him for dope."

"Dope? What sort of drugs did she do?"

"Just weed. She didn't even drink much. Maybe a beer, but not much more. She was all big on keeping her body a temple and all."

Except for putting marijuana smoke into it, thought Tate.

"So you don't think Gunner could have killed her? I mean if he was providing her with pot, he might have poisoned it."

"I don't think so." Everett suddenly seemed tired. "But who knows? You should check him out."

"Anyone else?"

"No, man, that's what's so weird. Everyone loved Merilee. Even when you were pissed at her, you still loved her. She was like that. Funny and sweet and…man, I can't believe she's gone. Anyway, I keep thinking it was one of those rockstars or something. They slipped something to her."

"Why would they do that?"

"I don't know. Maybe they didn't know it was poisoned. Maybe it was an accident."

An accident? How did that happen? He knew people were accidentally poisoned all the time, but arsenic? Who didn't know arsenic was dangerous?

"You gotta figure out what happened to Merilee, man. You just gotta. I can't hardly sleep at night for thinking about it, and then when they hauled me in for questioning, I damn near pissed myself, I was so afraid."

Tate frowned at that. If that was true, Everett didn't make much of a murder suspect. "I'll do my best," he told the kid.

The kid nodded, then turned on his heel and headed for the door.

* * *

By 6:00, Tate felt exhausted. There'd been a steady stream of customers and when there was a lull, he used the time to update the books and work on inventory. He was behind on both. As he made a deposit at the bank, he decided he didn't feel like cooking for himself tonight. Looking down Main Street, he watched the decorative streetlamps go on and he heard music coming from the *Bourbon Brothers*. People sat at the outdoor tables, laughing and talking. The temperature was just about perfect and darkness wouldn't fall for another three hours, but the sun had dipped below the mountains, bathing Sequoia in a dusky glow.

He pocketed the truck's keys and wandered down the street. As he passed *Trinkets by Trixie*, Trixie herself stepped out of the door with her husband Joe behind her. Trixie's red painted lips turned up when she saw him.

"Hey, Tate," she said.

"How's it going, Tate?" said the bigger man with the balding head.

"Hey, Trixie, Joe, I'm doing good," he said, pausing beside them. "How are you?"

"Doing awesome," said Joe.

Trixie locked the shop door, testing it before she dropped her keys into her oversized purse. "You going to the *Bourbon Brothers* for dinner. I hear they've got live music tonight."

Tate frowned. "Live music? Daryl didn't say anything."

Trixie hooked one arm through Tate's, the bangles on her wrist jangling, and the other through her husband's, steering them down the street. "Apparently there's an impromptu concert happening. We're gonna grab some dinner and a mug of beer." She tilted back her platinum blond head. "It's too beautiful a night to go home."

"Perfect night for some barbecued pork," said Joe.

She gave him a shake of her head, her false eyelashes fluttering. "You think every night is perfect for pork."

"Should be a slogan," said Joe and they all laughed.

When they got to the door, Joe pulled it open. The sounds of a guitar wafted out on the smell of barbecued heaven. Tate drew a deep breath, feeling his shoulders relaxing. He followed the older couple into the crowded restaurant, surprised to see so many people gathered around. It was standing room only and the line for the register went almost to the door.

Daryl waved to him, then went back to taking orders. Tallah wove her way through the crowd, carrying a tray.

"Hey, Tate," she said.

"Hey, Tallah." He thought to go back out, but he spotted Zion waving to him from the side of the room where a makeshift stage had been erected. Jaguar sat on a stool in the middle of the raised platform, strumming on a guitar and singing.

Tate pushed through the crowd and stopped at the booth, smiling down at Zion, her mother, and Dee. They had a pitcher of beer and three glasses. Gabi and Dee occupied one side of the booth, while Zion sat on the other by herself. They had a perfect line of sight to the stage.

Tate marked that two massive men sat on either side of the platform, glaring at anyone who got too close. They must be Jaguar's famed bodyguards.

"Sit down," Zion said, patting the seat beside her.

Tate slid into the booth, even though his conscience told him he should walk back out again. A moment later, Cheryl appeared beside him, putting another glass in front of his spot. She laid a hand on his shoulder.

"Glad you could stop by," she shouted over the noise.

He nodded. "This is insane."

Cheryl looked around, smiling. "It's a boon and I'm not looking a gift horse in the mouth. What you want to eat, baby?"

"The usual."

"You and my husband are going to need bypass surgery before you're fifty," she scolded, but she patted his shoulder and walked away.

Zion filled his glass with beer. "How was the rest of your day?" she said over the music.

"Not as interesting as yours was I'm guessing." He leaned his head down close to her. "Everett Hughes came to see me."

"What?" Her green eyes went wide.

"Nahuh," said Gabi, shaking a finger in front of their faces. "We are not talking about the case tonight. We're here to enjoy the music and bask in the beauty of living. Right, Deimos?" she said, patting his hand.

He gave Tate a hang-dog look, but he forced a smile for Gabi. "Yep, we're living in the moment."

Tate raised his brows at that, but he lifted his beer and held it out. "To living in the moment," he said.

The other three lifted their own beers. He gave Zion a smile, then turned to watch the rockstar singing a mellow ballad with adoring fans gathered all around him. Sinking down in the seat, he stretched out his legs and sighed. He could take a few minutes at least to enjoy this, he thought.

And he did.

CHAPTER 13

Zion tiptoed out of the house Sunday morning, forgoing a cup of coffee and her usual toast with jam. Gabi had declared all sugar off limits in the cottage and had thrown out the beautiful jar of preserves Carmen had made for her. Zion loved her mother dearly, but this new health food and yoga craze was worse than the piano playing had been.

She made it to the Optima and climbed behind the wheel, starting the car and backing down the driveway. She pulled over in front of Tate's house and looked at the dark windows. Last night at dinner, he'd promised to let her go with him to interview Gunner. Of course, she'd had to ask him in a moment when Gabi was distracted by the music because her mother had declared it was a no work night.

Picking up the phone, she tapped out a text and sent it to him.

Just a moment came his response.

Zion turned off the car and put it in park, then she dialed her father's number. She might as well use the time and this call was long overdue.

"Hello, my girl," came her father's cheery voice.

Zion drew a deep breath, then exhaled. "You have to tell Mom to come home."

There was a long pause on the line.

"Dad?"

"Look, kiddo, your mother wants to help you out right now. She knows you're short handed with everything that's going on and…"

"She's not working in the coffee house, Dad."

"Oh, what's she doing?"

"She's doing yoga with Dee in the front yard. They're both wearing yoga pants.'

"Oh dear. Why the front yard?"

"The energy's better out there."

"Really? I would have thought the trees in the back would have improved the energy flow."

"Dad!"

"She's worried about you, kiddo. She wants to make sure everything's all right. This whole murder thing is frightening both of us. She just wants to be close in case you need her."

"She made brussel sprout soup, Dad."

Another pause. Then, "Not the brussel sprout soup."

"Oh, yeah, and she threw out my homemade strawberry preserves because…"

"Refined sugar is causing diabetes," they said together.

"And every morning it's a smoothie with kale and Brewer's yeast." Zion shuddered. "I can't get the smell out of my nose." She could hear the pleading tone in her voice. "Please, Daddy, you've got to tell her to come home."

"I can't," he said, his voice miserable.

Zion pulled the phone away and looked at the display. Yep, her father. "What? What do you mean you can't?"

"I can't. Not yet. Give me another few days, please, kiddo."

Now Zion was concerned. "What? Why?"

"My stomach can't take it. All that kale and Brewer's yeast and brussel sprouts and broccoli. I thought I was going to die. My intestines were in knots, but they're healing now, Zion. I just need a few more days, then I should be okay for a few weeks."

Zion braced her forehead in her hand. "How long do you think this one's going to last?"

"I may die before it's over."

"Should we tell her?"

Another long pause. "Rascal's happier without the piano."

"I'll bet the neighbors are as well," she remarked.

"Look, this has been going on for about a month now. I say give it another month or so and we might be on the other side of this. Just give me a few more days, please, kiddo. Save your old man from a bleeding ulcer."

Zion closed her eyes. "Fine. You've got a few more days. We'll just have to tag team this one until it's over."

"Thank you. Thank you so much."

Zion almost laughed at the relief in her father's voice. "Don't thank me yet. You think this one's bad? Well, just wait until the next thing. It could be running with the bulls."

Her father went silent. After a moment, she could hear rustling on the line. "Gotta go, kiddo. I need to take some more antacids."

Zion laughed. "Bye, Daddy."

"Bye, sweet girl," he said and disconnected the call.

* * *

Gunner Bishop agreed to meet in the library at the community college where he was taking summer school classes. Zion pulled the Optima into the parking lot and found a space close to the building. Tate looked out at the trees and the squirrels racing up and down the trunks, then he exhaled.

"You okay?" she asked.

He looked over at her, forcing a smile. "Every time we question someone new, this case just gets more slippery. I keep feeling like I'm missing something."

"Well, maybe this guy can give us an idea."

He studied her face for a moment. "You shouldn't be doing this with me, Zion."

She frowned. "Why not? We agreed to work the case together."

"Yeah, but someone was murdered and…"

"And nothing. I can take care of myself."

He exhaled again. "This is interfering with your business."

"My business is better than it's ever been. What are you really getting at?" She felt a knot form in her stomach. If he told her he didn't want to work with her anymore, she knew she'd be disappointed, very disappointed. She'd actually been excited this morning at the prospect of going on this errand with him, spending time with him. She liked that he'd had dinner with them last night.

Sure, David was her guy, but she always felt like she had to be at her best with David, wear makeup, do her hair, wear nice clothes. With Tate she could be herself and that was so liberating. She didn't think she had romantic feelings for him. True, sometimes he made her pulse beat a little faster, but she didn't think that was anything serious. David sometimes did that too, but with Tate, the friendship just didn't feel as forced. She felt they were on the same wavelength, wanted the same things.

"Forget it," he said, forcing another smile, then he pushed open the Optima's door and got out.

Zion followed him to the sidewalk, clicking the button to lock the car. As they entered the library, the cool air smote them. In fact, the library was over air-conditioned and Zion wished she'd thought to bring a sweater. A woman behind the counter gave them a kind smile.

Tate paused in front of her, removing his badge. "We're looking for Gunner Bishop."

"He said he'd be somewhere among the study carrels on the second floor. He told me to expect you."

Tate thanked her and motioned to the wide wooden stairs leading to the second story. As Zion followed him, she looked around at the shelves choked with books and the smattering of students, sitting among the tables, working on laptops. She couldn't help but wonder how long such places would continue to exist with the wealth of knowledge sitting at the tips of people's fingers now.

They stepped out onto the second floor. More floor to ceiling shelves lined the walls and in the middle of the room was a metal sculpture of three triangles designed to look like they were sliding in and out of each other. Individual tables were scattered throughout this space, the tops covered in wooden carrels. Only one was occupied.

A young man with flowing brown hair reaching nearly to the middle of his back hunkered over a large textbook. A backpack rested against the leg of his chair, the top unzippered with folders and more books showing. He held a highlighter in one hand and his other was spread over the book, holding it open as he read.

Tate approached him, clearing his throat.

The young man looked up. He wore glasses and had a thick beard and moustache. High cheekbones peeked over the top of his beard and his lips were unusually red. He wore a hooded sweatshirt with a t-shirt beneath it and shorts. His feet were bare, a pair of flip-flops shoved under the desk, resting on top of one another.

"Gunner Bishop?" asked Tate.

He turned his chair to face them and eyed Zion, then he nodded. "You found me."

Tate glanced around, then he grabbed two chairs from the nearest carrels and set them up at an angle to Gunner. Zion took a seat, pulling her notebook out of her purse. Gunner's eyes tracked over her again, then shifted to Tate.

"She's my assistant," Tate told him, bracing his forearms on his thighs.

"Cool. So, before you start, I was at an all night study group the night Merilee died. I got there at seven and I didn't leave until seven the next morning." He reached into the backpack and pulled out a piece of paper, holding it out to Tate. "Here's a list of everyone that was at the study session. They can vouch for me. I never left the room, except to go to the bathroom, and the door to the bathroom was within sight of the people at the study group."

"Okay," said Tate, glancing at the paper. "Did you know Merilee well?"

"We were becoming good friends. I was helping her in our English class. We edited each other's essays."

"You met her here?"

"Yes. She was taking classes, so she could transfer to Humboldt State. That's where I'm headed in the fall."

"Were you and Merilee romantically involved?"

Zion crossed her legs and braced the pad on her thigh, waiting for the young man to speak.

"I wanted to be, but she said she had to focus on her school."

"And yet you got into an argument with Everett Hughes in the *Bourbon Brothers Barbecue*."

Gunner shook his head in disgust. "He wasn't any good for her. He distracted her from her classes."

"So what were you fighting with Everett about?"

"She asked me to go to dinner with a couple of her friends. Everett showed up and told her he wanted her to go with him. She said no, but he wasn't taking that answer. I told him to get lost. We bumped chests a few times, then the owners broke it up and told us to get out." Gunner shook his head. "She had so much potential, Merilee. She was going to do good things."

Tate nodded, folding the paper. "You smoke pot with Merilee, Gunner?"

Gunner's jaw clenched. "No, I was trying to get her away from that stuff."

"But she kept doing it?"

"She said she was through with Everett. Then she started hooking up with that other loser, that Dee. Next thing you know, she was back, smoking joints with him. She told me she was going to quit."

"Did that make you mad? That she didn't quit?"

Gunner straightened, his eyes cutting to Zion. "You sound like a cop now."

"Well…" Tate held out his open hands.

Gunner leaned forward, accentuating each word, the light from the overhead track reflecting in his glasses. "I didn't hurt Merilee. I wanted her to go to Humboldt. I wanted her to get away from here. She was too good for this place. She deserved more."

Tate nodded, tapping the paper against his other palm. "Do you know if Merilee had any enemies? Anyone who might want to do her harm?"

"Besides Everett."

"You think he wanted to hurt her?"

"He wouldn't take no for an answer. She told him it was over like a billion times and he wouldn't listen. He just couldn't let her go. He couldn't believe she didn't want to hang with him anymore."

"Do you ever smoke pot?"

"No, I don't touch the stuff. I want a future. I want to do something. I'm studying environmental science and I want to protect the earth, not rape and pillage her."

"Right," said Tate. "So you've never bought it?"

"Nope."

"Not once."

"No. Merilee said she got that. She said she treated her body like a temple."

"But she still smoked pot with Everett and Dee?"

Zion scribbled the *body like a temple* line. They'd heard it more than once.

"How did she reconcile that philosophy with the fact that she smoked pot?" continued Tate.

Gunner made a stabbing motion at Tate. "Exactly. That's what I said to her. You can't treat your body like a temple, watch everything you put into it, then suck smoke into your lungs, even marijuana. It was a contradiction."

"You got any idea who might have wanted to do Merilee harm?" Tate asked again.

Gunner leaned back in his chair. "Here's the thing. I just can't. I mean, I'd take a closer look at Everett, but even that guy doesn't seem like he'd do something like this. He really cared about Merilee. He really thought they were going to get together again." He stared at his hands, resting in his lap. "I can't believe this happened to her. She was so smart and funny and pretty."

Zion looked up, hearing the wistful quality in his voice. He'd cared about this girl. That was how everyone spoke about her. She met Tate's gaze. She knew he was frustrated that they didn't have any viable suspects, but she really didn't think Gunner Bishop was one.

"If you think of anything else, will you call the sheriff's office?" Tate asked.

Gunner nodded. "I promise."

Tate and Zion rose, then Tate returned their chairs.

"Thank you for talking with us," said Zion.

He nodded, then his brow furrowed. "You work at the *Caffeinator*, don't you?"

"I own it," she said.

"Right. Dee works for you."

"Yeah, he does."

"Did they really arrest him for Merilee's murder?"

Zion looked at Tate, not sure she should answer.

"We haven't narrowed down our suspect pool yet," said Tate.

Gunner nodded. "I heard you've got Jaguar from *Anaconda* working for you. Is that true?"

"Yeah, that's true."

"Jaguar from *Anaconda*? What's his deal?"

"He's trying to get back in touch with his music. He believes working with his hands might help."

Gunner considered that for a moment. "That's pretty righteous," he said. "Man, no way am I going back to my first job."

"What was that?" Zion asked.

"Picking up horse shit at the fairgrounds when they had a horse expo, which was damn near every two weeks."

Zion gave him a commiserate shrug. "It was honest work."

"Sure. That's what they say when they can't find anything else positive to say about it."

Yep, Zion was sure this self-deprecating young man had not harmed anyone. "Come in for a coffee and see Jaguar in action," she told him.

"I will," he said. "Yeah, I will."

"Thank you again," she answered and backed away from him. He immediately returned to studying his textbook as she and Tate descended the stairs.

* * *

By two in the afternoon, the coffee shop was humming along. Every table was filled and people were standing in groups outside the front door, sipping lattes and talking. Zion was wondering if she should add a few outside tables the way the Ford brothers had at the barbecue.

Jaguar was a blur of motion, running the espresso machine, making foam designs on the coffees, or spraying whipped cream with a flourish. The people ate it up.

Zion had to laugh at the way he worked a crowd. Whether as a rockstar or a barista, he had everyone in thrall. When he finished a drink, rather than calling out the names, he sang them. His two bodyguards sat in the kitchen, out of the way, one playing a game on his phone, the other reading a book on a tablet. They'd finally relaxed enough to let Jaguar do his thing without hovering. Zion felt better for it.

She found herself actually having fun as she took orders. Every customer seemed to be in a good mood and the tip jar was overflowing. She didn't know if this little experiment was helping Jaguar's creative juices to flow, but it was sure helping her bottom line.

When the door opened and David walked inside, she felt her smile fade and her stomach muscles contract. For a moment, she found herself lost in the surprise of that reaction, then she forced a smile as he came up to the counter.

"What's up?" she said, trying to keep the dread out of her voice.

"You got a moment to talk?" he asked, looking around the room. "Or, probably not?"

Jaguar glanced over. He was busy sprinkling chocolate shavings onto the top of an iced coffee. "Go. I got this. Maddog," he called into the kitchen, "get out here and ring up some orders."

"I don't think…"

"I got this," said Jaguar firmly, giving her a pointed look from those blue eyes of his.

Zion finished the order she was taking and then motioned for David to meet her at the end of the counter. She didn't know why she was so reluctant to talk to him, but she was. If he was going to break things off, it was probably for the best, she realized, but still, she wished he wouldn't do it here at work.

She led the way into her office and pushed the door almost shut behind him. She wanted to be able to hear what was happening in the coffee shop, although she knew Jaguar could handle it without her. His days as a barista had returned to him as easily as if he'd been working the coffee shop last week.

"What's up?" she said, going around her desk and taking a seat. She marked that David hadn't given her his usual kiss. That couldn't bode well for their continued relationship.

He stood before her desk, clasping his hands. He wore a charcoal grey suit with a red tie, the white cuffs of his shirt showing just the right amount below his jacket sleeves. "I owe you an apology."

She blinked at him. She wasn't sure where this was going, but that hadn't been what she'd expected him to say. "For what?"

"The other night. Look, I'm gonna be honest with you. I'm having a bit of a problem with you working with Tate."

"Why?"

He gave her a bewildered look. "Where to start? Um, you're working a murder case and you aren't a cop and two, I think he has feelings for you."

Zion considered that for a moment. Did Tate have feelings for her? She had to admit she'd caught him staring at her a few times and there were those awkward moments when she almost thought he might…what? She wasn't sure.

"I'm just taking notes in a murder case and as far as Tate goes, we're neighbors."

"I'm not sure he sees it that way."

Zion didn't respond. She wasn't sure where he was going with this and she wasn't sure she thought he had a right to oppose anything she did. True, they were seeing each other, but beyond a few movie nights at her house and some dinner dates, they hadn't moved to a more intimate relationship yet. She didn't call him her boyfriend and they'd never talked of being exclusive with each other. Of course, she knew she was the reason why they hadn't taken that next step, but she wasn't going to voice that out loud, not yet.

"Anyway, the point is I trust you. It doesn't matter what Tate thinks as long as we're good."

"Okay?"

"What I'm trying to say is I want us to move our relationship to the next level, Zion."

Zion nodded slowly. "I see."

"I think we should go away for a few days. Next weekend in fact. I got us a reservation in Chico at a bed and breakfast. We'll leave Sunday morning and come back Monday afternoon. It's not too long away from the coffee shop, but it'll be good to get out of town. Just the two of us. You told me Sunday and Monday are your slowest days." His expression grew so expectant, Zion felt a tug at her heart. "What do you say?"

What did she say? He knew she was short-handed. How was she supposed to fill two days, especially since Tallah couldn't be in the shop with Jaguar by herself? But he looked so hopeful and she knew that if they didn't move their relationship forward, it didn't stand a chance. They couldn't stay in this high school dating zone forever. Shouldn't she give it a chance? Shouldn't she see if there was something more between them? A weekend away would definitely tell her that.

"Let's do it," she said.

He laughed, then leaned on the desk, kissing her. "I think this is going to be a great weekend," he said, looking into her eyes.

She smiled, enjoying his enthusiasm. She liked David. She liked him a lot and it was nice to know someone cared about her, wanted to spend time with her. "It'll be fun. Good to get away."

He beamed and kissed her once more. "I gotta get back to work, but I'll send you the link to the B&B, so you can check it out."

"Sounds good."

"I'll call you soon and we'll do dinner or something."

"Okay."

He backed to the door. "This is going to be so good. I know it."

She nodded and waved to him as he left. Then she just sat and stared at her desk. After a moment, she took out her phone and dialed Rebekah's number. Rebekah Miles was her best friend in San Francisco. They'd worked in the insurance company together for years, but while Rebekah was moving up in the ranks, Zion had been stuck as a customer service rep/administrative assistant.

Rebekah had a very clear cut idea about men. The more money, the better the catch. She'd agreed to marry her doctor boyfriend, mostly because she felt it was an advantageous match for her first marriage. Yep, Becks thought in those terms.

She was the perfect one to call at this moment. Becks would be able to see this whole situation in the proper light (well, a light) and she never failed to share her opinions.

Based on how crazy Becks' response, Zion would be able to evaluate her own hesitation.

The video chat connected and Rebekah's perfectly coiffed and polished face filled the screen.

"What's up? Something must be wrong because you usually don't have time to talk to me during the day."

Zion braced her chin in her hand. "How are you? I'm doing fine."

"You need a blow-out and a color wash. What's going on with your hair and have you been in the sun? Your freckles are showing."

Zion sighed. The criticism was from a point of love, but sometimes she wished Becks wouldn't be so cosmopolitan. "I'm embracing my true self."

"Rock on," said Becks, smiling at her.

"Speaking of rocking on, hold that thought." Zion got up and opened her office door, turning the camera so it could catch her barista in action, dancing around behind the counter adding the last flourishing touches to his latest concoction, then he threw back his spiky blond head and sang out the name on the cup. Applause went up in the room.

"Hold on a damn minute," said Becks. "Is that…"

"Shh," hissed Zion, slipping back behind her desk. "Do you know *Anaconda*?"

"Yeah, they were huge about five years ago, but lately…"

"Well, that lately is why I have their lead singer and rhythm guitarist as my barista."

"What? Why didn't you tell me this?"

"I'm telling you right now."

"He's working in a coffee shop?"

"Yep. He thinks it'll help him get his mojo back."

"That's insane."

Zion shrugged. "He used to work here when he was in high school."

"Nuts."

"His bodyguards spend his entire shift sitting in the kitchen, playing on their phones."

Becks laughed. "I miss you," she said.

"I miss you too."

"I know you didn't call me about Jaguar. What's up?"

Zion braced her chin again. "David asked me to go away for a weekend with him. Next weekend, in fact."

Becks' perfectly plucked eyebrows shot up. "Well, that's moving things along."

"Yeah. He wants to take our relationship to the next level."

"That means…well, you know what that means. He's not getting twin beds, Lucy."

"I know." Zion frowned. "Did you just make an *I Love Lucy* reference?"

"I know my classic TV." Becks leveled a practiced eye on her. "What's the real problem?"

There it was. Zion needed to be honest, if not with herself, then with her best friend. "I don't know if I want to take things to the next level."

"So you told him no?"

"I told him yes."

"Now you're confusing me."

Zion dropped her head on the desk. "I know. I'm confusing myself."

"The desk blotter is fascinating, Zion," said Becks dryly.

Zion picked up the phone and lifted her head. "Tell me what's wrong."

"Honestly, I've never understood you. He's a lawyer, he makes big money."

"He makes Sequoia money."

"Well, it's big money in Sequoia. And he's crazy about you. Why aren't you locking this one down?"

"I don't know."

"Yes, you do. You've had commitment issues ever since you broke it off with Lucas."

Zion was pretty sure that wasn't the problem. She'd be willing to make a commitment, if she felt she was ready for one. Right now, she was enjoying her independence too much.

"Look, girl, he's got the right credentials. He's handsome, he's taller than you, and he wants to be exclusive. What more do you want?"

Put that way, she just didn't know what she wanted. David treated her well, he cared what she thought, he never pushed her faster than she wanted to go, and he pretty much accepted her for who she was. Sure, he didn't like her working a murder case and he especially didn't like her working with Tate, but he hadn't forbidden her from doing it.

"You're right," she said. "I don't know what more I could want."

Becks nodded triumphantly. "Now," she said, leaning close to the screen. "Get me a picture of *Anaconda* boy's tight rear end."

"You're engaged to be married."

"Right. That doesn't mean I'm dead, sister."

Zion laughed. "You're terrible and I love you."

"Right back at you, babe," said Becks. "Talk to you soon. I gotta go. Franklin's bellowing for me." Franklin had been their demanding boss, who didn't believe in advancement beyond his own.

"Talk to you soon," said Zion and disconnected the call.

* * *

About half an hour before closing, Trixie Taylor of *Trinkets by Trixie* walked into the *Caffeinator*. She smoothed a hand over her platinum blond hair and sidled up to the cash register.

"Hi, Zion," she said, but her eyes were fixed on the rockstar.

"Hey, Trixie. How are you?"

"Just fine." She fluttered a perfectly manicured hand at her throat. "Thought I'd get a latte for the road."

Zion punched in the order, hiding her smile. Trixie had never come in to get a coffee for the road before. As far as Zion knew, Trixie lived closer to Main Street than she did.

"Latte for Trixie," Zion called out to her famous barista.

"Latte for Trixie," Jaguar repeated, giving Trixie a flirtatious wink.

Trixie made a strange twittering sound and her hand fluttered against her throat again. Jaguar wasn't quite young enough to be her son, but it was close. She handed over her credit card, still without taking her eyes from the rockstar.

"He's quite…um, colorful," she said, nodding at his tattooed arms. She finally glanced at Zion. "Fascinating, isn't he?"

"Sure," said Zion, passing the card back. She leaned close to Trixie. "Want an autograph?"

Trixie's eyes widened. "I'm too old for an autograph."

"Beatrice and Carmen Sanchez got one for Carmen's granddaughter…Carmen."

Trixie laughed. "I can't do that." She thought for a moment, then passed Zion her phone. "But you could snap a picture of me with him in the background."

Zion took the phone and Trixie positioned herself by the pickup counter, striking a sultry pose. Zion lifted the camera, but before she took the picture, Jaguar moved up next to Trixie and put an arm around her shoulders, then bent over and kissed her cheek. Zion snapped the shot as Trixie's eyes went wide and her mouth made an O.

"Latte for Trixie," Jaguar sang and passed her the cup.

Trixie giggled, doing a little dance, then reached for her phone as Zion held it out to her. Zion couldn't help but smile. She was beginning to warm to the over-bearing rockstar with every little gesture he made.

CHAPTER 14

Sheriff Wilson walked into the *Hammer Tyme* shortly after Tate opened on Monday. He had his hat tilted to the back of his head as always and his thumbs tucked into his belt.

"Morning," he called to Tate, then gave Logan a nod where he was straightening up the shelves of nails. They could never seem to stay in their boxes.

"Morning, Sheriff," said Tate. "Can I get you a cup of coffee?"

"Nope. I'm good." He leaned against the counter, dropping his voice so Logan couldn't hear. "Followed up on Everett Hughes' alibi and it all checks out. One of our patrol officers even remembers him at the river. He pulled over to talk to the kids and asked to see some ID's since they were drinking. He entered all the ID's into the system. Hughes' information was there."

"What if he poisoned the joints before he went to the river? We don't have a real good idea of when she got the poison."

"Or if it was from a joint," said Wilson. "Where are you on suspects?"

"We talked with Gunner Bishop yesterday. I don't think he did it. He wanted Merilee to leave Sequoia and go to college at Humboldt State."

"He have any idea who might want to hurt her?"

"He suggested Hughes, then took it back. He said he couldn't believe he really wanted to harm her."

"Did he think Deimos might?"

"He mentioned Merilee hooking up with Dee, but he didn't say anything against him, except that he was a loser." Tate shrugged.

Wilson drummed his fingers on the surface of the counter. "What's your next move?"

"I think we need to go out to the fairgrounds. Merilee was either poisoned there or at Dee's apartment. It couldn't have happened earlier. The maintenance guy, Walter Kennedy, has come in here a few times, grumbling about drug addicted rockstars. That might be an angle."

"Good. You also might talk to Sabrina Clark. She's the event planner out there. I told her you'd be contacting her."

Tate grabbed the pad of paper they kept by the cash register and the pen, then he scribbled the name in the middle of it. "You think she had anything to do with the after party? I mean arranging it."

"Yeah, that would be in her department. She said she's at the fairgrounds every weekday between 9 and 5."

"Thanks." He folded the paper and put it in his back pocket.

"So as I understand it, you haven't eliminated anyone."

"Not yet, no, but my instincts say none of the people we've been looking at are guilty."

"I can't convict on instinct, Tate."

"I got that. I'm working as fast as I can." His phone rang and he fished it out of his pocket, seeing Darcy's name on the display. He showed it to Wilson. "Here's a call about the case right now." He thumbed the phone on. "Hey, Darce, you got something for me?"

"Hey, Tater Tot. I don't have a lot, but here it is."

"Hold on." Tate's gaze slid over to Logan where the boy was eavesdropping, although trying to pretend he wasn't. Tate walked to the counter and lifted it, motioning the sheriff to step inside. They headed into the storage room and Wilson took a seat at the table. "Okay, go on."

"Everett Hughes has no priors, no juvie record, no parking tickets. The kid's squeaky clean. Not even picked up for underaged drinking."

"Damn," said Tate. "Okay, what about Dr. Jerm?"

"Dr. Jerm is another matter, although it's nothing too grim. He was picked up for selling pot before it became legal and he served four years probation. He also did some community service, picking up trash along the highway. Since then, he's not been in trouble."

Tate sighed. "Thanks, Darce. I appreciate it."

"Sorry I wasn't more help."

"Hey, you at the terminal right now?"

"You know I am."

"Think you can just run a quick check for me."

"Tater Tot…" she moaned.

"I'll include a box of *Godiva* chocolates," he said.

"Fine. Give me a name."

"Desmond Hifler."

"Desmond Hifler?" she said, her fingers tapping on keys. "Who's he?"

"The manager for *Anaconda*."

"You think he'd lace their joints with arsenic?"

"Stranger things have happened. What if one of the band members die unexpectedly and everyone remembers how much they loved their music a few years ago? Albums suddenly go platinum."

Wilson's brows rose at Tate's comment and he leaned the chair back on two legs.

"That's true," said Darcy, her fingers tapping away. "Okay, give me a moment."

Tate pulled out a chair and sank into it. He needed to spend more time on the shop, he needed to see about hiring Bill Stanley part-time, but this part of an investigation always excited him. He thought he might be onto something here.

He was beginning to wonder if Merilee had, in fact, been the target, or had been collateral damage. He couldn't find a good enough motive for wanting Merilee dead, but he could for any of the band members – in fact, he could think of multiple motives for wanting one of them dead.

"Hmm," came Darcy's voice in his ear. "This is interesting."

"What?"

"Desmond Hifler was arrested for assaulting a young woman at a concert in San Diego. According to the report, she came to the concert and demanded to be let backstage. She said she was a friend of Jaguar."

"Really?" Tate motioned at Wilson for a pen and paper.

Wilson rose and went out to retrieve it. He appeared a moment later, passing Tate the pad and paper. Tate took some brief notes.

"How did he assault her?"

"She insisted on coming backstage, but Hifler blocked her because she didn't have a pass. She told him she had to talk to Jaguar. It was important. Hifler told her no and called for security. Once she saw the security guards approaching, she tried to slip past Hifler, but he blocked her, knocking her down. She hit her head on a piece of equipment and had to be transported to the hospital. She pressed charges and Hifler was arrested."

"What happened to the case?"

"It never went to court. I'm not sure why. You'll have to get a warrant to pull the records from the San Diego county courthouse."

"Does it say the name of the girl?"

"Uh, Nancy Spencer," said Darcy and Tate scribbled her name next to Hifler's. "Hifler made bail and the case disappears from our databases. I'll bet you dollars to donuts, he paid her off."

"Probably."

"It's a pretty far leap from shoving someone trying to get backstage to poisoning someone, Tater Tot."

Tate blew out air, tapping the pen on the pad. "You're right, but it's all I've got."

"Then you ain't got much, partner," she said in a country drawl.

"When you're right, you're right," he said wearily and glanced up at Wilson.

Wilson removed his hat and scratched his head, looking out into the hardware store. Tate could swear he felt the man's frustration as his own.

* * *

"So apparently, the girl tried to get backstage, but Hifler prevented it," Tate told Zion as they drove out to the fairgrounds. It was 10:30 and he had to have Zion back by noon. He'd been hoping they could stop for lunch at the pizza parlor Dee had bought the pizza from the night Merilee died, but there just wasn't enough time. "What if you're a little late getting back?"

She glanced over at him. "Dottie and Tallah will stay until I get there." She took out her phone. "I'll just text and let them know. How late do you think I'll be?"

"Around 1:00?"

She nodded. She was adding his notes from Darcy's call to her own notebook. "So Hifler pushed her and she fell."

"Right."

"Then they transported her to the hospital and she filed charges against him."

"Exactly."

"How does this relate to poisoning one of the band members?"

"It shows that Hifler isn't opposed to getting physical to get his way."

Zion tapped the pen against her bottom lip. "True, but I like your other angle better."

"What?"

"The one that says Hifler meant to poison a band member to make record sales increase. That's a direct line from point A to point B."

"Yeah, which means I may have to go down to LA to talk to Hifler again. You wanna do a road trip?" The words were out of his mouth before he thought about it. He held his breath, not sure what he hoped. He wanted her to go with him, but if she said yes, he'd have a harder time hiding his feelings from her.

Zion's pen stilled on the pad and she looked up. "When would you go?"

He started breathing again. There was a curious note in her voice, not accusation, just interest. She must not realize he had a terrible crush on her. "This weekend? We could fly in and fly out the next day."

She didn't answer right away. She shifted in the seat and looked out the window.

"Or not," he said quickly. "It's not a big deal, but if Hifler's my primary suspect, I think it might be a good idea to question him before he leaves the state."

"It's not that. I think you're right. It's just, I don't think I can go."

He didn't answer right away, fighting down his disappointment. "I understand. You've got a coffee shop…"

"It's not that." She rubbed a hand over her jaw. "David asked me to go away with him. He wants to go to Chico, stay in a bed and breakfast."

"I see. Sure, yeah, no worries."

"But the case is more important," she hedged and Tate glanced over at her. Did she not want to go away with her boyfriend? Why?

"It'll hold. I can question him myself," he said, trying not to sound passive aggressive about it.

She looked at him. He felt the weight of her gaze. "No," she said. "I want to be there. I should be there."

"Look, Zion, it's not a big deal. I'll just go myself and then let you know what happened when I get back. Besides, it'll be nice to see some of my co-workers again."

She frowned. "It's only Monday. Can you give me a few days?"

"Of course. We can just grab standby tickets or something." He shot another look at her. "Maybe drive."

She smiled. "You did say road trip."

"I did." He smiled back.

They pulled into the parking lot of the fairgrounds, driving under the archway that proclaimed it the *Best Rodeo in California* and pulled up to the parking kiosk. A teenage boy slid open the window and leaned on the sill as Tate rolled his down.

"We're closed," the boy said in a bored voice.

Tate showed him his badge. It was funny how the mannerisms of a cop had come back to him so fast. "We're here to talk to Walter Kennedy and Sabrina Clark."

The kid picked up a walkie talkie and pressed the button. "Patrick, there's a cop here, says he's supposed to see…" He paused and looked at Tate.

"Walter Kennedy," said Tate slowly.

"Walter Kennedy," the boy repeated.

"And Sabrina Clark," Tate finished.

"Sabrina Clark." Her name fell on a weary exhalation.

Static sounded over the walkie talkie, then a man's voice. "Direct them to the administration building. Clark's in there. I'll find Walt and send him over there too."

"Okey dokey," said the kid, rolling his head on his shoulders and looking at Tate through his bangs. He set the walkie talkie down and leaned out the window. "The admin building's over there," he said, pointing to their right. "There's signs all over, so you can't miss it."

"Thanks," said Tate, driving forward and rolling up the window.

They found the admin building easily, just as the kid said, but it wasn't so much a building as a trailer. Climbing out of the truck, they walked up the plank walkway to a door marked *Events* and Tate knocked. The door opened on a blast of air conditioning and a petite blond poked her head out.

She had to be about thirty, five two or five three, her blond hair in a long ponytail. She wore a pair of capris with sandals and a tank/sweater set combo. "Yes?" she said.

"Sabrina Clark?"

"Yes." She pushed open the door. "Are you Tate Mercer?"

"Right."

"Come in." She thrust out her hand. "Sabrina Clark." She shook his hand briskly, then held it out to Zion. "Sabrina Clark."

"Uh." Zion accepted her hand and got the same brisk shake. "Zion Sawyer."

"Nice to meet you." She pointed to a folding table with folding chairs arranged around it. "Sit, please. You want water? Coffee? Tea?"

Tate and Zion took a seat and Zion pulled out her notepad. "Nothing for me," said Tate, glancing at his companion.

"No, thank you," Zion said, her pen poised to take notes.

Sabrina perched on the edge of a chair. "You wanted to talk about the *Anaconda* concert at *Redwood Stock*."

"Yes. As you know, a young woman named Merilee Whitmire died after the concert."

"Right. Terrible tragedy."

"Yes, it was. So we're trying to nail down where she was poisoned."

"Not here."

Tate blinked and glanced at Zion. "I'm sorry."

"She wasn't poisoned here."

"How do you know?"

"The after party was catered and the food was tested. In addition, samples of the food for sale from the concert vendors and the fair vendors was tested and no traces of arsenic were found."

"I understand the band was smoking joints…"

"Drug use is not allowed on the fairgrounds," said Sabrina.

"It may not be allowed," said Tate, trying to soften his words with a smile, "but it happened. Multiple people have reported it was going on."

"That is not authorized."

"Authorized or not…"

"Deputy Mercer. It is deputy, right?"

"Right."

"If drugs were consumed on the fairgrounds, it was not with the permission of fairground personnel. You will have to take that up with the band."

Tate wasn't sure what to say. He stared at her in disbelief.

"A girl died," said Zion. "I get you're trying to protect the fairgrounds, but a girl died."

For the first time, Sabrina's abrupt mannerism cracked a bit. "I know that."

"We need any help you can give us. Did you notice anything strange? Did you hear anything?"

Sabrina stared at Zion for a moment, then she sighed. "We don't usually have people like that here."

"What does that mean?" asked Tate.

"Musicians and their groupies. We mostly host horse shows and the rodeo each year. Some home improvement events. We've never had a *Redwood Stock* before."

"A lot more people showed up than you usually have, right?" said Zion.

"Right."

Tate nodded at Zion to continue. She'd broken through to this woman, so she might as well continue.

"Some of the employees of the fairgrounds were upset by the clientele the festival attracted. Were you aware of that?" Zion asked.

"I know a lot of the regular employees complained about it, but the Chamber of Commerce wanted the concert and there was no where else to hold it. It generated a lot of revenue."

Zion laid her pen on her notepad. "It did. I'm still getting a benefit from it. I run the *Caffeinator* in town."

"Oh, I thought you looked familiar."

Zion smiled. "Come for coffee whenever you're in town. My treat."

"Thank you."

Zion's expression sobered. "Sabrina, arsenic isn't all that hard to get ahold of. Rat poison used to contain it and they used to treat pressurized wood with it. According to the medical examiner, if someone ground up some of that wood, they could get enough arsenic to poison someone." She looked around the trailer. "The fairgrounds have been here a long time."

Sabrina's brown eyes widened, then she laughed. Zion and Tate looked at each other in surprise. "Oh, you don't know, do you?"

"What?"

"You didn't know the fairgrounds burnt down five years ago?"

"Neither of us are from here. I just came a few months ago and Tate's only been here two years."

Sabrina bounced to her feet and retrieved a photo album, laying it on the table before them. She flipped open to a page at the back and pointed to a picture of burnt wood and twisted metal. "This is the day after the fire. The entire structure was completely rebuilt. That's why my office is in a trailer."

Tate slumped back in his seat. If the fairgrounds had been rebuilt five years ago, there was no way it was made with old pressure treated lumber.

"What about rats? Do you have a rat problem?" Zion asked.

"We use the Disney method."

"I'm sorry?"

"Stray cats. They live in the fairgrounds and they keep our rat population down. People like the cats and it's eco-friendly."

"Yes, it is," Zion answered, giving Tate a helpless look.

Tate rested his ankle on his thigh and picked at a hanging thread on his boot. Damn, he didn't know where else to look for suspects. Nothing was panning out. When he didn't immediately respond, Zion faced Sabrina again.

"We were supposed to talk to Walter Kennedy."

"Oh, he's off today. Do you want me to give you his address so you can talk to him at home?"

Zion glanced at Tate. Tate shook his head. What was the point? He hadn't really suspected Walter Kennedy and the two modes of poisoning he'd thought of were a red herring.

"No, that's okay." Zion thought for a moment, then she picked up her pen. "Can you give me the name of the caterer you used for the after party?"

"But her food was tested."

"I know, but we're running short on leads and I'm reaching here."

Sabrina bounced to her feet and went to a bookshelf, grabbing a binder and laying it on the table. *Redwood Stock* was emblazoned on the cover in thick black script. Sabrina opened the binder and ran her finger down a row of dividers, then flipped the pages until she came to a contract. Tate had to give her credit for being organized.

"The caterer is *Cater 2 U Event Catering*. Here's the address." She rattled it off and Zion wrote it down. "My contact was Nancy Osborn. She owns the business, I think. Nice lady."

"Thank you." Zion gave Tate another look.

"Thank you," he responded and pushed himself to his feet. They shook hands with Sabrina once more and Zion accepted her business card, then they went back out into the hot mid-morning sunlight.

Tate walked to the truck, feeling completely defeated.

Zion kept pace beside him. "Look at it this way, we just checked off another avenue. We're getting closer to finding the right one." She stuffed the notebook in her purse.

"Right," he said, unlocking the vehicle.

"What's next?"

He shook his head. "I'm not sure. I thought we'd check out the pizza parlor, but we both need to get back to our businesses."

"What about tomorrow? You can pick me up at 10:00 and we'll go get lunch at the pizza joint."

He climbed behind the steering wheel. "I think that's a dead-end too, but sure, why not?"

"Why not?" she said brightly, pulling on her seatbelt.

Tate paused, watching the way the sunlight caressed her red hair. "You did good in there, Zion," he said.

She looked over at him, startled, then a smile burst across her face. He felt his heart catch and for a moment, he had a mental image of himself leaning over and kissing her. He shook it away.

"It was fun," she said, clicking her seatbelt in place. "Who knows? Maybe I'll get deputized too."

He laughed and started the engine. "Criminals everywhere, beware. Zion Sawyer is on the case."

She laughed with him as he drove toward the exit.

* * *

The buzzer over the door sounded just as Tate was clearing out the register and Logan was restocking some shelves. Tate looked up, surprised to see David Bennett walk into his store. David looked around, appearing uncomfortable in his suit and jacket, his tie perfectly in line. He rubbed his hands together as he made his way to the counter, as if he were afraid being in such a place would instantly attract all manner of dirt to him.

He forced a tense smile as he stopped at the counter. "Tate."

"David, how are you? I've never seen you in here before."

David gave a strained laugh and looked around again. "No, I guess not." He ran a hand over his hair, although not a strand was out of place. "It's…um…nice."

Tate left it at that. "What can I do for you?"

"I thought we could talk about Zion."

Tate's brows rose. He wasn't going to talk about Zion behind her back, and not with this man. "I think that's not a good idea."

David held up a hand. "Wait. Understand, I'm just concerned."

"About?"

"About her helping you on this case."

"She's helping me because Dee's involved and she cares about him."

"I know that, but she got involved in Vivian's case too."

"Vivian was her mother."

"Still, I thought that after Vivian, she'd let it go, not get involved in another case."

Tate closed the drawer on the register with a satisfying click. "She's just taking notes. That's all."

"But it's a murder case."

"A very specific murder case. The victim was probably targeted because of who she was. Zion's not really in any danger."

David took a step closer, but he avoided touching the counter. Tate could see Logan's head pop up. The kid was obviously eavesdropping again. "I worry about her. She's got enough on her plate with learning how to run a business. She doesn't really need any other…" He tilted his head slightly. "…distractions."

Tate could read between the lines. The case wasn't a distraction, but he was. David felt threatened, which surprised

Tate because so far Zion hadn't expressed a bit of interest in him. "I think you don't have anything to worry about," he told the other man, although it annoyed the hell out of him.

He actually liked David Bennett. He was a decent guy and it wasn't his fault that his girlfriend liked solving murder cases with another man. David couldn't know that Zion wasn't interested in him romantically. All he knew was that his girlfriend was spending time with someone else.

David's expression hardened and he straightened, displaying his impressive height, but Tate already knew David was taller than him. "I didn't want it to come to this, but I'm asking you, man to man, to leave Zion out of it. She isn't trained as a police officer, so she's putting herself at risk." He glanced over his shoulder, but Logan had ducked back behind the shelving. "If you care about her, as I'm pretty sure you do, you'll respect my wishes."

Tate didn't respond. He wasn't sure if he was angry or if he felt sorry for the poor guy. He didn't think David was right for Zion. David was too straight-laced, while Zion had a zest for life. But it wasn't his place to interfere in their relationship. Zion had never indicated that she wanted to end things with David. He had to respect that, and he had to respect the other man's wishes, even if he didn't like them.

He nodded, nothing more, but it satisfied David, who turned on his heel and walked out of the hardware store.

As soon as he was gone, Logan popped up from behind the shelf. "What a jerk!" he said, giving Tate a bewildered look. "Zion deserves better than that."

Tate pushed the button on the cash register and withdrew the cash, beginning his count all over again. "It's Zion's decision," he said, trying to put enough nonchalance into his voice to end the conversation.

"Then it should be her decision whether she wants to work the case with you or not."

Tate's hands still on the money, Logan's words rolling around in his mind.

The boy walked over and grabbed the vacuum cleaner, turning it on. The roar of sound snapped Tate back to the task at hand and he started counting again, but when he'd counted the same bill three times, he stopped and considered the situation.

Logan had a point, but it was the point of a teenager, not a grown man. Zion wasn't a deputy. She had no law enforcement experience, so he really had no business letting her in on the cases. On the other hand, she was just taking notes and if she hadn't been there today, he would have been stonewalled by Sabrina Clark. Still, he was stepping on another man's toes and that wasn't fair. He knew David felt threatened, but he'd gone over to Zion's house numerous times behind David's back. And he didn't have platonic feelings for her. That much was probably obvious to everyone but Zion.

If he wanted a different outcome, he should come clean to Zion, but the thought of that made his stomach clench. After his divorce from Cherise, Tate hadn't allowed himself to care for anyone else, until Zion had come along and now, he was too afraid to take that risk again.

God, he was pathetic.

CHAPTER 15

The phone rang the next morning as Zion was pouring herself a mug of coffee. Gabi glanced over from her spot in front of the blender. She and Zion had come to an agreement. Zion could drink coffee if she agreed to drink a smoothie for breakfast. She didn't tell Gabi that most of the kale smoothies wound up in the toilet at the *Caffeinator*. What her mother didn't know wouldn't hurt her.

She picked up the phone and glanced at the display. Tate. She swiped a finger across it and lifted it to her ear. "I'll be ready in a few minutes. Do you want me to drive?"

There was a hesitation on the line, then Tate cleared his throat. "Actually, I was thinking I'd take this one myself. If you don't mind."

"What?" Zion set down the mug. "I thought we agreed to work the case together."

"I know, but I just think it might be better if I go it alone from here on out."

Zion leaned a hip against the counter. Gabi turned and gave her a curious look. "What gives? Yesterday you said I did a good job with Sabrina, but today, you want to go alone. What happened since I last saw you?"

He hesitated. When he spoke again, she could hear the distance in his voice. "I just think it's better if you stay out of this, Zion. You're not a trained officer and maybe the difficulty I'm having with the case is because of that."

Zion felt stung. She thought she was helping him. Yesterday he'd said as much, but now he thought she was hindering his case. What had happened in the last few hours? "I see," she said, trying to keep the hurt out of her voice, but she felt pretty sure she failed. "I guess that's your final decision."

"It is," he said. "I'll talk to you later, okay?"

"Sure," she forced out, but she wanted to tell him off, tell him not to call her again. Something stopped her though. She didn't want to be cut off from Tate's life.

"I'm sorry, Zion, but I think it's for the best."

"Look, Tate," she said, her temper snapping. "I get you don't want me involved, but don't treat me like a child. I'm a grown woman. I can take it."

"I didn't mean…" he began.

"I gotta go," she said and disconnected the call. Setting the phone on the counter, she stared at the display, feeling hurt and confused. What had happened between their trip to the fairgrounds and this morning?

Gabi came over and rubbed her back. "I'm sorry, honey," she said. "I know this is frustrating for you."

"No, it's fine," Zion lied, picking up her mug, but she didn't take a sip. "I don't understand it, Mom. Just yesterday he told me I did a good job. Why's he sidelining me now?"

"Maybe the sheriff doesn't want you involved."

"He hasn't said anything before this. Why would he suddenly object to it?"

"Men," said Gabi, returning to her blender.

Zion took the coffee mug and sank into a chair at the table. Cleo lay on her regular chair where a spot of sunlight filtered into the kitchen. She mewed at Zion, stretching all four feet. Zion reached over and petted her furry belly.

The blender whirred and Gabi added something that looked like parsley into the mix. Zion just couldn't understand what had happened. Reaching into her purse, where it sat on the table, Zion pulled out her notepad and opened it to the first page. The blender stopped grinding and Gabi removed the pitcher, taking the lid off and filling two glasses that stood at the ready.

Zion tried to ignore the unpleasant plopping noise the liquid made as it hit the bottom of the glasses. Gabi set a glass in front of her and took a third unoccupied chair across the table from her.

"Are those the notes you've been taking on the case?"

"Yeah. I know Tate's frustrated because all of our leads are coming up empty, but I don't know why he's decided to go it alone. He suggested I was messing things up."

"Dee's going stir crazy. He really wants to get back to work."

"I know. I miss him at the coffee shop. Jaguar's good, but he attracts so much attention. It's always packed in there."

"But that means you're making money."

"I know, but I liked the coffee shop the way it was. It was a quiet place to come and socialize. I had my regulars and a few new customers, but everything was low-key. Not anymore."

"So you said the leads keep coming up empty. What suspects do you have?"

"Well, no one's been completely eliminated yet, but the main one Tate's looking at is Desmond Hifler, the band manager."

Gabi frowned. "Why?"

"Maybe he tried to poison one of the band members to increase interest in the band, and thereby increase record sales."

"Okay, so that's an idea."

"Yeah, but he's in LA. Tate asked me if I wanted to go to LA with him this weekend, but now, I guess that's off."

"I thought you were going away with David this weekend."

"I know. I promised him I would, but the case is more important."

Gabi frowned at that, taking a sip of her smoothie. "Is it?"

Zion leveled a *don't start* look on her mother.

Gabi held up a hand in surrender. "Where were you and Tate going today before he canceled?"

"To the pizza parlor where Dee bought the pizza. Tate's still trying to establish the method of poisoning."

"I see. That seems like a long-shot."

"I think it is, but that's how slim our suspect list is. I think it's more likely Hifler spiked the joints they were smoking."

"But he's in LA?"

"Right." Zion rubbed her fingers against her forehead. "We need to go to LA or get Hifler to come back here. I wonder if Jaguar could help."

"Maybe, but the motive for that seems pretty weak. I mean greed is a powerful motivator, but wouldn't it be better for the band to just have a new hit, rather than killing one of them off and risk being caught. And how come only Merilee got sick? That doesn't make sense."

Zion sighed. "You have a point."

"Okay, so you're sidelined from the pizza parlor. What else do you have?"

Zion braced her chin on her hand. "Nothing," she said, flipping through the notebook. "Not a darn thing." Her fingers stilled on the page of notes she'd taken the previous day. "Except…"

"What?"

Zion shook her head. "It's silly. They tested the food. Apparently they tested all the food."

"What food?"

"The food at the after party. The fairgrounds hired a caterer, but they took the food to the lab and screened it for arsenic. They also screened the vendors' food too."

Gabi leaned forward. "Why don't we check out the caterer?"

"What? No," said Zion, then she gave her mother a questioning look. "Really? What would be the motive?"

"Who knows?" said Gabi, shrugging. "We sure won't until we investigate."

Zion absently reached for the smoothie glass and took a sip, then shuddered when the metallic, grassy taste filled her mouth. "God, Mom, how can you drink this stuff?" she complained.

"I can feel the energy just coursing through my body," Gabi said. "Health is its own high."

Zion gave her a skeptical look. "I think you're dizzy from malnutrition," she said wryly.

Gabi waved her off. "What do you say?" She leaned forward again. "Wanna do some sleuthing ourselves? We could dress in black and wear wigs."

Zion couldn't help but smile at the thought of Gabi in black spandex yoga pants and a hoodie, wearing a femme fatale wig and speaking with a Russian accent. "How about we just go introduce ourselves and discuss a retirement party for Dad?"

"Ah," said Gabi, pointing at her. "A ruse. That's good."

"Right. A ruse."

"Just let me change," said Gabi, jumping to her feet and scuttling out of the kitchen.

Zion waited until she'd gone, then she got up and dumped the smoothie down the sink, running the water to make sure it all disappeared.

* * *

David called as Gabi and Zion got into the Optima. Zion put the phone on Bluetooth and pulled out of the driveway.

"Hi, David, what's up?" she said.

"You headed to the *Caffeinator*? I can hear the car."

"No, Mom and I are on our way to check out a lead."

Silence met that comment.

"David?" Zion shot a look at Gabi.

Her mother shrugged.

She had indeed chosen a pair of black yoga pants, but it was too hot for a hoodie, so she wore a black t-shirt and her sneakers. Zion had opted for her pink capris and her *Caffeinator* t-shirt because she had to be at work by noon.

"You're doing what?" asked David.

"We're checking out a lead in the Merilee Whitmire case."

"Why?"

"Why? Because Dee's a suspect and I need him to come back to work."

"What happened to Tate?"

Zion pulled up to a stop sign, tamping down on the hurt she still felt. "He bailed on me. He's going to check out a lead by himself."

"Zion, let him check this one out too. Does he know what you and Gabi are doing?"

"No, he doesn't and it's none of his business. He decided it was none of mine. Well, he doesn't need to know about this either."

"I don't like this, Zion."

"David!" said Zion sharply, pulling away from the stop sign. "No offense, but I didn't ask your opinion, did I?"

He didn't immediately answer.

Gabi laid a hand on her arm. "Easy," she whispered.

"You're right," he finally said. "Hey, let me take you to dinner to make up for it. We haven't been to *Corkers* in a while. We can talk about our plans for this weekend."

Zion fought down her frustration. No use having a fight with another man over this. "Sure. Pick me up at 7:00, okay?"

"Sounds good. See you then."

"Bye," she said and ended the call.

Gabi stared out the windshield, but Zion knew she was dying to say something.

"What?" she demanded of her mother.

"Don't fight with me, my girl. I don't have man parts."

Zion burst into laughter and her mother followed. The rest of the drive went by in companionable silence. God, she loved her mother.

Cater 2 U was in a cute pink cottage, the sort of building her biological mother would have loved, with gingerbread shingles and white trim. She parked the Optima in the small parking lot beside the building and they climbed out, walking up the cobblestone walkway to the charming front porch.

A sign beside the door read OPEN, so Zion turned the antique doorknob and they stepped inside. A wind chime sounded as they entered a small living room, turned into a waiting room. At the opposite end, a beaded curtain covered the archway, leading to other rooms in the repurposed house.

A few antique sofas were arranged in the middle of the room around a tray coffee table. Photo albums lay on the table's surface. Zion opened the first one and they saw a wedding buffet laid out on white tablecloths with an ice sculpture in the middle of it. Other pages revealed more table settings, silver chafing dishes, and urns for coffee or tea.

"Is anyone here?" asked Gabi after they'd waited for a few minutes.

Zion shrugged, then moved to the beaded curtain and parted it. Beyond the curtain was another larger room with a desk and a leather chair, a table covered in binders with padded chairs arranged around it, and a fireplace on the sidewall with an ornate wooden mantle. The floors throughout the building had to be original hard wood, but oriental carpets in both the waiting room and this inner room softened the look. Pastel paintings of landscapes covered the walls and another beaded doorway led to what Zion assumed to be the kitchen. She could see a table against the wall in the kitchen that held the chafing dishes and urns they'd seen in the photo albums.

"Hello?" Zion called.

She heard a noise and looked to the right where another archway must lead to the bedrooms. A woman walked out of the hallway, her hand pressing a tissue over her mouth. She looked up in surprise when she saw Zion.

"Oh, I'm so sorry, I didn't hear the door," she said, hurrying forward.

Her face was pale and her mascara had run a little. Her eyes, a light brown, looked bloodshot and her brown bob was a bit mussed. She smoothed it down with her hand, patting her lips with the tissue. She might have been pretty, but she was unbelievably thin, her cheekbones pronounced and her figure almost boyish. Zion estimated she must be around her own age.

"Sorry, are you okay?" Zion asked as Gabi stepped into the inner room.

"Yeah, I'm fine." She waved off the comment. "How can I help you?"

"Are you Nancy Osborn?"

"I am."

"My name's Zion Sawyer and this is my mother Gabi." Zion touched the center of her chest. Seeing this woman, she actually felt bad for why they were here. She didn't look like she felt well and Zion hated to upset her. "I own the *Caffeinator* in town, the coffee shop."

"Right. I knew Vivian Bradley when she owned it. She was a nice lady."

"She was my biological mother."

"I heard something about that." She motioned to the table. "Won't you sit down?"

Gabi and Zion went to the table and took a seat.

"Can I get you some tea or coffee?"

"We're fine," said Zion.

Nancy grabbed a bottle of water off her desk and took a sip, then she sank into the seat as if every muscle in her body hurt. Gabi and Zion exchanged a concerned look.

"Are you sure you're all right?" Gabi asked.

"I'm fine. I just haven't been getting the rest I need. Business is booming, which is good, but…" She held out her hand to Zion. "…you know how it is."

"I do." Zion realized she couldn't carry through with the ruse she and Gabi had planned. She didn't want to promise this young woman business that she wasn't going to get. "I need to be honest with you, Nancy. I'm here about the catering job you did at the fairgrounds for the *Anaconda* after party."

Nancy's head lifted, but her expression remained the same. "That was unfortunate. Horrible," she said, shaking her head. "I can't believe that girl died."

"I know. My barista was with her and he's a suspect in the murder."

"That's too bad."

"I'm trying to help the sheriff's office solve the case, so he can come back to work."

Nancy nodded. "That's nice of you, but I don't know how I can help."

"You catered the event."

"And they tested the food. Did they tell you that?"

"Yes, but I was wondering if you noticed anything strange when you were setting up. Anyone hanging around backstage or anything?"

Nancy thought for a moment. "I mean, there were the usual people. An older man was working on the toilet, but he had a badge for the fairgrounds. I didn't catch his name."

That must have been Walter, thought Zion, but she thought Jaguar had said he came in at midnight.

"Some roadies and two burly bodyguards. They watched everything I did."

"Did you catch their names?"

"No, but I think they were there for the band."

"Did you ever leave the food unattended?"

"Not until I left. It was all covered with plastic wrap." She took another sip of her water. "I wish I could help you, but it was a pretty small job. Just some shrimp cocktail, some bottles of beer, a few cold cuts and a cheese platter."

"Would you have a list of what you provided?"

"Sure." She rose and went to her desk, opening a laptop and clicking on some windows. "You don't think someone tampered with my food, do you? God, that would be horrible."

"We can't establish how the girl got poisoned, but I wouldn't worry about it. Everything you provided was checked."

Zion could hear the printer start up. Nancy took the paper that came out of it and started back to the table, but a little girl appeared, rubbing sleep from her eyes. She came up to Nancy, holding up her arms, as the young woman took a seat again. Nancy passed the paper to Zion and pulled the child onto her lap, tucking her head under her chin. The little girl curled her hand in Nancy's blouse and laid her head on her shoulder.

Zion smiled at her. She had light brown hair, hanging halfway down her back, and huge blue eyes. "Is this your daughter?"

"Yes, this is Sophia. She starts kindergarten in the fall, but it's summer and I can't afford daycare right now."

"She's beautiful," said Gabi, waving her fingers at the child.

"She is," echoed Zion.

Nancy curled her arms around her. "She's the best thing that ever happened to me."

Zion folded the paper and shoved it into the notebook in her purse. "We won't take anymore of your time," she said, rising. Gabi rose with her.

When Nancy started to get up as well, Zion motioned her back down. "We can show ourselves out." She started to turn away, then she stopped. Clearly Nancy needed business. Catering an afterparty for a rock concert didn't happen that often and she'd mentioned she couldn't afford daycare. Her main work seemed to be in weddings, but this far into the summer, the weddings must be tapering off. "Do you have some business cards? I could put them in my shop and do a little cross advertising for you."

"Really? That would be wonderful," said Nancy. She leaned forward and shuffled a few papers on the table, locating some business cards. "I'd really appreciate it. If you want to bring some cards here, I could give them out to customers as well."

"I've got a better idea. Why don't you come to the *Caffeinator* sometime this week and I'll buy you a cup of coffee or tea? We can talk then. I might have some ideas that would help both of our businesses."

"That sounds really good. What about Thursday?"

"Thursday it is. I work at noon, so can you come by in the morning?"

"Actually, that will work. My sister agreed to take care of Sophia that morning. She has three kids of her own, so it doesn't happen very often, but once in a while I get lucky." Her expression clouded over. "It'll have to be around 9:00. I have a doctor's appointment at 11:30."

"Perfect," said Zion. She touched Sophia's shoulder. "I'll send Mommy home with some of Dottie's cinnamon breadsticks and frosting. You'll love them."

The little girl gave her a smile, then tucked her face into her mother's neck.

The three women laughed.

"See you Thursday," said Zion, then she and Gabi turned and made their way to the front door.

As soon as they got in the car, Gabi leaned forward and looked up at the building. "She's not well."

"I thought the same thing. I think she must have been throwing up before we got there. She had that look about her. Could she be pregnant again?"

Gabi shrugged, reaching for her seatbelt. "If she was, she'll be raising this one by herself too."

"Why do you say that?"

Gabi looked over at her. "She wasn't wearing a wedding ring."

Zion didn't think that meant anything, but she couldn't deny that Nancy talked like a woman who was struggling to hold things together without much support from a life partner. Goodness, this day was turning out to be a bummer.

* * *

Returning from the kitchen with a new batch of chocolate chip cookies to put in the display case, Zion stopped cold as grumpy Jim Dawson from the *Cut & Print* walked through the door. Zion could count how many times Jim Dawson had darkened her door and this made the second one. The first was for Vivian's memorial service.

Jim was a portly man in his mid-sixties with a full beard and moustache. His salt and pepper hair was thinning and he gave everyone younger than him the stink-eye. Zion placed the tray in the display case and smiled at him as he made his way to the counter.

"How are you, Mr. Dawson?" she said.

Jaguar turned from the espresso machine, his face lighting up. "Mr. Dawson!" he boomed. "Would you look at you? Twenty pounds heavier around here…" He motioned to his own flat belly. "And twenty pounds lighter here," he said, waving a hand over his spiky hair.

Zion gasped in horror, but to her surprise, Jim Dawson smiled, shaking a finger at Jaguar. "Jerome Jarvis, don't get cheeky with me!" he scolded.

Jaguar made a production out of looking around. "It's Jaguar, Mr. Dawson," he stage whispered. "You're gonna blow my street cred."

"Street cred. I knew you when you were a pimply faced teenager, boy."

Jaguar handed the coffee off to the adoring young girl waiting for it, bumping Zion with his shoulder. "Old man Dawson was my English teacher in high school."

Zion nodded. For some reason, she kept forgetting her rockstar barista had grown up here.

"Worst student I ever had," grumbled Jim.

"I wrote some damn good poetry."

"Blither blather," said Jim, but his words lacked their usual heat.

Jaguar laughed, slapping the counter. "What can I make you? I'll bet you like mochas." He motioned to Jim's bulging middle again.

"Still cheeky as the day is long," said Jim. "Fine. Make me a mocha."

Jaguar set to making the drink, while Jim walked over to the register, handing her his credit card. "He doing right by you?" he asked her as she rang up his order.

"Can you see how busy it is in here? It's been crazy since he started working."

"Yeah, no parking on the street. My shop is blocked all the time," he grumbled as Zion passed him back his card.

She smiled and handed him a receipt. "So was he really a bad student?"

"The worst. Always late, daydreaming, chasing the girls."

"They chased me!" Jaguar shouted over the espresso machine.

Jim waved him off, but he nodded in the affirmative to Zion. "Barely graduated as I remember."

Jaguar poured the mocha and topped it off with a perfect swirl of whipped cream, drizzling chocolate artfully over the top.

"This is about all he's good for," said Jim, holding up the drink for Zion to see. He took a tentative sip, smacking his lips. "It'll do."

Jaguar shook his head, smiling fondly on the older man.

Jim leveled a serious look at him. "How's your mother, boy?"

The smile faded. "She's not doing good, Mr. Dawson."

"She's not doing well." Jim gave Zion a disgusted look. "Horrible grammar."

Zion and Jaguar laughed.

Jim turned for the door. "Tell her I said hello, boy, you hear?"

"I hear, Mr. Dawson."

And without another backward glance, Jim Dawson left the *Caffeinator*, letting the door swing shut behind him.

"He was always a crotchety old coot," said Jaguar, shaking his head. "But he secretly loved me."

Zion laughed again. She didn't doubt it. Jaguar's blustery personality was hard not to like.

* * *

Zion wore a floral sundress with her hair in a loose bun for her dinner with David. Of course, he wore his usual business suit – this one navy with a pale blue shirt and a black tie. The number of times she'd seen him in casual wear had to be less than fingers she had on her two hands. She wondered what he planned to wear on their weekend getaway. Was he a boxers or briefs sort of guy? She figured he was probably briefs, pun totally intended.

She felt her cheeks heat as she thought about that, letting him guide her to his usual table in the dining room and pulling out the chair for her. She sat and lifted the white napkin, settling it across her lap.

A waiter approached. "Can I get you a cocktail?"

David opened the wine list, although he ate here enough, he ought to have it memorized. As usual, he ordered a bottle for them, red, never white. Zion preferred white. Actually, she preferred blush, but she knew that would seem uncultured to her lawyer boyfriend.

After the waiter departed, David clasped his hands on the edge of the table and smiled at her. He was everything Rebekah wanted for her. Polished, poised, educated, wealthy, with a healthy 401K or so she figured, and he was handsome, just an added bonus. Why didn't she feel more excited about this? He was into her, he showered her with attention. Just tonight, he brought her and her mother flowers. Who did that?

"How was your day?" he asked her. Even that was something to give him props for. He wanted to know about her day, not spend the night talking about his own. Yep, she was definitely the problem. He was perfect. She wasn't going to find a better guy.

"Fine," she said, adjusting her purse at her feet. "How was yours?"

"Busy, but most days are."

"Right." She forced a smile. Shouldn't this be easier? Shouldn't they be past the awkward by now?

"How'd it go with the caterer?" She sensed the strain in his voice.

"It went fine." She wanted to drop it. She didn't want to fight with him and she especially didn't want to talk about the case. She felt like a fool that Tate had sidelined her, but somehow she knew that would make David happy.

"She give you any information?"

Zion exhaled. "Can we drop it? I don't really want to talk about it tonight, okay?"

David's shoulders lowered and he gave a grateful sigh. "Yes, we can drop it. Absolutely."

Zion frowned. "What does that mean?"

He picked up his napkin and shook it out, placing it on his lap. "Just that I'm glad that's beyond us."

The waiter arrived with the wine. David never drank a bottle of wine without going through the whole wine tasting ritual. Zion stewed as she waited for it to finish. Finally the waiter poured them each a glass and set the bottle on the table, folding his hands behind his back.

"Can I tell you the specials?"

"Please," said David.

"In a moment," said Zion. She gave him a tense smile. "Can you give us just a minute?"

"Of course," said the waiter, offering them a short bow, then he backed away from the table.

Zion waited until he was out of earshot. "What exactly do you think is beyond us?"

David paused in the midst of picking up his wine glass. "This whole investigating thing. I already told you I don't like it, Zion. I think it's dangerous and frankly, I'm put out that Sheriff Wilson hasn't stopped it before this."

"Sheriff Wilson? What does he have to do with this?"

"He made Tate a deputy. Not you. He should have told Tate to keep you out of it, not make me do it."

Zion's back stiffened and David slowly lowered the wine glass to the table. "Make you do what?"

"Nothing. You were right in the first place. Let's not talk about this tonight."

"No," said Zion, "tell me what you meant. What did you do?"

"I just reminded Tate that he was putting you in danger, that's all."

"You did what?"

David glanced around the restaurant, then held up a hand. "Please, Zion, let's not do this."

"Tell me what you said."

"I told him I thought it was irresponsible of him to involve you in a murder case."

Zion grabbed her napkin and threw it on her plate. She was getting out of here. How dare he! No wonder Tate had canceled on her this morning. "You had no right…"

"I'm worried about you!" said David, placing a hand against his chest. "Did you think about that? Did you think for once that maybe I'm scared something might happen to you?"

That took the wind out of Zion and she sat back down.

David glanced around again, then leaned back. "Merilee Whitmire is dead, Zion. Someone poisoned her and you admitted Tate has no leads. Am I wrong to worry about your safety?"

No, he wasn't, but she didn't like him interfering in her life. "I understand that, and I appreciate it, David, but you can't go around talking to people behind my back."

He nodded. "You're right. I felt horrible about it the moment I did it. I knew it was wrong."

Well, that was something. She brushed a curl back from her eyes and looked around too. No one seemed to be aware of their argument. "Please don't do something like that again."

"I won't. I promise." He held up his wine glass. "Can we put it behind us? Have a nice dinner?"

She reached for her own glass and touched it to his. "Sure," she said, taking a sip. They could put it behind them and have a nice dinner, but it wasn't over. Not by a long shot. Except, oddly enough, she wasn't as mad at David as she was at Tate. Damn Tate, why the hell would he listen to anything David said?

CHAPTER 16

A knock sounded at Tate's door on Wednesday morning. He rinsed off his toothbrush and grabbed his t-shirt off the towel rack, heading into the living room. He yanked open the door, pulling the t-shirt over his head.

Zion stood on his porch, her eyes trailing down his body as he tugged the shirt down over his chest. He caught his breath as her green eyes rose to his face. For a moment, the tension between them was so thick, Tate could swear it was more than platonic. She had her hair in a loose bun, wearing her typical *Caffeinator* uniform, but he once more envisioned himself stepping forward and pulling her into his arms.

"Zion." His voice came out huskier than he'd intended, so he cleared it. "I wasn't expecting you."

She leaned on the doorjamb, looking beyond him into his house. "I guess not." She crossed her arms. "You're a putz!"

He blinked. "Excuse me?"

"We need to talk, so you can either let me in or you can come out here. It's another beautiful day."

He stepped back and held the door wider. The interior of his house was dark. He didn't often open the blinds. In fact, he didn't think about it. She stepped inside and looked around, walking over to his lamp/side table combination.

"You get this at an antique store?"

"Yeah, *70's R Us*," he said, smiling.

She looked over her shoulder, smiling too. Moving aside his glasses, she read the cover on his book. "Historical fiction, huh?"

He shrugged. "I'm a sucker for a good war book."

She turned and faced him. "I like science fiction."

His brows rose. He hadn't expected that. He shut the door and started toward the kitchen. "You want some coffee?"

"Sure." She followed him.

For the first time, he took a look at his 70's kitchen and thought it seemed shabby – formica countertops, pine cabinets with water stains, and appliances that had been in fashion twenty years before. He hadn't even bothered to remove the brown wallpaper with the coffee mugs on it.

"Oh, wow! This is a blast from the past."

He laughed, going to the coffee pot and pouring out two mugs. "Yeah, I sort of moved in two years ago and that was that. I haven't really done any updating."

She pulled a chair out from the formica table and gave the cracked vinyl a jaundiced eye, then she sat down. He brought the coffee to her and placed it before her spot. She lifted it to her lips and took a sip as he sat down across from her.

"It's not as good as your coffee, I'm afraid."

She made a choking sound and forced a smile. "It's fine."

"Want some milk?"

She nodded. "And sugar?"

"Sure," he said, fetching both for her.

As she doctored her coffee, he studied the pattern of freckles on her cheeks, the way the muted sunlight touched her hair. The sight of her sitting across from him at his breakfast table filled him with longing. He could imagine her tousled from sleep, sitting down to share a morning meal with him before they both took off for their shops. He liked the image. It was so different from Cherise who would never come to the table without makeup and perfectly prepped hair.

She looked up and caught him staring, but instead of looking away, she held his gaze and raised the mug to her lips, taking a sip. "Much better," she said, lowering it again.

He smiled. God, he could get used to this.

"You're a putz!"

Or maybe not.

"Why did you let David intimidate you?"

Tate frowned. "Intimidate me?"

"He told you not to let me work the case with you and you listened to him."

"It wasn't exactly like that…" Tate began.

"How exactly was it?"

"He asked me man to man if I would back off, and I agreed." He shrugged.

"You agreed. So the two of you decided you'd handle my life for me and you didn't need any silly little ideas in my head interfering with your male bonding?"

Tate tried to hide his amusement, but it wasn't working. After a moment of glaring at him, Zion's angry facade cracked and she fought a smile. He sort of figured she wasn't someone who stayed angry for long.

"Look, Tate, David and I are…" Her voice trailed away and she looked at the table. "Well, I'm not sure what we are, but he doesn't decide what I do with my life. I asked you to work this case and you told me I did a good job with Sabrina Clark."

"You did."

"Then don't sideline me. Please. This is too important to me."

He fingered the handle on his mug. "David's right about one thing, Zion. It could be dangerous."

"So is driving a car, or walking out of the house, or slipping in the bathtub. Besides, this was a very specific murder. Someone was the target and it was executed with the knowledge that only one person would die."

Tate considered what she said. Something about that rang true. "You have a point, which means the arsenic had to be delivered very specifically so it would only affect the person it was intended to affect."

Zion nodded.

"Which means the motive behind Hifler doing the poisoning is flawed. If he'd laced the joints, he had to know the band would pass them around, so that couldn't have been the mode of delivery. Merilee must have taken a drug that the rest of them didn't or eaten something they didn't."

He got up and headed toward the spare bedroom he'd turned into a sort of office. The file with the autopsy report was on top of his desk. He grabbed it and went back to the kitchen flipping it open. He scanned down the report. No remaining stomach contents, so whatever food she'd eaten had been purged. The tox panel had been preliminary and it was positive for THC-COOH, a non-psychoactive by-product of marijuana, so she'd definitely been smoking, but there was no other indication that she'd taken anything else. A visual exam of the body didn't report any track marks from needles or other unusual puncture wounds.

Tate flipped back to the front cover and found the coroner's information. He pulled his phone from his pocket and punched in the phone number, lifting the phone to his ear.

"What are you doing?" Zion asked.

"Checking to see if we have a more detailed tox screen." The line connected.

"Angela Davenport," came the female voice on the other end.

"Dr. Davenport, this is Tate Mercer, I'm an acting deputy with the Sequoia sheriff's department."

"Yes, Deputy Mercer, Sheriff Wilson told me you might call."

"I'm looking at Merilee Whitmire's autopsy report. I was wondering if the full tox screen had come back yet."

"Let me pull up her information," came the reply and Tate could hear her clicking on computer keys. After a moment, Davenport's voice was back on the line. "We don't have a complete tox screen back yet. That could take weeks. It has to go to San Francisco for processing."

"I understand."

"But on preliminary examination, I did note she had THC-COOH in her system along with a lethal level of arsenic."

"Right. You also don't indicate there were any puncture marks on her body."

"There weren't."

"Did she have arsenic in her lungs?"

"Yes, but the most significant amount was in her bloodstream."

"Meaning what? Injection?"

"No, I felt pretty certain it was ingested. The trace amounts in her lungs could have come from inhaling it while eating. I estimated she lived for hours after her poisoning. If she'd inhaled the lethal amount, her death would have been quicker after exposure."

Tate nodded. "Thank you," he said, considering. "Will you contact me as soon as you get the full tox screen back from the lab?"

"Absolutely. Why don't you give me your cell phone number now?"

Tate rattled it off, repeating it twice. "Thank you again, Dr. Davenport."

"I wish you God's speed, Deputy Mercer," she said in response and disconnected the call.

"What did she say?" asked Zion.

"She's pretty sure Merilee ingested the poison."

"Ingested it? You mean ate it?"

"Right."

"Wouldn't she know she was eating poison?"

"Not arsenic. It has a garlic odor and taste, so the issue is what has garlic in it."

"Pizza," said Zion.

Tate pointed a finger at her. "Bingo. What do you say we go have lunch?"

And Zion smiled. They were back on an even-keel again.

* * *

Tate and Zion walked into the *Slice & Dice* pizza parlor at 11:00. It would give them enough time to get lunch and make it back to Main Street for Zion to take over her shift at noon. Tate felt a little guilty about letting Logan open without him, but the kid said he could handle it. Tate guessed he'd find out.

He hadn't worked Merilee's case at all yesterday. Every time he thought he'd head out to the pizza parlor, something came up that needed to be handled at the store. In exchange, he figured he owed the majority of today to Merilee. He didn't want to admit that he'd been reluctant to go without Zion and she had the grace not to comment on it.

Slice & Dice was in a strip mall on the opposite end of town from the sheriff's office. The pizza parlor wasn't much of a parlor. It sat in the middle of the mall with a karate joint on one side and a juice bar on the other.

Zion gave the juice bar a critical look. "I'll bet Mom would love this place." She squinted through the window. "Yep, I see grass growing on the top shelf there. Perfect for her new diet."

Tate squinted in as well. Sure enough, growing out of a tray on the top shelf was a strip of grass. "Seriously? Who eats that? Besides cows?"

"My mother. She says she can feel the health coursing through her."

Tate didn't know how to respond. Gabi Sawyer was a character and he liked her a lot. He pulled open the door of the pizza parlor. A few two-person tables were arranged in front of the windows, but the rest of the space was occupied by a long counter that stretched across the width of the room and behind it were the pizza ovens. A number of people moved around in the back, shoving pizzas into the ovens or pulling them out. A second counter in the far back was where a team of people added toppings to the pizza or cut and boxed it.

No other customers were in the shop, but the smell of yeast and spices lay heavily on everything. Tate felt his stomach rumble in response and he placed his hand over it, reaching into his back pocket with his other hand to get out his badge.

They approached the pimply-faced kid behind the register. He was tall and lanky with brown hair escaping his *Slice & Dice* baseball cap. "What can I get you?"

Tate showed him the badge. "I need to talk to a manager."

The boy's eyes widened. "Yo, Roger, dude's here with a badge."

A portly man with jet black hair walked out of the back and up to the counter. He glanced at the badge and then gave Tate a lift of his bushy black eyebrows. "I'm Roger Mancuso. I own the joint. What can I do for you?"

"I'm investigating the death of Merilee Whitmire."

Mancuso didn't look like the name meant anything to him.

The kid nudged his arm. "That's the girl that bought it after the *Anaconda* concert."

Recognition dawned on Mancuso's face. "Right. I heard about that."

Tate nodded. "We're trying to narrow down the way she was poisoned."

"Not by my pizzas," said Mancuso emphatically.

"Well…"

The bushy brows lowered again.

Zion moved closer to the counter. "We're not suggesting you had anything to do with it, Mr. Mancuso," she said gently.

Mancuso continued to glare at Tate, but he relaxed visibly. "Just what are you saying?"

"One of the suspects mentioned he had leftover pizza in his fridge from your establishment," said Tate. "He said he and Merilee might have eaten it just before she died."

"Might have?" said Mancuso.

Zion held up a hand. "He was high, Mr. Mancuso. He has a spotty memory of that night."

"You think he put poison on my pizza and gave it to this girl."

"We're trying to find that out."

But no, Tate wanted to say. He didn't think that. He was just trying to narrow things down – to what, he wasn't sure. He had a whole lot of nothing right now.

"Who's this guy?"

"It's Deimos," said the boy. "I read about it in the *Sequette*."

Zion gave Tate a puzzled look.

"The local paper," he said wryly. "Sequoia and Gazette mashed together – Sequette."

Zion made a face.

"Deimos? Deimos Hendrix?" said Mancuso. "He's your suspect?"

"He's *a* suspect."

"He's not a suspect," said Mancuso, waving him off with a beefy hand. "Frankie, look up on the computer and see the last time he bought a pizza." The boy began messing with something on the register. Mancuso shifted his attention to Tate and Zion again. "He eats here at least three times a week, but he ain't been around lately. Guess you got him in the slammer, eh?"

"No, he hasn't been charged with anything."

"Then why you asking about my pizza? I got good pizza here. I have organic vegetables and I source all my meats locally."

"We're trying to narrow down something that Merilee ate..." *Or smoked,* he thought. "…that no one else did. Dee admitted they ate pizza when they returned to his apartment, or he thinks they ate pizza."

"The last time he ordered a pizza was for pickup," said Frankie, tapping Mancuso's shoulder.

"When was that?" Mancuso said.

"Two weeks ago."

"Two weeks?" said Tate and Mancuso together.

"That's the last record I can find."

"What if he paid cash?" asked Tate. "Would that show in the computer?"

Mancuso patted the machine with his thick palm. "Every order is stored in here. If he ordered and we airmailed it to him, it's in here."

"He hasn't ordered since then?" asked Tate.

"He's been hanging out with Mom a lot, drinking smoothies," said Zion.

Tate turned to her. "There's no way he offered her two week old pizza, did he?"

"He couldn't have been that high."

"So what did he offer her?"

"He may never remember, Tate."

"You need something else?" said Mancuso.

Tate stared out the windows of the pizza parlor. It suddenly hit him that someone may have gotten away with murder. Unless they got a break really soon, Merilee Whitmire's murderer may never be caught.

* * *

Bill Stanley was waiting for Tate when he got back to the *Hammer Tyme*. Tate shook hands with the older man and motioned him to follow him into the break room. He passed Logan the rest of the pizza he and Zion had ordered and lifted the counter, stepping through.

"Thanks for coming in, Bill," he said, watching Logan lift the lid on the pizza box.

"*Slice & Dice*?" Logan said with awe. "God, I love their pizza."

"Go take a break and eat it," said Tate.

Logan hurried past him and headed toward the front of the store and fresh air. Tate knew the kid liked to eat in the little park at the end of Main Street, watching the other kids skateboard.

"You gonna leave the store unattended?" asked Bill.

"The buzzer over the door will alert us if a customer walks in. Take a seat." He motioned to the chairs. Bill walked over and pulled one out. "You want some water or coffee."

"Water's good."

Tate grabbed two water bottles out of the dorm fridge he kept below the coffee pot and carried them back to the table, taking a seat. He slid a bottle over to Bill and twisted the cap off his own. Taking a sip, he sighed. He might be jumping the gun a little by hiring another employee. If he didn't find Merilee's murderer, Sheriff Wilson might never give him another case.

"So?" said Bill, playing with the label on the bottle. "You wanted to talk to me?"

"Yeah, I was wondering if you wanted a part-time job here."

Bill's brows rose and he scratched the side of his baseball cap. "Here? In the *Hammer Tyme*?"

"Yeah, Logan's going back to school in the fall and I'm sort of working with the sheriff's department. I need someone in the morning."

"I'm up in the morning," said Bill.

Tate nodded.

Glancing around the storeroom, Bill said, "What's the pay?"

"Um." Tate hadn't thought about that. "Probably minimum?"

Bill's eyes shifted back to him. "And the hours?"

"Part time, say 10:00 to 2:00, Monday through Friday. Logan will come in after school, I think that gets out at 3:00, and he'll do the weekends."

"I could do part-time," he said. "But I gotta talk to the wife. I mean, it's ultimately her decision. She may not want me away from the house that much."

Tate figured she might. She might like to have some time to herself. It might be the very reason she kept giving Bill so many chores to complete, requiring so many trips to the hardware store.

"Of course. Let me know whenever you can. I'm not in a hurry right now."

Bill nodded, then looked around again. "What's your position on employee discounts?"

Tate gave a huffing laugh. Yeah, he'd just bet money that Mrs. Stanley would be more than happy to have her husband take a part-time job.

* * *

After he and Logan closed the *Hammer Tyme* for the day, Tate sat in his truck, staring out at Main Street. The lights were on, but the sun hadn't set yet. He could go get dinner at the Fords' place, but Cheryl might be right about his hardening arteries, especially after the pizza this afternoon.

He could go get a coffee at the *Caffeinator*, but he could see the crowd of people hanging around the door and he didn't want to fight his way inside. Boy, that Jaguar character could really draw them in. He wondered how long Sequoia's fascination with the rockstar would last.

He brooded about Merilee's murder. He just didn't know how she'd been poisoned or when. If he could figure out either of those things, he'd be able to nail this case down, but the odds of that happening now were getting slim.

He knew murders went unsolved, but he hated to think of Merilee's father, facing a life of not knowing why his daughter was dead. It made him anxious. He couldn't accept that. He couldn't accept defeat. There had to be something he was missing.

He started the truck and drove over to the sheriff's office. Climbing out, he met Emilio Vasquez coming into the building.

"How's it going?" said the senior deputy.

"Not great. How are you?" said Tate.

"Just checking out some vandalism on the other side of town. We just get done with the summer tourists and we're staring down ski season." He held the door for Tate. "Probably sounds silly to you, eh? You coming from LA and all."

Tate walked through the door. "I don't know. I'm working a murder case that has no suspects. Seems a lot like LA to me."

Emilio laughed and used his key to open the inner door. "You coming in?"

"Yeah, thanks. I don't have keys yet. Do you think the sheriff is still here?"

"I saw his SUV out front, so I figured as much. You let me know if you need help, okay?"

"Thanks."

Tate walked back to Wilson's office and knocked on the door.

"Enter," came Wilson's voice.

Tate pushed the door open and stepped inside. Wilson had his head braced on his hand, staring at the computer screen. His hat lay on the desk next to him.

He glanced up and shook his head, shoving the mouse across the mouse pad. "Damn thing. It never does what I want it to do."

"They're contrary that way."

"Tell me about it. I'm trying to buy the missus some flowers. I miss when you could just walk into a florist and place the order that way, but now everything's online."

Tate took a seat before Wilson's desk. "You do something that warrants flowers?"

"It's our anniversary in two days. I'm trying to get out ahead of it, or I was." He folded his hands together. "What's up?"

"I'm stuck."

"I figured as much. Man, this case is a bear, ain't it?"

"Sure is."

"So tell me who your suspects are?"

"I'm down to one."

"Okay?"

"Desmond Hifler, the band manager. He's the only one I can pin a motive on and it's a thin one at that."

"I see. And he's in LA."

"Yep."

"So we gotta get him back here or send you down there."

"Well, before we do that, I was wondering if you could get a warrant for some arrest records."

"On Hifler?"

"Yeah, he had an altercation at a concert with a young woman. She was injured and pressed charges. The case never went anywhere, but I'd still like to see the records."

Wilson rolled back his chair and opened his top desk drawer, taking out a pad of paper. "Write down what you need and we'll get on it."

Tate took the pad. "I'm sorry I don't have more for you, Sheriff."

"Ah, I figured this case was gonna be a brain tickler. Why you think I brought you on?"

Tate blew out air. Frankly, he was beginning to wonder that himself.

CHAPTER 17

Zion showed up at the *Caffeinator* by 8:00 on Thursday to meet the caterer, Nancy Osborn, by 9:00 like they'd planned. She was pleased to see that Dottie and Tallah were handling the morning rush with efficiency. She slipped behind the counter and went into her office to catch up on some paperwork that needed doing. She didn't want it to seem like she was checking up on her employees.

She'd lost track of time when Tallah poked her head inside the office. "Hey, Zion, there's a woman here to see you."

Zion glanced up, then clicked off the inventory list she was making and rose to her feet. "Thank you. Hey, how's it been going?"

The girl shrugged. "It's fine. I wish you'd let me go back to my previous hours. I liked sleeping in."

Zion turned her by the shoulders and propelled her through the doorway back into the coffee house. "That's not it at all. You just want to be here when Jaguar is."

"Well, I don't know why you and Mom don't trust me. He's awesome, but I'm not planning on doing anything but look."

"It's not that we don't trust you," said Zion, depositing her beside Dottie.

"They don't trust that sexed up rockstar with the tight pants," said Dottie.

Tallah put her hands on her hips. "And just how do you know he has tight pants, Dottie?" she asked with a sly smile.

Dottie ducked her head, looking at her through her lashes. "I'm not dead yet, child," she remarked, making Zion and Tallah both laugh.

Glancing up, Zion saw Nancy sitting at a bistro table before the window. Sunlight filtered in from the street, bathing her in its glow. Her shoulders were hunched and her skin looked almost translucent. Zion just knew that something wasn't right with this woman's health.

"Hey, Nancy," she called.

Nancy looked over, her expression tense. "Hey, Zion," she called back.

"What can I get you?"

"Tea would be nice."

"I love our Chai teas. You want one of those?"

"Sure," said Nancy.

Zion started the prep work for the tea as Dottie and Tallah went back to serving customers. Carrying the two paper cups over to the bistro table, Zion took a seat, passing one cup to Nancy.

"How's Sophia?"

"Great," said Nancy, a ghost of a smile crossing her lips.

"She's such a beautiful child."

"Thank you. She's so excited to start school in the fall. I wish I could have sent her to nursery school, but I couldn't afford it."

"I understand. It's sort of nice that your job gives you some flexibility."

"Yes, it is."

"How is the catering business?"

"Great in the spring and summer. I do weddings mostly. Then it falls off, but usually it picks up around Christmas and New Year's. Anyway, I make a go of it."

Zion nodded. She wanted to ask her about her health, but she didn't know her well enough. The skin under Nancy's eyes seemed bruised and she was unnaturally thin.

"So, where are you originally from?" Nancy asked, playing with the top on her tea.

"San Francisco. I grew up there. Where are you from?"

"Here." Nancy looked out the windows. "Born and raised. I went to school here."

"So did Jaguar, the lead singer from *Anaconda*. In fact, I think the band met here."

Nancy's smile faded. "We were all in high school together."

"Did you know them then?"

"No, we didn't run in the same crowd. I was a cheerleader, if you can believe that. Jaguar and his bandmates, well, they weren't much into the whole school scene."

"That's what I understand from Jim Dawson." She pointed across the street at the print shop. "He taught Jaguar English. He said he was a terrible student."

Nancy gave a closed-mouth smile.

"You ever think of leaving?" Zion asked when the conversation didn't seem to be picking up.

"I used to. I used to dream about traveling the world, then I had Sophia."

"Are you raising her by yourself?"

Nancy dropped her eyes, her fingers picking at the lid. Zion wondered if she'd gone too far, pushed too much. She'd just opened her mouth to apologize for prying, when Nancy started talking.

"I was married for about three years. Allen was a little older than I was. We had Sophia shortly after we got married and we wanted more kids, but it didn't work out. He left when we found out we couldn't have any more."

"I'm so sorry, Nancy. Does Sophia see her father?"

Nancy looked up into Zion's face. "No, she doesn't. It's better that way."

"It must be hard raising her alone."

"It's not easy, but she's a really good girl." Nancy rubbed a hand against her neck. "I've been sick lately. It's hard to keep up with the business. A lot of doctor's appointments."

"I'm sorry. Is there anything I can do?"

Nancy shrugged. "Just listening to me babble about my problems means a lot. I appreciate that."

"Sure, but if you think of anything else, just ask."

"Thank you." Nancy smiled. "It's nice to have another friend."

Zion nodded.

"Anyway, when things seem the bleakest, I just look at Sophia and I think it's all worth it. Every part of it. It's worth it. She's the best thing that happened to me and I'd do anything to protect her. I just wish I could give her more."

Zion took a sip of her own tea. "I got this place from my biological mother. She left it to me when she died."

"I remember hearing about that."

"Well, when the lawyer called me to tell me about her death, I was worried my mother, my adoptive mother, would be upset."

"That's the woman who came to the shop with you?"

"Right. Well, I didn't answer the lawyer for a while because I was so worried about that, but you know what?"

"What?"

"She wasn't. She supported me. She came with me to find out what Vivian had left me. She had my back – she's always had my back." She looked out the window. "We didn't always have everything that I thought I needed growing up, but I never lacked for anything really important. Still, when I need her, my mom is always there for me and that means so much more than any material gain I could have gotten. Your daughter will understand this too when she grows up."

A teenage girl approached the table. "Excuse me?" she said, sidling forward. "Can you tell me when Jaguar's going to be here?"

Zion glanced up at her, marking the many piercings and tattoos she sported. "He comes in at noon."

Nancy grabbed her phone off the table and looked at the display. "Goodness, I need to get going," she said, rising to her feet. She grabbed her purse off the chair and picked up her tea. "I'm sorry I can't stay longer."

"That's okay," said Zion, confused by her abrupt departure.

"Thank you for the tea," she said, gazing down at her.

Zion rose also as the teenager walked out, disappointed. "You're welcome," she told Nancy. "Maybe we could do this again sometime?"

"Sure," said Nancy, edging to the door. "Talk to you soon."

Then she was gone.

Frowning, Zion watched her hurry down the street. She was afraid that Nancy was sicker than she let on. She wondered if she should have come out and asked her about it, but they'd just met. It was too soon to get that involved in her new friend's life. Still, it worried her. Sophia needed her mother. That was clear.

* * *

Betty and Barney Brown owned the *Fast & Furriest* pet store next door to the *Cut & Print.* Betty was stout and Barney was spare, but they both had identical bowl haircuts and wore jeans, sneakers, and usually a buttoned-up shirt (Betty's in pink, Barney's in blue). The married couple had the endearing habit of finishing each other's sentences and Zion had gotten to know them fairly well the last few months because she shopped in their store for Cleo's kitty needs.

As they entered the shop, Barney carried a circular, plastic container in his hands. The day was nearing the 6:00 PM closing time and the store had thinned out a little. Jaguar sat in the bistro seat before the windows and strummed on his guitar, a circle of besotted teenagers sitting around him on the floor, Tallah among them.

Zion smiled at the Browns as they made their way through the store, glancing over their shoulders at the rockstar. "How are you two?" she asked.

Barney placed the plastic container on the counter. "We're not here for coffee, Zion."

"No, we're not. We're here to bring a welcome home present."

"A welcome home present?"

"To Sequoia's favorite son," said Barney.

"Most famous son," said Betty.

Zion pointed at the container. "This?"

"Yes, it's a pie."

"Barney baked a pie."

"I baked a cherry pie because this is the season for cherries."

"They're locally grown cherries."

"We thought we might share."

"Pie for everyone."

Zion enjoyed the Browns, so she couldn't hide her smile. "Just let me close up shop and we'll have pie," she said.

The Browns beamed at her.

"Last call," said Zion. "We're closing in five."

Jaguar immediately stopped playing and rose, headed for his guitar case in Zion's office. The teenagers groaned and reluctantly pushed themselves to their feet, then they made their way to the door. Tallah hung back, looking longingly after Jaguar.

"Text your mom and tell her you're staying for pie," said Zion as she held the door open for the last of the customers to make their way out.

Tallah squealed in delight and grabbed her phone, texting rapidly as she moved toward the counter. Jaguar's bodyguards came out of the kitchen, Maddog rubbing his eyes with his fists. Zion suspected they took frequent naps in the back while they waited.

Jaguar also emerged from the back, passing the guitar case to Bruno and removing his apron. Bruno headed toward the front door, intent on getting the limo to take their boss home.

"Wait," said Zion, throwing the lock. "The Browns brought homemade cherry pie and I was just going to cut it."

Bruno looked at Jaguar and Jaguar shrugged. Zion motioned Jaguar out from behind the counter. "This is Betty and Barney Brown, Jaguar. They run the *Fast & Furriest* across the street."

Jaguar affably shook hands with the couple. "Nice to meet you," he said.

Barney held up the pie. "We wanted to welcome you home to Sequoia."

"Sorry it's taken so long, but we've been busy," said Betty.

Jaguar rubbed his hands together. "Well, I appreciate it. Thank you. How about I get us some coffee?"

The Browns nodded and Jaguar went behind the counter to pour the remaining coffee into mugs. Zion went to the kitchen and grabbed plates, forks, and a pie knife, carrying everything out to the dining room.

Barney placed the pie in the middle of the closest bistro table and removed it from its protective plastic holder. Zion handed him the pie knife and he began cutting slices while Jaguar placed the filled mugs on the counter. As Barney cut, Zion distributed. Taking two plates, she carried one of them to Jaguar.

"No, thank you," he said, smiling.

"It's homemade," she told him, giving him a piercing look. She didn't want to be rude to the Browns.

Betty and Barney looked up, their eyes going wide.

Jaguar offered them his most charming smile. "It looks delicious, but I'm sorry. I have to be careful with my diet. I'm gluten intolerant."

Zion went still. Gluten intolerant? Where had she heard that before?

Merilee Whitmire had a gluten allergy, which is why her father hadn't believed she would have eaten pizza at Dee's apartment.

"Wait. What did you say?"

"I'm gluten intolerant." He flashed that smile again at the Browns. "You wouldn't want to see what happens when I make a mistake and eat it."

"Who knows this?" Zion said.

He gave her a puzzled look. "What?"

"It's all right," said Barney. "I should have asked."

"Yes, we should have checked first," said Betty.

Zion set down both pie plates. "Who knows about your gluten intolerance?"

Jaguar shrugged. "Bruno and Maddog."

"What about Hifler?"

"Desmond?"

"Yes."

"Zion, what's going on?" asked Tallah.

Zion ignored the girl. "It's important, Jaguar. Did Desmond Hifler know you were gluten intolerant?"

"Um, yeah. Of course he did."

"At the after party, did you eat any of the food?"

"I ate things that didn't have flour in them." He looked at the bodyguards. "I think I had some shrimp and um, cheese."

The two men nodded.

"I usually don't eat until I get back to wherever I'm staying. I'm pretty ramped up after a concert and not really hungry." He gave her a curious look. "What's going on?"

"I need to go. We need to close up the shop."

Jaguar looked around at the espresso and coffee makers. They all needed to be cleaned. "Okay. Well, Tallah and I can get things ready for tomorrow, but I don't have a key to lock up."

Zion looked over at the girl. She'd promised Cheryl and Dwayne Tallah would never be alone with the rockstar. She couldn't back out on that now.

Betty and Barney started packing up the rest of the pie. Both Maddog and Bruno looked disappointed.

"Tallah, I'll pay you overtime if you help Jaguar clean," Zion told her.

"Sure," said Tallah, taking a bite of her pie.

Betty and Barney offered the two bodyguards slices that had already been cut. "Can we just take our plates with us? We can bring them back tomorrow morning."

Zion didn't care about the plates as she reached for her phone. She needed to talk to Tate. "Sure, that's fine. I'm sorry, you two."

"No problem. We understand," said Betty.

"We should have asked about the gluten," said Barney.

Zion knew she should reassure them, but she was too busy trying to get Tate on the line. "It was very thoughtful. We'll do this another time," she said, holding the phone to her ear.

"Of course. I'll make it with gluten free flour next time," promised Barney.

"And apricots. Apricots make a nice pie," said Betty.

"Yes, they do. A very nice pie and we can get some lovely ones in Visalia."

"Yes, they have lovely apricots in Visalia."

Jaguar gave a laugh, watching them in amusement. "Sounds awesome," he said.

The phone connected and before Tate could speak, Zion blurted out, "I need you to come to the *Caffeinator* right now."

"Zion?" said Tate.

She waved goodbye to the Browns and moved toward her office. She needed to get her notepad. "Come to the *Caffeinator* before you go home. It's important."

"Is everything okay?" he asked, worry in his voice.

"No, we're solving a murder, if you haven't forgotten, and I just got a lead."

The line went quiet. Zion left the office door half ajar and hurried around her desk, yanking her purse out of the bottom drawer. She opened it and dug out the notebook.

"You have a lead?"

"That's right."

"I'll be right over," came Tate's response.

* * *

Zion tapped her finger on the notebook. "I wrote it down as close to verbatim as I could. Roger Whitmire said she never ate anything with gluten in it and whenever she went out, she was really careful about eating anything unless she was sure it didn't have gluten in it."

Tate rubbed his hands over his face and back through his hair. "Okay, but what does this prove?"

"Jaguar's gluten intolerant. He just told everyone out there."

Tate's eyes narrowed. "Really?"

"Yes. You kept saying it didn't add up, that everyone loved Merilee. Maybe they did. Maybe Merilee wasn't the target."

"Maybe it was Jaguar?"

"Right."

"That means Merilee was poisoned at the after party." He chewed on his bottom lip. "But the food was tested, Zion."

"The caterer's food was tested. Jaguar said he hardly eats at those things, but what if someone knew why he didn't eat at them and provided food just for him?"

"Desmond Hifler?"

"Right. He knew Jaguar was gluten intolerant."

"What's the motive, Zion? Jaguar's the cash cow. Why would Hifler risk that?"

"Jaguar's not the cash cow anymore. He's not able to produce the hits that he once did. That's why he's working here. He admits he's lost his mojo. But you said it yourself, Tate. Jaguar's the lead singer. He's the frontman. I've seen it in the coffee shop. People come from all over to see him." She motioned toward the dining room. "Every business owner, including grouchy Jim Dawson from the *Cut & Print*, has come to see him. If he dies…"

"Album sales go through the roof."

"Platinum. Everyone's going to remember *Anaconda* at its height. And Jaguar's young. It'll be a tragedy."

Tate blew out air. "I need to go to LA."

"What about Jaguar? Don't you think we should warn him."

Tate considered that. "As long as Hifler's in LA, I think he's safe."

"Is he? Shouldn't he know he could be the real target?"

Tate briefly closed his eyes. "Nothing fit with this case. Merilee just didn't work as the target. I kept thinking that."

Zion waited. She knew he was on the brink of deciding something.

"Okay. Let's go tell him."

They found Jaguar cleaning the espresso machine as if it were his prized possession. Tallah was sweeping the dining room and even the bodyguards had been pressed into service. Bruno washed the few remaining dishes in the kitchen and Maddog was cleaning the tables.

Tate gave Zion an amused look. She had to admit the whole scene was pretty ridiculous. He jerked his chin at the rockstar barista and Zion went over to him, touching his shoulder.

"We need to talk to you," she said.

Jaguar stopped fussing with the machine and gave her a narrow-eyed look from those remarkable blue eyes. "I knew something was up." He went over to the sink and washed his hands, then he followed Zion and Tate out into the dining room.

Tallah stopped sweeping, watching them and Maddog looked up.

"So, what's going on?" Jaguar asked.

They took a seat at the bistro table Jaguar had used earlier for his impromptu concert. Tate clasped his hands together, the panther tattoo flexing on his forearm. "We think you might have been the target," he said.

Jaguar's eyes moved between the two of them. "The target of what?"

"The murderer. We think you were the one that was supposed to die instead of Merilee Whitmire," said Tate matter-of-factly.

Tallah stepped closer and Maddog abandoned his cleaning, taking up a position at Jaguar's back.

"What?" demanded the bodyguard.

"Merilee Whitmire had a serious gluten allergy, Jaguar," said Zion. "She was just as careful as you are about what she ate."

"You think the arsenic was in something at the after party?" asked Jaguar.

Tate nodded. "Can you remember if anyone made anything just for you? Anything that they said was gluten free?"

Jaguar thought for a moment, then he looked up at Maddog. "Do you remember anything? I was doing that interview for the *Sequette* at the start of the party."

"I was with you," said Maddog.

"Jaguar, what's your relationship with Desmond Hifler?" asked Tate.

"Our manager?" His blue eyes shifted to Zion. "Is that why you wanted to know if he knew about my allergy?"

Zion nodded.

"You think Desmond tried to poison me?"

Maddog straightened, looming at Jaguar's back.

Tate's gaze rose to the man, then lowered to the rockstar. "It would be a way to get record sales up."

"Especially if he thought you were…" Zion's voice trailed away.

"Washed up," said Jaguar, bitterness in his voice.

Zion nodded again. She hated the look of betrayal in his eyes.

"I need to talk to Hifler," said Tate. "I'll fly down and meet him in his office in LA."

"What if I can get him to come up here?" said Jaguar.

Tate's brows rose and he exchanged a look with Zion. "That would be better. How would you get him to come here?"

A crafty look came into Jaguar's eyes. "I'll tell him I've got the perfect comeback song and I want to play it for him. I'll say I tried it out in the coffee shop and everyone went crazy. He'll be on the next flight out."

"You think that will work? Why won't he want you to come to him?"

"Because he knows I'm here to see my mother. Besides…" Jaguar's expression darkened. "Trust me. Hifler's all about the bottom-line."

And Zion felt sure they'd finally found their man.

CHAPTER 18

Tate met Zion and Jaguar in front of the sheriff's office. Tate thought it was best to keep Jaguar close until they were sure they had their man. He'd expected Jaguar to show up with his bodyguards, so he was surprised to find him here with Zion. Tate had gotten to the sheriff's office early to get to work on a warrant to search Hifler's office and house in LA while Hifler was in Northern California, but Zion had texted him that she was coming in and to meet her in front.

Jaguar hadn't shaved and it looked like he hadn't even showered. His spiky hair was in more disarray than usual. Tate shifted his attention to Zion. She looked perfect. He couldn't deny that every time he looked at her he felt a flutter in his belly and he wished like hell she wouldn't go away with David Bennett on Sunday.

"How are you this morning?" he said to the rockstar.

"Didn't sleep much last night."

"Where are your bodyguards?" He gave Zion a speculative look.

Jaguar dropped his eyes, rubbing the back of his neck. "I gave them the day off."

"Why? Why would you give them the day off when…"

"Tate," said Zion in warning.

Jaguar glanced up then. "Look, right now, I'm not sure who I can trust. I've know Hifler for a long time and you're telling me he might be behind this? I just thought it might be better to trust in people that couldn't have been involved." His gaze shifted to Zion.

Tate nodded, although he didn't like Zion being this involved. "Okay. So how did you get Hifler to agree to come up here today?"

"I called him last night and told him I really needed to talk to him. After thinking about it some more, I figured a new song wouldn't get him up here, but me quitting the band might."

"What exactly did you say?"

"I told him my mom is getting worse, which is true, and that I need to spend as much time with her as I can. I said we needed to talk about where to go from here without the rest of the band involved right now."

"That was good thinking. Do you have any idea when he'll arrive?"

"He texted me this morning. His plane lands at 9:00 in Fresno."

Tate nodded and opened the glass door. He led them to the inner door and unlocked it. Sam Murphy had met him with his own set of keys when he arrived this morning. Wilson had assembled all of his deputies and they milled around the desks, getting coffee or talking in groups. The realization of how small Wilson's office was struck him. He knew Sam Murphy and Emilio Vasquez, but besides those two, Wilson had four other patrol officers.

Everyone stopped as soon as Jaguar entered the room. Tate realized that *Anaconda* might be on the decline, but the hometown band still drew attention in Sequoia. Jaguar gave Zion a nervous look. He'd asked for her to come with him and Tate couldn't help but worry a little at their growing closeness. Maybe Tate wasn't a rival for David, but Jaguar sure could be.

Wilson crossed the room, holding out his hand. "Welcome home, son," he said to Jaguar.

Jaguar shook his hand. "The last time I saw you you busted me for smoking pot behind the high school gym."

Wilson laughed. "I damn near forgot that." He motioned to the rest of his staff. "Come meet my people."

As Jaguar moved off with Wilson to greet the other officers, Sam Murphy approached Tate, holding out a folder. "Here's the arrest record you asked for on Hifler."

"Thanks," said Tate, flipping it open. He glanced up as Jaguar made the rounds, shaking hands and signing autographs, then he looked down at the report. For a moment, he was distracted by the faint vanilla scent of Zion's perfume as she stood next to him, then he forced himself to concentrate.

The altercation had happened backstage at an *Anaconda* concert. Nancy Spencer had appeared without a pass, demanding to talk to Jaguar. Hifler had stopped her at the door and told her she couldn't enter. She got combative and tried to get past him. He called for security. When she saw the security guards moving towards her, she'd rushed Hifler, who reacted by shoving her.

She'd fallen and cracked her head on an amplifier. In an abundance of precaution, the concert hall had called 911 and transported her to the hospital. Hifler had called the cops and reported she'd tried to force her way backstage, but when they arrived at the hospital to question Spencer, she told them she wanted to press charges against Hifler. Hifler was scheduled to be arraigned two weeks later, but Spencer unexpectedly dropped the charges.

"Does it say anything?" asked Zion.

Tate glanced up at her, closing the file. "Not much. Hifler was arrested for assault, made bail in a few hours, and then the woman dropped the charges. It doesn't say why."

"He paid her off, didn't he?"

"That's what I'm guessing."

Wilson strode over to Tate. "I got the flight information from Jaguar and I'm sending Murphy and Vasquez out to meet the plane. We'll bring him in for questioning."

"You aren't going to be able to hold him long. I don't have any evidence connecting him to this. A man like Hifler's going to lawyer up immediately."

"Which is why we need to get him to confess. I need you to question him, Tate. You got more experience at this than any of my guys. I'm figuring his lawyer's in LA. We'll have a few hours to question him before the lawyer gets here and makes him shut up."

Tate nodded.

"We'll keep Jaguar occupied here until we have Hifler in custody, but why don't you go over to your store and get things set up for the day. I'll call you when Hifler arrives."

"Okay. I'll do that." He looked at Zion. "You're not gonna stay, are you?"

Her gaze shifted to Jaguar. "No, I need to get to the shop too. I need to get things in order if I'm going out of town on Sunday. Just let me tell Jaguar and I'll walk out with you."

"Sounds good," said Tate, watching her cross the room to the rockstar. She touched his shoulder and he turned immediately to her, his expression anxious.

Wilson shifted around to face Tate again. "You ever gonna tell her what you feel for her?"

"What?" Tate frowned. "She's with David Bennett."

"Right," said Wilson, shifting weight and tucking his thumbs into his belt. "How sure are you that Jaguar's the real target?"

"Pretty sure. It makes a whole lot more sense than Merilee. When all's said and done, people are motivated to murder by two things – passion and money, and nine times out of ten, money's the bigger motivator."

"That's a pretty grim view of humanity."

Tate shrugged. "I wish I could tell you differently."

* * *

Tate had never liked interrogating suspects. People were so unpredictable when confronted with a crime. He'd seen innocent people sweat and fidget and confess to things he knew they hadn't done just because they felt pressured. The minute a person was brought into a police department and given his Miranda Rights, all bets were off. He might confess to assassinating JFK just because he was in a hot panic.

Staring at Hifler through the two way glass, Tate noted that the portly man displayed those very characteristics. He picked at his cuticles and he bounced his leg on the floor, his eyes darting around the room. According to Sam Murphy, as soon as they'd met him coming off the plane, he'd demanded to call his lawyer, even though Murphy and Vasquez had made it clear they just wanted to ask him some questions, that they weren't arresting him.

"We got maybe two hours at the outside," said Wilson at Tate's side. "Then that lawyer will be on us and Hifler will be gone. We don't have any evidence to hold him in Sequoia."

"I know. Just give me a moment."

Wilson nodded, tilting his hat to the back of his head.

Tate took a couple of deep breaths, then he scrubbed his hands on his jeans and picked up the file on Merilee Whitmire. Murphy opened the interrogation room door for him and he walked as steadily as he could to the table, setting the file on it.

Hifler's eyes focused on Tate's face, then lowered down to his jeans and t-shirt. "You're a cop?"

"Deputy," said Tate, taking a seat.

"My lawyer said not to talk to you."

"That's fine, but I still need to ask you questions." He adjusted the chair so he was facing Hifler. "You're not under arrest, Mr. Hifler."

"Then why am I sitting here."

"You know we're investigating Merilee Whitmire's death."

"The girl at the afterparty?"

"Right."

Hifler ran a hand through his unnaturally black hair, combing strands over the bald spot at the back of his head. Tate noted that his belly hung over his belt and that he had broken blood vessels on his cheeks. *Drinker*, Tate thought, but kept the thought to himself.

"I already told you everything I know about that when you came to the bed and breakfast."

"You didn't tell me that Jaguar's gluten intolerant."

Hifler reared back, making a face. "What? Why would I tell you that? What does that have to do with anything?"

"Merilee Whitmire was also gluten intolerant."

Hifler's eyes widened. "Is that how she was poisoned? Through something she ate?"

Tate nodded, although that hadn't been confirmed by the coroner and probably never would be.

Hifler's brow lowered in a frown and he stared at the file under Tate's hand. "But what does that have to do with me?"

"You knew Jaguar was gluten intolerant."

"Of course. It's my job to know everything about them."

"Do you usually make arrangements for his allergy?"

"What do you mean?"

"Do you usually have gluten free offerings made for him?"

"Of course. It's always a stipulation."

"Did you do that for this event?"

"What?"

Tate drew a breath for patience. He had Hifler talking and he didn't want a chance that he might shut down again. "When you made the arrangements for the after party, did you inform the fairgrounds that Jaguar was gluten intolerant?"

Hifler gave a bewildered look, shaking his head. "I'm sure I did. I made all the arrangements with that event planner at the fairgrounds." He tapped his forehead. "What was her name?"

"Sabrina Clark?"

Hifler snapped his fingers. "That's the one. Right. I made the arrangements with her."

"You told her Jaguar was gluten intolerant?"

"Yes," said Hifler emphatically.

Tate fingered the edge of the folder. "*Anaconda's* sales are down, aren't they?"

Hifler shrugged. "It's a difficult business. You go viral one day, the next no one remembers your name."

"But *Anaconda's* been big for a few years now. Why do you think they've fallen out of favor?"

"If I knew that, I'd be the richest man in the world, wouldn't I, Deputy?"

"I guess," said Tate, giving him a wane smile. "You gotta stay in the news to keep the public focused on you, don't you?"

"That's the God's honest truth."

"So, if one of the band members died, unexpectedly, it would probably increase album sales, don't you think?"

Hifler went still and the smile dried on his face. "What exactly are you saying, Deputy?"

"If Jaguar were to suddenly die…"

"I'm not listening to this anymore."

"It would definitely increase interest in the band. I mean, Jaguar's the face and voice of *Anaconda*, isn't he?"

"We're through here," said Hifler, crossing his arms and leaning back in the chair. He looked at the two way mirror. "You hear me? We're done. I'm not saying anymore."

Tate scratched his forehead, then he opened the folder and took out the autopsy picture of Merilee Whitmire. The young woman lay on the slab, a white sheet draped over her body. He slid the picture in front of Hifler.

The man's eyes were drawn to it involuntarily.

Tate tapped the picture. "This is Merilee Whitmire, Mr. Hifler. She wanted to study environmental science at Humboldt State. She has a father, who's gutted at the loss of his only child. She didn't deserve what happened to her."

Hifler's eyes rose to Tate's face, but he didn't speak.

"I can understand if it was a mistake. If you meant for it to poison Jaguar, but Merilee got it instead. You couldn't know she was gluten intolerant."

Hifler leaned forward, his face twisting. "I didn't poison anyone. I told that Sabrina Clark woman Jaguar was gluten intolerant. I don't even know if she listened to me. I can't remember if there was even anything on the table that was gluten free. I mean, you people tested the food and it didn't come back with any arsenic in it, now did it?"

"That's true, but we only tested the food provided by the caterer and the fair vendors. We didn't test anything that might have been provided by you."

"I didn't provide any food!" Hifler yelled. "Everything on that table was from the caterer! Everything on that table was on blue serving dishes with little signs saying what they were..." Hifler's voice trailed off and his eyes went wide.

Tate sat up straighter. "What did you just remember?"

Hifler shook his head.

"Mr. Hifler, please, a girl is dead because of this. What are you remembering?"

"Everything was on the blue caterer's serving dishes except this paper plate, a plate of brownies that said it was gluten free."

"Brownies?" Tate grabbed the folder and began searching through it for the list of food that was tested. "I don't remember brownies on the list."

Hifler nodded. "They were there. It said gluten free brownies. I remember it because..."

Tate stopped searching and looked up at the man. "You remember it because?"

"It was just sitting there. Not arranged like the rest of the stuff. It was just there on a paper plate and it was the only thing with a label. It was the only thing that said it was gluten free."

"But you asked for gluten free items, didn't you? You asked Sabrina Clark?"

"Yeah, but I mean there was shrimp cocktail and cheese and lunch meats, so I figured that was good enough. But there was this plate of brownies and this girl…" He covered his mouth with a hand.

"This girl? What about the girl?"

"A girl at the afterparty took one and ate it. She said it tasted weird, like garlic."

Tate felt his mouth go dry. "They tasted like garlic." He leaned forward and tapped Merilee's picture. "Was this the girl?"

"I don't know," said Hifler. "I was so busy and I'd had a few shots."

"Shot?"

"Tequila. Look, I was running around backstage, trying to get interviews set up and keep everyone happy. The girl told me the brownies tasted like garlic. I didn't know what the hell that meant, but they were gluten free. I mean that stuff tastes like shit anyway, but she kept talking about it, so I grab the damn things and I…"

"You what? What did you do with the brownies?"

"I couldn't find a garbage can and this reporter wanted to talk to me. I gave them to a roadie and told him to get rid of them. They weren't from the caterer and the girl said they tasted funny, so I just said to get rid of it. I don't know what he did with it. I mean, how much could the girl have eaten?"

Enough to kill her, thought Tate. "Do you remember which roadie?"

Hifler shrugged. "I told you I had a few shots."

"A few?"

"Okay!" Hifler barked. "I was pretty hammered. It was an after party. The booze and joints were flowing. Who the hell thinks about remembering everyone they talked to?"

"When we talked about the poisoning, you didn't tell me this," demanded Tate. "Why?"

"I didn't remember it until just now. I mean, it was just a plate of brownies and you said you'd tested all the food. Why would I remember the brownies when you said that?"

Tate slumped back in his chair. If Hifler had even mentioned this when they talked with him, Tate could have searched the fairgrounds for the brownies. As it was now, they'd probably wound up in the landfill. He rubbed his hand over his face and closed his eyes.

"Can I go now? I need to get back to LA," said Hifler.

Tate looked at the man and he wanted to smash his face with his fist. If he'd only told them about the damn brownies, they might have the evidence they needed now, but his concern was with going back to LA. If Tate had his way, Desmond Hifler would be charged as an accessory, but even as he thought it, he knew he wasn't being fair.

There was no way for Hifler to know how important any little detail like that might be. He didn't know that any evidence they had to convict a murderer was probably gone. The very real fear that Tate had, that someone was going to get away with killing Merilee Whitmire seemed more and more likely.

But a more disturbing thought kept running through Tate's mind. What was he going to do to make sure Merilee's murderer didn't get a second chance to kill?

CHAPTER 19

Zion stared at the time stamp on her computer screen. It was 11:30. Dee was scheduled to come in at noon, returning to his regular shift. Since the investigation had zeroed in on Hifler, Zion didn't feel it was necessary to keep Dee from work. His voice had trembled when she'd called him, he was so emotional.

Having Dee return to work solved another problem. She figured Wilson would keep Jaguar on a short leash today until they could get a confession out of Hifler or at least until Hifler lawyered up and went back to LA. Jaguar's days of working in the coffee shop were probably over. She felt a stab of disappointment at that thought. She gotten used to him and his bodyguards being around. Still, it would be quieter in the *Caffeinator* and she could get caught up on the paperwork she'd been neglecting while helping Tate with the case.

A knock at the office door startled Zion. "Come in," she said and Dee pushed the door open, stepping inside.

Zion jumped to her feet and hurried around the desk to hug him. "I'm so glad to see you."

He laughed, patting her back. "Reporting for duty, ma'am," he said, giving her a mock salute.

Looking out of her office, she could see Dottie and her mother beaming at them. "Did my mom bring you in?"

"Yeah, we did some yoga this morning and then she brought me to work. She's a great lady, your mom."

"I know." Zion waved her into the office.

"I'm gonna get to work," said Dee, but he halted and gave Zion a broad smile. "Thank you for believing in me. You and your mom. I don't know what I would have done if it hadn't been for the two of you."

Zion hugged him again. "I'm just so glad you're back."

Dee left the office as Gabi entered.

"Thanks for bringing him down."

"No worries," said Gabi, "I needed to come into town anyway. Cleo's out of kitty food."

"Oh, well, let me get that."

"You don't have to. I can handle a few cans of kitty food for my grandcat."

"Cleo's my responsibility, Mom. I'll pay for her food." Zion opened the desk drawer and grabbed her purse, setting it on the desk. "I've got a twenty. Get her some litter too."

"Fine," said Gabi, taking a seat. "So, I thought I'd stay here through Monday until you get back from your trip with David. That way you don't have to make arrangements for Cleo."

"That would be great." Zion dug in her big bag for her wallet. "Are you sure Dad isn't missing you too much?"

"I'll go home Tuesday morning." Gabi leaned forward, dropping her voice. "I think he's been cheating on his diet."

"No!" said Zion with mock severity. She removed her notebook and set it on the edge of the desk, while she hunted for her wallet in the bottom of the bag.

Gabi huffed. "I'm telling you, you'd feel so much better if you'd just drink my smoothies."

"That *is* what you keep telling me," she said, locating the wallet. She opened it and pulled out a twenty, leaning across the desk to hand it to her mother. As she did so, the notebook fell and a piece of paper fluttered to the floor.

Zion dropped the wallet in her purse and bent to retrieve the notebook and the paper. She'd forgotten the menu Nancy Osborn had given her for the after party. Something caught her eye and she read it more carefully.

As she read, the color drained from her face.

"Zion?" asked Gabi, rising to her feet.

Zion stared at the paper, her brain just not processing what she was reading.

"Zion, are you all right?"

Zion's gaze lifted to Gabi. "She made gluten free brownies," she said.

"What?" Gabi frowned. "What are you talking about?"

"She has them listed here. She made gluten free brownies." Grabbing her purse, Zion searched her desk for her keys. "Mom, can you stay here for awhile? See if there's anything that Dottie needs help doing."

"Where are you going?"

But Zion was already out the door and headed for her car.

* * *

Zion yanked open the sheriff's office door and raced across the lobby, hitting the buzzer. She hit it again for good measure. Finally the window slid back and Sam Murphy gave her a glare.

"Something better be on fire!" she scolded.

Zion looked beyond her into the office. "Tate! Tate!" she called, then she looked at Murphy. "Is he still here?"

Murphy started to answer, but Tate appeared out of the hallway on the right. "Zion, what's wrong?"

He went to the door and pulled it open. Zion ran over to it and shoved the paper at him. "Nancy Osborn made gluten free brownies."

He took the paper.

Zion was aware that other officers and Sheriff Wilson were appearing. Tate shook his head, holding the paper away from himself to read it. "Who's Nancy Osborn?"

"She's the caterer the fairgrounds hired for the after party. She owns *Cater 2 U*." Zion grabbed the paper from him and pointed at the tiny print near the middle of the list. "See, she made gluten free brownies. She listed all the food with a GF that were gluten free, including the brownies."

Tate held the paper out to Wilson. Wilson took it, rubbing a hand over his jaw.

"She went to school with Jaguar and the rest of the band," she said.

Tate put his hands on her shoulders and turned her to face him. "Slow down. How do you know this?"

Zion fell silent, realizing she hadn't told him about her independent investigation. "The other day when you sidelined me because of David, Mom felt bad, so she suggested we track down a lead."

"What?" said Tate, his grip tightening.

"You and your mother tracked down a lead?" asked Wilson.

"We went to *Cater 2 U*. I remembered Sabrina Clark saying that was who made the food."

"We tested the food," said Wilson.

"I know, but I just thought it was worth looking into. Nancy and I hit it off and she gave me the list of food she'd made for the after party. I didn't think anything of it and I stuffed the list into my purse. I invited her to come to the *Caffeinator* for coffee on Thursday."

Tate dropped his hands. "And did she?"

"Yes, just before her doctor's appointment."

"Was Jaguar there then?"

"No, but we were talking about him and she mentioned she went to school with him. Something's wrong with her, Tate. She looks like she's sick."

"Did she say she knew Jaguar well?" asked Wilson.

"No, she said they didn't run in the same crowds. She was a cheerleader."

"What's the motive then?" said Wilson, shaking the list. "And if she was going to poison him, why would she write it on here?"

Zion shrugged. "I don't know that."

Tate's face had gone grim. "It corroborates Hifler's claim about the plate of brownies. He said they weren't on the caterer's blue trays, but that doesn't mean she didn't put it there. He said it was the only thing that was clearly labeled gluten free."

"But why put it on the list?" said Wilson, shaking the paper again.

"Maybe she wanted to get caught. Often people make mistakes like that because they secretly want to be stopped," said Tate. "It matches, Sheriff. In profiling, poisoning is primarily a woman's mode of killing. Maybe some part of her was reluctant to do it, so she put it on a different plate and labeled it so Jaguar would be the only target. Maybe she was trying to minimize the collateral damage."

"But why does she want him dead?" said Wilson.

"We need to ask her. We need to bring her in."

Wilson nodded. "Murphy, take Jones and head out to this *Cater 2 U*. Vasquez, grab Lewis and find her home address." They started moving, but Wilson held up a hand. "Murphy, tell Jaguar he needs to stay put for a little longer. Where is he?"

Sam Murphy went still. "What?"

"Where's Jaguar?"

"I let him go. He said he was worried about his mother. She's having an off-day. I figured it was okay since we had Hifler here."

Wilson scratched his head under his hat. "Okay." He turned to Zion. "You call him and tell him to stay put at home until we have this Osborn woman in custody."

Zion nodded and reached for her phone.

"Update me as soon as you have her," said Wilson to his people and everyone dispersed.

Tate turned Zion to face him again and she curled the phone in her hand. "You should have told me you went out there."

"You shouldn't have listened to David."

"Fine, but what if she got spooked by your questions and attacked you and your mother? This is why David's right about this. It's too dangerous."

"I may have solved this case!" Zion said, jutting out her chin. "Why can't you just tell me I did a good job? Why do you have to scold me?"

Tate went still and his hands fell away again. "Because you could have been hurt."

She gave him an arch look, then she pressed the icon for Jaguar. "We can talk about this later," she said, turning away from him.

* * *

Zion tried Jaguar's number again, but it went to voicemail. She disconnected the call and squirmed in her seat. They were sitting in Wilson's office, listening to the patrol officers on the radio as they tried to find Nancy Osborn.

Tate suddenly moved, grabbing a file off Wilson's desk and opening it. He had to hold it away from himself to read.

"Why don't you carry your glasses with you?" she said, still feeling angry with him. Men and their vanity. Why did everything have to be about not looking weak?

He shot her a tense look and went back to reading, but Wilson snickered.

"We've been here twenty minutes, Sheriff," came Murphy's voice over the radio. "The sign on the door says she opens at 10:00. I don't think she's showing."

Wilson exhaled. "Okay. Vasquez, anything at the house?"

"Nothing, Sheriff."

"Tell Dispatch to send her license plate number and car model out to everyone on patrol. Start searching the streets for her. You have her sister's address, Murphy. Get over there and have her call Nancy. Maybe she can get her to turn herself in." He released the radio button and looked at Zion. "Try Jaguar again."

Zion dialed, listening to the ringing phone.

Tate looked up. "Sheriff, the name on the complaint about Hifler? The woman who filed charges against him when she tried to see Jaguar backstage?"

"Yeah?"

"It's *Nancy* Spencer."

The phone went to voicemail. Zion disconnected the call. "Something's wrong, Sheriff."

"Maybe we should bring Jaguar back in," said Tate. "Just until she's caught."

"I've got everyone out looking for her," said Wilson. "She tried to poison him before. What's she going to do now? Show up at his door with brownies again. I'll bet she skipped town. She got wind we were looking for her and she bailed."

"How would she know that?" asked Tate.

Wilson sighed. "Why would she go after Jaguar again?"

"We don't know why she went after him in the first place. Who knows what she'd do?"

"She's frail, Tate," said Zion, but something bothered her about the fact that Jaguar wasn't answering. And about the fact that a woman who had everything to lose would try to kill a man she barely knew. Unless she didn't barely know him and unless she had nothing left to lose. "I'll just drive out to his house. I have his address in my records at the *Caffeinator*."

"No!" said both Tate and Wilson.

Tate set the folder on the desk. "Call the *Caffeinator* and get his address. I'll drive out. That way you won't have to pull one of your guys off patrol," he told Wilson.

Wilson nodded.

Zion hesitated. "Let me come with you."

Tate shifted in the chair. "Zion, you need to go back to work. We've got this."

"He's right," said the sheriff. "You did a good job, but now let the professionals handle it."

He might have added *little lady* for all it was worth. Zion clenched her teeth, but she dialed her mother's phone to have her look up Jaguar's home address.

* * *

Zion had every intention of going back to the *Caffeinator*, but as soon as she got in her car and watched Tate drive off in his truck, she changed her mind. She had a bad feeling about this whole situation. There was no reason for Nancy to want Jaguar dead, or none that was readily apparent, and yet the evidence was starting to stack up against her. She also couldn't understand why Jaguar wasn't answering his phone. He had to know it was Zion calling him. Unless his mother had taken a turn for the worse, Jaguar's silence was ominous. Closing her eyes, she touched the address in the text message from her mother and waited for the directions to load on her phone.

Tate was going to kill her, but rather than turn right to head for Main Street, Zion turned left and followed the direction that Tate had taken. Jaguar's parents lived in a gated community on the other side of Sequoia. Zion sat before the gates, feeling a wash of relief. Maybe Nancy hadn't been able to get inside after all. In fact, the more she thought about it, the more Zion felt sure Wilson was right. Nancy had fled the scene. She'd probably left her daughter with her sister and gotten out of town.

With a squeal of poorly oiled metal, the gates suddenly began opening. Zion glanced behind her at the sedan waiting to get inside and marked she was blocking the way. She drove forward, through the gates and glanced in her rearview mirror, pulling to the side of the road.

The sedan turned left and continued on its way, unconcerned with who had entered the gates. Behind her the gates swung closed again. *So much for security,* she thought. Her phone announced she needed to make the next right turn. Zion pulled back onto the street and followed the directions. As she drove by the address for the house, she didn't see Tate's truck and there were no cars in the long driveway. The curtains were drawn over the front window and there were no people on the street. A wave of relief went through her. Likely, Jaguar and his parents had gone out for the day. She'd just head back to the *Caffeinator* and no one would know she'd disobeyed the sheriff.

Turning left to circle back to the gate, her eyes landed first on Tate's empty truck, then shifted to the vehicle before it. A small SUV with a vinyl side panel that read *Cater 2 U*. She felt her insides churn and she made a U-turn, pulling up behind Tate's truck. She looked up and down the street, searching for him, but this street was empty as well.

She put the Optima in park and set the brake, then she grabbed her phone and shoved her purse behind the driver's seat to hide it. Getting out of the car, she locked the doors and pocketed her key, then she hurried to the SUV and looked inside. She saw a booster seat in back and some coloring books. A doll with dark hair lay on the seat next to the booster. Moving to the front of the vehicle, she placed her hand on the hood. Warm. Nancy couldn't have been here long.

Jogging to Jaguar's street, she walked up to the house, then she hesitated, pausing to listen. She didn't hear anything and there was no sign of Tate. Taking a deep breath, she wondered if she should call Sheriff Wilson and wait for either Vasquez or Murphy to arrive.

Lifting her phone, she searched for the sheriff's office direct number and pressed the icon, lifting the phone to her ear. A dispatcher came on the line.

"Sheriff's office," she said brightly.

"I need to talk to Sheriff Wilson. It's urgent. Tell him Zion Sawyer's calling."

"Hold a moment."

Zion glanced around again, feeling the hair rise on the nape of her neck. It was so quiet here among these ranch style homes with their manicured yards and the looming presence of redwood trees overhanging everything.

"I'm sorry. Sheriff Wilson's very busy right now. Can I take a message?"

Zion pulled the phone away and stared at it. "You told him it was Zion Sawyer?"

"Of course, miss. Can I take a message?"

"Tell Sheriff Wilson I'm at the Jarvis house and I found Nancy Osborn's SUV. Tate Mercer is here somewhere, but I can't locate him. I'm going up to the house to see if everything's all right."

"Hold on, miss. I don't think…"

Zion disconnected the call. She didn't have time for this. Taking another deep breath and releasing it, she started up the paved walkway to the covered front porch. Climbing the two stairs, she lifted her hand to knock on the door, but it swung open and Jaguar filled the doorway.

"Go!" he said.

"Is everything all right?" she asked, trying to look beyond him.

"Zion, just go!"

"Bring her in," came a woman's voice. Zion thought she recognized it, but she wasn't sure.

Jaguar's eyes drifted down, then he opened the door wider. Zion stepped into a dated living room with antique furniture and wooden floors. An older woman sat in a rocker, while an older man stood beside her, holding her hand. Standing in front of both of them with a gun pointed at the woman was Nancy.

Zion felt a wave of disappointment. She'd thought she and Nancy were on the way to becoming friends. Some part of her really hadn't thought she was capable of murder. "Nancy, what are you doing?"

Nancy's hands shook, but she kept the gun pointed at the woman. "Close the door," Nancy ordered and Jaguar complied, moving up beside Zion.

"This has gone too far, Nancy," said Jaguar.

"Shut up!" she snapped, the gun dipping. "I don't want to hear anything more from you."

She looked horrible. She had a scarf wrapped around her head and her face looked grey. Understanding suddenly struck Zion.

"You have cancer, don't you?"

Nancy nodded. "High-grade glioma. Brain cancer."

Zion glanced around the room again. Where was Tate? "Nancy, please don't do this."

Nancy started to speak, but nothing came out.

Jaguar stepped in front of Zion. As he moved, Nancy whipped the gun around and pointed it at him. Zion gasped, reaching out to stop him from moving.

"I said don't move!" Nancy shouted at him. "I need to think."

"Nancy, I don't understand why you're doing this," he said. "We can talk about it."

"Shut up!" She braced the gun with her other hand. "Just shut up! I need to think."

Zion saw motion in the room behind Nancy. She thought it might be in the kitchen. She felt her heart pounding against her ribs and she wasn't sure what to do to stop this. The older woman in the chair began crying and the older man bent over her, trying to comfort her.

"Nancy, let them go," Zion said. "They haven't done anything to deserve this and you're scaring them."

"Why are you here?" Nancy demanded.

"I want to help you."

"Help me? Help me!"

"Yes. I don't believe you've thought this through. I think you might not be completely aware of what you're doing."

"I'm aware. I know exactly what I have to do." Her eyes shifted to Jaguar. "It's nothing personal, but I can't take a chance on you living past me."

Jaguar gave Zion a bewildered look. The older woman started crying harder, making Jaguar start toward her, but Zion grabbed his arm, holding him back. She could see the look in Nancy's eyes. She might be having a hard time just pulling the trigger while he stood there, but if he posed even the slightest threat she'd shoot.

"Don't move," Zion told him.

He gave his mother an anguished look, but he stayed. Zion thought she heard footsteps in the other room, but Nancy didn't react.

"Nancy, I can help you," said Jaguar. "I can find a doctor who can look at you…"

"They've all looked. They've all told me the same thing! There's nothing that can be done. Now, this is all I have left to do."

"What about Sophia, Nancy?" said Zion. "If you do this, you'll be robbing Sophia of the remaining time she has with you. What about your daughter?"

"I'm doing this for her!" said Nancy with a sob. "I'm doing this for her!"

Tate stepped through the doorway, his gun pointed at the back of Nancy's head. "Put the gun down, Nancy!" he ordered, bracing his back on the doorjamb.

The gun wavered in Nancy's hand, but she didn't lower it. "Stay back!" she screamed. "Stay back!"

Jaguar's mom collapsed over on herself, shuddering in fear. His father draped his body over hers to protect her.

Zion raised her free hand slowly. "Everyone, just calm down!" she said urgently. She felt like she was going to be sick, she was so afraid. The way Nancy's hand shook, it was anyone guess where a bullet would go if she fired. She tightened her grip on Jaguar's arm to hold him there.

"Nancy, Jaguar's parents are innocent. His mother isn't well and you're scaring her. I don't think you mean to do that, do you?" she said.

Nancy glanced at the woman, but she didn't answer.

"Whatever you think this is accomplishing, it's hurting the wrong people."

"I'm not trying to hurt anyone. I'm protecting my daughter. I don't have any other way to protect her."

"Then don't take her mother away from her. Not like this. Give her the rest of the time you have. Don't let her find out you died before it was time. And you will die here, Nancy. If you pull that trigger, you erase any remaining life you have, any remaining time you could spend with Sophia. Why would you deny her that?"

Nancy's eyes shifted from Jaguar to her. Zion held her gaze, even though she was trembling so hard her teeth clattered. Tate edged forward a few steps, his gun pointed at Nancy's head, his free hand outstretched.

"Don't deny Sophia her mother," Zion said.

With a violent shudder, Nancy lowered the gun. Before she'd brought it down all the way, Tate grabbed it and pressed his own gun to the side of her head. In the distance, Zion could hear sirens approaching before black spots completely covered her vision.

CHAPTER 20

Tate glared at Jaguar where he sat in the viewing room outside of interrogation. He'd almost gotten his parents and Zion killed. Damn him, why hadn't he come clean about his past? Tate guessed he'd never thought his careless actions would come back to bite him in the ass.

"Do you remember her?" asked Wilson.

Tate looked into the interrogation room at the thin woman hunched over, her arms crossed on the table, her head braced in a hand. He shifted and met Zion's gaze. He was still pissed at her too, but he couldn't deny if she hadn't been there, Jaguar would likely be dead by now.

"We went to high school together." Jaguar rubbed a hand against the back of his neck. "Look, Sheriff, I should be with my mother right now."

"Right now, we need a statement," said Wilson without budging. "So you went to high school together. Did you have history?"

Jaguar looked up, his blue eyes shifting to Zion. "A few years ago I ran into her in a bar…um, *Corkers*, I think. I'd come home to visit my mom."

"And?"

"And, she was upset. We had a few drinks and went back to the hotel I was staying in. Things happened."

"Things happened?"

"Yeah." He shrugged. "It was just one night."

"Do you remember when this was?" asked Wilson.

"Not really. Three or four years ago."

"What about more like five?" asked Zion.

"Could be," said Jaguar.

"She tried to see you in LA after a concert," said Tate. "Your manager prevented her from getting in. He shoved her and she fell, hitting her head."

Jaguar looked up, confused. “I don’t remember that.”

Wilson huffed. “See if she’s ready to talk,” he told Tate.

Tate wasn’t sure why he was the one questioning her, but he’d been the one to make the arrest, so he guessed it made sense. He’d agreed to help out on cases, but he was getting dragged in deeper and deeper it seemed.

Mentally centering himself, he walked out of the viewing room, crossing to interrogation. Sam Murphy opened the door for him and stepped inside as Tate took a seat at the table. Nancy Osborn lifted her head.

“You okay?” Tate asked her.

She gave a grim laugh. “No, I’m dying. I saw the doctor yesterday and he told me to sign up for hospice. He said I had maybe a month, maybe less. I can’t see much out of my left eye anymore.”

“I’m sorry.”

“Yeah, I know. Everyone’s sorry, but what you really mean is you’re just so damn grateful it isn’t you.”

Tate wasn’t sure what to do with that, so he didn’t comment. “Nancy, is Osborn your married name?”

“Yeah.”

“Where’s your husband?”

“He left. He’s living in Florida with his new wife.”

“What’s his name?”

“Allen. Allen Osborn.” She looked at the two way glass. “Are they recording this?”

“They are. We called the public defender. He should be here in a few hours. You don’t have to talk with me if you don’t want to.”

“I’m not trying to hide anything.”

“Okay. I’ll just get right to the point. Did you poison the brownies at the after party?”

“I did.”

“With what?”

“Arsenic. I found an old bottle of rat poison Allen had in the garage.”

"Why did you list the brownies on your menu?"

"The manager wouldn't agree to hire me if I didn't indicate what foods were gluten free. I wasn't thinking about killing Jaguar when I made the menu, then I guess I didn't care." She made a scoffing noise. "Jaguar. What a name. Seriously? His name's Jerome. What an idiot."

"Why did you decide to kill…um, Jerome? What has he done to you?"

"It's not really about him. I know he thinks everything revolves around him, but it doesn't."

"Then why did you want to kill him?"

She shifted in the chair, crossing one thin leg over the other and clasping her hands on her knees. "I needed my sister to agree to take Sophia."

Tate frowned. "What?"

"When I die, I want Sophia raised by my sister, but Pam keeps saying I need to get Sophia's father to do it. She has three kids of her own and they're strapped for cash, so I get it, but I want Sophia raised here. I don't want her living that lifestyle and I told Pam that. She didn't care. She said it wasn't right to deny Sophia her father."

"What lifestyle?"

"His lifestyle."

Tate glanced over his shoulder at the glass. "Jaguar's your daughter's father?"

Nancy nodded.

"Are you sure?"

"Well, it ended my marriage, so yeah."

"How did it do that?"

Nancy sighed, straightening the scarf on her head. "Allen and I had a rocky marriage right out of the gate. He was almost fifteen years older than I was."

"Okay."

"Six years ago, we had a really bad fight. I thought it was over. He left and he said he wasn't coming back. I thought we were headed for divorce. I was upset, so I went out for a drink and I wound up in *Corkers*."

"Where you met Jaguar?"

Nancy nodded, lifting a hand to adjust her scarf again. "I thought he was a real loser in school, but that night he was so kind and I really needed some kindness. I didn't mean it to happen, but…" She held out her empty hands. Tate noticed they were shaking. "A few weeks later I found out I was pregnant."

"So you went to LA to tell him?"

"Right. I tried to get backstage, but that manager stopped me. I don't know what I wanted, but I guess I just wanted someone to tell me it was going to be all right. The manager shoved me and I hit my head. When they did the MRI, that's when they found the cancer."

Tate tilted up his head. God, this woman knew she was doomed from that moment on. She must have hated Jaguar, blaming him for everything that had happened to her.

Nancy stared at the table, her eyes going distant in memory. "I'm actually glad I didn't see him that day. I don't know what would have happened if I had." She looked up at Tate, her expression tortured. "I might have had an abortion."

"But you didn't."

"No, I kept the pregnancy."

"Did they treat you for the cancer?"

"There wasn't much they could do. The tumor was small and it wasn't in a place they could operate and chemo wouldn't help. Besides, I couldn't take chemo while I was pregnant, so they said we'd wait until I had the baby. Allen and I got back together again and I didn't tell him. It didn't seem right."

"Did Allen think Sophia was his?"

Nancy nodded. "He always wanted kids, so I didn't think it would hurt, but almost immediately he knew something was wrong. Allen has really dark eyes and he couldn't understand why Sophia's eyes were so blue."

"But he stayed with you?"

"For three years. I knew I was getting worse, but I'd stopped going to the doctor. They said the chemo would just buy me time, there was no cure, and I didn't want to spend my last few years with my daughter unable to take care of her, so I just told myself everything was all right the way it was."

"Why did Allen leave the final time, Nancy?"

Nancy scraped her teeth across her lower lip. "He wanted another baby. We tried and tried for a year, but nothing happened." She fussed with the scarf again. "I didn't know it, but he went to a fertility doctor. Allen had mumps when he was a teenager and it made him sterile."

Tate drew a breath, then exhaled. Everything this woman did went from bad to worse. "So he knew Sophia couldn't be his?"

"He left the next day and I got divorce papers the following week."

Tate shifted in the hard metal chair. "Why did you want to kill Jaguar?"

Nancy cleared her throat. "Could I have some water?"

"Of course." Tate signaled to Sam Murphy and she went out the door.

"Pam said she couldn't take Sophia after I die. She started putting pressure on me to force Jaguar to have a paternity test."

"And you didn't want it to be revealed that he's Sophia's father?" Tate couldn't help but wonder how the rockstar was taking this news.

"Do you know the sort of life he leads? Do you know the drugs and booze and women he does?"

"So you decided to kill him and *Redwood Stock* gave you the opportunity?"

She nodded. "If Jaguar was dead, Pam wouldn't have any choice. She'd have to take Sophia in."

This was the sort of disordered thinking a desperate person would devise. Honestly, he wondered if the cancer could be contributing to this paranoia and delusion. "You killed an innocent girl, Nancy."

Nancy's face crumpled and she put her hands on her head. "I know. I didn't mean for that to happen." She curled her fist against her chest. "They made such a big deal about having gluten free things for Jaguar, I thought if I clearly labeled the dish, he'd be the only one to take any. I never dreamed anyone else would eat it."

That was just madness, thought Tate.

"Why did you go to his house today?"

"I'd dropped Sophia off with Pam and I went to meet with the hospice coordinators. As I was coming back, I saw the police at *Cater 2 U*. I knew you'd figured it out. I knew you were coming for me."

"Where did you get the gun?"

"It was Allen's. He left it for me when he moved to Florida." She gave a moan of misery and closed her eyes. "I didn't mean for anyone else to die. I just wanted to make sure Jaguar was out of the picture. I just wanted to make sure that Pam had no other choice."

Tate sat back in his chair as Sam Murphy entered the room, setting a bottle of water on the table in front of Nancy. Nancy took it, breaking the seal, her hand shaking violently. Tate watched this woman who had casually poisoned another and who justified it in the name of her daughter, and he wondered if he'd ever understand the workings of the human mind.

But worse still was the thought of Sophia. What would happen to the little girl whose mother would die in prison as a murderer and whose father was a washed-up rockstar? How would she ever overcome the misfortune of her birth?

EPILOGUE

Zion wheeled her suitcase into the *Caffeinator* and handed her car keys to Gabi. Gabi would drive the Optima home and keep it while she was away with David. Dottie looked up from her spot rolling out dough and Tallah dragged herself out of the back room, her eyes heavy with sleep.

"When can I stop getting up at the crack of dawn?" the teenager complained.

"Tuesday morning you get to sleep in," said Zion. "Everything will be back to normal then."

"Argh," growled Tallah, slumping in front of the espresso machine.

"Morning, Dottie," Zion called.

"Morning, sugar. What are you doing here? I thought you were off on your hot weekend get-away."

"David's picking me up here. I just wanted to make sure you had everything you need. Mom's promised to lock up after the store closes."

"You want an espresso, Mrs. Sawyer?" Tallah asked Gabi.

For a moment, Zion thought her mother might give in and allow some poison (caffeine) back into her system, but she straightened her back and lifted her chin. "No, I will not weaken," she said dramatically.

Zion rolled her eyes and kissed her cheek. "Good for you. I'm just going to make sure they have enough beans for the next two days."

"Do whatever you need to do," said Gabi, taking a seat at the window. "I'm just going to relax for a bit."

The outer door opened as Zion started toward the back and Jaguar, followed by his two bodyguards, walked into the room. Zion turned to face him. "You're up early?" she said, smiling.

"I haven't been to sleep yet. I've been at the hospital all night with Mom."

"How is she?" asked Zion.

"She's better. They're going to release her today. She doesn't remember what happened."

"That's sort of a blessing, isn't it?"

Jaguar shrugged. "I don't know at this point."

Zion gave him a warm look, rubbing his arm. "How are you doing?"

He shook his spiky head. "I honestly have no idea. I'm in shock."

"I'll bet. What are you going to do about Sophia?"

He sighed. "I don't know about that either. I agreed to a paternity test and Nancy's sister promised to keep her for now, but I don't know anything about being a father. Nancy wasn't wrong about me, or about that."

Zion tightened her hold on his elbow. "You'll figure it out." She pointed over her shoulder at the espresso machine. "If you can make that thing hum, you can handle this."

He laughed, then stepped forward and hugged her. "Thank you for everything. If it wasn't for you, I'd be dead."

Zion hugged him in return. "Don't be silly. You turned my profit margin from red to black five months early this year."

He laughed again and released her.

"How about a café au lait for the road? My treat?"

Jaguar nodded. "How about a café au lait all around and I'll treat." He looked at his bodyguards who nodded, then at Gabi.

Zion watched Gabi as well. "What the hell!" said her mother, throwing up her hands. "Café au lait all around!"

* * *

After Jaguar and his bodyguards left, Zion opened the coffee shop and slipped into the back to check the inventory. She was nervous leaving the shop for two days, although she knew Dee and Dottie had run it for quite awhile after Vivian died without her supervision. And she had a nice profit cushion even if everything went badly off the rails when she walked out the door.

Still she fussed and that made her think about why she was fussing. She wanted to go away, didn't she? She was looking forward to moving her relationship with David to the next level, right? She deserved some time off, especially after solving a murder, didn't she?

She stopped herself when she'd counted the same shelf of bean packets four times and still had no idea how many were there. Did she want to go away with David? To be honest, she wasn't sure. She hadn't seen David for a few days now and she didn't miss him the way she should. In fact, they hadn't even talked on the phone – nothing more than a few text messages to set up today's trip. Shouldn't that be more of a problem for her? Shouldn't she be longing for daily contact with him?

She closed her eyes and gently bounced her forehead against the edge of the shelf. What was wrong with her? Was Rebekah right and she hadn't gotten over Lucas yet?

That was ridiculous. She never thought about Lucas except when Rebekah mentioned him.

Maybe she was like Jaguar, incapable of making a commitment? But she didn't think that was it. She liked the idea of a monogamous relationship. It was just that when she thought of it, David wasn't the first guy to come to mind. In fact, while she was being honest, David wasn't even the second guy to come to mind. The first guy was…

"Zion!"

Tate.

She would recognize his voice anywhere. She set down her notepad and pen, smoothing her hands over her shorts and peasant blouse.

"Zion!"

She quickened her pace and moved through the kitchen to the counter. What was wrong now?

"I'm here," she said, crossing around the counter to meet him in the middle of the floor.

His eyes darted around the room and Zion became aware of everyone staring at them – Tallah behind the register, Dottie at her kneading board, her mother at the table before the window. A young couple sat on the couches to their right.

Focusing back on her, he drew a deep breath.

"What's up?" she asked him.

He opened his mouth to speak, then before she could react, he stepped forward, catching her face in his hands. Zion didn't move as he lowered his mouth and kissed her. And what a kiss! Her hands fluttered as he deepened the kiss, then finally they came to rest on his shoulders, pulling him toward her, rather than away.

After a moment, he broke off and braced his forehead against hers. "Don't go away with David," he said in a husky voice.

Oh boy, she thought, and then he kissed her again.

The End

Now that you've finished, visit ML Hamilton at her website: authormlhamilton.net and sign up for her newsletter. Receive free offers and discounts once you sign up!

The Complete *Peyton Brooks' Mysteries* Collection:

Murder in the Painted Lady, Volume 0
Murder on Potrero Hill Volume 1
Murder in the Tenderloin Volume 2
Murder on Russian Hill Volume 3
Murder on Alcatraz Volume 4
Murder in Chinatown Volume 5
Murder in the Presidio Volume 6
Murder on Treasure Island Volume 7

Peyton Brooks FBI Collection:

Zombies in the Delta Volume 1
Mermaids in the Pacific Volume 2
Werewolves in London Volume 3
Vampires in Hollywood Volume 4
Mayan Gods in the Yucatan Volume 5

***Zion Sawyer* Cozy Mystery Collection:**

Cappuccino Volume 1
Café Au Lai Volume 2

The Avery Nolan Adventure Collection:

Swift as a Shadow Volume 1
Short as Any Dream Volume 2
Brief as Lightning Volume 3
Momentary as a Sound Volume 4

The Complete *World of Samar* Collection:

The Talisman of Eldon Emerald Volume 1
The Heirs of Eldon Volume 2
The Star of Eldon Volume 3
The Spirit of Eldon Volume 4
The Sanctuary of Eldon Volume 5
The Scions of Eldon Volume 6
The Watchers of Eldon Volume 7
The Followers of Eldon Volume 8
The Apostles of Eldon Volume 9
The Renegade of Eldon Volume 10

Stand Alone Novels:

Ravensong

Serenity

Jaguar

Want to know more about Jaguar and his story?
Coming soon:

JAGUAR

For Jaguar, the lure of the lights and the crowds has filled his years since leaving Sequoia, but even the brightest lights fade. When his mother falls ill, he puts his career on hold to help her, but coming home after so much time away has its own pitfalls.

Jaguar's return creates a clash with his estranged father and a past lover who has secrets she's been hiding for five years. In the face of his personal turmoil, Jaguar is forced to make a choice between the boy he was and the star he became.

Even more so, he has to decide between fame and family.

Made in the USA
San Bernardino, CA
10 April 2017